D1310600

A Tale of Two Cities

CHARLES DICKENS

PRESTWICK HOUSE, INC.

"Everything for the English Classroom!"

© 2005 by Prestwick House, Inc.

ADAPTED BY: Peter Boysen

EDITED BY: Douglas Grudzina

DESIGN: Larry Knox

PRODUCTION: Jerry Clark

ISBN 978-1-58049-556-1

A Tale of Two Cities

CHARLES DICKENS

CONTENTS

Contents Continued

Book the Third. The Track of a Storm

To the Reader

MOST PEOPLE in the publishing and education industries agree that there are some books that everyone should read. While there might be a good deal of disagreement on exactly which books should be included on that must-read list, almost everyone agrees that some books are just so important that no one should be able to leave school without having read them.

The problem with many of these books, however, is that they were written in a time and place when the standards of written and spoken English were very different from twenty-first century American English—so different, in fact, that the language alone can block a full understanding of the plot, characterization, imagery, tone, or whatever it is that makes the work worth reading in the first place. By the same token, if you have to invest too much time simply decoding the text (the lowest level of reading comprehension), there's a good chance that you'll simply give up. Your English teacher probably sees this happen nearly every day.

One "solution" to this problem has been for publishers to offer "adapted" and "condensed" versions of these important works. The problem with these adaptations is that they are usually too condensed, oversimplified to the point that there is little left but the plot events. All of the rich texture of narrative voice, foreshadowing, irony, sophisticated characterization, and theme are cut, along with the archaic diction and syntax.

Another popular "solution" has been to bring film versions of great literature into the classroom. While there are some excellent reasons to conduct a "book-to-film" comparison, it is a disservice to everyone involved to assert that watching the movie and reading the book are similar experiences at all. Recognizing the need for a text that is accessible to the average reader, yet rich enough to maintain the original's literary quality, we developed the *Prestwick House Spotlight Edition*. Each Spotlight Edition is a complete and thoughtful adaptation that allows you to examine the structure, themes, character development, and richness of great literature without having to fight with the archaic language that makes much great literature such a challenge.

To further enhance your reading experience, we've added the sidebar commentary and guided reading questions to the margins. These are your aids—road signs as it were—to guide you through the text, to note the foreshadowing, and to follow the development of a character or the gradual revelation of plot facts.

You may choose to read this Spotlight Edition *instead* of the original. Or you may choose to use this Spotlight Edition as a resource *while reading* the original, referring to the adaptation to help clarify a particularly difficult passage. Use the sidebar commentary and guided reading questions as tools to help you navigate the unadapted original. Reading groups might find the sidebar comments and questions helpful in their discussion of either the Spotlight adaptation or the original. The offered writing opportunities invite even deeper thought.

Similarly, the research opportunities are not intended to be major papers or projects (unless your teacher wants them to be). The primary purpose of the research opportunities is simply to encourage you to examine the social, historical, and philosophical environments in which the text was written or on which the text was based. All of the research questions can be answered by consulting one or two magazine articles or by clicking on one or two links of a basic web search.

There is some apparent repetition of guided reading questions and writing and/or research opportunities in the book to illustrate that reading is often a recursive process in which you will re-encounter the same concept or question again and again, each time adjusting original impressions and theories to reflect new information, additional character growth, plot development, and so on. Each time an idea or question reappears, you should expand your understanding of the issue under consideration.

Most of all, enjoy the book. Get to know (to like, dislike, love or hate) the characters. Live as accurately and completely as possible in the setting. Delve into the history and culture. Let your foray into great literature truly be an excursion into a new world where you will learn as much about yourself as you will about the people you meet there.

A Tale of Two Cities

CHARLES DICKENS

BOOK THE FIRST. RECALLED TO LIFE

CHAPTER I
The Period

D EPENDING ON WHO you listened to, it was either the best of times, or it was the worst of times. Society had never been smarter, or more foolish. The Church was either at its strongest, or it was on its deathbed. Crime and the economy were either about to improve dramatically, or all were on the brink of starvation and ruin. In other words, that time wasn't so different from our own time—basically, politicians could be counted on to spout whatever rumor or innuendo would best improve their own chances of election, or, better yet, re-election.

England had a king with a large jaw and a queen with a plain face; France also had a king with a large jaw, but her queen was beautiful to look at. Appearance was far less important, however, than the idea shared by both rulers that the way things were was the way things would always be.

It was 1775. England seemed to be ahead of France in the arena of odd spiritual revelations. One of the "gifts" that Mrs. Southcott received for her twenty-fifth birthday was a vision from a prophetic private in the Life Guards, of a tremendous earthquake that swallowed up all of Westminster as well as all of London. The notorious Cock Lane ghost had only been still for

❷ *What is suggested by the title of the first "Book" of this novel?*

✅ *The pairing of opposites like this is a rhetorical device called "antithesis."*

✅ *This part of the novel takes place in 1775. The American Colonies have begun to rebel, but the Declaration of Independence has not yet been written. George III is the "king with the large jaw." The "queen with the plain face" is Charlotte of Mecklenburg-Strelitz, for whom Charles bought the "Queen's House" that was later enlarged to become Buckingham Palace. France's king was Louis XVI, who had just been crowned in August. The "beautiful" queen is the infamous Marie Antoinette.*

❷ Joanna Southcott was a self-proclaimed religious prophetess, who lived from 1750-1814. This vision was one of many she claimed to see.

❷ In 1762, the Parsons family, residents of a house in Cock Lane in London, claimed their house was haunted by the ghost of a woman who had died in the house two years earlier. Careful investigation eventually showed that the Parsons' eleven-year-old daughter was the source of the "hauntings" and that the Parsons had devised the scheme in order to accuse the husband of the "ghost" of his wife's murder and blackmail him. During the height of the sensation, such famous and influential people as Horace Walpole, Samuel Johnson, and Oliver Goldsmith showed extreme interest.

❷ Don't miss the sarcastic tone of this passage. Are the monks really lacking in self-esteem?

❷ What do you suppose is the "uniquely French death machine"?

❷ Note the personification of Fate and Death. This type of personification is a type of allegory. How does this personification contribute to the tone of this section?

a dozen years at this point in time. Equally disturbing news was coming from the American colonies—news that would prove to be more important in human history than any fortune telling arrived at by studying the chickens of Cock Lane.

France was not as spiritually gifted as England, nor were economic matters faring much better. The highly-valued French *franc* was suffering from the use of paper money instead of gold—each paper bill making her golden sister less and less valuable. The spiritual leaders of France also suffered from runaway inflation. They apparently lacked so much self-worth that, when a country boy failed to kneel in the rain when a procession of monks some fifty or sixty yards away passed by, the priests had his hands chopped off, his tongue ripped out with tongs, and then burned his body while his heart was still beating.

It is likely that Fate stood and watched this boy's execution, standing with his own axe in hand. There were trees in France and Norway on that very day that would later be used to make that uniquely French death machine, and Fate had to smile and shake his head at these priests, whose heads would soon be falling in a manner equally barbarous, but considerably more efficient.

Fate was no doubt also considering his partner, Death, who would be counting carts in the French countryside—carts that would be used to haul away bodies newly executed. While these carts might now house chickens and serve as latrines for pigs, in time they would indeed hold a far less natural cargo. However, anyone claiming to see these two conspirators at work, was very likely to be charged with treason—indeed, to be burned for discounting the absolute sovereignty of God.

To be fair, England did not have any right to claim superiority as far as social justice went. Families going on vacation were urged to store their furniture in locked warehouses; armed men would rob citizens throughout the capital at night; the person who sold dry goods by day was very likely to steal them back when the sun went down, and shoot anyone who recognized him in his disguise as the notorious "Captain." Seven bandits attacked the mail wagon—too many for the sole guard, who could only shoot three of them before being shot himself. Even the Lord Mayor of London was robbed in the middle of Turnham Green by one burglar, in full view of his own servants and assistants who enjoyed watching the humiliation of someone who held himself in such high regard. In the prisons, inmates fought wardens, despite the shot pellets flying all around them; thieves wandered into the parties of the aristocracy and snipped off necklaces; a team of musketeers raided St. Giles', to break up a black market, and ended up running from an angry mob. All of this, of course, was just another day in England. The hangman was busier than ever, hanging rows and rows of criminals—here a housebreaker, there a murderer, and over there a man who stole sixpence. When there were no criminals to hang, there were lesser thieves to brand on the hand, or rebellious pamphlets to burn.

So was the year 1775 in France and in England. Unseen, or unheeded, Fate and Death prepared the coming storm. The kings and queens and France, of course, foresaw nothing—their divine right to rule helped them to sleep every night. So the year went, and so the characters of this story crept down the roads that lay before them.

❷ *You know what happened in 1776 in the United States. What event(s) is Dickens laying the foundation(s) for in this section? How different are England and France at this time?*

❷ *What social problems might Dickens point out if he were writing about the United States today?*

Writing Opportunity:

Compare and contrast the political and religious conditions in England and France in 1775.

Research Opportunity:

Look up the conditions of the French economy in the 1770s. What struggles was the government facing? How did this contribute to social unrest?

A Tale of Two Cities

CHARLES DICKENS

CHAPTER II
The Mail

ON A FRIDAY NIGHT in late November, the road to Dover lay before the first person who has something to do with this tale. He saw the road crawling before him, past the wagon carrying the mail (and his luggage) to Dover. He walked uphill in the thick mud beside the wagon, with the rest of the passengers—not because he needed the exercise, but because the hill, the leather harness, the mud, and the mail had brought the horses to a stop three times already, and had almost convinced the horses to turn around and go back to Blackheath. The coachman and the guard had been forced to use their reins and whip to change the horses' firm opinion, which some say comes from sound Reason, and so the team of horses was still headed up this tiresome hill.

With their heads drooping and their tails shaking, the horses mashed their way through the morass, floundering and stumbling all the way, as though their hips and knees were about to fly apart. Every time the driver gave them a rest, the horse leading on the near side would shake his head and his entire body, as if to say that there was no way the mail coach would climb this hill. With every shake, the passenger we are interested in shook as well, gripped with worry.

Again, note Dickens's tone of mild sarcasm.

❷ How does Dickens's imagery
add to the suspense of this
section?

✅ This "Captain" is probably the
notorious bandit identified in
Chapter I.

✅ A blunderbuss was a type of
gun—either a long pistol or
a short rifle that was used for
firing at close range without
taking careful aim. Thus, it
would be sufficient protection
for a person who was not an
expert marksman.

✅ Again, note the mild sarcasm.

The valley was filled with a steaming mist, which also started to climb up the hill like an evil spirit seeking rest and finding none. Despite the steam, this mist was clammy and cold, rippling up the hills like a ghastly sea. All that was left of the light of the coach-lamps was the ghostly outline of each wave of this mist, and the shadow of the road, soaked with the odor of the sweat-soaked horses—as though the mist poured out of these horses with their perspiration.

This passenger had two fellow-passengers, plodding up the hill alongside the wagon. All three were wrapped up over their ears and up to their eyes, and all wore jackboots. None could have recognized any of the others later, based on what he saw that night. In those days, one never knew whether one was traveling with thieves—or those who were helping the "Captain" prey upon the innocent. Since landlords and stablehands alike enjoyed the extra income that graft provided, running into peril was as likely as not. These thoughts filled the mind of the wagon guard, upon that Friday night in November, 1775, as the soggy crew trod up Shooter's Hill, and so he was glad to feel the arm-chest before him, where his loaded blunderbuss lay upon six or eight loaded horse-pistols, which rattled on a pile of swords.

It was just another peaceful night for the Dover mail wagon: the guard suspected the passengers, who suspected each other and the guard—everyone suspected everyone else, and the horse driver was only confident in his horses—which he knew were unfit for the journey.

"Whoa-ho!" said the driver. "One more pull and you're at the top! Damn you for all the trouble I've had getting you to it! Joe!"

"What is it?" the guard replied.

"What time is it?"

"Ten minutes past eleven, at least."

"By my blood!" screamed the driver, "and not on top of Shooter's Hill yet? Yah! Get on with you!"

The horse which had startled the passenger with

his shaking, decided to make a scramble for the top of the hill, once he felt the driver's whip, and the other three horses followed. Once more, the Dover wagon crept on, amidst the sounds of the passengers' jack-boots squashing in the mud. The passengers had stopped with the wagon, and they stayed close beside it. Had any of them walked ahead into the dark mist, he would have instantly risked being shot as a highway robber.

This last burst of speed carried the wagon to the top of the hill. The horses stopped again to breathe, and the guard got down to brace the wheels, so that the wagon would not run away down the hill, and to let the passengers back into the wagon.

"Psst! Joe!" cried the driver, looking down from the box.

"What is it, Tom?"

They both listened.

"I hear a horse coming up at a canter, Joe."

"I hear a horse at a gallop, Tom," replied the guard, letting go of the door and hopping back on the wagon. "Gentlemen! In the king's name, all of you!"

With this hurried order, he cocked his blunderbuss, and stood at the ready.

The passenger of our story was on the step, about to get in the wagon, and the other two passengers were close behind him. However, he remained on the step, half in and half out of the coach, while they remained on the road behind him. They all looked back and forth from the guard to the driver, listening. The driver looked back; the guard looked back; even the emphatic horse looked back, without argument.

Without the noise of the rumbling coach or the shouting men, what had been a still night became very quiet indeed. The panting of the horses made the wagon quiver, as if it also were nervous. The hearts of the passengers beat loud enough, perhaps, to be heard, but the quiet pause was one of people out of breath, holding their breath, and feeling their pulses quickened by nervous anticipation.

Notice the use of repetitive sentence structure and diction to contribute to the suspense.

The sound of a galloping horse came fast and furiously up the hill.

"Ho!" the guard sang out, as loud as he could roar. "Yo there! Stand! I shall fire!"

The pace of the coming horse suddenly slowed and was joined by splashing and floundering. A man's voice called from the mist, "Is that the Dover mail wagon?"

"Never you mind what it is!" the guard spat back. "Who are you?"

"Is that the Dover mail wagon?"

"Why do you want to know?"

"I'm looking for a passenger, if it is."

"What passenger?"

"Mr. Jarvis Lorry."

The passenger of our story acknowledged that that was his name. The guard, the driver, and the other passengers eyed him with suspicion.

"Stay where you are," the guard called to the voice in the mist, "because if I make a mistake, it will never be set right in your lifetime. Mr. Lorry, answer straight!"

"What is the matter?" asked Mr. Lorry, with quavering speech. "Who wants me? Is it Jerry?"

The guard muttered to himself, "I don't like Jerry's voice, if it is Jerry. He's hoarser than suits me."

"Yes, Mr. Lorry."

"What is the matter?"

"A message sent after you from over yonder. T. and Co."

"I know this messenger, guard," said Mr. Lorry, getting down into the road—shoved more than helped by his fellow passengers, who hopped up into the wagon, shut the door, and pulled up the window. "He may come close; there's nothing wrong."

"I hope there ain't, but I can't make so sure of that," said the guard, in a gruff speech. "Hallo you!"

"Well! And hallo you!" said Jerry, more hoarsely than before.

"Walk your horse slowly! Do you see me? If you've

❶ Now we know the name of our first character.

❷ The names of Dickens's characters often indicate their personality or their function in the story. Look up the word "lorry" in the dictionary. What might this character's personality of function turn out to be?

got holsters on that saddle, don't let me see your hand go near 'em. For I tend to make quick mistakes, and when I make one, it's made of a lead musket ball. So now let's look at you."

The figures of a horse and rider came slowly through the mist, and came to the side of the wagon, where the passenger stood. The rider bent, looked up at the guard, and handed the passenger a small folded paper. The rider's horse was worn out, and both rider and horse were covered with mud, from hoof to hat.

"Guard!" said the passenger, in a tone of quiet business confidence.

The watchful guard, with his right hand on the stock of his blunderbuss, his left on the barrel, and his eye on the horseman, answered curtly, "Sir."

"There is nothing to worry about. I work for Tellson's Bank. You've heard of them in London. I am going to Paris on business. Here's a crown for you to buy a drink with. May I read this?"

"As long as you're quick, sir."

He opened it in the light of the wagon-lamp, and read (first to himself, then aloud): "'Wait at Dover for Mam'selle.' It's not long, you see, guard. Jerry, say that my answer was, RECALLED TO LIFE."

Jerry jumped in his saddle. "That's a strange answer, too," he said, at his hoarsest.

"Take that message back, and they will know that I received yours. Good night."

With those words, the passenger opened the wagon-door and got in; absent was the assistance of his fellow-passengers, who had quickly hidden their watches and purses in their boots, and were now pretending to sleep, if only to avoid the danger of appearing to do anything else.

The coach lumbered on again, slowly entering heavier mists as it went down the hill. The guard soon put his blunderbuss back in his weapon chest, checked his spare pistols in his belt, and checked to see that his torches and tinder-box were in a small chest under his seat. He was prepared, just in case the

❷ *Note that Mr. Lorry's response to the note is the title of this first book. What might it foreshadow?*

coach-lamps were be blown out, to shut himself inside the wagon and light them again. Sometimes he could re-light the lamps in five minutes, if he were lucky.

"Tom!" came softly over the wagon roof.

"Hey, Joe."

"Did you hear the message?"

"I did, Joe."

"What did you make of it, Tom?"

"Nothing at all, Joe."

"That's a coincidence too," the guard said, "for I made the same of it myself."

Jerry, now alone in the mist and the darkness, slid down from his horse, not only to give his animal a break, but to wipe the mud from his face, and shake the water from his hat-brim, which could hold half a gallon. After standing with the bridle over his soaked arm, until the wheels of the wagon had faded out of hearing, he turned to walk down the hill.

"After that gallop from Temple Bar, old lady, I won't trust your forelegs until I get you on the level," said Jerry to his mare. " 'Recalled to life.' That's a blazing strange message. Much of that wouldn't do for you, Jerry! I say, Jerry! You'd be in a blazing bad way, if recalling to life was to come into fashion!"

Journal Entry:

What has aroused your interest in the first two chapters? What do you think the messages—the one delivered by Jerry and Mr. Lorry's reply—mean? What type of story is beginning?

A Tale of Two Cities

C H A R L E S   D I C K E N S

CHAPTER III
The Night Shadows

IT IS A WONDERFUL fact that every person is created to be a deep secret and mystery to every other. It is a quiet thought, when I enter a large city at night, that every one of those dark houses clustered together contains its own secret; that every beating heart in each of the millions of bodies there is—in some of its thoughts—a secret to the heart of the person it loves most! The fear of death is similar to this, because we only get to spend such a short time with the ones we love. I can compare it to a book that I pick up, knowing that I will never get to read it all; to glimpses of buried treasure far beneath the surface of a lake, that I will never get to enjoy fully. It has long been determined that the book will snap shut, after I have read only a page; that the lake will be frozen forever while I still stand on the shore, peering down at the gold and jewels. My friend, my neighbor, my love, my soulmate, must die—this is the final sealing of the secret that each person carries, and that I will carry to my own grave. In any cemetery, is there a corpse that holds a more mysterious secret than the ones held by the innermost personalities of the busy inhabitants of London? Are any of these shadows more mysterious to me than I am to them?

Explain the metaphor of the book and buried treasure being similar to life.

❷ To what point about his story does the author bring his discussion of human secrets?

And so the messenger on horseback possessed the same secrecy as the King, the first Minister of State, or the richest businessman in London. So it was with the three passengers shut up in one lumbering old mail wagon. They were mysteries to one another, just as if each had been in his own wagon with six horses—or even sixty horses—with miles of distance between them.

The messenger returned to London at an easy trot, stopping fairly often in taverns to drink, but tending to keep to himself, with his hat down over his eyes, which fit well with his costume—being black on the surface, with no depth in color or shape, and very close together, almost as if they were too guilty to risk being apart. They had a sinister expression, under an old cocked-hat that looked like a three-cornered spittoon, and over a long muffler for the chin and throat, which hung down almost to his knees. He moved his muffler only to pour his liquor down his throat; as soon as that was done, his muffler covered his mouth again.

✔ A spittoon was a bowl into which gentlemen who chewed tobacco would spit the tobacco juice and saliva. Here the author is comparing the shape of the messenger's hat with a spittoon.

"No, Jerry, no!" he said to himself again and again as he rode. "It wouldn't do for you, Jerry, it wouldn't suit your line of business! Recalled—! Bust me if I don't think he'd been drinking!"

❷ What is this character's name?

His message was so confusing that, several times, he wanted to take off his hat to scratch his head. He was bald on top but had black hair, standing jaggedly stiff, everywhere else, seeming to grow all the way down to his broad, blunt nose. It looked like hair a blacksmith might have designed, more like the top of a spiked wall than a head of hair—the best leapfroggers in the world might well have decided not to jump over him.

✔ Note the joke.

❷ Again, how is Dickens continuing to build suspense?

While he trotted back with his message to Tellson's Bank, the message seemed to grow into the shapes he saw in the shadows of the night, and even his mare started to awaken from her private thoughts at the fearful illusions. There seemed to be many of these shadows, because she shied at every shape on the road.

At the same time, the mail-wagon lumbered, jolted, rattled, and bumped along its tedious road, with its three mysterious passengers inside. The same shadows that frightened Jerry and his mare took other forms in the dreams of these three travelers.

In Mr. Lorry's vision, there was a "run" on Tellson's Bank. As he slept in his corner, with one arm drawn through a leather strap, designed to keep him from pounding against the next passenger, the wagon's windows and lamp became the bank. The rattle of the harness was the chink of money, and more customers took their money out of the bank in five minutes than all of the branches of Tellson's Bank had ever served in fifteen minutes. His dream took him next to the basement of Tellson's, where the safes, containing valuables and secret documents, opened before him, and he wandered among them, finding them just as secure as he had left them.

However, even though his bank was always in his mind, and though the wagon (something like the feeling of pain through the hazy filter of drugs) was always in his mind, one thought refused to be displaced by his dreams: he was on his way to dig someone out of a grave.

Suddenly, a gallery of faces appeared before him, and the shadows of night kept him from seeing which was the face of the man he was supposed to rescue. All of the faces, though, had this in common: they were a man who was 45 years old, and whose hair had turned white long before its time. The faces differed in their passions, and in their early decay. He saw faces altered by pride, contempt, defiance, stubbornness, submission, and complaint; he saw sunken cheeks, deathly color, painfully thin hands and frames. A hundred times the passenger asked the faces this question:

Buried how long?

The answer was always the same: *Almost eighteen years.*

❷ What does it mean for there to be a "run" on a bank?

❷ What is the significance of Mr. Lorry's dream?

❷ Do you suppose this is a literal or metaphoric statement? What do these emotions have in common? What do they foreshadow?

❷ What do these emotions have in common? What do they foreshadow?

You had abandoned all hope of being dug out?
Long ago.
Do you know that you have been recalled to life?
They tell me so.
I hope you want to live again?
I can't say.
Can I show you to her? Will you come and see her?

Each face seemed to answer this question in a different way. Sometimes the broken reply was, *Wait! It would kill me if I saw her too soon!* Sometimes it was given tenderly, with tears: *Take me to her.* Sometimes it was staring and confused: *I don't know her. I don't understand.*

After each of these imaginary interviews, Mr. Lorry would dig inside his dream—now with a shovel, now with a large key, now with just his hands—to dig this wretched creature out. Once rescued, with dirt hanging from his face and hair, he would crumble into dust. Mr. Lorry would awaken, lower the window, and feel the real rain on his cheek.

However, even after the rain called him away from his dreams, the shadows outside would merge with the shadows in his mind, and he would return to the specter of his bank, his strongrooms below, and his mission. The ghostly face would rise out of it all, and he would interrogate it again.

Buried how long?
Almost eighteen years.
I hope you want to live?
I can't say.

He would dig, dig, dig in his mind, until a complaint from one of his fellow travelers would force him to pull up the window, slide his arm through the strap, and look upon the sleeping passengers, until his mind slid back into the bank and the grave.

Buried how long?
Almost eighteen years.
You had abandoned all hope of being dug out?
Long ago. He heard the words as clearly as if they had just been spoken—as clearly as any words he had

❷ *What is the effect of repeating this imaginary conversation three times in this chapter?*

ever heard in his life—and, all of a sudden, he found himself bathed in daylight, and the shadows of the night were gone.

He lowered the window, and looked out at the rising sun. He saw a ridge of plowed land, with the plow still waiting where the horses had left it when they were unyoked; beyond the plow was a quiet grove of trees, with many leaves of burning red and golden yellow still on the trees. The earth was cold and wet from the night's rain, but the sky was clear, and the sun was bright, calm, and beautiful.

"Eighteen years!" said Mr. Lorry, looking at the sun. "Gracious Creator of day! To be buried alive for eighteen years!"

❷ *On what note does Dickens end the first weekly installment of his novel?*

THIS IS THE END OF THE
FIRST WEEKLY INSTALLMENT.

A Tale of Two Cities

CHARLES DICKENS

CHAPTER IV
The Preparation

WHEN THE MAIL wagon finally arrived in Dover, later in the morning, the head servant at the Royal George Hotel opened the wagon door, as he usually did. He did it with the flourish of ceremony, because traveling with the mail from London during the winter was an achievement worthy of congratulations.

Only one traveler left the wagon at the Royal George because the other two had stopped at other destinations along the way. The mildewed wagon, with its damp and dirty straw, as well as its darkness, was much like a large dog-kennel. Indeed, Mr. Lorry, the passenger, resembled a large dog as he shook the straw from his coat, with his wrapper, hat, and muddy legs flying in all directions.

"Will there be a boat to Calais tomorrow?"

"Yes, sir, if the weather is good and the wind is fair. The tide will be suitable around two in the afternoon, sir. Bed, sir?"

"Not until tonight, but I do want a bedroom, and a barber."

"And then breakfast afterwards, sir? Yes, sir. That way, sir, if you please. Show him the Concord Room! Gentleman's suitcase and hot water to Concord. Pull off gentleman's boots in Concord. (You will find a fine sea-coal fire there, sir.) Fetch the barber to Concord. Move about there, now, for Concord!"

Because the Concord bedroom was always assigned to a passenger on the mail wagon, and since those passengers almost always arrived wrapped from head to foot, any new visitor was the object of a great deal of curiosity for the employees of the Royal George—one kind of man was seen to enter it, but all sorts of men came out of it, after their wrappings had been removed. And so another servant, two porters, several maids, and the landlady could be found loitering in the hallway outside the Concord room when a sixty-year-old gentleman emerged, formally dressed in a brown suit of clothes that was well worn, but very well kept, and headed to breakfast.

At this point late in the morning, the coffee room had no other customers. His table was pulled up in front of the fire, and as he sat, with the fire flickering on him, waiting for his meal, he sat so still that he might have been posing for a portrait.

He looked very orderly and methodical, with one hand on each knee, and a loud watch ticking deeply and solemnly under his vest, as though it were trying to challenge the cheerfulness of the fire. His legs looked good, and he was proud of them, because he chose stockings that fit sleek and close, and were of a fine texture; his shoes and buckles were also trim. His wig was odd—small, sleek, crisp, and made of flax, setting very close to his head. His wig was supposedly made of hair, but it looked far more like threads of silk or glass. His dress shirt, although not as finely made as his stockings, was kept as white as the tops of the waves coming in on the neighboring beach, or the dots of sail that glinted in the sunlight, far out at sea. His face was used to being serious and quiet, but it could not hide the bright, cheerful eyes that must have been difficult to control in the reserved attitude required of a banker in Tellson's. His cheeks were rosy, and his face, while lined, betrayed little worry.

❷ *Again, note the mildly sarcastic tone.*

❷ *What does Mr. Lorry's physical description reveal about his character?*

Since most of the cares of the confidential clerks of Tellson's were the cares of others, perhaps it was easy to shed those secondhand cares, much like secondhand clothes.

Mr. Lorry's stillness became complete as he dropped off to sleep. When his breakfast arrived, he woke up, and said to the servant, "Please prepare a room for a young lady who may come here at any time today. She may ask for Mr. Jarvis Lorry, or she may only ask for a gentleman from Tellson's Bank. Please let me know when she arrives."

"Yes, sir. Tellson's Bank in London, sir?"

"Yes."

"Yes, sir. We often have the honor to entertain your employees in their traveling back and forth between London and Paris, sir. There is a great deal of traveling, sir, in Tellson and Company's House."

❷ What important bit of information have we just been given?

"Yes. We are quite a large company in France, as well as in England."

"Yes, sir. I don't think you're much in the habit of traveling yourself, sir?"

"Not lately. It's been fifteen years since we—since I—came last from France."

"Indeed, sir? That was before my time, sir—even before the owners' time. The George was in other hands at that time, sir."

"I believe so."

"But I would lay a large bet, sir, that a bank like Tellson and Company was flourishing, a matter of fifty, not to speak of fifteen years ago?"

"You might triple that, and say a hundred fifty, and yet not be far from the truth."

"Indeed, sir!"

His mouth and eyes grew wide with surprise, as he backed from the table, and the head servant shifted his napkin from his right arm to his left, let his posture slacken into a comfortable pose. He stood, watching the guest while he ate and drank, as if he were in an observatory or a watchtower—as waiters have done throughout the ages.

When Mr. Lorry had finished his breakfast, he went out for a stroll on the beach. The little, narrow, crooked town of Dover hid itself away from the beach, and ran its head into the chalk cliffs, like an ostrich. The beach was a desert with heaps of seaweed and stones tumbling wildly about. The sea did what it liked, and what it liked was destruction. The sea thundered at the town and thundered at the cliffs, and so ate away madly at the coast. The air among the houses smelled so strongly of fish that one might have supposed that the sick fish went up to be dipped in the air, as sick people went down to be dipped in the sea. Some fishing was done at the port, and some more strolling was done at night, while looking out at sea: especially when the tide came in, and was near flood levels. Poor tradesmen, who had no apparent business at all, sometimes came into large fortunes without explanation, and these miracles happened in a neighborhood where no one wants the streetlights to be lit.

As Dover was an infamous entry point for smugglers, these are probably the "poor tradesman who had no apparent business at all" who find great fortunes at night at full tide. Of course these "businessmen" would object to installing streetlights as their illegal activities required the cover of darkness.

A bottle of good wine after dinner does no harm to a person tending a fire, except that it might put him to sleep. Mr. Lorry had been sitting a long time—and had just poured out his last glassful of wine looking as fully satisfied as an elderly gentleman with a fresh complexion who has finished an entire bottle of wine can look—when he heard wheels rattle up the narrow street and into the inn-yard.

He set down this last glass untouched. "This is Mam'selle!" he said.

In a very few minutes, the waiter came in to announce that Miss Manette had arrived from London, and would be happy to see the gentleman from Tellson's.

"So soon?"

Miss Manette had had dinner while traveling, and required none then. She was extremely anxious to see the gentleman from Tellson's immediately, if that suited were convenient for him.

The gentleman from Tellson's had no choice but

to drain his glass rather hastily, adjust his odd little flaxen wig at the ears, and follow the waiter. Miss Manette's chamber was a large, dark room, furnished like a funeral parlor with black horsehair, and filled with heavy, dark tables. The furniture had been polished with furniture oil so many times that the two tall candles on the table in the middle of the room were gloomily reflected on every surface, as if the two of them were buried in deep graves of black mahogany, and no light to speak of could appear until they were dug out.

The darkness was so thick that Mr. Lorry, picking his way over the carpet, thought that Miss Manette was not there until—after he passed the two tall candles—he saw a young lady, no older than seventeen, standing in a riding-cloak, still holding her traveling-hat by its ribbon in her hand. She was a short, slender, pretty figure with thick golden hair and blue eyes. She turned and looked into his eyes with a questioning look, and a furrowed forehead. As he looked at her, he suddenly remembered a child whom he had held in his arms on one cold passage across the English Channel, when the hail drifted heavily and the sea ran high. This memory passed quickly, like the fog a person might make by breathing on the mirror behind her. The mirror's carved frame depicted a morbid group of black cupids. Several of them were headless. All of them were crippled. In the carving, they were offering black baskets of black fruit to black goddesses.

Mr. Lorry bowed formally to Miss Manette.

"Please take a seat, sir." The voice was clear, and pleasantly young; with just a slight hint of a foreign accent.

"I kiss your hand, Miss," said Mr. Lorry, with the manners of days gone by, as he made his formal bow again, and took his seat.

"I received a letter from Tellson's Bank, sir, yesterday, informing me that some information—or discovery—"

❷ What is the author implying with this description of Miss Manette's room?

❷ How old is Miss Manette? How long has it been since Mr. Lorry last made the journey from Paris to London?

❷ *What do you suspect is developing? What clues from the beginning of the book suggest this?*

"Either word will do, Miss."

"—concerning the small property of my poor father, whom I never met—so long dead—"

Mr. Lorry moved in his chair and cast a troubled look toward the mirror and the black cupids, as if they had any help for anybody in those absurd baskets!

"—made it clear that I should go to Paris, there to communicate with a gentleman of Tellson's Bank, who would be dispatched to Paris for the purpose."

"That would be me."

"As I thought, sir."

She curtseyed to him (young ladies made curtseys in those days), and wanted to tell him how much older and wiser he was than she. He made her another bow.

"I replied to the Bank, sir, that I would indeed go to France if my advisors and guardians thought it necessary. But, as I have no family or friend to travel with me, I asked if I might be accompanied on the journey with the gentleman from the Bank who was to meet me in Paris. I was told that he had already left London, but a messenger would be sent out to try to intercept him and instruct him to wait for me."

"I am happy," said Mr. Lorry, "to be your escort and guide."

"Sir, I thank you indeed. I am very grateful. I was also told by the Bank that the gentleman would explain to me all of the details of the business, and that I must prepare myself to be surprised. I have done my best to prepare myself, and I am eager to learn these details."

"Naturally," said Mr. Lorry. "Yes—I—"

He paused, pressing his crisp wig against the tops of his ears.

"It is very difficult to begin."

He did not begin, but, in his indecision, met her glance. The young forehead was again wrinkled in curiosity and concern, which actually made it prettier. She raised her hand, as though trying to grasp a passing shadow.

"Have we ever met before, sir?"

"Haven't we?" Mr. Lorry opened his hands, and extended them outwards with a persuasive smile.

Between her eyebrows and just above her small, feminine nose—as delicate and fine as any he had ever seen—the thoughtful wrinkles deepened, and she sat in the chair she had been standing next to. He watched her as she thought, and—when she looked up at him again—he continued:

"In your adopted country, I presume, you live like—and are treated like—a young English lady, Miss Manette?"

"Indeed, sir."

"Miss Manette, I am a man of business. I have a business responsibility to perform. As you listen, don't react to me any more than you would if I were a loudspeaker—truly, I am not much else. With your permission, I will tell you, miss, the story of one of our clients."

"Story!"

He seemed to purposefully misunderstand the word she had repeated, when he quickly added, "Yes, clients; in the banking business, we usually call our customers our clients. He was a French gentleman; a scientist; a man of great achievements; a Doctor."

"Not from Beauvais?"

"Why, yes, from Beauvais. Like Monsieur Manette, your father, the gentleman was from Beauvais. Like Monsieur Manette, your father, the gentleman was well known in Paris. I had the honor of knowing him there. Our relationship was a business relationship, but quite intimate. I was working then at our French office, and had been for-oh!-twenty years."

"When was this—may I ask, when this was, sir?"

"I speak, Miss, of twenty years ago. He married—an English lady—and I was one of the trustees. His business, like the business of many other French gentlemen and families, was entirely in the hands of Tellson's Bank. I have been a trustee in the same way for dozens of other customers over the years. These

❷ *Note the repetition of the word "business" in Mr. Lorry's description of himself and the duties he is performing with Ms. Manette, here and later in the chapter. What is the rhetorical effect of this word?*

Note how Mr. Lorry insists that there be no personal connection between himself and his business clients.

are mere business relationships, Miss; there is no friendship, no emotional interest. I have moved from one to another, throughout my business life, just as I pass from one client to another during my business day; in short, I have no feelings; I am only a machine. To continue—"

"But this is my father's story, sir; and I begin to think"—here, the unusually lined forehead was very intent—"that when I was left an orphan, when my mother died only two years after my father, it was you who brought me to England. I am almost sure it was you."

She hesitantly extended her hand, and Mr. Lorry took it, putting it to his lips formally and coolly. He then led the young lady straight back to her chair and stood looking down into her face while she sat looking up into his.

"Miss Manette, it was I. And you will see how truly I spoke of myself just now, in saying that I had no feelings, and that all of the relationships I hold with other people are business in nature, when you consider that I have never seen you since. No; you have been in the care of Tellson's Bank since, and I have been busy with the other business of Tellson's Bank since. Feelings! I have no time for them, no chance of them. I spend my whole life, Miss, in turning an immense wheel of money."

After this description of his life of business, Mr. Lorry once more flattened his wig upon his head (which really was unnecessary, since it was impossible to flatten this wig any further), and returned to his former expression.

"So far, Miss—as you have said—this is the story of your poor father. Now comes the difference. If your father had not died when he did—Don't be frightened! How you jump!"

She did, indeed, jump. And she caught his wrist with both her hands.

"Please," said Mr. Lorry, in a soothing tone, covering her trembling fingers with his left hand: "please calm yourself—this is only a matter of business. As I was saying—"

Her expression disturbed him so much that he stopped, paced the room, and began again:

"As I was saying—if Monsieur Manette had not died—if he had suddenly and silently disappeared—if he had been kidnapped—if it were easy to guess where, even though no amount of effort could trace him—if he had a powerful enemy who could use a privilege that even the boldest people are afraid to speak of—the privilege of having anyone for any reason committed to prison for any length of time—if his wife had begged the king, the queen, the court, the clergy, for any news of him, with no success—then the history of your father would have been the history of this unfortunate gentleman, the Doctor of Beauvais."

"I beg you to tell me more, sir."

"I will. Can you bear it?"

"I can bear anything but not knowing."

"You speak calmly, and you—are calm. That's good!" (Although his expression was less satisfied than his words.) "A matter of business. Consider this only as a matter of business that must be done. Now if this doctor's wife—even though she were brave—had suffered so intensely because of her husband's confinement before her little child was born—"

"The little child was a daughter, sir."

"A daughter. A—a—matter of business—don't be distressed. Miss, if the poor lady had suffered so intensely before her little child was born, that she decided to protect the child from any part of the agony she herself had known, by raising her as though her father was dead—don't kneel! Why in Heaven's name should you kneel to me?"

"I kneel for the truth. O dear, good, compassionate sir, for the truth!"

"A—a matter of business. You confuse me; how can I transact business if I am confused? Let us be clear-headed. If you would please tell me now, for instance, what nine times ninepence are, or how

❷ *What is happening to Mr. Lorry's businesslike attitude?*

many shillings are in twenty guineas, it would be so encouraging. I would be so much more comfortable about your state of mind."

Without answering him, she sat so still when he gently lifted her up, and her hands that were still clasping his wrists became steadier than they had been, that he felt reassured.

"That's right, that's right. Courage! Business! You have business before you; useful business. Miss Manette, to spare you the pain of wondering where your father had gone, your mother decided to raise you as if he were dead. And when *she* died—I truly believe she died of a broken heart—having never stopped her fruitless search for your father, she left you, at two years old, to grow to be blooming, beautiful, and happy, without the dark cloud of uncertainty about your father's fate."

As he said the words, he looked down on the flowing golden hair, as though he imagined it was already tinged with gray.

❷ Why would Miss Manette's hair be turning gray?

"You know that your parents had no great wealth, and that what they had was left to your mother and to you. There has been no new discovery of money, or of any other property, but—"

He felt his wrist gripped more tightly, and he paused. The expression on her forehead had deepened into one of pain and horror.

❷ What do the title of this first book and Mr. Lorry's reply to his message mean?

"But he has been—been found. He is alive. Greatly changed, it is too probable; almost a wreck, it is possible; though we will hope for the best. Still, alive. Your father has been taken to the house of a former servant in Paris, and we are going there: I, to identify him if I can: you, to restore him to life, love, duty, rest, comfort."

A shiver ran through her frame, and from hers through his. She said, in a low, distinct, awe-stricken voice, as if she were saying it in a dream, "I am going to see his Ghost! It will be his Ghost—not him!"

Mr. Lorry quietly rubbed the hands that held his arm. "There, there, there! See now, see now! Now you know both the best and the worst. You are already well on your way to see this poor, wronged gentleman. With a good sea voyage and a good land journey, you will be soon by his side."

She repeated in the same tone, lowered to a whisper, "I have been free, I have been happy. His Ghost has never haunted me!"

"Only one more thing," said Mr. Lorry, stressing this as a good way to keep her attention: "he has been found under another name. He has long forgotten or long hidden the name 'Manette.' It would serve no purpose now to wonder which is the actual case; no purpose to wonder whether he has merely been overlooked all these years, or has been held intentionally; no purpose now to ask any questions at all, because it would be *dangerous*. It would be better now not to mention the subject, anywhere or in any way, and to remove him—for a while, anyway—out of France. Even I, safe as an Englishman, and even Tellson's, important as they are in the French economy, avoid all talk of the matter. I carry about me, not a scrap of writing openly referring to it. This is truly a secret mission. My credentials, entries, and memoranda are all comprehended in the one line, "Recalled to Life;" which may mean anything. But what is the matter? She doesn't notice a word! Miss Manette!"

Perfectly still and silent, not even fallen back in her chair, she sat under his hand, unaware of her surroundings, with her eyes open and fixed upon him, and with that expression of horror set on her forehead. Her hold upon his arm was so tight, that he was afraid to detach himself, because he might hurt her; therefore, he called out loudly for assistance without moving.

A wild-looking woman burst into the room. Even in his agitation, Mr. Lorry noticed that she seemed to be red all over—even her hair—and to be dressed in extraordinarily tight clothing, and to have on her head a bonnet that looked like a wheel of Stilton cheese. She laid a brawny hand upon his chest, and sent him flying back against the nearest wall.

I really think this must be a man! was Mr. Lorry's breathless thought, as he slammed against the wall.

"Look at you all!" bawled this figure, to the servants. "Why don't you go and fetch things, instead of just standing there staring at me? I'm not so much to look at, am I? If you don't bring smelling-salts and cold water—and quickly—then I will."

The servants immediately scattered to get these items, and she gently laid the patient on a sofa, and took care of her with great skill and gentleness: calling her "my precious!" and "my bird!" and spreading her golden hair aside over her shoulders with great pride and care.

"And you in brown!" she said, angrily turning to Mr. Lorry; "couldn't you tell her what you had to tell her, without frightening her to death? Look at her, with her pretty pale face and her cold hands. Do you call that being a Banker?"

Mr. Lorry was so upset. The woman's questions were very hard to answer, and he could only look at Miss Manette from a distance, with feeble sympathy and humility. The strong woman, who had banished the servants with the threat of "letting them know" something if they stayed there, brought the girl gradually back to consciousness, and coaxed her to lay her drooping head upon her shoulder.

"I hope she will feel better now," said Mr. Lorry.

"No thanks to you in brown, if she does. My darling pretty!"

"I hope," said Mr. Lorry, after another sympathetic and humble pause, "that you will accompany Miss Manette to France?"

"A likely thing, too!" replied the strong woman. "If it was ever intended that I should go across salt water, do you suppose Providence would have set me an island?"

Since this was another difficult question to answer, Mr. Jarvis Lorry returned to his room to consider it.

THIS IS THE END OF THE
SECOND WEEKLY INSTALLMENT.

❷ *Why does Dickens end the
second installment here? What
important information has he
revealed, and what plot line
has he foreshadowed?*

Research Opportunity:

*There were essentially two classes of prisoners in the Bastille,
those who were under suspicion of a crime based on some evidence or cause, and those who were imprisoned on "grounds
of precaution" or for purposes of "admonitory correction."
Because these had no right to an investigation or hearing,
the length of their imprisonment depended on the will of the
king. Dr. Manette was apparently this type of prisoner.*

*Look up "lettres de cachet" and explain their relevance to
Dr. Manette's imprisonment.*

A Tale of Two Cities

CHARLES DICKENS

CHAPTER V
The Wine Shop

A LARGE CASK of wine had been dropped, and broken, in the street. It had tumbled out of a cart, the hoops had burst, and it lay on the stones outside the door of the wine shop, shattered like a walnut-shell.

Everyone within reach had stopped their work— or their idleness—to run to the spot and drink the wine. The rough, irregular stones of the street, pointing in all directions, and designed, it might seem, to cripple all living creatures that stepped on them, had dammed the wine into little pools; each pool was surrounded by its own jostling group or crowd, according to its size. Some men kneeled down, put their hands together to make scoops, and sipped, or tried to help women, who bent over their shoulders to sip, before the wine had all run out between their fingers. Others—men and women—dipped little mugs made of dented clay, or even handkerchiefs from women's heads, into the puddles, and ran the wine into infants' mouths. Others made small dams of mud, to control the direction of the wine as it ran. Others, directed by spectators from windows high above, ran here and there, to cut off streams of wine that were headed in new directions. Others focused on the soaked pieces

❷ *What condition is Dickens establishing in this scene?*

✔ *Note that the description of this place is very different from the setting of the previous chapters. Dickens has begun his third weekly installment by changing the setting from England to France.*

of the cask, licking and even chewing the wine-rotted wood with eager appetites. Although there was no drainage to carry off the wine, it was all picked up, and so much mud along with it, that it looked like a scavenger had been plundering the street—if anyone on that street could have believed there was anything there to steal.

The shrill sound of laughter and of amused voices—men, women, and children—resounded in the street while this wine game lasted. There was some roughness, but more playfulness. There was a special bond among those who played. Everyone felt a strong desire to join with someone else, which led to some playful hugs, toasts, handshakes, and even to some dancing—a dozen people together. When the wine was gone, and the places where it had been deepest had been raked into a grill-pattern by fingers, all of this playfulness stopped as suddenly as it had started. The man who had left his saw sticking in the firewood he was cutting went back to it and started sawing again. The woman who had left her pot of hot ashes on the doorstep, where she had been rubbing them into her arms and legs, trying to ease the pain in her starved limbs, returned to it. Men with bare arms, matted hair, and deathlike faces, who had come out into the winter light from cellars, went back down; and a gloom fell upon the scene that seemed more natural than sunshine.

The wine was red wine, and had stained the ground of this narrow street in the suburb of Saint Antoine, in Paris, where it was spilled. It had stained many hands, and many faces, and many naked feet, and many wooden shoes. The hands of the man who sawed the wood left red marks on his work; the forehead of the woman who nursed her baby, was stained with the wine on the old rag she wound about her head again. Those who had been gnawing on the wooden fragments now had a tigerish smear about the mouth; one tall wiseguy was so stained that he

✔ *The Saint Antoine quarter of Paris is where the infamous Bastille stood.*

❷ *Consider the imagery of the wine-stained hands and faces. What do you suppose is being foreshadowed?*

scrawled upon a wall with his finger dipped in muddy wine the single word: BLOOD.

The time would soon come, when that wine too would be spilled upon these stones, and when the stain of it would be red.

As the temporary happiness in Saint Antoine faded, the gloom returned heavily—cold, dirt, sickness, ignorance, and poverty, were the nobles now visiting the blessed saint. All of them were nobles of great power, but especially poverty. Examples of a people who had endured a terrible grinding and regrinding in the mill—not in the miraculous one that made old people young—shivered in every corner, went in and out every door, looked out every window, and trembled in every fragment of a garment shaking in the wind. The mill that had ground these people was the one that makes young people old. The children had ancient faces and serious voices. Everyone's face wore the signs of Hunger. It was everywhere. Hunger was in the ragged clothing that hung upon poles and clotheslines. Hunger was in the patches on each garment, made of straw and rag and wood and paper. Hunger was repeated in each crumb of firewood that the man sawed off. Hunger stared down the smokeless chimneys, and jumped up from the filthy street with no scrap of anything to eat among the garbage. Hunger was the sign on the baker's shelves, written on every tiny, spoiled loaf in his shrinking stock. It was found in every dog's body that was prepared and sold at the sausage shop. Hunger rattled its dry bones among the roasting chestnuts in the turning cylinder. Hunger was shred into tiny fragments in every potato chip, fried with reluctant drops of oil.

❤ *Note the metaphor. Blood is "that wine" that would be spilled soon.*

❤ *Note the metaphor. Who or what is the "blessed saint"?*

❤ *The metaphor of the mill and the grindstone will occur several times throughout this book. A mill grinds things into very fine powder—coffee beans into coffee grounds, wheat kernels in flour, etc.—and the part of the mill that does this grinding is the grindstone. The reference to the "miraculous mill" that makes old people young is an allusion to a popular children's rhyme of Dickens's day.*

Research Opportunity:

Look up some of the conditions that contributed to this poverty and hunger.

Hunger's residence was anywhere it chose to haunt. It could be a narrow, winding street filled with crime and filth. The people seemed hunted, and yet there was the possibility of turning, and attacking their hunter. They were depressed, and they slunk from place to place, and yet here and there were eyes of fire; lips turned white with unspoken words; foreheads so wrinkled with thought that they looked like the hangman's rope which they knew would be used on them if they did not first use it on someone else. The tradesmen's signs all advertised Poverty. The butcher and the porkman had signs of plump cows and pigs, but only sold the leanest scraps of meat; the baker, the driest of insufficient loaves. The people who were pictured as drinking in the wine shops, croaked to one another over their tiny portions of diluted wine and beer, and glared at one another through eyes that conveyed secrets they dared not speak aloud. The only flourishing trades were tools and weapons: the cutler's knives and axes were sharp and bright, the blacksmith's hammers were heavy, and the gunmaker's stock was murderous.

The city itself was poorly laid out as if it had been designed for suffering. The hard and jagged paving stones of the street ended at the doors of the shops. The gutter ran down the middle of the street—when it ran at all, which was only after heavy rains. Then it would run, by crazy turns here and there, into the houses. Instead of the generous gas lamps of London, the foul streets of Paris were "lighted" by solitary lamps slung by ropes and pulleys across the streets, far apart from one another. This weak grove of dim wicks swung overhead, as if they were at sea. Indeed, in the neighborhood of Saint Antoine, all were at sea, and the ship and crew were in danger of a fatal storm.

Indeed, the time would soon come, when the gaunt scarecrows of Saint Antoine would watch the lamplighter using his ropes and pulleys, to learn how to improve upon his method, so that they could hang

❷ *In this metaphor, who would be the "ship" and the "crew"?*

❷ *Who are the scarecrows? And who are the birds?*

men by those same ropes and pulleys. However, that time had not yet arrived, and every wind that blew across France shook the rags of the scarecrows in vain, because the wealthy birds, beautiful in song and exquisite in feather, took no warning.

The wine shop was fortunately placed on a corner, higher than the neighboring shops in both appearance and status. Its owner could only watch, in his yellow vest and green trousers, at the fight for the lost wine. "It's not my problem," he said, with a shrug of his shoulders. "The people from the market dropped the barrel. Let them send me another."

Then, noticing the tall joker writing on the wall, he called to him across the street: "Say, then, Gaspart, what are you doing there?"

The man pointed to his joke to show its importance, as comedians often do. No one else understood the joke, as also happens with from time to time.

"What now? Do you want to be locked up?" said the wine shop owner, who crossed the road and wiped out the writing with a handful of mud. "Why do you write on walls in the public streets? Is there no other place to do this kind of writing?"

While talking, he laid his clean hand upon the joker's heart. The joker rapped it with his own hand, jumped up into the air, and came down with one of his stained shoes now in his hand, and held it out. He looked very much like a clown now.

"Put it on, put it on," said the wine shop owner. "Call wine what it is, and stop there." He wiped his muddy hand on the joker's clothes—on purpose, because he had dirtied his hand to help the joker out, and then went back to his wine shop.

The owner of the wine shop had a thick neck and resembled a soldier here in his thirtieth year, and he looked like a man with a quick temper. Although it was a bitter cold day, he had his coat slung only over his shoulder. His shirt-sleeves were rolled up, and his brown arms were bare to the elbows. His head's only covering was his own crisply curled, short, dark hair.

❷ *Why does the author use metaphor so extensively in this section?*

❷ *What did the Joker mean by writing "blood" on the wall, and why does the wine merchant wipe it out?*

He was a dark-looking person, with good eyes, set wide apart. He appeared to be a friendly fellow, but also a stubborn one. This was a man who would not change his mind, once his purpose was set.

Madame Defarge, his wife, was behind the counter as he came in. She was a stout woman, about the same age as her husband, with a watchful eye that seemed to rove and shift continuously over everything in her sight. Her large hand was heavy with rings, and her strong-featured face was steady and calm. She seemed like a person who did not often make mistakes that would harm herself or her plans. Since she was more sensitive to cold, she was wrapped in fur, and had a shawl wrapped about her head, showing only her earrings. Her knitting was in front of her, but she had set it down to pick her teeth with a toothpick. She said nothing when her husband returned, but coughed quietly, and lifted her eyebrows just enough for him to notice. Her husband knew that he should look around among the customers who had come in while he was out in the street.

❷ What do the descriptions of M. and Mme. Defarge suggest about them?

And so the wine shop owner scanned the room, until his eyes rested on an elderly gentleman and a young lady, who were seated in a corner. There were other customers: two playing cards, two playing dominoes, and three standing by the counter nursing small glasses of wine. As he passed behind the counter, he noticed that the elderly gentleman gave him a look of recognition.

❷ Who do you suppose the elderly gentleman is? The young lady?

"What the devil are you doing?" said Monsieur Defarge to himself, "I don't know you."

He pretended not to notice the two strangers, though, and started talking to the three customers drinking at the counter.

"How goes it, Jacques?" said one of these three to Monsieur Defarge. "Is all the spilled wine gone?"

"Every drop, Jacques," answered Monsieur Defarge.

When these names were given, Madame Defarge,

still picking her teeth, coughed and raised her eyebrows just so again.

"It doesn't happen often," said the second of
the three to Monsieur Defarge, "that these miserable
beasts get to taste of anything but black bread and
death, let alone wine. Isn't that so, Jacques?"

"It is so, Jacques," Monsieur Defarge returned.

With this second exchange of first names, Madame
Defarge, still calmly picking her teeth, coughed lightly
and raised her eyebrows again.

The last of the three now had his say, as he put
down his empty glass and smacked his lips.

"So horrible! Those poor beasts always have such
a bitter taste in their mouths, and their lives are so
hard. Am I right, Jacques?"

"You are right, Jacques," was the response of
Monsieur Defarge.

This third exchange made Madame Defarge take
her toothpick out and rustle in her seat.

"All of this is true!" muttered her husband.
"Gentlemen: my wife!"

The three customers pulled off their hats, bowing grandly, to Madame Defarge. She nodded her
response. Then, glancing around the wine shop, took
her knitting, and became focused her full attention on
it once again.

"Gentlemen," said her husband, who had been
watching her the whole time, "good day. The room,
furnished for a single man, that you wished to see, is
on the fifth floor. The doorway of the staircase is just
off the little courtyard close to the left here. But, now
that I remember, one of you has already been there,
and can show the way. Adieu!"

They paid for their wine and left their place. As
Monsieur Defarge studied his wife at her knitting, the
elderly gentleman walked from his corner and asked
to speak with him.

"Of course, sir," said Monsieur Defarge, and they
both stepped quietly to the door.

❷ *What important information is the author hinting at
in this conversation and in
Mme. Defarge's reaction?*

Their conversation was short, but very certain. From the beginning, Monsieur Defarge paid close attention. But the meeting did not last a minute— then, Defarge nodded and went out. The gentleman signaled to the young lady, and they too went out. Madame Defarge knitted with nimble fingers and a steady expression, and gave no evidence of having seen anything.

Mr. Jarvis Lorry and Miss Manette met Monsieur Defarge in the same doorway to which he had sent his three visitors just moments before. It opened onto a stinking little black courtyard, and was the public entrance to a great number of houses, inhabited by a great number of people. In this gloomy setting, Monsieur Defarge bent down on one knee to the child of his old master, and put her hand to his lips. It was a gentle action, but not done with gentle attitude: he had changed dramatically in the last few seconds. His smile had vanished; he had become a secret, angry, dangerous man.

As they began climbing the stairs, Monsieur Defarge warned them both: "It is very high; it is a little difficult. Better to begin slowly."

"Is he alone?" Mr. Lorry whispered.

"Alone! God help anyone who would be with him!" said the other, in a low voice.

"Is he always alone, then?"

"Yes."

"Is that what he wants?"

"It is what he *needs*. He hasn't changed at all since I first saw him after his jailers found him and demanded to know if I would take him and be discreet about it."

"Prison has changed him, then?"

"Changed!"

The wine shop owner stopped to strike the wall with his hand and mutter a foul curse; this answer was stronger than any direct one would have been. Mr. Lorry's spirits grew heavier, as he and his companions climbed higher.

Remember that in Chapter IV, Mr. Lorry told Miss Manette that her father had been taken to the house of a former servant. M. Defarge is that former servant.

Even in our own time, such a staircase, in the parts of Paris that are older and more crowded, would be unpleasant; at that time, it was disgusting to those who were not used to it. Every little apartment within the large building left its own pile of trash on the landing, and threw more garbage out the window into the street. The uncontrolled decay would have polluted any air—the poverty and scarcity made this air virtually toxic. It was through this air, though, climbing up a steep, dark shaft of dirt and poison, that these three had to go. Mr. Jarvis Lorry stopped twice to rest, each time over a small, sad ventilation grate that seemed to let all of the healthy air *out* of the building, while inviting all of the unhealthy air to come *in*. Through the rusty bars, one could sense what the neighborhood must be like; the only signs of healthy life were the two great towers of Notre-Dame cathedral, miles distant.

Finally, they reached the top of the stairs, and they rested a third time. However, a narrower, steeper, staircase still lay between them and their goal. At this landing, the wine shop owner, who had been walking slightly ahead of the other two, and keeping Mr. Lorry between himself and Ms. Manette, as though he wanted to avoid answering any of her questions, turned around, felt in his coat pockets, and took out a key.

"The door is locked then, my friend?" said Mr. Lorry in surprise.

"Ah, yes," was the grim reply of Monsieur Defarge.

"Do you think it is necessary to keep the unfortunate gentleman so confined?"

"I think it is necessary to turn the key." Monsieur Defarge whispered it closer in his ear, and frowned heavily.

"Why?"

"Why! Because he has lived so long, locked up, that he would tear himself to pieces in fright—die—if the door was left open."

❷ *Look up the "three estates" of pre-Revolutionary France. What is the significance of this reference to Notre-Dame?*

"Is it possible!" exclaimed Mr. Lorry.

"Is it possible!" repeated Defarge, bitterly. "Yes. And a beautiful world we live in, when such things are possible, and not only possible, but done—done!—under that sky there every day. Long live the Devil. Let us go on."

This conversation had been held in such a low whisper, that not a word of it had reached the young lady's ears. However, she was trembling so badly with emotion, and her face showed such dread and terror, that Mr. Lorry felt that he should speak a word or two of reassurance.

"Have courage, dear Miss! The worst will be over in a moment; all we have to do is pass the room-door, and the worst will be over. Then all the good, the happiness you bring to him, will begin. Let our good friend here help you up the stairs. Good, friend Defarge. Come now. Business, business!"

They went up slowly and softly. This staircase was short, and they were soon at the top. There, coming around a sharp turn, they suddenly saw three men, with their heads bent down close together at the side of a door, looking into the room through some chinks or holes in the wall. Hearing footsteps, they turned and rose—they were the three customers from the wine shop.

"I forgot them in the surprise of your visit," explained Monsieur Defarge. "Leave us, fellows, we have business here."

The three glided by, and went silently down the stairs.

Since there was no other door on this floor, and the wine shop owner went straight to this door when they were left alone, Mr. Lorry angrily whispered to him:

"Do you make a show of Monsieur Manette?"

"I show him, like this, to a chosen few."

"Should you?"

"I think I should."

"Who are these few? How do you choose them?"

"I choose them as loyal men who share my name—Jacques is my name. I choose them as men—for whom the sight of Monsieur Manette is likely to do good. Enough—you are English, and I do not expect you to understand. Wait here one moment, please."

Gesturing to keep them back, he stooped and looked in through the crevice in the wall. Raising his head again, he rapped on the door two or three times—only for the purpose of making noise. Similarly, he ran his key across the door three or four times, before he slid it clumsily into the lock, turning it as heavily as he could.

He pushed the door slowly inward, and he looked into the room and said something. A faint voice answered something—barely more than a single syllable on either side.

He looked back over his shoulder, and signaled them to enter. Mr. Lorry slid his arm securely around the daughter's waist, and held her; because he felt her sinking.

"Ah, business, business!" he urged, with a most unbusinesslike tear on his cheek. "Come in, come in!"

"I am afraid of it," she answered, shuddering.

"Of it? Of what?"

"I mean of him. Of my father."

Her state made him desperate to follow their leader, so he drew her arm over his neck, lifted her slightly, and hurried her into he room. He set her down just inside the door, and held her, as she clung to him.

Defarge pulled out the key, closed the door, locked it from the inside, took the key out again, and held it—all as loudly as possible. Finally, he walked across the room to the window, stopped, and turned around.

This attic, built for storing firewood and other things, was dim and dark; the window was really a door in the roof, with a crane over it for lifting up

✅ *We still use "French Doors" in building design today.*

❓ *On what note of suspense or surprise does Dickens end this third weekly installment?*

cargo from the street. Like any French-made door, its two sections closed in the middle. One half of this door was locked, and the other just barely open, to keep out the cold. So little light was let in this way, that it was difficult, at first, to see anything. Only after a long while in this room would one's eyes have adjusted to be able to do work requiring any detail.

Nonetheless, finely detailed work was being done in this room. With his back to the door, and his face toward the window, where the wine shop owner stood looking at him, a white-haired man sat on a low bench, stooping forward, very busy at making shoes.

THIS IS THE END OF THE THIRD WEEKLY INSTALLMENT.

Research Opportunity:

What was the Jacquerie? Why did these men refer to each other as "Jacques"?

A Tale of Two Cities

CHARLES DICKENS

CHAPTER VI
The Shoemaker

"GOOD DAY!" said Monsieur Defarge, looking down at the white head bent over the shoemaking.

The head rose for a moment, and a very faint voice said, as if from a distance: "Good day!"

"You are still hard at work, I see?"

After a long silence, the head rose again, and the voice answered, "Yes—I am working." This time, two tired eyes looked at their questioner, before the face dropped again.

The faintness of the voice was pitiful and frightening. This was not the faintness of physical weakness, but of solitude and disuse—much like the last echo of a sound made very long ago. This echo had lost the sound of life in a human voice, so that it seemed like the dried stain left behind by a once beautiful color. It was so suppressed that it sounded like a voice underground. It was so lost and hopeless, that it was the voice a starved, lost traveler would have used in the wilderness to remember family and friends before lying down to die.

After some more minutes of silent work, the eyes looked up again—not with any interest, but just awareness that the visitor was still standing where he had been.

Reread this paragraph just to notice the beauty of the description of the shoemaker's voice.

What is the narrator suggesting about the voice of the prisoner with this description?

"I would like," said Defarge, still looking at the shoemaker, "to let some more light in here. Is that all right with you?"

The shoemaker stopped his work and looked around—first, at the floor on one side; then, at the floor on the other side; finally, up at the speaker.

"What did you say?"

"Can you bear a little more light?"

"I must, if you let it in." (Just the slightest stress on the word "must.")

The opened door was pushed a little further ajar, and fastened at that point. Now a broad beam of light came into the attic and showed the workman with an unfinished shoe upon his lap. His tools and some scraps of leather were at his feet and on his bench. He had a white beard, raggedly cut, but not very long, a hollow face, and extremely bright eyes. These eyes would have looked large anyway, because of his thin face and dark eyebrows, but since they were naturally large, now they looked enormous. His shirt, ragged and yellow, was open at the throat, and showed a withered, worn body. He had turned to the same shade of parchment-yellow as his clothes and stockings, because of his long isolation.

He had put up a hand to shield his eyes from the light, and it seemed that even his bones were transparent. He sat there with a vacant gaze, looking at the floor on either side of him, then back up at his visitor. When he spoke, he seemed at first to forget what he was about to say.

"Are you going to finish that pair of shoes today?" asked Defarge, waving Mr. Lorry forward.

"I can't say that I mean to. I suppose so. I don't know."

The question reminded him of his work, and he bent over it again.

Mr. Lorry came forward silently, leaving the daughter by the door. After he had stood by Defarge for a minute or two, the shoemaker looked up. He showed no surprise at this new guest, but one of his fingers strayed to his lips (his fingernails and lips were both the color of pale lead), and then the hand dropped back to his work. The look and the action had taken just a second.

"You have a visitor," said Monsieur Defarge.

"What did you say?"

"Here is a visitor."

The shoemaker looked up again, but kept his hands on his work.

"Look!" said Defarge. "Here is a man, who knows a well-made shoe when he sees one. Show him that shoe you are working on. Take it, Monsieur."

Mr. Lorry took it in his hand.

"Tell Monsieur what kind of shoe it is, and the maker's name?"

After a longer pause than usual, the shoemaker replied, "I forget what you asked me. What did you say?"

"I said, would you describe the shoe, for the gentleman's information?"

"It is a lady's shoe. It is a young lady's walking-shoe. It is the current fashion. I never saw the model. I have had a pattern in my hand." He glanced at the shoe with a small look of pride.

"And the maker's name?" said Defarge.

Since his hands were now empty, he laid the knuckles of the right hand in the palm of the left, and then the knuckles of the left hand in the palm of the right, and then passed a hand across his chin, and so on in regular cycles, without pausing. Pulling him from the trance he sank into after speaking was like holding onto the spirit of a man headed for death.

"Did you ask me for my name?"

"Yes, I did."

"One Hundred and Five, North Tower."

"Is that all?"

"One Hundred and Five, North Tower."

With a weary sound that was neither a sigh nor a groan, he bent back to work, until the silence was broken again.

✔ *Remember that Mr. Lorry told Miss Manette that her father was using a name different from his own either because he had forgotten his name or thought it was dangerous to use it.*

❷ *What does the name Doctor Manette gives signify?*

"Are you not a shoemaker by trade?" said Mr. Lorry, looking directly at him.

His weary eyes turned to Defarge as if he expected him to answer for him; however, as no word came from the wine shop owner, his eyes went back to Mr. Lorry after looking down at the ground.

"No, I was not a shoemaker by trade. I learned it here. I taught myself. I asked permission to—"

He paused again, even more minutes, running his hands through the same cycles as before. His eyes came slowly back, finally, to Mr. Lorry's face; when they rested there, he started again, like a sleeper just waking up, but talking about the same topic as the night before.

"I asked permission to teach myself, and I got it with much difficulty after a long time, and I have made shoes ever since."

As he held out his hand to get his shoe back, Mr. Lorry said, still looking directly at him: "Monsieur Manette, don't you remember me at all?"

The shoe dropped to the ground, and the shoemaker looked fixedly at Mr. Lorry.

"Monsieur Manette—" Mr. Lorry laid his hand upon Defarge's arm, "do you not remember this man? Look at him. Look at me. Is there no old banker, no old business, no old servant, no old time, in your memory, Monsieur Manette?"

Some long hidden signs of intelligence began to appear on the shoemaker's forehead as he stared at Mr. Lorry and at Defarge, as though coming through a black mist. His forehead was deeply wrinkled exactly as the fair young woman's had been. She had crept along the wall to a point where she could now see him, and was looking at him, her hands raised—first in fear and compassion, but were now reaching out toward him with a desire to pull him to her and love him back to life and to hope. Their expressions were so similar, that it looked like a passing light, moving between the two of them.

But darkness soon returned to the shoemaker's

face. He looked at Defarge and Mr. Lorry, with less and less attention, and his eyes searched for the ground, and for his work. Finally, he picked up the shoe, and continued his work.

"Have you recognized him, Monsieur?" asked Defarge in a whisper.

"Yes, for a moment. At first, I thought it was hopeless, but, for a single moment, I saw the face that I once knew so well. Hush! Let us move back!"

She had moved from the attic wall, and stood very close to the bench where he sat. His failure to notice the figure that could have reached out and touched him was frightening.

Not a word was spoken; not a sound was made. She stood, like a spirit, beside him, as he bent over his work.

Eventually, he needed to change tools, and he reached for his shoemaker's knife. After he picked it up, his eyes caught the skirt of her dress. He raised his eyes and saw her face. The two spectators moved forward, but she stopped them with a motion of her hand; she had no fear of his striking at her.

He stared at her, frightened. After a while, his lips began to move, but no sound came out. As his breath quickened, the spectators heard him whisper, "What is this?"

With tears streaming down her face, she put her hands to her lips, and kissed them to him, then clasped her hands to her breast, as if she held his ruined head there.

"Are you the jailer's daughter?"

"No," she sighed.

"Who are you?"

She did not trust her voice, but instead sat down beside him. He shrank back, but she laid her hand upon his arm. A strange thrill struck him, and passed through his body. He set his knife down softly, and stared at her.

Her golden hair, worn in long curls, had been hurriedly pushed aside, and fell down over her neck. He slid his hand slowly, picked up her hair and looked at it. Suddenly, though, he let out another deep sigh and went back to his shoe.

But not for long. She released his arm and laid her hand upon his shoulder. He looked at it, two or three times, as if it might disappear, and then he set down his work, put his hand to his neck, and took off a blackened string with a scrap of folded rag attached to it. He opened it, carefully, on his knee, and it contained a very little quantity of hair: just one or two long, golden hairs, which had been wound, a long time ago, around his finger.

He took her hair in his hand again, and examined it. "It is the same. How can it be? When was it? How was it?"

As the look of concentration returned to his forehead, he recognized it on hers as well. He turned her to face the light, and looked at her.

What do you suppose is going on here? Who does Doctor Manette think his daughter is? Where do you think this golden hair came from?

"She had laid her head upon my shoulder, the night when I was called out—she was afraid, but I was not—and when I was brought to the North Tower, they found these hairs upon my sleeve. 'You will leave them for me? They will never help my body escape, but they may help my spirit,' I said. I remember those words very well."

He moved his lips to these words many times before he could actually say them. When the words came, they were clear, but slow.

"How was this? Was it you?"

Once more, the spectators jumped, as he turned upon her suddenly. However, she sat perfectly still in his grasp and said only, "I beg you, do not come near us, do not speak, do not move!"

"Hark!" he exclaimed. "Whose voice was that?"

Why is Miss Manette's voice such a shock to the prisoner?

As he uttered this cry, his hands released her, and flew up to tear his white hair. His frenzy wore out, as did everything but his shoemaking. He folded his little packet again, and tried to fasten it on his breast, but he still looked at her, and sadly shook his head.

"No, no, no; you are too young, too blooming. It

can't be. See what the prisoner is. These are not the hands she knew, not the face she knew, not a voice she ever heard. No, no. She was—and he was—before the slow years of the North Tower—ages ago. What is your name, my gentle angel?"

Hearing his soft tone and attitude, his daughter fell upon her knees before him, with her hands upon his chest.

"Sir, at another time you shall know my name, and who my mother was, and who my father was, and how I've never known their terrible story. However, I cannot tell you now or here. All that I may ask you is to touch me and to bless me. Kiss me, kiss me! O my dear, my dear!"

His cold white hair mixed with her radiant blonde curls, which shone on him like the light of Freedom.

"If my voice is anything like the voice that was once sweet music in your ears, weep for it! If my hair is anything like the beloved head that lay on your chest when you were young and free, weep for it! If my promise of a new Home is anything like your memories of a Home long ago, weep for it!"

She hugged him closer and rocked him on her breast like a child.

"If, when I tell you that your agony is over, and we go to England to live in peace, you think of your lost lifetime, and of the wickedness of France, weep for it! And if, when I tell you who I am, and who my mother and father are, weep for it! Weep for my mother and for me! Good gentlemen, thank God! I feel his sacred tears upon my face, and his sobs strike my heart. See! Thank God for us, thank God!"

He had sunk into her arms, and his face lay on her breast: a sight touching, and yet terrible because of the suffering that had come before it—so much so that the two beholders covered their faces.

After quiet had returned to the attic, and his tears and trembling had subsided, the two came forward to lift father and daughter from the ground. He had gradually fallen to the floor and lay there, worn out.

❷ *Why would Dickens develop this reunion scene so melodramatically?*

She had nestled with him, so that his head lay on her arm, and her hair was his curtain from the light.

"Could we leave Paris at once? From this very door?" Her questions caught Mr. Lorry in the middle of returning an air of business to his face.

"Is he fit for the journey?" asked Mr. Lorry.

"More fit for that, than to stay here in this city, so terrifying to him."

"It is true," said Defarge. "More than that, Monsieur Manette would be safer out of France. Shall I hire a carriage and horses?"

"That's business," said Mr. Lorry, returning to his methodical manners. "If there is business to be done, I had better do it."

"Then please," urged Miss Manette, "leave us here. Look how calm he is—there is no reason to fear leaving him alone with me. If you lock the door when you leave, I am sure that you will find him as quiet when you return as he is now. In any case, I will take care of him until you return, and then we will move him."

Both Mr. Lorry and Defarge were against this, preferring that one remain. However, since the journey needed not only a carriage and horses but traveling papers as well, even this late in the day, both of them hurried off to take care of their business.

As the darkness closed in, the daughter laid her head down on the ground by her father's side, watching him. As the darkness deepened, they both lay quiet, until a light gleamed through the chinks in the wall.

Everything was ready for the journey. In the carriage, the two men had placed traveling cloaks and wrappers, bread and meat, wine, and hot coffee, wrapping them on the shoemaker's bench. They awoke the captive, and helped him up.

No one could interpret the look of blank surprise on his face—whether he knew what had happened, what had been said to him, whether he was free or

❷ *Why might Dr. Manette still be unsafe in France?*

not. They tried speaking to him, but his confusion
frightened them, and so they agreed not to try to talk
to him. He had a wild way of clasping his head in his
hands, that none had observed before, but his daughter's voice was to him as the sun is to a plant—he
turned toward it whenever she spoke.

Note the analogy.

In the submissive way of someone long used to
prison, he ate and drank what he was given, and put
on the cloak and other wrappers that he was given. He
easily let his daughter draw her arm through his, and
took—and held—her hand in both of his.

They began to go down the stairs—Monsieur
Defarge first with the lamp, Mr. Lorry in the rear.
They had not made it halfway down the long staircase
yet when he stopped, and stared at the roof and at
the walls.

"Do you remember this place, father? Do you
remember coming up here?"

"What did you say?"

Before she repeated her question, he murmured his answer, "Remember? No. It was so very
long ago."

They heard him mutter "One Hundred and Five,
North Tower" as he looked around him. It was clear
that he did not remember being brought here from
his prison, and thought that the walls of this house
were the strong fortress-walls where he had been
confined. In the courtyard, he changed his steps,
expecting a bridge. But there was no bridge—only a
carriage. Confronted with this difference, he dropped
his daughter's hand and grabbed his head again.

There was no crowd around the door—not even
an accidental pedestrian in the street. The only soul
in this unnatural quiet was Madame Defarge—who
leaned against the doorpost, knitting, seeing nothing.

The prisoner got into the coach, and Mr. Lorry
was about to get in behind him, when the prisoner
asked for his shoemaking tools, and unfinished shoes.
Madame Defarge immediately shouted that she would

❷ *What effect is the author creating by repeating "seeing nothing?"*

go get them. She quickly brought them, handed them in, and returned to the doorpost, leaning, knitting, seeing nothing.

Defarge climbed up on the carriage, and ordered the driver "To the Gate!" The driver cracked his whip, and they clattered away under the dim, swinging lamps.

They passed under the lamps—brighter in the better streets, and dimmer in the worse—by lighted shops, happy crowds, bright coffee-houses and theater doors, to one of the city gates. Soldiers there asked for their papers, and Defarge pulled one of them apart from the others. "See here then, Monsieur Officer," he said, "these are the papers of the man inside, with the white head. They were given to me, with him, at the…" He dropped his voice, and the soldier approached the carriage door to examine the prisoner. "It is well. Forward!"

"Adieu!" said Defarge. And so the carriage went on, through the light of dimmer and dimmer lamps, out under the stars.

Beneath the great arch of the stars—some, so far away that we've never even seen their light—the shadows of the night were broad and black. As they did when he was traveling with the mail, the shadows asked Mr. Lorry the old question:

"Do you want to be recalled to life?"

And the old answer:

"I don't know."

THIS IS THE END OF THE
FOURTH WEEKLY INSTALLMENT.

THE END OF THE FIRST BOOK.

A Tale of Two Cities

CHARLES DICKENS

BOOK THE SECOND. THE GOLDEN THREAD

CHAPTER I
Five Years Later

EVEN BY THE standards of 1780, Tellson's Bank, located near the Temple Bar, was considered old-fashioned. It was small, very dark, very ugly, and very inconvenient. Its lack of fashion was a source of pride among the partners, who delighted in their bank's smallness, darkness, ugliness, and inconvenience. They bragged that, if the bank were more pleasant, it would be less respectable—a boast that they made to ridicule the more convenient banks. Tellson's needed no elbow-room—no bright lights—no fancy frills. Noakes and Co. might, and Snooks Brothers' might—but never Tellson's!

Had any of these partners' sons mentioned remodeling Tellson's, they would have been disinherited on the spot. This was similar to the attitude of England as a whole—anyone who suggested improvements in laws and traditions often received severe punishment.

And so Tellson's had become the perfection of inconvenience. After having to use all of your strength to push open a door that would rattle back at you, you fell down two steps and found yourself in a miserable little shop, with two little counters, where ancient men would make your check shake as if a strong

The Temple Bar is the westernmost boundary of the City of London, before the entrance to Westminster. In the late 1700s, this was a wall containing a stone archway, which was designed by the famous architect Sir Christopher Wren. As mentioned in the story, the heads of traitors were mounted on pikes that were set up on this barrier.

Noakes and Co. and Snooks Brothers' were rival banks to Tellson's.

What is the author saying about the British government? How does this compare to the situation in France?

breeze were whistling through the room, while they examined the signature through windows continually spotted and crusted by mud from Fleet Street, and criss-crossed by their own iron bars. If you had to see "the House" (a manager), you were put into a holding tank in the bank, where you thought about the mistakes you had made in life, until the House could see you. Your money was held in old wooden drawers with worms as companions—wood that would shed particles every time the drawers were opened or closed. Your money smelled like decomposing rags; your silver was hidden in one of many filthy vaults, where even the best polish was corrupted in a day or two. Your documents were placed in rooms converted from kitchens, and so were soon dried out. Your other family papers went into an old dining room that never had a meal, and had only recently been placed out of the view of the condemned, mounted across the way at the Temple Bar.

In those days, executions were an appropriate punishment for people of all trades and professions. Death is Nature's solution for all things—so why not the Law's solution? And so, the forger was put to Death; the slanderer was put to death; the mail thief was put to death; the petty thief was put to Death; the horse thief was put to Death; the counterfeiter was put to Death; at least three out every four criminals were put to Death. The idea was that this would prevent crime; however, it seemed to do the opposite. One benefit, though, was the fact that no one had to worry about the future of criminals dangling from ropes. In fact Tellson's, in its day, had successfully pressed charges against so many criminals, that if you laid all their heads in front of the windows, any remaining light would have been entirely blocked out.

In Tellson's you would see the oldest of men, cramped in by shelves and cabinets, gravely at work. When a young man was hired at Tellson's London branch, they hid him somewhere until he was old. They would store him in the dark, much like an aging cheese, until he had a similar flavor and blue-mold growing on him. Only then could he be seen in his decay, spectacularly examining large books.

Standing outside Tellson's—and only permitted in if he was needed—was an errand-man—occasionally a courier and messenger. He was never absent during business hours, unless he was on an errand, and even then he was represented by his son, a dirty child of twelve. People understood that Tellson's, in a dignified way, tolerated the errand-man. The house had always tolerated someone in that job, and fate had sent this person to the post. His last name was Cruncher, and upon his baptism, in the eastern parish church of Hounsditch, he had received his first name, Jerry.

Our scene now was Mr. Cruncher's home in Hanging-sword-alley, Whitefriars. The time, 7:30 on a windy March morning, 1780.

This home was not in a pleasant neighborhood, and had only two rooms, including a closet with a single pane of glass for a window. However, the rooms were kept very clean. Even this early, the room where Jerry still lay in bed was already scrubbed, and a sparkling white tablecloth lay on his breakfast table.

Mr. Cruncher rested under a patchwork window, like a Harlequin at home. At first, he slept heavily, but he gradually began to roll and turn in bed, until he rose up, with his spiky hair looking as though it would tear the sheets to ribbons. At this point, he exclaimed, in a voice of deep frustration, "Bust me, if she ain't at it agin!"

A clean and careful-looking woman rose hastily and nervously from her knees in a corner.

"What?" said Mr. Cruncher, looking for a boot. "You're at it again, are you?"

After greeting her twice in this way, he threw a boot at her. It was a very muddy boot—which was unusual, since he often came home from work with clean boots, only to wake up with them covered in clay.

☑ Note the mild sarcasm in the simile.

☑ Remember that Mr. Lorry—a man of business—has been at Tellson's for over forty years, over twenty in the Paris office and now twenty since he left Paris with Miss Manette as a child.

☑ In Dickens's London, Whitefriars was a relatively unfashionable neighborhood, the site of an old monastery.

☑ The Harlequin was a character in a medieval drama form known as the commedia dell'arte, in which the characters represent extreme forms of human impulses. Like the Jester, the Harlequin was usually in a multi-colored costume with a diamond-shaped pattern (like Jerry's quilt), and originally was the Devil's messenger, coming from the underworld with blackened fingers—which was not so unsuitable, considering the rust Jerry constantly has on his own fingers.

"What," said Mr. Cruncher, changing his greeting after the boot missed the woman—"what are you up to, Aggerawayter?"

"I was only saying my prayers."

"Saying your prayers! That's wonderful! What do you mean by flopping yourself down onto the floor and praying against me?"

"I was not praying against you. I was praying *for* you."

"You were not. And if you were, I won't let you do it. Here! Your mother's a nice woman, young Jerry, going and praying against your father's success. You've got a dutiful mother, my son. You've got a religious mother, my boy, going and flopping herself down, and praying that the bread-and-butter may be snatched out of your mouth—the mouth of her only child."

Master Cruncher (who was in his shirt) was very upset, and, turning to his mother, strongly objected to her depriving him of his own personal food.

"And what do you suppose, you conceited female," said Mr. Cruncher, "that the worth of your prayers may be? What would you charge for your prayers?"

"They come only from the heart, Jerry. They are worth no more than that."

"Worth no more than that," he repeated. "They ain't worth much, then. I won't let you pray against me. I can't afford it. I'm not going to be made unlucky by your sneaking. If you must go flopping yourself down, flop in favor of your husband and child, and not against them. If I had a decent wife, and if this poor boy had a decent mother, I might have made some money last week instead of being prayed against and undermined and manipulated into the worst of luck. Bust me!" said Mr. Cruncher, who had been dressing during this outburst. "If piety and one thing after another, haven't brought me as bad luck as an honest worker ever met! Young Jerry, get dressed, and keep your eyes on your mother while I clean my boots. If you see any signs of her flopping, give me a call. I won't be betrayed like this. I am as rickety as a hackney-coach. I'm as sleepy as an opium addict. My joints are so stiff that I wouldn't know which are mine and which are someone else's except for the pain. Yet, I've got no money to show for it. I think you've been at it from morning to night, praying to keep me from making any money, and I won't put up with it, Aggerawayter, and what do you say now?"

While growling and continuing to spout insults at his wife, Mr. Cruncher turned back to cleaning his boots and getting ready for work. His son, whose hair had the same spikes as his father's, just in a softer form, kept watch over his mother. He would run out of the closet where he slept, where he was getting ready, and yelled, "You're about to flop, mother! Father!" After raising these false alarms, he would run back into his closet with an undutiful grin.

Mr. Cruncher's mood had not improved when he came to breakfast. He especially resented Mrs. Cruncher's saying grace.

"Now, Aggerawayter? What are you up to? At it again?"

His wife explained that she had merely "asked a blessing."

"Don't do it!" said Mr. Cruncher, looking about, as if he expected the bread to disappear as a result of his wife's prayers. "I ain't a-going to be blessed out of house and home. I won't have my vittles blessed off my tables. Keep quiet!"

Looking red-eyed and grim, as if he had been at an all-night party that had gone wrong, Jerry Cruncher harassed rather than ate his breakfast, growling over it as if he were an animal and it was feeding time at the zoo. Around 9:00 he smoothed his expression and, looking as respectable as he could, left his house to meet the day.

He referred to himself as an "honest tradesman," and yet what he did could hardly be called a "trade." His supplies consisted of a wooden stool, which his

While introducing us to a new character who will play a very important role later in the story, and building suspense as to the nature of Jerry's occupation, Dickens also offers his readers a comic scene, similar to comic relief in a tragedy.

son carried every morning to the bank window. After adding a handful of straw to keep his feet warm, that was his "shop" for the day. At his post, Mr. Cruncher was as well-known to Fleet Street and the Temple, as the Bar itself—and almost as gruesome-looking.

Jerry took up his post at 8:45, in time to greet the oldest of men as they came into work at Tellson's, with young Jerry by him, when he was not running through the Bar to bully younger boys. Father and son, sitting and watching the morning traffic, resembled each other—and looked much like a pair of monkeys. This resemblance was increased by the older Jerry's habit of biting and spitting out straw, while the younger Jerry's eyes restlessly watched his father, and everything else in Fleet Street.

The head of one of the indoor messengers popped through the door, and shouted, "Porter wanted!"

"Hooray, father! Here's an early job to begin with!"

Having sent his father off with a blessing, young Jerry seated himself on the stool, took up his father's interest in chewing straw, and thought.

"Always rusty! His fingers is always rusty!" muttered young Jerry. "Where does my father get all that iron rust from? He don't get no iron rust here!"

❷ *Where does he get rusty hands? And why are his boots muddy when he wakes up?*

Writing Opportunity:

Write an essay in which you analyze Dickens's use of humor in this chapter.

A Tale of Two Cities

CHARLES DICKENS

CHAPTER II

A Sight

"I'M SURE YOU know the Old Bailey well?" said one of the oldest clerks to Jerry.

"Ye-e-es, sir," returned Jerry, somewhat doggedly. "I do know the Bailey."

"Just so. And you know Mr. Lorry."

"I know Mr. Lorry, sir, much better than I know the Bailey. Much better, than I—as an honest trades-man—wish to know the Bailey" said Jerry—much like a reluctant witness inside that same Old Bailey.

"Very well. Find the door for witnesses, and show the door-keeper this note for Mr. Lorry. He will then let you in."

"Into the court, sir?"

"Into the court."

Mr. Cruncher crossed his eyes as if one wanted to ask the other, "What do you think of this?"

"Am I to wait in the court, sir?" he asked the clerk.

"I am going to tell you. The door-keeper will pass the note to Mr. Lorry, and you make a sign to Mr. Lorry, so he can see where you are standing. Then, stand there until he wants you."

"Is that all, sir?"

"That's all. He wishes to have a messenger at his

The Old Bailey is the criminal court in London—thus Jerry is proud that he only has limited knowledge of its operations.

disposal. This is to tell him you are there."

As the ancient clerk folded and wrote on the outside of the note, Mr. Cruncher, asked, "I suppose they're trying Forgeries this morning?"

"Treason!"

"That's quartering," said Jerry. "Barbarous!"

"It is the law," remarked the ancient clerk. "It is the law."

"It's cruel of the law to spill a man, I think. It's cruel enough to kill him, but it's very cruel to spill his insides into the street, sir."

"Not at all," replied the ancient clerk. "Speak well of the law. Take care of your chest and voice, my good friend, and let the law take care of itself. That's my advice."

"It's the damp, sir, that settles on my chest and voice," said Jerry. "I leave you to judge what a damp way of earning a living mine is."

"Well, well," said the old clerk, "we all have our various ways of earning a living. Some of us have damp ways, and others have dry ways. Here's the letter. Go along."

Jerry took the letter, and, remarking to himself less respectful of the ancient man than his outward manner suggested, "You're a skinny, old thing, too." With this, he made his bow, told his son where he was going, and went on his way.

Hangings were out at Tyburn, in those days, so the street outside the Newgate Prison did not have the same awful reputation that it does now. However, it was still a vile place, where all sorts of evil were committed, and where such deadly diseases were bred, that would come into court with the prisoners—even right up at the judge himself. It had happened more than once, that the Judge in the black cap would catch a disease like typhus and pronounce his own death sentence along with the prisoner's, sometimes even dying before him. The Old Bailey was famous as a kind of deadly hotel courtyard, where countless pale travelers started their journey, in carts and carriages, on a violent passage into the other world, crossing two and a half miles of public street and roads, to the hangman's noose. The Old Bailey was also famous for the pillory—a wise institution that inflicted a punishment with consequences that no one could foresee, also famous for the whipping-post, very humanizing and softening to watch in action, also, for extensive dealing in blood-money, which led to every imaginable mercenary sort of crime. Altogether, the Old Bailey was a prime example of the idea that, "Everything that is, is right"—a proverb that would prove to be as final as it was lazy, because it implied that nothing that ever was, was wrong.

Making his way through this tainted crowd, through all these attractions, Jerry found the door he was looking for, and handed in his letter through a slot. Back then, people had to pay to get into the Old Bailey, just as they paid to see a play in Bedlam—but the courtroom entertainment was much more expensive. Therefore, all the doors were well guarded—except the doors for the criminals, which were always wide open.

After some delay and denial, the door grudgingly opened, and allowed Mr. Cruncher to squeeze himself into the room.

"What's going on?" he whispered to the man next to him.

"Nothing yet."

"What's coming up?"

"The Treason case."

"The quartering one, eh?"

"Ah!" returned the man with enjoyment; "he'll be drawn on a hurdle to be hanged until he's not quite dead. Then he'll be taken down and sliced before his own face, and then his insides will be taken out and burnt while he looks on, and then his head will be chopped off, and he'll be cut into quarters. That's the sentence."

In 1783, a platform was built outside the prison, which replaced the public gallows at Tyburn. Public executions were finally abolished in 1868, but prisoners continued to be hanged inside Newgate until 1901. The prison was finally closed and demolished in 1902.

Again, compare Dickens's description of London's criminal justice system with his earlier description of France's. What do you suppose is his point?

Again, note the touch of sarcasm and irony.

"Bedlam" refers to Bethlehem Hospital, originally built in the sixteenth century to house and care for "lunatics." A new and grander hospital was built in 1676. It was a popular tourist attraction from the beginning of the seventeenth century. The admission was approximately two pence. This was a considerable source of revenue for the hospital until the practice was stopped near the end of the eighteenth century.

"If he's found guilty, of course?" Jerry added.

"Oh! They'll find him guilty," said the other. "Don't worry about that."

Mr. Cruncher's attention was diverted to the doorkeeper, who was making his way to Mr. Lorry, with the note in his hand. Mr. Lorry sat at a table, among the gentlemen in wigs, not far from the prisoner's attorney, who had a large pile of papers before him, nearly opposite another gentleman in a wig who seemed to be staring at the ceiling. After some loud coughing and rubbing of his chin and signing with his hand, Jerry attracted the attention of Mr. Lorry, who had stood up to look for him, and who quietly nodded and sat down again.

"What's he got to do with the case?" asked the man he had spoken with.

"Darned if I know," said Jerry.

"What have you got to do with it, if I may ask?"

"Darned if I know that, either," said Jerry.

The Judge entered, causing a great stir and then settling down the court, including this conversation. All eyes were focused on the dock. Two jailers, who had been standing there, went out and brought the prisoner in.

Everyone in the room, except the one man staring at the ceiling, gazed at the prisoner. Eager faces strained around pillars to get a sight of him. Spectators in the back stood up, not to miss even a hair of him. People on the floor of the court put their heads on the shoulders of those in front of them, stood on tiptoe, climbed up on ledges, stood on anything that would hold the edge of a shoe, just to get a view of him at any cost. Jerry was among this last group, looking like one of the spikes on the wall of Newgate come to life, sending his beery breath toward the prisoner with other waves of gin, tea, coffee, and a thousand other odors, which broke upon the windows behind the prisoner in a foul mist.

This prisoner at whom everyone was staring was a young man of about twenty-five, good-looking, with

❷ *Why are there men wearing wigs in a courtroom?*

❷ *Like the Temple Bar, Newgate was another gate at one of the boundaries of the City of London. It was also used as a place to put the heads of executed criminals on pikes for public exhibit.*

sunburned cheeks and a blackened eye. He dressed and looked like a young gentleman. He was plainly dressed in black, or very dark gray, and his long, dark hair, was gathered in a ribbon at the back of his neck. The overall paleness of his complexion—apparent despite the sunburn on his cheeks—showed how strong was the fear of his soul. Otherwise, he was calm, bowed to the Judge, and stood quietly.

The interest this crowd showed in this prisoner was simple bloodlust. If he had not faced a sentence of quartering, there would have been much less fascination. This body that would so soon be brutally mangled, was a sight to see; this immortal creature that was to be so butchered and torn, was a sensation. No matter what anyone in the room said, each person's interest was no better than an ogre's.

Silence in the court! Charles Darnay had yesterday pleaded Not Guilty to an indictment accusing him of being a false traitor to our serene, illustrious, excellent, and so forth, prince, our Lord the King, by reason of his having, on several occasions, and by several methods, assisted Lewis, the French King, in his wars against our said serene, illustrious, excellent, and so forth; that was to say, by coming and going between the dominion of our serene, illustrious, excellent, and so forth, and those of the said French Lewis, and revealing to the said French Lewis what forces our said serene, illustrious... (you get the idea), *had prepared to send to Canada and North America.* This much, Jerry made out with huge satisfaction—the legal terms agitating his hair more and more—and so he understood that Charles Darnay stood before him upon his trial, and that the Attorney-General was getting ready to speak.

The accused who was (and knew he was) being mentally executed by everyone there, neither flinched, nor put on a theatrical air. He was quiet and attentive, watching the opening with serious interest, and stood with his hands resting on the slab of wood in front of him, so calmly, that they had not displaced a leaf of the herbs with which it was covered. The court was

✅ Again, notice how Dickens apparently mocks the high-sounding language of the charge against the prisoner.

❓ What sort of treason is Charles Darnay accused of committing?

"Jail Fever" was a particularly contagious form of typhus. In 1750, two infected Newgate prisoners who were on trial in the Old Bailey spread the disease to the entire courtroom, including the judge. Forty people died of the outbreak. This is probably the incident to which Dickens is alluding on page 68.

covered with these herbs and sprinkled with vinegar, as a precaution against jail air and jail fever.

There was a mirror over the prisoner's head, throwing light down upon him. Hundreds of wicked and wretched souls had been reflected in this mirror, and had left its surface and this earth's at the same time. That courtroom would have been terribly haunted, if that glass could have ever given back its reflections, as it is said that the ocean will one day give back its dead. It may be that the prisoner thought about the disgrace for which this mirror was used. In any event, when he became aware of a bar of light across his face, he looked up; his face flushed, and his right hands pushed the herbs away.

He was facing the side of the court that was on his left. He noticed two people on the same level. When he saw them, his expression changed so that all the eyes that had been looking at him, turned to look at them.

The spectators saw a young lady, barely twenty years old, and a gentleman who was evidently her father, remarkable in the absolute whiteness of his hair, and the intensity of his face—not outward, but thoughtful and inward. This expression made him look old. But when the intensity was lightened, as it was now, while he was speaking to his daughter, he became handsome—not past the prime of life.

His daughter had one of her hands drawn through his arm, and the other pressed upon it. She had moved close to him, dreading the scene, pitying the prisoner. Her forehead revealed terror and compassion, sensing only the danger of the accused. This terror was so noticeable, and so powerful, that even the ogres in the galley below wondered aloud, "Who are they?"

Jerry, who had been looking around the room, while sucking the rust off his fingers, stretched his neck to hear who they were. The answer soon wafted through the crowd to Jerry:

"Witnesses."

"For which side?"

Who do you suppose they are?

"Against."

"Against which side?"

"The prisoner's."

The Judge, who also looked up at the witnesses, leaned back in his seat, and looked steadily at the man whose life was in his hand, as the Attorney-General rose to spin the rope, grind the axe, and hammer the nails into this man's scaffold.

❷ *Explain the symbolism involved in the description of the Attorney-General's task.*

❷ *Create a list or chart of the characters we have met so far and their relationships to each other.*

THIS IS THE END OF THE
FIFTH WEEKLY INSTALLMENT.

Writing Opportunity:

How is Dickens using Jerry Cruncher in this chapter to express his own views about capital punishment? Use evidence from the text to support your answer.

A Tale of Two Cities

CHARLES DICKENS

CHAPTER III

A Disappointment

THE ATTORNEY-GENERAL had to inform the jury that, although the prisoner was young, he was old in betraying his country. That the prisoner had been trading secrets with France for years. That he had been traveling back and forth between France and England on a secret business that he could not explain. That only Providence had discovered the scheme and revealed it to his Majesty's Chief Secretary of State and the Privy Council. That this loyal patriot would testify before them. That this patriot was in a sublime position. That he had once been the prisoner's friend, but had felt that he could no longer love someone who would betray his country, and so he had decided to sacrifice the prisoner. That, if it were a British custom to make statues of public heroes, as it used to be in Greece and Rome, this patriot would have one. That Virtue was contagious—especially such a bright virtue as patriotism, or love of country. That this patriot's virtue had spread to the prisoner's servant, who had searched in the prisoner's table drawers and pockets, to take his papers. That the Attorney-General expected the defense to attack the patriot's character, but that the Attorney-General himself liked the patriot more than his own mother

What Dickens is calling the "Attorney-General," we would call the District Attorney, the prosecutor in the case.

What is Providence? What is Dickens implying about the prosecution's case?

What effect is created by the shortened syntax in this paragraph, and throughout the testimony in this chapter?

or father. That the jury would soon feel likewise. That the evidence of these two witnesses, along with the documents that had been stolen, would show that the prisoner had received lists of the King's forces, and of how they had been prepared and sent, by sea and land, and that the prisoner had given that information to a hostile power. That these lists were not in the prisoner's handwriting—but that was just evidence of how tricky the prisoner was. That the proof would go back five years—even to the beginning of the action between the British and the Americans. That, for these reasons, the jury—being loyal and responsible (as he knew they were), must find the prisoner Guilty, and execute him, like it or not. That they could never go to sleep at night—let alone permit their wives or children to go to sleep at night—unless the prisoner's head was taken off. That the prisoner was as good as dead and gone.

When the Attorney-General stopped, a buzz of conversation arose around the prisoner, like a cloud of gnats. When order returned, the blameless patriot, the Attorney-General's star witness—entered the witness-box.

The Solicitor-General now questioned the witness, a man who gave his name as John Barsad, and his occupation as "gentleman." His story was exactly as the Attorney-General had described it—too exactly, in fact. Having gotten this burden off his chest, he got up as if to leave, but the wigged gentleman seated near Mr. Lorry wanted to ask him a few questions. The other wigged gentleman still stared at the ceiling of the court.

Had Barsad ever been a spy himself? No, he laughed at the silly claim. How did he earn a living? Income from his property. Where was his property? He didn't precisely remember. What was it? No one's business. Had he inherited it? Yes. From whom? Distant relative. Very distant? Yes. Ever been in prison? Of course not. Even in a debtors' prison? He didn't see what that had to do with anything. Never

❷ *What action between the British and Americans is Dickens referring to? Why does he need to refer to it?*

❸ *The Solicitor-General is the English equivalent of our Public Defender.*

in a debtors' prison? Yes. How many times? Two or three times. Not five or six? Perhaps. Of what profession? Gentleman. Ever been kicked downstairs? Absolutely not; once received a kick at the top of a staircase, and fell downstairs on purpose. Kicked for cheating at dice? So it was said by the intoxicated liar who committed the assault, but it was not true. Swear it was not true? Absolutely. Ever live by cheating at gambling? Never. Ever live by gambling? No more than other gentlemen. Ever borrow money from the prisoner? Yes. Ever pay him? No. Was his relationship with the prisoner forced upon the prisoner in carriages, hotels, and boats? No. Was he sure he saw the prisoner with these lists? Certain. Knew no more about the lists? No. Had not acquired them himself, for instance? No. Expect to get anything from this evidence? No. He wasn't being paid by the government to lay traps? Goodness, no. Or to do anything? Goodness, no. Swear to that? Over and over again. No motives except for absolute patriotism? None whatsoever.

Roger Cly, the prisoner's servant, gave his testimony quickly. He had started working for the prisoner four years ago. He had asked the prisoner, aboard the boat to Calais, if he wanted someone handy, and the prisoner had hired him. He had not asked this as act of charity. He began to suspect the prisoner, and to keep an eye on him, soon afterwards. While arranging the prisoner's clothes, he had seen lists in the prisoner's pockets, over and over again. He had taken these lists from the drawer of his desks—no, he had not put them there first. He had seen the prisoner show these lists to French gentlemen in Calais and Boulogne. He had testified because he couldn't bear seeing his country betrayed. As far as criminal background of his own, he had never been suspected of stealing a silver teapot—it had been only a silver-plated mustard-pot. He had known Barsad—the first witness—seven or eight years, but that was only a coincidence. He didn't call it a curious coincidence, because most coincidences *were* unusual. Nor was it a curious coincidence that both were motivated only by true patriotism—he was a true Briton, and hoped that there were many more like him.

The gnats buzzed again, and the Attorney-General called Mr. Jarvis Lorry.

"Mr. Jarvis Lorry, are you a clerk in Tellson's Bank?"

"I am."

"On a certain Friday night in November, 1775, did business cause you to travel between London and Dover on the mail carriage?"

"It did."

"Were there any other passengers?"

"Two."

"Did they get out on the road in the course of the night?"

"They did."

"Mr. Lorry, look at the prisoner. Was he one of those two passengers?"

"I cannot say for certain."

"Does he resemble either of the two passengers?"

"Both were so wrapped up, and the night was so dark, and we all kept to ourselves, and so I cannot swear even to that."

"Mr. Lorry, look at the prisoner again. Imagine him wrapped up as those two passengers were. Is there anything in his bulk or stature to make it unlikely that he was one of them?"

"No."

"You will not swear, Mr. Lorry, that he was not one of them?"

"No."

"So at least you say he may have been one of them?"

"Yes. Except that I remember both of them to have been—like me—afraid of highwaymen, and this prisoner does not seem afraid of anything."

"Did you ever see false fear, Mr. Lorry?"

"I certainly have seen that."

"Mr. Lorry, look again at the prisoner. Have you seen him, to your certain knowledge, before?"

"I have."

"When?"

"I was returning from France a few days afterwardss, and, at Calais, the prisoner came on board the ship in which I returned, and made the voyage with me."

"What time did he come on board?"

"Just after midnight."

"In the dead of the night. Was he the only passenger who came on board at that untimely hour?"

"He happened to be the only one."

"Never mind about 'happening,' Mr. Lorry. Was he the only passenger who came on board in the dead of night?"

"He was."

"Were you traveling alone, Mr. Lorry, or with any companion?"

"With two companions. A gentleman and lady. They are here."

"They are here. Had you any conversation with the prisoner?"

"Hardly any. The weather was stormy, and the passage long and rough, and so I lay on a sofa almost the whole trip."

"Miss Manette!"

The young lady stood up, and all eyes returned to her. Her father rose with her, and kept her hand drawn through his arm.

"Miss Manette, look upon the prisoner."

Her look of pity, and her young beauty, were much harder on the prisoner than the attitude of the crowd. Standing with her, as it were, on the edge of his grave, he found the nerve to remain still. His right hand shredded the herbs in front of him. The buzz of the gnats was loud again.

"Miss Manette, have you seen the prisoner before?"

"Yes, sir."

"Where?"

"On board the ship just now mentioned, sir, and on the same occasion."

"You are the young lady just now mentioned?"

"Oh! I am sorry to say that I am!"

Her compassionate tone merged into the hard tone of the Judge, as he said fiercely, "Simply answer the questions, please, and do not comment on them."

"Miss Manette, did you have a conversation with the prisoner on that trip across the Channel?"

"Yes, sir."

"Please tell us about it."

After a profound silence, she began softly, "When the gentleman came on board—"

"Do you mean the prisoner?" asked the Judge, knitting his brows.

"Yes, my Lord."

"Then say 'the prisoner'."

"When the prisoner came on board, he noticed that my father"—here she turned her eyes lovingly toward the old man—"was very tired and weak. My father was so ill that I was afraid to take him indoors. I had made a bed for him on the deck near the cabin steps, and I sat at his side to take care of him. There were no other passengers that night besides the four of us. The prisoner was so kind as to ask me if he could help me shelter my father from the wind and weather. He was very kind and gentle about my father. That was how we started talking."

"Let me interrupt you for a moment. Did he come on board alone?"

"No."

"How many others were with him?"

"Two French gentlemen."

"Had they spoken to each other?"

"They talked until the last moment, when the French gentlemen had to be taken ashore in their boat."

"Did they hand any papers to one another, similar to these lists?"

"They did exchange some papers, but I don't know what they said."

"Did they look like these, similar shape and size?"

"Maybe, but I don't know. Even though they were very close to me, they were up at the top of the cabin steps under a dim lamp, and they spoke very quietly, so I didn't hear what they said, and only noticed that they were looking at papers."

"Now, tell me about your conversation with the prisoner, Miss Manette."

"The prisoner was as open with me as he was kind, and good, and useful to my father. I hope,"— and here she started to cry—"I may not repay him by doing him harm today."

The gnats buzzed again.

❷ *Who are these gnats?*

"Miss Manette, the prisoner—and the rest of us—can certainly sense your reluctance in giving this evidence. Please go on."

"He told me that he was traveling on difficult and delicate business, that might get people into trouble, and so he was using an assumed name. He said that this business had taken him to France, and might take him back and forth between France and England for a long time."

"Did he say anything about America, Miss Manette? Be specific."

"He tried to explain to me how the quarrel arose, and he said that it seemed to him foolish on England's part. He added, as a joke, that perhaps George Washington might gain almost as great a name in history as George III. He was only making a joke, though."

❷ *In our own time, this is clearly ironic—since George Washington did become as famous as George III of England. Would Dickens's readers have understood this humor?*

Just as audience members will often imitate the strong facial expressions of actors they are watching, both the prosecutor and defense attorney saw how the audience in court imitated the way Lucie Manette's forehead was creased in nervous anxiety. The effect was so strong, the even the Judge saw it when he looked up from his papers to glare at her for her brash heresy about George Washington.

The Attorney-General now called Dr. Manette, the lady's father.

"Dr. Manette, look at the prisoner. Have you ever seen him before?"

"Once. He came to my home in London, three or three and a half years ago."

"Can you identify him as your fellow-passenger on board the ship, or confirm his conversation with your daughter?"

"Sir, I can do neither."

"Is there any specific reason why you cannot?"

He answered, in a low voice, "There is."

"Did you suffer a long imprisonment, without trial or even accusation, in your native country, Dr. Manette?"

He answered in a tone that chilled every heart: "A long imprisonment."

"Had you just been released on the night in question?"

"They tell me so."

"Have you no memory of this occasion?"

"None. My mind is a blank, from some time—I do not know when—when I employed myself, in prison, in making shoes, to the time I found myself living in London with my daughter. I had remembered her, thanks to God's grace, but I'm unable to say how. I have no memory of the process."

The Attorney-General sat down, and the father and daughter sat down together.

An unusual event then happened. Since the prosecutor's object was to show that the prisoner traveled with the Dover mail carriage on that Friday night in November, got out during the night, at a place where he did not stay, but traveled back more than a dozen miles, to a garrison and a dock, where he collected information, a witness was called to identify him as having been, at the precise time required, in the coffee lounge of a hotel, waiting for another person. Under cross-examination, this witness said only that he had never seen the prisoner on any other occasion. The wigged gentleman who had been staring all the while at the ceiling, wrote a couple words on a piece of paper, balled it up, and tossed it to the prisoner's attorney. Opening this paper, he looked with great curiosity at the prisoner.

"You say again you are quite sure that it was the prisoner?"

The witness was quite sure.

"Have you ever seen anyone who looks a lot like the prisoner?"

Not close enough (the witness said) that he could be mistaken.

"Look upon that gentleman, my learned friend there," said the attorney, pointing to the man who had tossed the paper to him, "and then look closely at the prisoner. What do you say? Do they look much alike?"

Taking into consideration the "learned friend's" sloppy appearance, they were close enough to surprise, not only the witness, but everyone in the courtroom. When the Judge reluctantly asked him to take off his wig, the similarity was even more striking. The Judge then asked Mr. Stryver (the prisoner's attorney) if they were going to try Mr. Carton (the learned friend) for treason? Mr. Stryver responded that if the witness made a mistake once, he might well make it twice. He wanted to smash this witness like a piece of pottery.

By this time, Mr. Cruncher had chewed a good deal of rust off his fingers. He now listened as Mr. Stryver summarized the case—how the patriot, Barsad, was a hired spy and traitor, an unblushing seller of blood, and one of the vilest scoundrels since Judas Iscariot—whom he certainly looked like. How Cly, the servant, was actually Barsad's friend and partner; how these perjurers had seen Darnay as a victim, because of his French citizenship and family affairs. How the evidence that had been warped and wrested from the young lady was simply the innocent conversation between any young gentleman and lady similarly thrown together, except for the joke about George Washington. How the Attorney-General was trying to gain popularity using the most basic fears of the citizens; how his case rested upon nothing except two dishonest witnesses—a strategy too often used in State Trials. At this point, though, the Judge intervened, saying he would not tolerate any more comments like that.

Mr. Stryver then called his witnesses, and it was time for the Attorney-General to attempt to ruin the suit of clothes that Mr. Stryver was trying to tailor—showing how Barsad and Cly were even more virtuous than he had thought, and the prisoner far worse. Finally, the Judge summarized the case, fitting the suit of clothes into a funeral outfit for the prisoner.

Then the jury turned to consider, and the gnats buzzed ever louder.

Explain the extended metaphor used to describe the way Mr. Stryver, the Attorney-General, and the Judge all view and interpret the case against Darnay.

Mr. Carton still sat staring at the ceiling, even in this excitement. While Mr. Stryver piled his papers, whispered to those around him, and glanced nervously at the jury; while the spectators moved around, and formed themselves into new groups; while even the Judge arose from his seat, and slowly paced up and down his platform—causing the rumor that he had become feverish; while everything and everyone around him was in an uproar, this one man sat back, with his torn gown hanging off him, his dirty wig looking as though it had just happened to land on his head, his hands in his pockets, his eyes still gazing up to the ceiling. There was something reckless—even wicked—in his look that greatly lessened his resemblance to the prisoner, and several people sitting around him said they would never have thought the two looked so very alike. Mr. Cruncher commented to the person next to him, "I'd bet half a guinea that he don't get no law-work to do. He don't look like the sort to get any, do he?"

However, Mr. Carton took in far more than he appeared to; for now, when Miss Manette's head dropped upon her father's breast, he was the first to see it, and to ask an officer to help her father remove her from the courtroom.

There was much sympathy for her as she was removed, and much sympathy for her father. It had obviously been a great distress to him, to think back to his imprisonment. He had shown a great deal of internal struggle when he was questioned, and the brooding look which made him old, had been on his face ever since. As he left, the jury spoke, through their foreman.

They were not in agreement, and wished to retire. The Judge showed some surprise, but agreed that they should retire under guard, and retired himself. The trial had lasted all day, and lamps were now being lighted. There were rumors that the jury would be out a long time. The spectators left to get dinner, and the prisoner went to the back of the dock and sat down.

Mr. Lorry, who had gone out with the young lady and her father, now reappeared, and signaled to Jerry, who could now easily get near him in the less crowded room.

"Jerry, if you wish to get something to eat, you can, but stay around. You will be sure to hear when the jury come in. Don't be a moment behind them, because I want you to take the verdict back to the bank. You are the quickest messenger I know, and will get to Temple Bar long before I can."

Jerry rubbed his knuckles on his forehead after this compliment and a shilling. Mr. Carton came up at that moment and touched Mr. Lorry on the arm.

"How is the young lady?"

"She is greatly distressed, but her father is comforting her. She feels much better out of court."

"I'll tell the prisoner. A respectable bank gentleman like you shouldn't be seen speaking to him publicly."

Mr. Lorry reddened as though he had had that

⚫ *The dock was an enclosure in the courtroom in which the prisoner was placed during his trial. For most of the trial, the prisoner would stand at a rail at the front of the box, but there was a bench at the rear of the dock for the prisoner to sit during recesses.*

same thought, and Mr. Carton made his way outside. The way out of court lay in that direction, and Jerry followed him, all eyes, ears (and spikes).

"Mr. Darnay!"

The prisoner came forward.

"You will naturally be interested to hear about the witness, Miss Manette. She is feeling much better. You have seen the worst of her agitation."

"I deeply regret having been the cause of it. Could you tell her for me?"

"Yes, I could. I will, if you ask it."

Mr. Carton was so careless that he seemed disrespectful. He stood, half turned from the prisoner, lounging with his elbow against the bar.

"I do ask it. Accept my cordial thanks."

"What outcome do you expect, Mr. Darnay?" asked Carton, still only half turned toward him.

"The worst."

"That's the wisest thing to expect, and the most likely. However, their withdrawing is in your favor."

Jerry heard no more, since loitering on the way out of court was not allowed. So he left them—so like each other in looks—standing side by side, both reflected in the mirror above them.

An hour and a half limped heavily away in the passages below, even after mutton pies and ale. Jerry, seated uncomfortably after eating his meal, had slipped into a doze, when a loud murmur and swift tide of people carried him along with them.

"Jerry! Jerry!" Mr. Lorry was already calling when he got the door.

"Here, sir! It's a fight to get back in. Here I am, sir!"

Mr. Lorry handed him a paper through the throng. "Quick! Have you got it?"

"Yes, sir."

Hastily written on the paper was the word "ACQUITTED."

❷ *What would "recalled to life" have meant this time?*

"If you had sent the message 'Recalled to Life'

again," muttered Jerry, as he turned, "I would have known what you meant this time."

He had no opportunity to say—or think—anything else, until he was clear of the Old Bailey; for the crowd came pouring out and nearly took him off his legs, and the gnats were dispersing in search of other victims.

❷ *What important pieces of information is the reader given during this weekly installment?*

THIS IS THE END OF THE
SIXTH WEEKLY INSTALLMENT.

Review and Predict:

Given the characters, the settings, and the relationships we have been introduced to, where do you think the plot is likely to lead?

Writing Opportunity:

Analyze the initial description of Sydney Carton. What sort of person is the reader prepared to expect Carton to be? Support your answer with evidence from the text.

A Tale of Two Cities

CHARLES DICKENS

CHAPTER IV
Congratulatory

THE LAST SEDIMENT of the human stew boiling all day in the Old Bailey slowly strained out, and Dr. Manette, Lucie Manette, his daughter, Mr. Lorry, the solicitor for the defense, and the defense attorney, Mr. Stryver, stood around Mr. Charles Darnay—just released—congratulating him on his escape from death.

Even in a much brighter light, it would have been difficult to recognize Dr. Manette as the former shoemaker in that Paris attic. However, no one could have looked at him, without looking again—even without hearing his low, grave voice, or noticing the distraction that would cloud his face over, for no apparent reason. While any reference to his long agony would cause him to remember the past, and drag him back into gloom, at times that gloom would come over him all of its own accord, and any casual observer might think he stood in the shadow of the actual Bastille— even though that building was 300 miles away.

Only Lucie could drive this gloom from his mind. She was the golden thread that bound him to a Past back before his misery, and to a Present after his misery; the sound of her voice, the light of her face, and the touch of her hand, almost always had a warm-

Note this wonderful metaphor: the mix of people in the courtroom are a stew, and the last, gawking thrill-seekers to leave are the sediment straining out.

Bastille is a French word meaning "castle" or "stronghold." Used as a single word ("la Bastille" in French, "the Bastille" in English) it invariably refers to the former Bastille Saint-Antoine—Number 232, Rue Saint-Antoine—in Paris.

Note this metaphor.

ing influence on him. There had been a few times when even she could not bring him around, but they were few and far between, and she believed them to be over.

Mr. Darnay had kissed her hand fervently and gratefully, and had warmly thanked Mr. Stryver. This attorney was barely thirty years old but looked almost fifty—stout, loud, red, brash, and lacking any delicacy. He had a way of pushing his way (morally and physically) into any company or conversation—it was this way that had helped him shoulder his way up in life.

What are we being told about Mr. Stryver?

He still had his wig and gown on and, shouldering into the group with such energy that he bounced the innocent Mr. Lorry out of the conversation. "I am glad to have brought you away with honor, Mr. Darnay. It was a hateful prosecution—extremely so; but sometimes simple hatred is enough to convict an innocent person."

"Now I owe you my life—in two senses," said Mr. Darnay, taking his hand.

"I have done my best for you, Mr. Darnay; and my best is as good as another man's, I believe."

Since someone was clearly obligated to say, "Much better," Mr. Lorry said it—with the object of getting himself back into the group.

Note the mild irony and humor in the lawyer and banker jockeying for position in the conversation, and the lawyer's fishing for compliments.

"You think so?" said Mr. Stryver. "Well! You have been present all day, and you should know—being a man of business."

"And, as a man of business," said Mr. Lorry, now back in the group, "I will ask Dr. Manette to break up this conference and order us all home. Miss Lucie looks ill, Mr. Darnay has had a terrible day, and we are all worn out."

"Speak for yourself, Mr. Lorry," said Stryver; "I have a night's work to do yet. Speak for yourself."

"I do speak for myself," answered Mr. Lorry, "and for Mr. Darnay, and for Miss Lucie. Miss Lucie, don't you think I may speak for us all?" He asked her pointedly, with a glance at her father.

His face had frozen in a very strange look at Darnay: an intent look, deepening into a frown of dislike, distrust, even fear. With this strange expression, his thoughts had wandered away.

"Father," said Lucie, softly laying her hand on his.

He slowly shook the shadow off, and turned to her.

"Shall we go home, my father?"

With a long breath, he answered, "Yes."

Mr. Darnay's friends had all left, thinking that he certainly would not be released that night. The lights were nearly all out in the hallways. The iron gates were being closed with a jar and a rattle, and the dismal place was deserted, until tomorrow's interest in the gallows, pillory, whipping-post and branding-iron, would fill it again. Lucie walked out into the fresh air, between her father and Mr. Darnay. A carriage was called, and the father and daughter climbed into it.

Mr. Stryver had left them inside, to work his way back to the robing-room. Another person, who had neither joined the group nor talked to any of them, but who had been leaning against the wall in the shadows, walked out after the rest, and watched until the carriage drove away. He now joined Mr. Lorry and Mr. Darnay on the pavement.

"So, Mr. Lorry! Men of business may speak to Mr. Darnay now?"

Nobody had mentioned Mr. Carton's part in the day's proceedings—nobody had remembered it. He was now unrobed, and looked no better in his street clothes.

"If you knew what conflicts erupt in the business mind, when it is divided between the good-natured impulse and business appearances, you would be surprised, Mr. Darnay."

Mr. Lorry reddened, and said, with emphasis, "You have said that before, sir. We men of business, who work for a company, are not our own masters. We have to consider the company more than ourselves."

❷ *Why is Dr. Manette so intent upon studying Darnay's face?*

❷ *What point is the author making about Sydney Carton?*

❷ *Whose words is Carton mocking?*

✔ *The "chair" that Mr. Lorry calls for was probably a litter, a type of carriage, consisting of a platform, usually padded and enclosed. The sides were usually curtained, for privacy. The litter was either carried by footmen, or slung on the sides of horses, at the back and front. It was a slow method of travel.*

❷ *What "other" world is Carton talking about?*

"I know, I know," replied Mr. Carton, carelessly. "Don't get upset, Mr. Lorry. You are as good as another, I have no doubt: even better, I'd say."

"Indeed, sir," Mr. Lorry went on, paying him no attention, "I really don't know what you have to do with the matter. If you'll excuse me, as someone much older than you, for saying so, I don't really think it is your business."

"Business! Bless you, I have no business," said Mr. Carton.

"It is a pity you do not, sir."

"I think so, too."

"If you had," Mr. Lorry added, "maybe you would attend to it."

"Lord love you, no! I wouldn't," said Mr. Carton.

Annoyed by his indifference, Mr. Lorry cried, "Well! Business is a very good thing, and a very respectable thing. If business imposes its own restrictions, then Mr. Darnay, as a generous young man, knows how to make allowances. Mr. Darnay, good night. God bless you, sir! I hope that this day has saved you for a prosperous, happy life. Chair there!"

Perhaps a little angry with himself, and with Mr. Carton, Mr. Lorry climbed into his chair, and was carried off to Tellson's. Carton, who smelled like wine and did not appear to be sober, laughed, and turned to Darnay:

"This is a strange coincidence that throws us together. Is this strange to you, standing alone here with your virtual twin on these cobblestones?"

"It doesn't feel," replied Charles Darnay, "that I'm back in this world yet."

"That doesn't surprise me—it hasn't been so long since you were on your way to another. You speak faintly."

"I think I might faint."

"Then have some dinner! I did, myself, while those numbskulls were deciding which world you belong to. Let me show you the nearest tavern where you can get a good meal."

Pulling his arm through his own, Carton took Darnay down Ludgate Hill to Fleet Street, and, up an alley, into a tavern. Here, they were shown into a little room, where a plain dinner and good wine were soon strengthening Charles Darnay, while Carton sat opposite him, with his own bottle in front of him, his half-disrespectful manner on full display.

"Do you feel like you belong to this world again, Darnay?"

"I am very confused about time and place—but even that confusion is an improvement."

"How satisfying it must be!" He said it bitterly, and filled up his glass again—which was a large one. "As for me, I would truly like to forget that I belong to this world. It has no good for me—except wine like this—nor I for it. So you and I are not much alike in that regard—indeed, I think we are not very much alike at all."

Confused by the day's emotions, and feeling that this dinner with his double was like a dream, Charles Darnay did not know how to answer. He, therefore, remained silent.

"Now that your dinner is done," Carton presently said, "why don't you make a toast, Mr. Darnay?"

"What toast?"

"Why, it's on the tip of your tongue. It ought to be; it must be; I'll swear it's there."

"Miss Manette, then!"

"Miss Manette, then!"

Looking at Darnay full in the face while he drank the toast, Carton flung his glass over his shoulder against the wall, where it shattered to pieces; then, he rang the bell, and ordered another glass.

"That's a pretty young lady to help into a carriage in the dark, Mr. Darnay!" he said, filling his new glass when it came.

A slight frown and an abrupt "Yes," were his only answer.

"That's a pretty young lady to have pity you and cry for you! How does it feel? Is it worth being on

❷ *The term* toast *comes from the Roman practice of dropping a piece of burnt bread into wine. The charcoal in the toast reduces the acidity of slightly bad wine making it more fit to drink. In the 1700s, party-goers even liked to toast the health of people not present—especially beautiful women. A woman who was often toasted in this way, came to be known as the "toast of the town."*

❷ *What is Carton suggesting?*

trial for your life, to have someone like her feel such sympathy and compassion for you, Mr. Darnay?"

Again, Darnay gave no answer.

"She was *very* pleased to get your message, when I gave it to her. She didn't show it, but I could tell that she was."

This comment reminded Darnay that this man—although he seemed to be quite an unpleasant person—had willingly helped him in the trial. He thanked him for it.

"I don't want or deserve any thanks. It was nothing, and I'm not even sure why I did it. Mr. Darnay, let me ask you a question."

"Willingly—a small repayment for your good deeds."

"Do you think I like you?"

"Really, Mr. Carton," Darnay answered, confused, "I haven't even thought about it."

"Think about it now."

"You have done me a great favor; but I don't think you do."

"I don't think I do, either," said Carton. "However, I do begin to respect your understanding."

"Nevertheless," Darnay continued, as he rang the bell, "that shouldn't prevent my paying the bill, or us parting without bad feelings on both sides."

Carton answered, "No, it certainly should not!"

Darnay rang again. "Are you paying the whole bill?" said Carton. Receiving a nod, he said, "Then bring me another pint of this same wine, waiter, and come wake me at ten."

Charles Darnay rose and said good night. Carton rose too, with something bitter in his manner, and said, "A last word, Mr. Darnay. Do you think I am drunk?"

"I think you have been drinking, Mr. Carton."

"Think? You know I have been drinking."

"Since I must say so, yes, I know it."

"Then you shall also know why. I am an unhappy

The use of two negatives to suggest a positive is called litotes.

Why does Carton seem to be going out of his way to be unpleasant to Darnay?

drone, sir. I care for no man on earth, and no man on earth cares for me."

"That's quite a shame. You might have used your talents better."

"Maybe so; maybe not. But don't get too excited by your uprightness, though—you don't know where it might lead. Good night!"

After Darnay had left, Carton picked up a candle, walked to a mirror, and examined himself in it.

"Do you honestly *like* the man? Why would you like a man who looks like you? There is nothing in you to like. Is that a good reason for liking a man—that he shows you what you might have been? If you changed places with him, you might have been looked at by Lucie Manette's blue eyes as he was, and pitied by that agitated face as he was! Admit it! You hate Charles Darnay."

He turned back to his wine for consolation, drank it all in a few minutes, with his head on his arms, his hair straggling all over the table, and a long sheet in the candle dripping down on him.

Writing Opportunity:

Explain the metaphorical significance of the name Mr. Stryver, based on evidence in the text describing this lawyer.

A Tale of Two Cities

CHARLES DICKENS

CHAPTER V
The Jackal

THOSE WERE DAYS when men drank a lot. In our time, we would consider the amount of wine and rum punch that one man would drink in one night to be a ridiculous exaggeration. Lawyers were no different than other men in their Bacchanalian habits; neither was Mr. Stryver behind any other lawyer, in his drinking as well as in the drier aspects of the practice of law.

Now a favorite at the Old Bailey, and at Sessions, Mr. Stryver had started to solidify his hold on opportunities. Now Sessions and Old Bailey had to call him to come and handle special cases, and he could be seen every day, moving toward the Lord Chief Justice in the Court of King's Bench, pushing up like a sunflower from among a garden filled with competitors.

His colleagues and other officers of the court had once noticed that, while Mr. Stryver was a smooth speaker, unscrupulous, and had initiative, he could not take a heap of statements and boil them down to a main idea—a necessary skill for an attorney. Then he suddenly began to improve—the more business he got, the better he became at finding the substance of an issue. No matter how late he stayed out drinking

✔ *Whereas the Old Bailey was a criminal court, the Sessions court primarily involved civil matters—lawsuits involving property and damages, rather than criminal acts.*

✔ *Explain the simile of the sunflower.*

The Hilary Term was one of the four yearly terms of the British court, lasting from January 11–January 31. Michaelmas refers to the Christian Feast of St. Michael, traditionally on September 29. So Carton and Stryver's drinking bouts would begin in early January and last to the end of September.

What is being implied about who has the real legal ability in this odd partnership?

The jackal is a dog-like animal that hunts in packs and howls at night. It used to be believed that jackals would run before lions and hunt down their pray for them. This is most likely what the author means when he says that Carton was Stryver's "jackal."

The King's Bench Walk and the Paper Buildings are two streets in the Temple area of London.

with Sydney Carton, he always had his main ideas at hand in the morning.

Sydney Carton, idlest and most unpromising of men, was Stryver's great ally. What the two drank together, between Hilary Term and Michaelmas, might have floated a king's ship. Stryver never had a case going without Carton at his side, hands in his pockets, staring at the ceiling of the court. They traveled the same legal Circuit, and even on the road would drink late into the night, and Carton might be seen in the morning, sneaking back, a bit unsteadily, to his lodgings, like a promiscuous cat. At last, the reputation spread that, while Sydney Carton might never become a lion, he was an amazingly good jackal, and that he was Stryver's jackal.

"Ten o'clock, sir," said the man at the tavern, whom Carton had told to wake him—"ten o'clock, sir."

"What's the matter?"

"Ten o'clock, sir."

"What do you mean? Ten o'clock at night?"

"Yes, sir. You asked me to call you."

"Oh! I remember. Very well, very well."

After trying to get to sleep again, Carton was frustrated by the loud efforts of the waiter to stir the fire for five minutes, so he got up, tossed his hat on, and walked out. He entered the Temple District, walked around the King's Bench Walk and the Paper Buildings to awaken himself, and entered Stryver's chambers.

Stryver's clerk had long ago gone home, and Stryver himself opened the door. He was wearing a loose sleeping-gown and his slippers. His eyes had that wild, strained, blood-shot look, typical of those who drink too much.

"You are a little late, Mr. Memory," said Stryver.

"It's the usual time—maybe fifteen minutes later."

They went into a dingy room lined with books and littered with papers, where there was a blazing fire. A kettle steamed on its stand, a table shone in the middle of the chaos, with plenty of wine, brandy, rum, sugar, and lemons.

"It looks like you've already had your bottle of wine, Sydney."

"Two tonight, I think. I've been dining with today's client, or at least, watching him dine—it's all the same!"

"That was ingenious of you, Sydney, to mention how alike you and Darnay looked. When did you think of it?"

"I thought he was rather handsome, and I thought I might have looked much the same, if I had had any luck."

Mr. Stryver laughed until his ample belly shook.

"You and your luck, Sydney! Get to work, get to work."

Now sullen, the jackal loosened his collar, went into the next room, and came back with a large jug of cold water, a basin, and a towel or two. He soaked the towels in the water, wrung some of the water out, folded them on his head, sat down, and said, "Now I am ready!"

"Not much work tonight, Mr. Memory," said Mr. Stryver, happily, as he looked down at his papers.

"How much?"

"Only two sets of them."

"Give me the worst first."

"There they are, Sydney. Fire away!"

The lion then lay on his back on a sofa on one side of the table, while the jackal sat at his own paper-covered table, with the bottles and glasses ready at hand. Both drank without stopping—the lion mostly reclining with his hands in his waistband, looking at the fire, sometimes picking up a small document, and the jackal, so deep in his task, that his eyes wouldn't even follow his hand to the glass, and so it often had to grope around for a minute or more before it could find it. Two or three times, the legal matters he was dealing with became so complex, that the jackal had

❷ *What do you suppose the cold water and towels suggest?*

✔ *Note the continuation of the lion and jackal metaphor.*

❷ *What do you think of Carton
and Stryver's relationship?
What does it say about
Carton? About Stryver?*

to get up and soak his towels again. His deep concentration and serious facial expression made this damp
headgear even more ridiculous.

Eventually, the jackal had put together a small
meal for the lion, and offered it to him. The lion took
it with care and caution, chose what he wanted, made
his remarks, and the jackal served him. When they
were finished, the lion put his hands in his waistband
again, and lay down to "meditate." The jackal then
refilled his glass, put on fresh towels, and worked on
a second meal. He served this to the lion in the same
way, and was not done until three in the morning.

"Now that we've done, Sydney, fill a bowl of
punch," said Mr. Stryver.

The jackal took the towels from his head, which
had been steaming again, shook himself, yawned,
shivered, and did as Stryver asked.

"You were absolutely right, Sydney, about the
crown's witnesses today. Every question helped."

"I am always right, am I not?"

"I don't disagree. What has made you upset?
Calm down and have some punch."

With a sarcastic grunt, the jackal again did as
Stryver commanded.

"The old Sydney Carton of old Shrewsbury
School," said Stryver, nodding as he thought about
Carton in the present and the past, "the old seesaw
Sydney. Up one minute and down the next; now
excited, now depressed!"

❷ *What are we learning about
Carton's past? What impact
did this behavior probably
have on his reputation and
his career?*

"Ah!" replied the other, sighing, "Yes! The same
Sydney, with the same luck. Even then, I did work for
other boys, and seldom did my own."

"And why not?"

"God knows. It was my way, I suppose."

He sat with his hands in his pockets and his legs
stretched out before him, looking at the fire.

"Carton," said his friend, facing him with a bullying air, "your way is, and always was, a lazy way. You
have no ambition. Look at me."

"Oh, botheration!" replied Sydney, with a

lighter and happier laugh, "don't you start preaching morals!"

"How have I done what I have done?" said Stryver; "how do I do what I do?"

"Partly through paying me to help you, I guess. But to preach to me about it is as worthwhile as preaching to the air. You do what you want to do. You were always at the top of the class, and I was always behind."

"I had to get to the top of the class; I was not 'well born,' was I?"

"I was not present at the event, but I suspect you were," said Carton. At this, he laughed, and then they both laughed.

"Before Shrewsbury, at Shrewsbury, and ever since Shrewsbury," Carton went on, "you have fallen into your place, and I have fallen into mine. Even when we were fellow-students in the Student-Quarter of Paris, picking up the French language, French law, and other French women, you were always somewhere, and I was always…nowhere."

The ambiguity of this conversation is in the contrast between someone's rank based on birth and based on effort.

"And whose fault was that?"

"Upon my soul, I'm not sure that it wasn't yours. You were always pushing and striving and elbowing your way and passing others by—so much so that all I could do was rust and rest. It's depressing, though, to talk about the past, at dawn. Let's change the topic before I go."

"Well then! Put in a good word for me with that pretty witness," said Stryver, holding up his glass. "Would she make a better topic of conversation?"

Apparently not, for Carton became gloomy again. "Pretty witness," he muttered, looking down into his glass. "I have had enough of witnesses today and tonight. Who do you mean?"

"The beautiful doctor's daughter, Miss Manette."

"Was she pretty?"

"Isn't she?"

"No."

"Man alive, the whole Court was admiring her!"

"Forget the whole Court! Who made the Old Bailey a judge of beauty? She was a golden-haired doll!"

"Sydney," said Mr. Stryver, looking at him sharply, and running his hand across his flushed face, "do you know, at the time, I thought that you felt sorry for that 'golden-haired doll.' You were awfully quick to make sure that 'golden-haired doll' was all right."

"Quick to make sure! If a girl-—doll or not—faints within a yard or two of a man's nose, he can see it without a magnifying glass. I'll put in a good word, but I deny the beauty. No more to drink; I'm off to bed."

When Mr. Stryver walked him out to the staircase with a candle, to light his way down the stairs, the dawn was coldly looking in the grimy windows. The air outside was cold and sad, the dull sky overcast, the river dark and dim, the whole scene like a lifeless desert. Wreaths of dust were spinning round and round, as if the desert sand had risen from the ground far away, and a storm were advancing on the city.

Forces of waste at work inside him, and a desert all around, this man stood still as he crossed a silent terrace and saw, for a moment, a mirage of honorable ambition, self-denial, and perseverance. In this vision, he saw balconies from which gods of love and grace smiled at him, gardens where the fruits of life hung ripening, waters of Hope that sparkled in his sight. Then, it was gone. Climbing up to a high room in a tangle of houses, he threw himself down—still in his clothes—onto his unmade bed, and covered his pillow with wasted tears.

And so the sun rose, sadly—upon no sadder sight than this man of good abilities and emotions, but incapable of using them, incapable of helping himself, incapable of making himself happy, aware of his own decay, and accepting his soul's demise.

THIS IS THE END OF THE
SEVENTH WEEKLY INSTALLMENT.

❷ *Note the personification and the strong imagery. What is the weather most likely supposed to parallel?*

❷ *What is the significance of this "vision"?*

✔ *Attributing a human emotion like sadness to an inanimate object like the sun is a special type of personification called a Pathetic Fallacy.*

Writing Opportunity:

Explain the significance of the extended metaphors in this passage: Mr. Stryver as the lion and Mr. Carton as the jackal.

Research Opportunity:

What sort of education was required of a lawyer in Dickens's time? How is that similar or different to the requirements in our own time?

A Tale of Two Cities

CHARLES DICKENS

CHAPTER VI

Hundreds of People

DOCTOR MANETTE'S QUIET lodgings were in a quiet corner not far from Soho Square. One fine Sunday afternoon, four months after the trial for treason, Mr. Jarvis Lorry walked along the sunny streets from Clerkenwell, where he lived, to dine with the Doctor. After falling back several times into a business frame of mind, Mr. Lorry had become the Doctor's friend, and this quiet street-corner was the sunny part of his life.

On this certain Sunday, Mr. Lorry walked toward Soho, early in the afternoon, for three reasons of habit. First, he often took long walks on fine Sundays, before dinner, with the Doctor and Lucie; second, because, on unpleasant Sundays, he was used to being with them as the family friend, talking, reading, looking out the window, all day long; third, because he had a problem on his mind, and knew that he might find the solution in the Doctor's household.

There were no corners more pleasantly unusual than that where the Doctor lived in all of London. It was closed, like a cul-de-sac, and so the front windows of the Doctor's lodgings had a domestic view of a quiet, peaceful street. There were few buildings—in those days—north of Oxford Road, so forest trees

✔ *Notice the contrast between the descriptions of this home and the Doctor's lodging with the Defarges and in the Bastille in Paris.*

flourished, wild flowers grew, and the hawthorn blossomed in fields that have long since been developed. Country breezes circulated freely in Soho in those days, instead of limping into the neighborhood like stray paupers with no welfare, and many walls facing south had peaches ripening on them.

The summer light shone brilliantly in the corner early in the day, but when the streets became hot, the corner was in shadow—shadow without a glare. It was a cool spot, quiet but cheerful, a wonderful place for echoes, and a refuge from the raging traffic.

Such a calm dock implies a quiet ship, and so there was. The Doctor occupied the two upper floors of a large, quiet house, where several businesses made little noise during the day and closed their doors at night. In a building at the back was an organ builder, and traders in silver and gold. The Doctor and Lucie saw very little of any of these businesses, or of other persons they had been told also inhabited the building. And so the sparrows in the tree behind the house had their way from Sunday morning to Saturday night, undisturbed by noisy commerce.

Patients came to see Dr. Manette, attracted by his reputation, and by whispers of his story. His knowledge of science and his diligence in conducting experiments, made him a popular researcher, and so he earned as much money as he wanted.

All of this was going through Mr. Jarvis Lorry's mind when he rang the doorbell at this tranquil house, on the fine Sunday afternoon.

"Is Doctor Manette at home?"

Out, but back soon.

"Is Miss Lucie at home?"

Out, but back soon.

"Is Miss Pross at home?"

Possibly, but not possible for a handmaid to determine.

"Since I'm at home myself," said Mr. Lorry, "I'll go upstairs."

Although the Doctor's daughter knew nothing

❷ *What image is conjured by this simile? Why would Dickens choose to bring this image to mind at this time?*

✔ *Note the metaphor.*

❷ *What does Mr. Lorry mean when he says he is "at home"?*

about her France, her native country, she seemed to have inherited the ability to make much out of little from her French ancestors. The furniture was simple, and the decorations were simple—having value only in that they showed Lucie to be a woman of good taste—and so the home she made for herself and her father was delightful. The arrangement of everything in the rooms—colors, sizes, variety, and contrast—was so pleasant, and so expressive of Lucie, that, as Mr. Lorry stood looking around him, the very furniture seemed to ask him, whether he approved.

Each floor had three rooms, and, since the doors were all open to permit the air to circulate freely, Mr. Lorry, sensing Lucie's strong desire for approval all around him, walked from one to another. The first room was the best—with Lucie's birds, flowers, books, desk, work-table, and box of watercolor paints. The second was the Doctor's examination room, and also the dining room. The third was the Doctor's bedroom. There, in a corner, stood the shoemaker's bench and tray of tools—now unused—much as it had stood on the fifth floor of the dismal house by the wine shop, in the suburb of Saint Antoine in Paris.

❷ *Why does Dickens pause to have Mr. Lorry walk through the rooms?*

"I can't believe," said Mr. Lorry, pausing as he looked around, "that he keeps that reminder of his sufferings around him!"

"And why not?" was the abrupt question that made him jump.

It came from Miss Pross, the wild, red woman; with massive, strong hands; whom he had first met at the Royal George Hotel in Dover; and had since come to know.

"I would have thought—" Mr. Lorry began.

"Pooh! You'd have thought!" said Miss Pross, and Mr. Lorry stopped.

"How do you do?" inquired that lady—sharply, yet gently.

"I am pretty well, thank you," answered Mr. Lorry meekly. "How are you?"

"Nothing to brag about," said Miss Pross.

"Indeed?"

"Indeed!" said Miss Pross. "I am very upset with my Ladybird."

"Indeed?"

"Say something besides, 'indeed,' or you'll make me fidget to death," said Miss Pross, whose personality (but not figure) was shortness.

"Really, then?" said Mr. Lorry.

"Really, is bad enough," replied Miss Pross, "but better. Yes, I am very upset."

"May I ask why?"

"I don't want dozens of young men, who are not worthy of Ladybird, to come calling on her," said Miss Pross.

"Do dozens come for that purpose?"

"Hundreds," said Miss Pross.

One of this lady's characteristics was, that when someone questioned something she said, she would then exaggerate it.

"Dear me!" said Mr. Lorry, as the safest remark he could think of.

"I have lived with the darling—or she has lived with me, and paid me for it; which she certainly would never have done, if I could have afforded to keep either her or me for nothing—since she was ten years old. And it's really very hard," said Miss Pross.

Not seeing just quite what was very hard, Mr. Lorry shook his head.

"All sorts of people, who are not in the least worthy of her, keep turning up," said Miss Pross. "When you began all this—"

"*I* began it, Miss Pross?"

"Didn't you? Who brought her father back to life?"

"Oh! If that was beginning it—" said Mr. Lorry.

"It wasn't the end of it, was it? I say, when you began it, it was hard enough—not that I have a problem with Doctor Manette, except he is not worthy of such a daughter—but no one could be, under any circumstances. However, it is doubly hard to have crowds and multitudes of people turning up after him to take Ladybird's affection away from me."

Mr. Lorry knew that Miss Pross was very jealous, but he also knew her to be—underneath her oddities—one of those unselfish creatures—found only among women—who will serve, with absolute adoration, other women who have the youth they have lost, the beauty they never had, the accomplishments they never gained, and the hopes they never had. He knew enough of the world to know that nothing is better than the faithful service of the heart, and so he considered Miss Pross to be very close to the lower Angels in heaven—much closer than ladies much more beautiful and much more highly bred, who had savings accounts at Tellson's.

"There has only ever been—and will only ever be—one man worthy of Ladybird," said Miss Pross," and that was my brother Solomon, if he hadn't made a mistake in life."

Mr. Lorry had discovered that her brother Solomon was a worthless scoundrel who had stolen everything she possessed, to use as an investment, and had abandoned her in poverty forever, with no sign of guilt or regret. Her faithful belief in her brother contributed to Mr. Lorry's good opinion of her. "Since we are both alone, and are both people of business," he said, when they had gone back to the drawing room and sat down. "Let me ask you—does the Doctor, in talking with Lucie, ever refer to the shoemaking time?"

"Never."

"And yet he keeps that bench and those tools beside him?"

"Ah!" replied Miss Pross, shaking her head. "I didn't say that he doesn't *think* about it."

"Do you believe that he thinks of it much?"

"I do," said Miss Pross.

"Do you imagine—" Mr. Lorry had begun, but Miss Pross stopped him with:

"I never imagine anything. I have no imagination at all."

❷ *Who are probably two of the "dozens" of young men who call on Lucie?*

✐ *Think about what the narrator has just said about women.*

❷ *Why is the choice of Solomon for this character's name ironic?*

"I stand corrected. If you don't *imagine*, do you *suppose*, sometimes?"

"Now and then," said Miss Pross.

"Do you suppose," Mr. Lorry went on, with a twinkle in his eye, as he smiled gently at her, "that Dr. Manette has any theory of his own, as to why he was so oppressed—even as to the name of his oppressor?"

"I don't suppose anything about it, except what Ladybird tells me."

"And that is—?"

"That she thinks he does."

"Now, don't get mad at all these questions, because I am only a dull man of business, and you are a woman of business."

"Dull?" Miss Pross calmly inquired.

Regretting that adjective, Mr. Lorry replied, "No, no, no. Surely not. To return to business—isn't it remarkable that Dr. Manette, innocent of any crime, should never raise that question? Not even with me—not even with his daughter? Believe me, Miss Pross, I'm not curious—I'm very interested."

"To the best of my understanding, he is afraid of the whole subject."

"Afraid?"

"It's plain enough, I think, why he might be. It's a terrible memory. Besides that, he lost himself there. Since he doesn't know how he lost himself—or how he found himself—he may never feel sure that he won't lose himself again. That, alone, would make the subject unpleasant, I would think."

This was a more profound remark than Mr. Lorry had looked for. "True," he said, "and frightening to think about. However, I wonder, Miss Pross, whether it is good for Dr. Manette to have that suppression always shut up inside him. It is this doubt that has led me to this conversation."

"It can't be helped," said Miss Pross, shaking her head. "If you get close to that topic, he instantly becomes worse—better to leave it alone. Sometimes,

❷ *What does Miss Pross mean when she says that Dr. Manette "lost himself"?*

✔ *Look up the psychological phenomena of "suppression" and "repression."*

he gets up in the middle of the night, and we can hear him, pacing up and down in his room. Ladybird has figured out that his mind is pacing in his old prison. She hurries up to him, and they walk together, up and down, up and down, until he is calm. However, he never says a word of the true reason for his pacing, and she does not hint at it. They walk in silence until her love and companionship have restored him."

For someone with no imagination, Miss Pross certainly seemed to perceive the pain of being haunted by one sad idea, when she repeated the phrase, walking up and down.

This corner, which we've already pointed out was wonderful for echoes, now resounded with coming feet.

"Here they are!" said Miss Pross, rising to end the conversation, "and now we will have hundreds of visitors soon!"

The acoustics in this corner were such, that as Mr. Lorry stood at the open window, hearing Doctor and Lucie Manette approach, he imagined that they would never arrive. The echoes would die away, followed by echoes of other steps, and then those too would die away as they seemed nearby. However, father and daughter did finally appear, and Miss Pross met them at the street door.

Although she was red, and wild, and grim, Miss Pross was a pleasant sight, taking Lucie's bonnet off as she came upstairs, dusting it with her handkerchief, and smoothing Lucie's rich hair with as much pride as she might have taken in her own. Lucie was a pleasant sight too—hugging and thanking her, and jokingly protesting at all the trouble Miss Pross was taking. The Doctor was a pleasant sight, too, teasing Miss Pross about how much she spoiled Lucie, still showing with the expression in his own eyes and in his own tone of voice that he would spoil Lucie just as much, if not more. Mr. Lorry was also pleasant, grinning at the entire scene in his little wig, thankful that he had found such a family in his elder bachelor

Think what Dickens might be foreshadowing and symbolizing in the sound of footsteps, always approaching, but never arriving.

years. However, Miss Pross' "hundreds of people" never seemed to come.

It was time for dinner, and the "Hundreds" were still absent. Miss Pross was in charge of the lower floor of the apartment, and did a marvelous job. Her dinners were so well-cooked and well-served that, even though they were plain meals simply served, nothing could be better. She had found a few poor French immigrants in Soho and had paid them shillings and half-crowns to teach her French cooking. She had learned such secrets that her two household servants saw her as a sorceress, or Cinderella's godmother, who could turn a bird, rabbit, or a vegetable, into anything she liked.

On Sundays, Miss Pross ate at the Doctor's table, but on other days insisted on eating in the kitchen, or in her own room on the second floor—a blue room, where only her Ladybird was permitted. On this night, Miss Pross, responding to her Ladybird's pleasant face and pleasant efforts to please her, became very friendly; and so the dinner was very pleasant, too.

The heat was oppressive, and, after dinner, Lucie suggested that they move outside under the plane-tree to drink their wine. As that household revolved around her, they did as she suggested without question. She had made herself

Mr. Lorry's cup-bearer and kept his glass filled as they talked.

Still, the "hundreds of people" never showed up. Mr. Darnay presented himself while they were under the plane-tree, but he was only One.

Dr. Manette and Lucie received him kindly. However, Miss Pross suddenly became afflicted with twitches in the head and body, and went into the house. This "fit of the jerks" often came upon her.

The Doctor was feeling his best, and looking quite young. The resemblance between him and Lucie was very strong at these times, and as they sat side by side, their likeness became quite striking.

✔ *The character of the spinsterly governess who absolutely dotes on her beautiful, young charge, is a stock character popular in many novels of Dickens's day. Part of Dickens's genius, however, was his ability to develop his characters beyond their mere stereotypes. It will be interesting to see what Dickens has in store for Miss Pross.*

❷ *Review: Who is Mr. Darnay?*

❷ *What is the author suggesting?*

The Doctor had been talking all day, and had been unusually lively. "Doctor Manette," said Mr. Darnay, as they talked about the old buildings of London, "have you seen much of the Tower of London?"

"Lucie and I have been there, but only as visitors. We have seen enough to know that many people are interested in it—little more."

"I have been there, as you remember," Darnay said with a smile, tinged with anger, "in a different situation. They told me something unusual when I was there."

"What was that?"

"Some workmen found an old dungeon, built over and forgotten, when they were making some alterations. Every stone of its inner wall was covered with inscriptions that had been carved by prisoners— dates, names, complaints, prayers. Upon one corner stone, a prisoner had carved three letters, as his last work. Eventually, they figured out that the three letters were DIG. After digging, they found the ashes of a piece of paper and a leather bag. What the unknown prisoner had written will never be read, but he had written something, and hidden it from the jailer."

"Father!" exclaimed Lucie, "You are ill!"

He had suddenly jumped it, his hand to his head. His behavior and expression terrified them all.

"No, my dear, not ill. There are large drops of rain falling, and they made me jump. We'd better go in."

He recovered almost instantly. Rain was really falling in large drops, some of which were on the back of his hand. However, he made no mention of the discovery Darnay had mentioned, and the business eye of Mr. Lorry noticed that Dr. Manette was looking at Charles Darnay as he had in the passages of the Court House.

His recovery was so quick, however, that Mr. Lorry questioned his business eye. Dr. Manette remarked that small surprises still made him jump, and that the rain had startled him.

Tea-time came, and Miss Pross made tea, with

❷ The Tower of London was originally built as a fortress and palace, but had also been used throughout British history as an infamous prison.

❸ Speculate why this anecdote is at all important, and why does the Doctor react to it as he does?

another fit of the jerks upon her. However, no "hundreds of people" came. Mr. Carton had lounged in, but he made only Two.

The night was so hot and humid, that the heat overpowered them, even with doors and windows open. When the tea was gone, they all moved to a window, and looked out into the heavy twilight. Lucie sat by her father. Darnay sat beside her. Carton leaned against a window. The curtains were long and white and twirled like ghostly wings as the thunder-gusts blew into the room.

"The raindrops are still falling, large, heavy, and few," said Dr. Manette. "It comes slowly."

❷ *Don't miss the ominous tone of Carton's sentence. Dr. Manette is talking about the rainstorm. What "storm" is Carton speaking of?*

"It comes surely," Carton said.

They spoke quietly, as people do as they are watching and waiting—especially if they are in a dark room, waiting for Lightning.

People ran through the streets to get shelter before the storm broke, footsteps echoing throughout the corner, but with no owners coming into view.

"A multitude of people, and yet a solitude!" said Darnay after a while.

"Isn't it impressive, Mr. Darnay?" asked Lucie. "Sometimes I've sat here in the evening, until I've imagined, when all is black and solemn—"

"Let me shudder too. We may know what it is."

"It will seem like nothing to you. I think such whims are only impressive in our own minds—they are not to be shared. I have sat here until I've imagined that these echoes are the footsteps that will soon be entering our lives."

✔ *Important foreshadowing*

"If that is so, there is a huge crowd coming into our lives one day," Carton added, in his moody way.

The footsteps would not stop, and they became more and more rapid. The corner echoed and re-echoed with the sounds of feet. Some sounded as if they were right under the windows. Some sounded as if they were actually in the room. Some sounded as if they were coming, some going, some pausing, some completely stopping—yet there was not one person within sight.

"Are all these footsteps coming for all of us, Miss Manette, or will they be divided among us?"

"I don't know, Mr. Darnay; I told you it was foolish, but you asked for it. I've been alone when I had these thoughts, and I've imagined that these would be people who are to come into my life, and my father's."

"I take them into mine!" said Carton. "I ask no questions and make no requirements. There is a great crowd bearing down on us, Miss Manette, and I see them—by the Lightning."

"And I hear them!" he added after a peal of thunder. "Fast, fierce, furious!"

The rush and roar of rain echoed Carton's words, and he stopped, because the noise drowned him out. A storm of thunder and lightning broke with that sweep of water, and there was not a break until after the moon rose at midnight.

The great bell of Saint Paul's Cathedral was striking *One* in the calm air, as Mr. Lorry, escorted by Jerry—high-booted and carrying a lantern—returned to Clerkenwell. There were lonely and dangerous stretches of road along the way, and Mr. Lorry always hired Jerry for this service, although it was usually done a good two hours earlier.

"What a night! Almost a night, Jerry," said Mr. Lorry, "to bring the dead out of their graves."

"I've never seen the night myself, master—and I don't expect to—that would do that," answered Jerry.

"Good night, Mr. Carton," said the man of business. "Good night, Mr. Darnay. Shall we ever see such a night again, together?"

Perhaps. Perhaps they would also see the great crowd of people with its rush and roar, bearing down upon them too.

THIS IS THE END OF THE
EIGHTH WEEKLY INSTALLMENT.

He added the last words, after a vivid flash showed him lounging by the window. Note how each of the three characters, Darnay, Lucie, and Carton react to the notion that the footsteps represent people coming into their lives.

Violent storms, especially thunder and lightning storms, often symbolize mental, emotional, or physical violence. Note that this storm begins to arrive just as Darnay is talking about the prisoners' documents hidden in the Tower of London.

Again, a reference to bringing the dead out of their graves.

Writing Opportunity:

Explain the irony and tension Dickens establishes in this installment, contrasting the apparent peacefulness of the Manette residence with the ominous foreshadowing. Use evidence from the book to support all of your assertions and speculations.

A Tale of Two Cities

CHARLES DICKENS

CHAPTER VII

Monseigneur in Town

MONSEIGNEUR, ONE OF the great lords in power at the French Court, held his fortnightly reception in his grand hotel in Paris. He was in his inner room—the Holiest of Holies for the crowd of worshippers in the outer rooms, about to have his chocolate. He could easily swallow many things—and was rumored to be swallowing France whole—but he needed four men, not counting the cook, to drink his chocolate.

Yes, it took four men, all glowing with gorgeous decorations, their leader unable to exist with fewer than two gold watches in his pocket—an attitude similar to that of Monseigneur—to carry the happy chocolate to Monseigneur's lips. One lackey carried the chocolate-pot into Monseigneur's sacred presence. A second mixed and stirred the chocolate with the utensil he carried, just for that purpose. A third held out the napkin, and the fourth (the one with the two gold watches) poured the chocolate. It would have been impossible for Monseigneur to get rid of one of these attendants and hold on to his high status. His reputation would have been ruined had only three men brought him his chocolate. If there had been only two, he would have died of shame.

Again, note that this installment begins with a "change of scene." We are again in France.

"Monseigneur"(from mon, "my" and seigneur, "elder" or "lord") was the proper form of address for any member of the French aristocracy. It is used in this chapter for one specific person—the host of the party—but it is also used in this novel in general to represent members of the noble class—thus Monsieur the Marquis is also referred to as "Monseigneur."

"Holiest of Holies" is an allusion to the Temple in Jerusalem, which was essentially a series of courts, each one higher and more holy than the previous one. Anyone, even non-Jews, could enter the outermost court. The second court was for Jewish women, the third for Jewish men. The fourth court was reserved for the priests, but only the High Priest could enter the innermost chamber, the Holy of Holies.

Remember the sarcasm Dickens used earlier when he was talking about the French clergy.

King Charles I of England
dissolved both houses of
Parliament and attempted to
rule alone. He ran into trouble when the Scots invaded,
and Charles was forced to
pay the Scottish war expenses,
in exchange for their retreat.
He had to call Parliament
into session to ask for
money—a Parliament
session that would last 20
years. Charles attempted to
use the military to dissolve
Parliament again, and
ended up being overthrown
by the Puritan army, led by
Oliver Cromwell. They were
called Roundheads because
of the style of their haircuts.

Psalm 24:1—The earth is
the LORD's, and the fullness
thereof…

In pre-Revolution France,
a Farmer-General was a
person who had paid a fee
to the crown for the right to
levy taxes within a particular
district.

Note the irony that the
Monseigneur is broke
and relies on the Farmer-
General's money, but,
because the Monseigneur is
of "better blood," he and his
sister (the Farmer-General's
wife) look upon him with
contempt.

As he did most nights, Monseigneur had gone out last night to a little dinner with fascinating company. Last night, he also went to the Grand Opera. He was so polite and impressionable that his entertainment influenced his opinions about politics more than the actual needs of his country. The leaders of England were much the same, when the Roundheads overthrew King Charles I. The Monseigneur believed that the best way to handle general public business was to let it go its own way; in specific matters, he believed that it should go his way—benefit his power and wallet. He believed that the world was made to fulfill his personal pleasures. He only had to alter the Old Testament by one word to make his basic belief: "The earth and the fullness thereof are mine, saith [Monseigneur]."

As a result of indulging his greed and his pleasures, Monseigneur had essentially run out of money and amassed considerable debts. To repair the political damage, he had allied himself with a Farmer-General. Because he could not levy taxes, he enjoyed that the Farmer-General could. Because he could not live under a budget, and Farmer-Generals were rich, he found the financial contributions to be helpful. And so Monseigneur had removed his sister from a convent, before she could take her vows, and gave her to a very rich Farmer-General. The wealthy brother-in-law was now among the throng in the outer rooms waiting to see Monseigneur, carrying a cane with a golden apple on top. All of the other guests doted and fawned on him—all the guests except those who were superior in blood, like the Monseigneur, and even the Farmer-General's own wife, who looked upon him with the proudest contempt.

This Farmer-General was wealthy. He had thirty horses, twenty-four male servants, and six attendants for his wife. Since he openly pretended to do nothing but rob and grab where he could, the Farmer-General was the one who lived most like his outward image among the guests at Monseigneur's hotel that day.

If any of the poor scarecrows in rags and night-caps in Saint Antoine, or any of the other poor neighborhoods in France, had seen the Monseigneur's rooms, there would have been a riot indeed. Everyone at his party was a fraud: military officers who knew nothing about war; naval officers who knew nothing about ships; politicians who knew nothing about how to govern; bold clergymen, who knew nothing about self-denial; all in the room were unfit for their professions, and all told horrible lies to keep them. All were in the same social class as Monseigneur, and therefore received all government jobs that could give them any money or status. There were people in private employment here, who were also frauds in their profession: doctors who made great fortunes out of fancy medicines for imaginary illnesses; analysts who had figured out every solution for the minor problems in France, except the solution of personal responsibility and morality. Agnostic philosophers, who were remodeling the world with words, and making their own Towers of Babel out of playing cards, talked with agnostic chemists, who talked about changing lead into gold, at Monseigneur's party. Exquisite gentlemen of the highest class, which was (and has been since) recognized by its indifference to natural topics of human interest, filled the rooms. The spies in this room—at least half of the occupants—would have had a hard time finding one wife who looked like a mother. Indeed, except for the act of bringing a troublesome creature into the world, there was no such action performed in this class. Peasant women nursed the inconvenient babies, raised them, and charming grandmothers dressed, ate, and danced at sixty as they had at twenty.

The leprosy of fraud disfigured every human creature at Monseigneur's gathering. In the outermost room were half a dozen truly exceptional people who had had, for a few years, vague qualms about the way things were going in France. Half of these had joined a religious sect of Convulsionists, and were even

We have seen the image of the scarecrow to describe the residents of Saint Antoine before.

These references to agnostics are digs at the eighteenth-century "Enlightenment" during which philosophers questioned all of the traditional notions of God.

The Tower of Babel is the Old Testament story of humankind attempting to build a tower high enough for humans to see God. To prevent this, God made all of the workers speak different languages. This allusion refers to the idea that the philosophers, by rejecting God, were conducting similar errors in their ways of thinking.

List all of the criticisms—explicit or implicit—in this paragraph.

Note the metaphor.

Convolutionists were a radical sect of French Catholics
who fell in convulsions
and spasms of ecstasy and
prophesy. The prophesies dealt
with the future destruction
of the French Church and
Government. Violence and
excessive behavior eventually
brought the movement to
an end.

then deciding whether they should foam, rage, roar, and have a fit on the spot—sending a message to the Monseigneur. The other three had joined another sect, whose solution to problems was some nonsense about "the Center of Truth"—which believed that humanity had abandoned the Center of Truth (easily proven) but had not yet escaped the Circumference, and could head back to the Center by fasting and seeing ghosts. These people held a number of séances, which allegedly did a world of good—but not that anyone could see.

All of these worrisome factors were hidden by the fact that everyone at Monseigneur's hotel was perfectly dressed. If Judgment Day were a measure of the quality of one's clothing, everyone there would have been saved. All of the frizzling, powdering, sticking up hair, all of the artificial preservation of delicate skin, all of the gallant swords, all of the perfumes and colognes, would surely keep anything going, forever. The gentlemen wore trinkets that chinked as they slowly moved around the rooms. Golden chains rang like precious little bells. It was this ringing, and the rustling of silk, brocade, and fine linen, that may well have set a flutter in the air of Saint Antoine and his devouring hunger.

Fashion was the one unfailing symbol used to keep all things in their places. Everyone who could, in those days, dressed for a Fancy Ball that was never supposed to end. Even the executioner was required to do his duty "frizzled, powdered, in a gold-laced coat, pumps, and white silk stockings." At the gallows (the axe was rarely used), all the executioners dressed in this manner. No one at the Monseigneur's party, that day in 1780, could possibly doubt that this system would outlast the stars!

After relieving his four men of their burdens and drunk his chocolate, the Monseigneur had the doors of the Holiest of Holies thrown open, and he went forth. What submission, what servility, what humiliation! After bowing down to the Monseigneur so fervently, these characters had nothing left to give to Heaven—which may have been one reason why so few members of this class ever entered it.

Monseigneur passed through the rooms affably, making a promise here, giving a smile there, all the way to the room where the Circumference of Truth met. There, he turned and came back again, and so he was shut up in his sanctuary by his chocolate acolytes, and was seen no more.

With the show over, the conversation got louder, and the nobles went ringing their ways downstairs. Soon, there was only one person left, and he, with his hat under his arm and his snuff-box in his hand, slowly passed among the mirrors on his way out.

"I devote you," said this person, stopping at the last door, turning in the direction of Monseigneur's chamber, "to the Devil!" With that, he shook the snuff from his fingers as if he had shaken the dust from his feet, and walked quietly downstairs.

He was about sixty years old, handsomely dressed, haughty in manner, with a face like a fine mask. His face was so pale as to look transparent, every feature clearly defined. The nose, mostly beautiful, was slightly pinched at the top of each nostril—it was in these two pinches that the only change in his expression ever appeared. Sometimes these would change color, and sometimes seem to grow and shrink, as though they were pulsating—at that time, they gave him a cruel, treacherous look. Even with a face that seemed too round and too thin, he came across as handsome, even remarkable.

The owner of this face went downstairs, got into his carriage, and drove away. Not many people had talked to him at the reception. He had stood off by himself, and Monseigneur had not been very friendly to him. In his mood, he enjoyed watching the common people scatter in front of his horses, often barely escaping being run down. His servant drove as if he were charging an enemy, and he paid no attention. There had been the occasional complain from the

In other words, the "worshippers" waiting outside Monseigneur's door gave so much "honor and glory" to Monseigneur, there was none left for God.

In the New Testament, Jesus instructs his disciples to shake the dust off their feet every time they leave a town where they have found no hospitality. This man obviously has such a sense of self-importance that he takes his rejection by the Monseigneur to have monumental significance, and he responds in kind.

rabble that carriages such as this drove too fast and too recklessly in sections of the city where the streets were narrow and there was little room for pedestrians. But, as was the case of most of the complaints of the common barbarians, no one of the upper classes really cared. Let the rabble care for their own.

The carriage tore through streets and around corners, with women screaming and men yanking each other and children out of its way. At last, flying around a street corner by a fountain, one of the wheels made a sickening little jolt. There was a loud cry from a number of voices, and the horses reared up and plunged.

If the horses hadn't stopped, the carriage probably would not have: carriages would often leave their wounded behind—and why not? However, the frightened driver had gotten down in a hurry, and now twenty hands held the horses' bridles.

"What has gone wrong?" said Monsieur, calmly looking out.

A tall man in a nightcap had picked up a bundle from among the feet of the horses, and had laid it on the base of the fountain. He then collapsed in the mud and wet, howling over it like a wild animal.

"Pardon, Monsieur the Marquis!" said a ragged, submissive man, "It is a child."

"Why does he make that abominable noise? Is it *his* child?"

"Excuse me, Monsieur the Marquis—it is a pity—yes."

The fountain was some way off; the street opened into a space about twelve yards square. The tall man suddenly got up from the ground, and came running at the carriage. Monsieur the Marquis grabbed for the hilt of his sword.

"Killed!" shrieked the man, in wild desperation, extending both arms high above his head, and staring at Monsieur the Marquis. "Dead!"

The people closed around them, and looked at Monsieur the Marquis. There was no visible menace

Note the Marquis's callousness.

or anger on their faces—only eager watchfulness. The
people said nothing—they had been silent since their
first cry. The voice of the submissive man who had
spoken was flat and tame. Monsieur the Marquis ran
his eyes over them all, as if they had been mere rats
coming out of their holes.

He took out his purse.

"It amazes me," he said, "that you people cannot
take care of yourselves and your children. One of you
is always in the way! You've probably injured one of
my horses. See! Give him that."

He threw a gold coin down for the driver to pick
up, and everyone looked forward to see it as it fell.
The tall man called out again in his unearthly way,
"Dead!"

Another man hurried through the crowd, and
grabbed the tall man, who fell on his shoulder, sob-
bing and crying, and pointing to the fountain, where
some women were bending over the motionless
bundle, and moving gently around it. They were,
however, as silent as the men.

"I know it all, I know it all," said the man to the
tall man. "Be a brave man, my Gaspard! It is better for
the poor little plaything to die so, than to live. It has
died in a moment without pain. Could it have lived
an hour as happily?"

❷ What consolation does this
second man offer Gaspard?

"You are a philosopher," said the Marquis, smiling. "What do they call you?"

"They call me Defarge."

"What is your trade?"

"Monsieur the Marquis, I am a vendor of wine."

"Pick up that, philosopher and vendor of wine,"
said the Marquis, throwing him another gold coin,
"and spend it as you will. The horses there; are they
all right?"

Without bothering to look at the crowd a second
time, Monsieur the Marquis leaned back in his seat,
and was just about to leave, with the attitude of a
gentleman who had just broken some everyday thing,
and had paid for it—could afford to pay for it—when

his complacency was disturbed by a coin flying into his carriage, and clanging onto the floor.

"Hold!" said Monsieur the Marquis. "Hold the horses! Who threw that?"

He looked to the spot where Defarge the vendor of wine had stood, a moment before, but the wretched father was groveling on his face on the pavement there now, and next to the father was now a dark stout woman, knitting.

"You dogs!" said the Marquis, but smoothly, and with a calm face, except for the spots on his nose. "I would ride over any of you very willingly, and exterminate you from the earth. If I knew which rascal threw this coin back at the carriage, and if that vermin were near enough, I would crush him under my wheels."

Their condition was so cowed, and they were so familiar with what a man as powerful as Monsieur the Marquis could do to them— both within the law and beyond it—that not a voice, or a hand, or even an eye was raised. Among the men, not one. But the woman who stood knitting looked up steadily, staring the Marquis in the face. It was not worth his dignity to notice it. His contemptuous eyes passed over her, and over all the other rats, and he leaned back in his seat again, and gave the word "Go on!"

He was driven on, and other carriages came whirling by in quick succession; the Minister, the State-Projector, the Farmer-General, the Doctor, the Lawyer, the Bishop, the Grand Opera, the Comedy, the whole Fancy Ball in a bright continuous flow, came whirling by. The rats had crept out of their holes to look on, and they stayed looking on for hours, soldiers and police often passing between them and the parade, making a barrier behind which the rabble slunk, and through which they peered. The father had long ago taken up his bundle and hidden himself away with it, when the women who had watched the bundle while it lay at the base of the fountain, sat there watching the running of the water and the

We will learn later the significance of this knitting.

rolling of the carriages—when the one woman who had stood conspicuous, knitting, still knitted on with the certainty of Fate. The water of the fountain ran, the swift river ran, the day ran into evening, so much life in the city ran into death according to rule—time and tide waited for no man—and so the rats were sleeping close together in their dark holes again, the Fancy Ball was lighted up at supper, all things ran their course.

There were three Fates in Greek mythology, sisters who spun the thread and wove the tapestry that governed the events of human life. This allusion is suggesting that this woman has some power over others' lives as did these three sisters.

Writing Opportunity:

Write an essay in which you describe the verbal and non-verbal language used by Monsieur the Marquis to show his condescension toward the peasants in the streets of Paris. Support your answer with evidence from the text.

Research Opportunity:

The French Revolution came at the end of an intellectual movement known as the Enlightenment, which held that human reason could solve any problem and was vastly superior to the human passions or emotions. Analyze Immanuel Kant's essay "What is Enlightenment" and explain his main ideas. Consider the causes of the French Revolution, and how it turned out that many of Kant's ideas were wrong.

A Tale of Two Cities

CHARLES DICKENS

CHAPTER VIII
Monseigneur in the Country

ENVISION A BEAUTIFUL landscape, with the corn bright, but not abundant, in it. There are patches of poor rye where corn should have been, patches of poor peas and beans, patches of most coarse vegetable substitutes for wheat. Just like the people who grow them, these crops seem to be growing unwillingly and seem to be more likely to give up, and wither away.

Monsieur the Marquis in his travelling carriage (which seemed heavier than usual for some reason), pulled by four strong horses ridden by two drivers, struggled up a steep hill. Monsieur the Marquis now appeared to be blushing—but it was not an insult to his high breeding; it was merely the setting sun.

The sunset shone so brilliantly into the traveling carriage when it reached the hill-top, that its occupant was crimson. "It will die out," said Monsieur the Marquis, glancing at his hands, "directly."

In fact, the sun was so low that it set at that very moment. When the brake had been placed against the wheel, and the carriage slid down the far side of the hill in a cloud of dust, the red glow departed quickly; the sun and the Marquis going down together, there was no glow left when the brake was taken off.

There was a stretch of open, broken country yet to

One of the factors leading to the French Revolution was a harsh winter in 1787 and poor harvest in 1788, leading to widespread hunger among the poor. Of course, the wealthy took the first fruits of what food was produced, leaving virtually nothing for the masses of hungry.

Note how the author establishes the Marquis' elevated opinion of himself by equating him with a heavenly body—the sun and the Marquis set together.

cover, a little village at the bottom of the hill, a broad sweep and rise beyond it, a church tower, a windmill, a forest for hunting, and a rocky hill with a fortress used as a prison on it. The Marquis looked at all of these objects as the night drew on, with the air of one who was coming near home.

Research Opportunity:

Look up the "Three Estates" of France and the tax structure prior to the French Revolution. What factors contributed to the severe economic depression of that time in France?

❷ *In Greek and Roman mythology, the Furies were three sisters whose function was to relentlessly pursue and torment evildoers and sinners, especially those who had committed heinous crimes beyond the scope of human justice. While the Furies were undeniably cruel, they were also renowned for being very fair. They were often pictured as repulsive winged women wearing black robes. Sometimes they were shown with snakes twined through their hair, piercing red eyes that dripped blood, and pitch-black bodies with bat wings. Even with the snakes twined in their hair, the Furies should not be confused with the Gorgons who were sisters who had snakes growing out of their heads instead of hair. What might Dickens be suggesting by using this allusion in connection with the Marquis?*

The village had one poor street, with a single poor brewery, poor tannery, poor tavern, poor stable yard for relays of post-horses, poor fountain, all the usual poor ingredients of a poor country village. It had its poor people too. Many of them were sitting at their doors, shredding spare onions and the like for supper, while many were at the fountain, washing leaves, and grasses, and any similar small bits of the earth that could be eaten. Evidence of the source of their poverty, was not everywhere: everywhere were signs announcing that state tax, the church tax, the feudal tax, local and general taxes, were due to be paid. The wonder was, that there was any village left that hadn't been swallowed up by one tax or another or the sum total of all the taxes combined.

There were few children to be seen, and no dogs. As to the men and women, their choices on earth were clear to the observer—they could accept Life on the lowest terms that could sustain it, down in the little village under the hill or endure captivity and Death in the prison on the crag.

Announced by a messenger in advance, and by the cracking of his drives' whips, which twined snake-like about their heads in the evening air, as if he came attended by the Furies, Monsieur the Marquis drew up in his traveling carriage at the posting-house gate. It was very close to the fountain, and the peasants stopped to look at him. He looked at them, and saw in them, without knowing it, the effects of a slow, sure decay of humanity that would lead the English to consider the French to be weak and starved for about a hundred years longer than they actually were.

Monsier the Marquis cast his eyes over the submissive faces that drooped before him, just as his had dropped before Monseigneur of the Court—only the difference was, that these faces drooped merely to suffer, with no chance of gaining any favors. A grizzled road worker joined the group.

"Bring me that fellow!" said the Marquis to the messenger.

The fellow was brought, cap in hand, and the other fellows closed round to look and listen, in a manner similar to the people at the Paris fountain.

"Did I pass you on the road?"

"Monseigneur, it is true. I had the honor of being passed on the road."

"Coming up the hill, and at the top of the hill, both?

"Monseigneur, it is true."

"What did you look at so closely?"

"Monseigneur, I looked at the man."

He stooped a little, and with his tattered blue cap pointed under the carriage. All his fellows stooped to look under the carriage.

"What man, pig? And why look there?"

"Pardon, Monseigneur; he swung by the chain of the brake."

"Who?" demanded the Marquis.

"Monseigneur, the man."

"May the Devil carry away these idiots! Who was the man? You know all the men of this part of the country. Who was he?"

"Please be merciful, Monseigneur! He was not from this part of the country. In all my entire life, I have never seen him before."

"Swinging by the chain? Was he in danger of being suffocated?"

> ✔ *Note the similarity between the "reverence" the peasants pay the Marquis and the "reverence" paid by the Marquis to Monseigneur, but also note the significant difference.*

> ✔ *Notice how the road worker addresses Monsieur the Marquis as "Monseigneur."*

"With your gracious permission, that was the wonder of it, Monseigneur. His head was hanging over—like this!"

He turned sideways to the carriage, and leaned back, with his face thrown up to the sky, and his head hanging down; then recovered himself, fumbled with his cap, and made a bow.

"What did he look like?"

"Monseigneur, he was whiter than the miller. All covered with dust, white as a ghost, tall as a ghost!"

The image made an immense sensation in the little crowd, but all eyes, instead of looking at each other, looked at Monsieur the Marquis—maybe to observe whether he had any ghosts on his conscience.

"It was truly courageous of you," said the Marquis, reminding himself not to be perturbed by that such vermin, "to see a thief accompanying my carriage, and not open that great mouth of yours. Bah! Get him out of my way, Monsieur Gabelle!"

Monsieur Gabelle had the twin jobs of Postmaster and tax collector. He had come out with great humility and servility to assist at this interrogation, and had held the road-mender by the sleeve in an official manner.

"Bah! Go away!" said Monsieur Gabelle.

"Lay hands on this stranger if he seeks to stay in your village tonight, and make sure that his business is honest, Gabelle."

"Monseigneur, I am flattered to devote myself to your orders."

"Did he run away, fellow? Where is that Accursed fellow?"

The Accursed was already under the carriage with six friends, pointing out the brake chain with his blue cap. Six more friends promptly hauled him out, and presented him, breathless, to Monsieur the Marquis.

"Did the man run away, Idiot, when we stopped for the brake?"

"Monseigneur, he jumped over the hill-side, head first, just as a person dives into the river."

"Go find him, Gabelle. Go on!"

The half-dozen who were peering at the chain were still among the wheels, like sheep; the wheels turned so suddenly that they were lucky to save their skins and bones; if they had not been so skinny, they might not have been so lucky.

The jolt with which the carriage started out of the village and up the slope beyond was soon slowed by the steepness of the hill. Gradually, the carriage slowed to a walking pace, swaying and laboring upward among the many sweet scents of a summer night. The drivers, with a thousand shimmering gnats circling about them instead of the Furies, quietly mended the tips of their whips. The valet walked by the horses. The messenger could be heard trotting on ahead into the dim distance.

At the steepest part of the hill there was a little graveyard, with a Cross and a new large figure of Our Savior on it. It was a poor carving in wood, done by some inexperienced rural carver, but he had made a lifelike figure—like his own life, maybe—for it was dreadfully spare and thin.

At the foot of this rude Crucifix—that could be taken to symbolize the severe hardship in France that still had not reached its worst—knelt an old woman. She turned her head as the carriage came up to her, rose quickly, and presented herself at the carriage door.

"It is you, Monseigneur! Monseigneur, a request." With an exclamation of impatience, but with his unchangeable face, Monseigneur looked out.

"How, then! What is it? Always requests!"

"Monseigneur. For the love of the great God! My husband, the forester."

"What about your husband, the forester? It is always the same with you people. Does he have a debt he cannot pay?"

"He has paid all, Monseigneur. He is dead."

"Well! What then? Can I bring him back to life?"

"Alas, no, Monseigneur! But he is buried over

✏ Notice how she too addresses Monsieur the Marquis as "Monseigneur."

there, under a little heap of poor grass."

"So?"

"Monseigneur, there are so many little heaps of poor grass."

"Again, so?"

Although she looked like an old woman, she was actually quite young. Her passionate grief showed in her veined, knotted hands, which she clasped together with wild energy, and then laid on the carriage door—as if caressing it—as if it had been a human breast, and could feel the appealing touch.

"Monseigneur, hear me! Monseigneur, please hear my request! My husband died of poverty. So many die of poverty. So many more will die of poverty."

"Again, so? Can I feed them?"

"Monseigneur, the good God knows whether you can or not; but that is not what I ask. My request is simply that a tiny bit of stone or wood, with my husband's name, may be placed over him to show where he lies. Otherwise, the place will be quickly forgotten and will never be found when I am also dead of poverty, and I shall be laid under some other heap of poor grass. Monseigneur, the poor are so many, they increase in number so fast, there is so much poverty. Monseigneur! Monseigneur!"

The valet moved her away from the door, and the carriage broke into a brisk trot. The drivers quickened the pace, and she was left far behind. Monseigneur, again escorted by the Furies, was rapidly heading for his chateau.

The sweet scents of the summer night rose all around him, and on the dusty, ragged, and around toil-worn group at the fountain—since scents are free. This group was entertained by the road-mender, who told them about the ghost, over and over again. Slowly, when they could bear no more, they dropped off one by one, and lights came on in little windows. As the stars came out, it looked as if these lights had shot up into the sky instead of having been extinguished.

Monsieur the Marquis emerged from his carriage

❷ *What is literally happening here? Why does Dickens return to his allusion to the Furies?*

into the shadow of a large high-roofed house, and
of many overhanging trees. Almost immediately, the
shadow was illuminated by the light of a torch, as the
great door of his chateau was opened to him.

"Has Monsieur Charles arrived from England?"

"Monseigneur, not yet."

THIS IS THE END OF THE
NINTH WEEKLY INSTALLMENT.

❷ *On what suspenseful and
foreshadowing note does
Dickens end this weekly
installment?*

Writing Opportunity:

*How does Dickens use the setting sun in the beginning of this
chapter? Explain the rhetorical idea behind the imagery.*

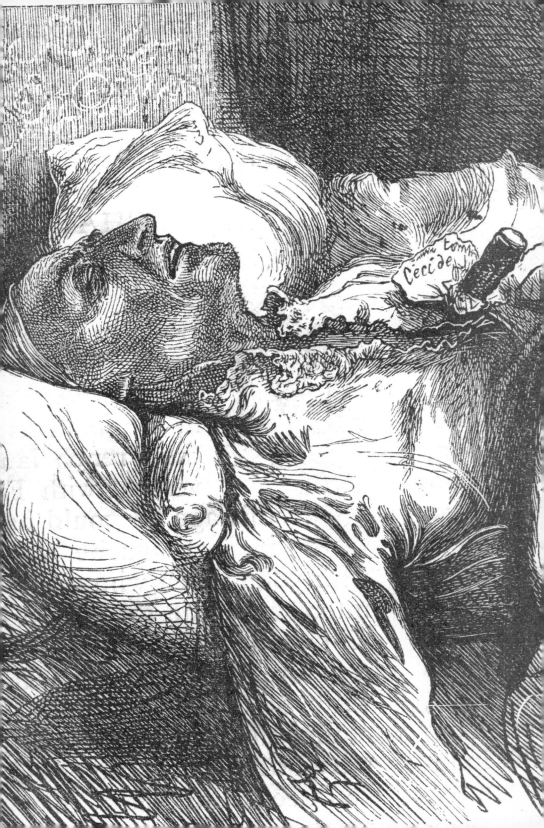

A Tale of Two Cities

CHARLES DICKENS

CHAPTER IX
The Gorgon's Head

THE CHATEAU WAS a heavy mass of building, with a large stone courtyard in front of it, and two wide stone staircases meeting in a stone terrace before the main door. It was a stony business altogether, with heavy stone balustrades, and stone urns, and stone flowers, and stone faces of men, and stone heads of lions, in all directions, just as if the Gorgon's head had surveyed it, when it was finished, two centuries ago.

An owl was angered by the disturbance made by the Marquis' slow progress up the shallow steps, preceded by candlelight. Everything else was so quiet that the torch carried up the steps and the other torch held at the great door burnt as brightly as if they were in a small parlor, instead of being in the open night air. There was no other sound than the owl's voice except the splashing of a fountain into its stone basin; for, it was one of those dark nights that seem to hold their breath by the hour together, and then heave a long low sigh, and hold their breath again.

The great door clanged behind him, and Monsieur the Marquis crossed a hall decorated grimly with old boar-spears, swords, and hunting knives. The gruesome effect was made even grimmer by heavy riding-rods

✔ *In Greek Mythology, the Gorgons were three sisters who had live snakes growing out of their heads instead of hair, scales covering their necks, tusks like a wild boar's, golden hands, and bronze wings. The most famous of the three sisters was Medusa, who was once a notoriously beautiful woman. Boasting of her beauty, and claiming to be more beautiful than Athena, she was cursed by the goddess, stripped of her beauty, and turned into the hideous snake-haired monster. She was so ugly that anyone who looked at her was instantly turned into stone. Being the only mortal among her sisters, she was eventually killed by Perseus. From her blood, the winged horse Pegasus was said to have sprung. Perseus presented the Gorgon's head to Athena, who placed it in the center of her shield. That is why pictures of Athena show the image of a snake-haired woman on her shield.*

❓ *Given the context, what does the entrance to the Marquis' chateau say about him?*

❷ *What is ironic about this description of the Marquis?*

and riding-whips, many of which had striped the back of a peasant, when his master was angry.

Avoiding the larger rooms, which were dark and locked for the night, Monsieur the Marquis, following his torch bearer, climbed the staircase to a door in a corridor, which contained his own private three-room apartment: his bed-chamber and two others. These were high-ceilinged rooms with cool, uncarpeted floors, and all the luxuries fitting the status of a Marquis in a luxurious age and country. The decoration was primarily in the fashion of King Louis XIV, but it was diversified by many objects that were illustrations of old pages in the history of France.

In the third room, a supper table was set for two. It was a round room, in one of the chateau's four towers. It was small and lofty, with its window wide open, and the wooden blinds closed, so that the dark night only showed in slight horizontal lines of black, alternating with their broad lines of stone color.

❷ *Who is this nephew most likely going to turn out to be?*

"My nephew," said the Marquis, glancing at the supper preparation; "they said he was not arrived."

He had not, but, he had been expected to arrive with Monseigneur.

"Ah! He will probably not arrive tonight. However, leave the table as it is. I will be ready in a quarter of an hour."

In a quarter of an hour Monseigneur was ready, and sat down alone to his sumptuous and luxurious supper. His chair was facing the window, and he had eaten his soup, and was raising his glass of Bordeaux to his lips, when he put it down.

"What is that?" he calmly asked, looking with attention at the horizontal lines of black and stone color.

"Monseigneur? That?"

"Outside the blinds. Open the blinds."

It was done.

"Well?"

"Monseigneur, it is nothing. The trees and the night are all that are here."

The servant who spoke, had thrown the blinds wide, had looked out into the vacant darkness, and now looked round for instructions.

"Good," said the calm master. "Close them again."

That was done too, and the Marquis went on with his supper. He was halfway through it, when he again stopped with his glass in his hand, hearing the sound of wheels, approaching quickly, up to the front of the chateau.

"Ask who is arrived."

It was the nephew of Monseigneur. He had been some few miles behind Monseigneur, early in the afternoon. He had closed the gap rapidly, but not so rapidly as to meet Monseigneur on the road. He had heard that Monseigneur had passed some of the posting-houses before him.

Monseigneur gave orders to tell the nephew that supper awaited him immediately, and that he was asked to come to it. In a little while he came. He had been known in England as Charles Darnay.

Monseigneur received him politely, but they did not shake hands.

"You left Paris yesterday, sir?" he said to Monseigneur, as he took his seat at table.

"Yesterday. And you?"

"I come direct."

"From London?"

"Yes."

"You have been a long time coming," said the Marquis, with a smile.

"On the contrary; I come direct."

"Pardon me! I mean, not a long time on the journey; a long time since your last visit."

"I have been detained by"—the nephew stopped a moment in his answer—"various matters."

"No doubt," said the polished uncle.

As long as a servant was present, no other words passed between them. When coffee had been served and they were alone together, the nephew, looking at

❷ *What has probably kept Darnay in London?*

the uncle and meeting the eyes of the face that was like a fine mask, opened a conversation.

"I have come back, sir, as you expected, pursuing the goal that was my original reason for leaving. It brought me great danger, but it is a sacred goal and if it had caused my death, I hope it would have sustained me.

"Not your death," said the uncle, "it is not necessary to say your death."

"I doubt, sir," replied the nephew, "whether—if my endeavor had carried me to the very brink of death—you would have bothered to stop me there."

The cruel face made no sign of protest, beyond that which was called for by polite manners. This was not reassuring to the nephew.

❷ *What is the "danger" Darnay is speaking of, and what is he suggesting here?*

"Indeed, sir," pursued the nephew, "for all I know, you may have actually worked to make my circumstances look even more suspicious than they were."

"No, no, no," said the uncle, pleasantly.

"However," resumed the nephew, glancing at him with deep distrust, "I know that you would stop me in any way you thought you could, and would find no means to be unethical."

"My friend, I warned you," said the uncle, with a fine pulsation in the two marks on his nose. "Do me the favor to remember that I warned you a long time ago."

"I recall it."

"Thank you," said the Marquis very sweetly indeed.

His tone lingered in the air, almost like the tone of a musical instrument.

❤ *Remember two things: We first met the Marquis standing outside a higher noble's suite, and he was essentially snubbed by Monseigneur; also, the* Lettres de Cachet *could have a person imprisoned without charge or trial.*

"In effect, sir," pursued the nephew, "I believe it to be your bad luck, and my good luck that has kept me out of a prison here in France."

"I do not quite understand," returned the uncle, sipping his coffee. "Dare I ask you to explain?"

"I believe that if you were not in disgrace with the

Court, a letter would have sent me to some fortress indefinitely."

"It is possible," said the uncle, with great calmness, "that for the honor of the family, I could even resolve to harm you to that extent. Excuse me!"

"I understand that—luckily for me—the Court reception of the day before yesterday was—as usual— a cold one for you," observed the nephew.

"I would not say 'luckily,' my friend," returned the uncle, with careful politeness. "I would not be sure of that. A favorable position in Court might help you far more than it would harm you. But it is useless to discuss the question. I am, as you say, at a disadvantage. These tools of correction that honorable families use, are difficult to get. They are sought by so many, and they are granted to comparatively few! It was not always this way, but France in all such things is changed for the worse. It wasn't that long ago that our families had the right of death over the commoners. From this room, many such dogs have been taken out to be hanged. In the next room, my bedroom, one fellow, to our knowledge, was stabbed on the spot for admitting some indiscretion with his daughter—his daughter! We nobles have lost many privileges; a new philosophy has become the mode; and returning to the old way of things would cause us real inconvenience. All very bad, very bad!"

The "tools of correction" are the Lettres de Cachet.

"We have always demanded the dues of our station, both in the old time and in the modern time also," said the nephew, gloomily, "that I believe our family name to be more hated than any name in France."

"I certainly hope so," said the uncle. "The lower classes praise us the most in their hatred of us."

"I cannot look at a single face in this entire country," continued the nephew, in his former tone, "that looks at me with any other emotion than fear and hatred."

"That is a compliment," said the Marquis, "to the grandeur of the family, well deserved for the way in which the family has maintained that grandeur. Hah!"

What essentially is the Marquis saying about the actions and attitudes of his family?

And he took another gentle little pinch of snuff, and lightly crossed his legs.

However, this fine mask looked at his nephew with a stronger concentration of sharpness, closeness, and dislike, than was compatible with its outward expression of indifference.

"Repression is the only lasting philosophy. The dark respect of fear and slavery, my friend," observed the Marquis looking up to the ceiling, "will keep the dogs obedient to the whip, as long as this roof shuts out the sky."

That might not be so long as the Marquis thought. If he'd seen a picture of the chateau as it would look in five years—and fifty chateaux like his after five years—he might have had difficulty recognizing his own among the fire-charred ruins. His roof, that he praised so highly, would soon become lead in a thousand muskets—shutting out the sky permanently for thousands across France.

"Meanwhile," said the Marquis, "I will preserve the honor and peace of the family, even if you will not. But you must be tired. Shall we stop our conference for the night?"

"A moment more."

"An hour, if you desire."

"Sir," said the nephew, "we have done wrong, and are reaping the fruits of wrong."

"*We* have done wrong?" repeated the Marquis, with an inquiring smile, and delicately pointing, first to his nephew, then to himself.

"Our family; our honorable family, whose honor is so important to both of us, in such different ways. Even in my father's time, we did a world of wrong, injuring every human creature who came between us and our pleasure, whatever it was. Why do I need to remind you of my father's time, when it is equally yours? Can I separate my father's twin brother, joint inheritor, and next successor, from himself?"

"Death has done that!" said the Marquis.

"And it has left me," answered the nephew,

The Marquis' face has already been compared to a mask, but notice how now it is not even a person speaking to Darnay, but the non-human "mask."

The lead in the nails and rain gutters would be melted by French Revolutionaries and used to make musket balls.

Charles Dickens's novels are famous for their coincidental events and characters who appear and reappear in odd relationships. Check your list of characters and relationships and predict where you think this story might go.

"bound to a system that is horrible to me, responsible for it, but powerless to change it; seeking to carry out the last request of my dear mother's lips, and obey the last look of my dear mother's eyes, which begged me to undo the harm our family has caused."

"If you want me to help you take our system apart, my nephew," said the Marquis, touching him on the breast with his forefinger—they were now standing by the hearth—"you are asking in vain, be assured."

Every fine straight line in the clear whiteness of the Marquis' face, was cruelly, craftily, and closely compressed, while he stood looking quietly at his nephew, with his snuff-box in his hand. Once again he touched his nephew on the breast as though his finger were the fine point of a small sword, with which he ran him through and said, "My friend, I will die, serving the system under which I have lived."

When he had said it, he took a decisive pinch of snuff, and put his box in his pocket.

"It is better to be a rational creature," he added then, after ringing a small bell on the table, "and accept your natural destiny. But you are lost, Monsieur Charles, I see."

"This property and France are lost to me," said the nephew, sadly. "I renounce them."

"Are they yours to renounce? France may be, but is this property? It is scarcely worth mentioning; but, is it yours yet?"

"I would not claim it, if it passed from you to me tomorrow—"

"Which I have the vanity to hope is not probable."

"—or even twenty years from now—"

"You do me too much honor to wish me so long a life," said the Marquis; "still, I prefer that idea."

"—I would abandon it, and live by other means in another place. It's not much to give up. What is our property but a jungle of misery and ruin!"

"Hah!" said the Marquis, glancing round the luxurious room.

❷ *The Enlightenment was a philosophical way of thinking that promoted pure reason as superior to passion, and taught its adherents to believe in reason and logic as the primary methods of decision-making. One result of this philosophy was the idea that the way things were had to be logical, since things had turned out that way—an idea used by the nobles in France, as elsewhere, to justify the inequity of economic conditions.*

❷ *What must occur in order for the property to pass from the Marquis to Darnay?*

"To the eye it is beautiful enough, here, but seen through more just eyes, under the sky, and by the daylight, it is a crumbling tower of waste, mismanagement, bribery and blackmail, debt, mortgage, oppression, hunger, nakedness, and suffering."

"Hah!" said the Marquis again, in a self-satisfied manner.

"If it ever becomes mine, I will let someone manage it who can release these people from the crushing burdens of debt and obligation. But, I will not manage the property myself. There is a curse on it, and on all this land."

"And you?" said the uncle. "Forgive my curiosity; how do you, under your new philosophy, graciously intend to live?"

"I will do what others of my countrymen have done, what even with present aristocracy, may have to do some day—work."

"In England, for example?"

Darnay is not the actual name of the family.

"Yes. The family 'honor', sir, is safe. I cannot harm the family name in England, for there I do not use it."

The ringing of the bell signaled a servant to come and light the neighboring bed chamber. It now shone brightly, through the door between it and the parlor. The Marquis looked that way, and listened until his valet started walking away.

"I am surprised you admire England so, considering how poorly you have prospered there," he observed then, turning his calm face to his nephew with a smile.

"I have already acknowledged that your support has helped me to prosper there. Nonetheless, it will become my permanent Refuge."

"They say, those boastful English, that it is the Refuge of many. Do you know a fellow Frenchman who has found a Refuge there? A Doctor?"

"Yes."

"With a daughter?"

"Yes."

"Yes," said the Marquis. "You are tired. Good night!"

As he bent his head in his most courtly manner, his nephew noticed a sarcastic air of secrecy come across his face, that struck him in a most unpleasant manner

"Yes," repeated the Marquis. "A Doctor with a daughter. Yes. So begins the new philosophy! You are fatigued. Good night!"

It would have been as useful to question one of the stone faces outside the chateau as to question the Marquis' puzzling face. The nephew looked at him, unable to understand the uncle's self-satisfied expression, in passing on to the door.

"Good night!" said the uncle. "I look forward to seeing you again in the morning. Sleep well! Give light to my nephew and lead him to his chamber there!" he said to the servant holding a lighted candle. "And burn Monsieur my nephew in his bed, if you will," he added to himself, before he rang his little bell again, and summoned his valet to his own bedroom.

The valet being finished with his preparations and leaving, Monsieur the Marquis paced back and forth in his loose dressing gown to prepare himself gently for sleep on that hot, still night. Rustling about the room, his softly-slippered feet making no noise on the floor, he moved like a refined tiger, looking like some wicked and magical being—who could change back and forth into a tiger at will.

He moved from one end of his luxurious bedroom to the other, recalling the events of the day. The fountain in his little village reminded him of the Paris fountain, the little bundle lying on the step, the women bending over it, and the tall man with his arms up, crying, "Dead!"

"I am cool now," said Monsieur the Marquis, "and may go to bed."

So, leaving only one candle burning on the large hearth, he let his thin gauze bedcurtains fall around him, and heard the night break its silence with a long sigh as he lay down to sleep.

The stone faces on the outer walls stared blindly at the black night for three heavy hours. For three heavy hours, the horses in the stables rattled at their racks, the dogs barked, and the owl made a sound quite unusual for an owl. However, it is the stubborn habit of such creatures hardly ever to say what they are supposed to say.

For three heavy hours, the stone faces of the chateau, lion, and human, stared blindly at the night. Dead darkness lay on all the landscape, dead darkness added its own hush to the hushing dust on all the roads. At the burial-place, the heaps of grass were indistinguishable, and the Cross could not be seen. In the village, taxers and taxed were fast asleep. Dreaming, perhaps, of banquets, as the starved usually do, and of ease and rest, as the driven slave and the yoked ox may, its lean inhabitants slept soundly, and were fed and freed—until the morning.

The fountain in the village flowed unseen and unheard, and the fountain at the chateau dropped unseen and unheard—both melting away, like the minutes that were falling from the spring of Time— through three dark hours. Then, the gray water of both began to be ghostly in the light, and the eyes of the stone faces of the chateau were opened.

The morning became lighter and lighter, until at last the sun touched the tops of the still trees, and poured its radiance over the hill. In the glow, the water of the chateau fountain seemed to turn to blood, and the stone faces crimsoned. The song of the birds was loud and high, and, on the weatherbeaten sill of the great window of the bed-chamber of Monsieur the Marquis, one little bird sang its sweetest song with all its might. A new stone faced seemed to stare amazed, with its eyes bulging open and its jaw permanently fixed.

Now, the sun was full up, and movement began in the village. People came forth shivering— chilled

Notice how the adjective "heavy" emphasizes the humidity and the stillness of the night in addition to the length of time.

What effect is the author creating with the repetition of the word "dead"?

What is happening literally in this passage? What is being suggested by the choice of words in establishing the imagery?

by the morning air, and went to work—some, to the fountain, some to the fields, men and women here, to dig and delve; men and women there, to see to the poor livestock, and lead the bony cows out to whatever pathetic pasture as could be found by the roadside. In the church and at the Cross, there was a kneeling figure or two. One cow searched for a breakfast among the weeds at its foot while its owner prayed.

The residents of the chateau awoke later, as fitted their status. First, the lonely boar-spears and knives of the hunt had been reddened as they had been in years past; then, they gleamed in the morning sunshine. Doors and windows were thrown open. Horses in their stables looked around over their shoulders at the light and freshness pouring in the doorways. Leaves sparkled and rustled at iron-grated windows. Dogs pulled hard at their chains, and reared impatient to be let loose.

Again, the imagery of the hunting weapons shining red in the morning sun suggests bloody violence.

All these trivial incidents were a part of the routine of life, and the return of morning. But what was happening? The great bell of the chateau was ringing—people running up and down stairs, hurrying around the terrace, saddling horses quickly, and riding away!

How did the road-mender sense this disturbance, already at work on the hill-top beyond the village? He'd his lunch with him—not much to carry, not even worth a crow's time to peck at it. Had the birds somehow told him? But however he became aware of the emergency, the mender of roads ran—as if for his life—down the hill and didn't stop till he got to the fountain.

All the people of the village were at the fountain, standing about in their typical depressed manner, whispering quietly, but showing no other emotion than grim curiosity and surprise. The cows, hastily brought back in and tied to anything that would hold them, were looking stupidly on, or lying down chewing their cud. Some of the people of the chateau and some of those of the posting-house, and all the tax-collecting authorities, were armed, and were crowded on the other side of the little street standing and staring purposelessly. Already, the mender of roads had made his way into the center of a group of fifty, and was hitting himself in the breast with his blue cap. What did all this mean? What did the swift hoisting-up of Monsieur Gabelle behind a servant on horseback mean, and what did it mean that Gabelle and his servant galloped away?

Apparently there was now one stone face too many, up at the chateau.

The Gorgon had surveyed the building again in the night, and had added the one stone face wanting; the face of the house of Evremonde, for which it had waited through about two hundred years.

It lay back on the pillow of Monsieur the Marquis. It was like a fine mask, suddenly startled, made angry, and petrified. Driven home into the heart of the stone figure attached to it, was a knife. Around its hilt was a scrap of paper, on which was scrawled:

"*Drive him fast to his tomb. Jacques.*"

THIS IS THE END OF THE
TENTH WEEKLY INSTALLMENT.

✔ *Now we know the true family name of the Marquis and Charles Darnay.*

❷ *Who probably killed the Marquis? What evidence do we have to suggest this? What does the note mean?*

❷ *What important information have we received at this end of this weekly installment? What is now Charles Darnay's true, "official" identity?*

Research Opportunity:

What happened to the chateaux owned by the Aristocracy in the first few years of the French Revolution? Prepare a report explaining how the Republic handled the property of the former Aristocracy in France.

A Tale of Two Cities

CHARLES DICKENS

CHAPTER X
Two Promises

ANOTHER YEAR HAD come and gone, and Mr. Charles Darnay was established in England as a higher teacher of the French language who was familiar with French literature. Today, he would have been a Professor, but in that time, he was called a Tutor. He taught young men who had the time and interest to study a "living" language, one actually spoken all over the world. He could write *about* literature in perfect English, and *translate* literature into perfect English. Such teachers were not, at that time, easily found. In these days immediately before the beginnings of revolutions throughout Europe, Fallen Princes, and Deposed Kings had not yet sunk to the Teacher class. No ruined aristocracy had yet found their fortunes seized and their prospects dwindled to becoming either a cook or a carpenter. As a talented tutor, whose students found that they actually learned—and enjoyed learning, and as an elegant translator whose translations had voice and mood in addition to correctness of language, young Mr. Darnay soon became fairly well known. In addition, he was very aware of what was happening in his own France, and the growing threat of revolution was of great

The eleventh weekly installment begins with the passage of time and a change of setting back to England.

Why would the English aristocracy be at all interested in affairs in France?

interest to the wealthy English who hired him so he found he never lacked work.

In London, he had not expected to walk on streets of gold, or to lie on beds of roses. If he had had any fantasies like that, he would not have prospered. He had expected to work hard, and he did work hard, and he built a life for himself. This was his definition of success.

He spent a part of his time at Cambridge where he taught undergraduates as a sort of tolerated smuggler who had a contraband trade in European languages. The rest of his time he passed in London.

Now, from the days when it was always summer in Eden, to these days when it is mostly winter and sin, the world of a man has always turned in one direction—Charles Darnay's direction—the way of the love of a woman.

He had loved Lucie Manette ever since his trial. He had never heard a sound so sweet and dear as the sound of her compassionate voice. He had never seen a face so tenderly beautiful as hers when she could possibly put him in grave danger. However, he had not yet spoken to her about his feelings. Even a year after the assassination of his uncle, he had not told her how he felt.

He had his reasons, however. It was again a summer day when he approached the quiet corner in Soho, intending to find a chance to reveal his feelings to Doctor Manette. It was evening, and he knew Lucie to be out with Miss Pross.

He found the Doctor reading in his armchair at a window. The Doctor's energy had gradually been restored to him, and so he was now a very healthy man indeed, strong in both will and body. In his recovered energy he was sometimes a little fitful and jumpy, as he had at first been when his mind was returning to him, but this had never happened frequently, and had grown more and more rare.

Prior to the middle of the twentieth century, the only languages thought appropriate for study at University were "dead" languages like Latin and ancient Greek. To learn a "living" language was considered "middle class." Still, there were many good reasons for studying foreign languages, so men like Darnay—who were not "real teachers"—would be hired on a part-time basis to teach material that was useful, but not considered an essential part of the curriculum.

He studied much, slept little, and was nearly always cheerful. Seeing Charles Darnay enter the room where he was sitting, he closed his book, stood, and extended his hand.

"Charles Darnay! I am so glad to see you. We have been counting on your return these three or four days past. Mr. Stryver and Sydney Carton were both here yesterday, and both made you out to be more than due."

"I am obliged to them for their interest in the matter," he answered—not all that happy to hear about *them*, but very happy to see the Doctor. "Miss Manette—"

"Is well," said the Doctor interrupting him, "and your return will delight us all. She has gone out on some household matters, but will soon be home."

"Doctor Manette, I knew she was not at home. I took the opportunity of her being from home, to beg to speak to you."

There was a blank silence.

"Yes?" said the Doctor, with evident hesitation. "Bring your chair here, and speak on."

He did indeed move his chair, but found it difficult to continue speaking.

"I have been very happy, Doctor Manette, to have felt so welcome here," he finally began, "for about year and a half. And I hope what I am about to say will not—"

He paused when the Doctor put out his hand to stop him. After a long pause, the Doctor asked, "Is Lucie the topic?"

"She is."

"It is hard for me to speak of her. It is *very* hard for me to hear her spoken of in that tone of yours, Charles Darnay."

"It is a tone of fervent admiration, true homage, and deep love, Doctor Manette!" he said respectfully.

There was another blank silence before her father rejoined:

"I believe it. I do you justice; I believe it."

Darnay's hesitation was obvious. It was likewise obvious that it arose from the Doctor's unwillingness to approach the subject.

"Shall I go on, sir?"

Another blank.

"Yes, go on."

"I think you know what I have come here to say, though you cannot know how earnestly I say it, or how earnestly I feel it. You also cannot know my secret heart, and the hopes and fears and anxieties with which I have long been burdened. Dear Doctor Manette, I love your daughter fondly, dearly, devotedly. If any man ever loved a woman, I love her. You were in love once yourself. Surely you sympathize with what I am feeling!"

The Doctor sat with his face turned away, and his eyes on the ground. At Darnay's last words, he stretched out his hand again, and cried, "No! Better to leave those memories alone! I order you, never to refer to that!"

His cry was so much like a cry of actual pain, that it rang in Charles Darnay's ears long after the Doctor was again quiet. He motioned with the hand he had extended, and it seemed to ask Darnay to wait.

"I beg your pardon," said the Doctor, more quietly, after some moments. "I have no doubt you love Lucie." He turned toward Darnay, but did not look at him, or raise his eyes. His chin dropped upon his hand, and his white hair overshadowed his face. "Have you spoken to Lucie?"

"No."

"Nor written?"

"Never."

"I thank you for taking my feelings into consideration."

He offered his hand, but he still would not look at Darnay.

"I know," said Darnay, respectfully, "how can I not understand, Doctor Manette, that the love that you and Lucie share is unique, even among the closest of fathers and daughters. I know, Doctor Manette—how can I fail to know—that, mingled with the affection and duty of a adult daughter, she also loves you as a child loved her father. I know that—since she had not parent to love in her childhood, her love for you is doubly strong—that of an adult daughter, and of a small girl. I know perfectly well that if you genuinely *had* been restored to her from the dead, you could not be to her more a god than you are now. I know that when she hugs you, the hands of baby, a girl, and a woman, all in one, are around your neck. I know that in loving you, she sees and loves her mother at her own age, sees and loves you at my age, loves her mother broken-hearted, loves you through your dreadful trial and in your blessed restoration. I have known this, night and day, since I have known you in your home."

Her father sat silent, with his face bent down. His breathing was a little quickened, but he repressed all other signs of being upset.

"Dear Doctor Manette, being aware of this, I have waited to speak my mind as long as a man can wait. I believe that to bring my love—even mine—between the two of you would be to pollute your lives. But I love her. Heaven is my witness that I love her!"

"I believe it," answered her father, mournfully. "I have suspected before now. I believe it."

"But, do not believe," said Darnay, who felt a twinge of guilt, hearing the mournful tone of the Doctor's voice, "that—if I were fortunate enough to be Lucie's husband—I would ever separate the two of you. That would be a low, and base move on my part. I could not touch your hand honorably if I had any other thought in mind."

He set his hand upon the Doctor's as he spoke.

"No, dear Doctor Manette. Like you, I am a voluntary exile from France. Like you, driven from it by its terrible, terrible problems. Like you, striving to live away from it by my own hard work, and trusting in a happier future. I ask only to share your fortunes, share your Life and home, and be faithful to you to death. Not to steal Lucie from you as your child, companion, and friend; but to come in support of it, and bind her closer to you, if such a thing were possible."

His touch still lingered on her father's hand. Answering the touch for a moment, but not coldly, her father rested his hands upon the arms of his chair, and looked up for the first time since the beginning of the conversation. His face was struggling between hope and a dark dread.

"You speak with such feeling, Charles Darnay, that I thank you with all my heart, and will open all my heart—or nearly so. Have you any reason to believe that Lucie loves you?"

"None. As yet, none."

"Are you asking me as to the state of her mind?"

"Oh no! I might not have the hopefulness to declare my love to her for weeks; I might (mistaken or not mistaken) have that hopefulness tomorrow."

"Do you seek any guidance from me?"

"I ask none, sir. But I have thought it possible that you might be able to offer some."

"Do you seek any promise from me?"

"I do."

"What is it?"

"I fully understand that, without you, I have no hope of winning Lucie's hand. I well understand that, even if Miss Manette loved me half as much as I love her—and do not think I have the presumption to presume so much—her love for me could never rival the love she feels for you. For that reason, I also fully understand, that a single word from her father in any suitor's favor, would hold more influence with her than even her own feelings. But I would never ask that you try to sway her."

"I understand that. Charles Darnay, mysteries exist between people who love each other, as well as between dread enemies. In the case of lovers, these mysteries are subtle and delicate, and difficult to penetrate. My daughter Lucie is, in this one respect, such a mystery to me. I can make no guess at the state of her heart."

"May I ask, sir, if you think she is—" As he hesitated, her father supplied the rest.

"Is sought by any other suitor?"

"Yes."

Her father considered a little before he answered. "You yourself have seen Mr. Carton here. Mr. Stryver is here too, occasionally. If she has any other suitor, it can only be one of these."

"Or both," said Darnay.

"I had not thought of both. But I do not think that she loves either one. You want a promise from me. Tell me what it is."

"It is, that if Miss Manette were to come to you and tell you that she loves me—of her own free will—I ask that you tell her what I have told you. And I would hope that you would not say anything against me. I say nothing more of my stake in this. This is what I ask. If you have any conditions, I am prepared to fulfill them." "I give that promise," said the Doctor, "without any condition. I believe your object to be—purely and truthfully—as you have stated it. I believe your intention is to strengthen—and not to weaken—the ties between me and my daughter. If she should ever tell me that you are essential to her happiness, I will give her to you. If there were—Charles Darnay, if I had any—"

The young man took the Doctor's hand gratefully as the Doctor spoke. "If I had any doubts about the man she loved—if any fears resurfaced from the past—but things that were not his fault—they would vanish from my mind. She is everything to me, more to me than suffering, more to me than injustice, more to me—Well! This is idle talk."

So strange was the way in which he faded into silence, and so strange his fixed look when he had ceased to speak, that Darnay felt his own hand turn

❷ *This has been a long conversation to come to this point. What is the promise Darnay is asking of the Doctor?*

cold in the hand that slowly released and dropped it.

"You said something to me," said Doctor Manette, breaking into a smile. "What was it you said to me?"

He did not know what to say, until he remembered having spoken of a condition. Relieved as he remembered that, he answered, "Your confidence in me ought to be returned with full confidence on my part. My present name, though only slightly changed from my mother's, is not, as you will remember, my own. I wish to tell you my name, and why I am in England."

"Stop!" said the Doctor of Beauvais. "I wish it, that I may better deserve your confidence, and have no secret from you."

"Stop!"

For an instant, the Doctor even covered his hands with his ears. For another instant, he even covered Darnay's mouth with his hands.

"Tell me when I ask you, not now. If you should be successful, if Lucie should love you, you shall tell me on the morning of your wedding. Do you promise?"

"Willingly."

"Give me your hand. She will be home very soon, and it is better she should not see us together tonight. Go! God bless you!"

It was dark when Charles Darnay left him, and it was an hour later and even darker when Lucie came home. She hurried into her father's study alone— for Miss Pross had gone straight upstairs—and was surprised to find his reading chair empty.

"My father!" she called to him. "Father dear!"

There was no answer, but she heard a low hammering sound in his bedroom. Passing lightly across the room, she looked in at his door and came running back frightened, crying to herself, with her blood all chilled, "What shall I do! What shall I do!" Her uncertainty lasted but a moment; she hurried back, and tapped at his door, and softly called to him. The hammering stopped at the sound of her voice,

Remember that Dr. Manette is French. The town he is from is not "BEE—vis." It is "Bo—VAY."

Why is the doctor's hometown mentioned here?

What do you suppose is happening in the Doctor's bedroom?

and he presently came out to her, and they walked up and down together for a long time.

She came down from her bed, to look at him in his sleep that night. He slept heavily, and his tray of shoemaking tools, and his old unfinished work, were all as they had been.

❷ *What are the "two promises" suggested by this chapter's title?*

Writing Opportunity:

Explain how the Doctor's reaction to Charles's avowal of love, combined with the Marquis' remarks about a Doctor and his daughter, serve to foreshadow the coming troubles for these characters.

A Tale of Two Cities

CHARLES DICKENS

CHAPTER XI
A Companion Picture

O N THE SAME NIGHT (or early morning) that Charles Darnay had his conversation with the Doctor, Mr. Stryver said to his jackal, "Sydney, mix another bowl of punch. I have something to say to you."

Sydney had been working double duty that night, and the night before, and the night before that, and a good many nights in a row, completely clearing Mr. Stryver's papers before the beginning of the Long Vacation. The clearance was finished at last. The Stryver affairs were caught up. Everything was put away until November would bring its fogs to London—in the atmosphere and in the law. Sydney was no more lively and no more sober despite all the work. It had taken a good number of wet towels to pull him through the night; an extra quantity of wine had been drunk before the toweling; and he was in a very intoxicated condition, as he now pulled his turban off and threw it into the basin in which he had steeped it at intervals for the last six hours.

"Are you mixing that other bowl of punch?" said Stryver the stout, with his hands in his waistband, glancing round from the sofa where he lay on his back.

A "companion piece" or "companion picture" is a second picture that offers a slightly different view or treatment of a theme established in the original. In this chapter, therefore, we should expect to see the theme of marriage, specifically marriage to Lucie from a different perspective.

In England, there were formerly four terms in the year during which the superior courts were open: Hilary term sat January 11-31. Easter term sat April 14-May 8. Trinity term sat May 22-June 12; and Michaelmas term sat November 2-25. The rest of the year was called "vacation." The night Darnay spoke of his love to Dr. Manette was identified in the last chapter as a "summer day." Therefore, the "long vacation" that Stryver is preparing for is the period between the closing of the courts on June 12 and their reopening on November 2. Note again Dickens's sarcasm that November would bring not only atmospheric fog, but also fog in the law.

❷ Note how Stryver thinks it is important to mention that he is not marrying for money. Whom do you suppose he intends to marry?

"I am."

"Now, look here! I am going to tell you something that will surprise you, and that perhaps will make you think I am not quite as smart as you thought. I intend to marry."

"Yes. And not for money. What do you say now?"

"I don't feel moved to say anything. Who is she?"

"Guess."

"Do I know her?"

"Guess."

"I am not going to guess, at five o'clock in the morning, with my brains frying and sputtering in my head. If you want me to guess, you must ask me to dinner."

"Well then, I'll tell you," said Stryver, sitting up slowly. "Sydney, I don't believe you'll ever understand me, because you are such an insensitive dog."

"And you," returned Sydney, busy mixing the punch, "are such a sensitive and poetical spirit."

"Come!" rejoined Stryver, laughing boastfully, "though I don't prefer any claim to being the soul of Romance, still I am more tender than you."

"You are a luckier, if you mean that."

"I don't mean that. I mean I am a man of more... more—"

"Say *gallantry*, while you're going on about yourself," suggested Carton.

"All right! I'll say *gallantry*. But what I mean is that I am a man," said Stryver, puffing out his chest, "who *wants* more to be agreeable, who *tries harder* to be agreeable, who *knows better how to be* agreeable, while in the company of women, than you do."

"Get out of here," said Sydney Carton.

"No. But before I go on," said Stryver, shaking his head in his bullying way, "I'll settle this with you. You've been at Doctor Manette's house as much as I have. Maybe even more than I have. And I have been ashamed of your moodiness there! Your manners have been of that silent, brooding kind, and, I swear that I have been ashamed of you, Sydney!"

"I'm amazed that a lawyer would be ashamed of anything." returned Sydney.

"You're not going to get out of this that easily," rejoined Stryver. "No, Sydney, it's my duty to tell you—and I tell you to your face for your own good—that you are a devilish ill-mannered fellow in that sort of society. You are a disagreeable fellow."

Sydney drank a cup of the punch he had made, filled to the brim, and laughed.

"Look at me!" said Stryver, squaring himself, "Being a successful lawyer, I do not need to make myself attractive as much as you do. So why do I do it?"

"I never saw you do it yet," muttered Carton.

"I do it because it's in my best interest. I do it on principle. And look at me! I succeed."

"Tell me about your matrimonial intentions," answered Carton, with a careless air. "I wish you would keep to that. As to me—will you never understand that I am what I am and nothing will ever change me?" He asked the question with a tone of scorn.

"You have no business to be hopeless," Stryver answered harshly.

"I have no business to be *anything* that I know of," said Sydney Carton. "Who is the lady?"

"Now, don't let my announcement of the name make you uncomfortable, Sydney," said Mr. Stryver, now acting friendly to prepare him for the confession he was about to make, "because I know you don't mean half of what you say. But even if you had meant this, it wouldn't matter. I say this, because you once mentioned this young lady to me in slighting terms."

"I did?"

"Certainly; right here in these rooms."

Sydney Carton looked at his punch and looked at his self-satisfied friend. He gulped his punch and looked at his self-satisfied friend again.

"You spoke of the young lady as a golden-haired doll. The young lady is, obviously, Miss Manette. I didn't resent your remark, because I know you are completely insensitive. I didn't resent it any more than I would resent a dog not appreciating a work of art."

Sydney Carton gulped even more punch; gulped another glassful, and then another, looking at his friend.

"Now you know all about it, Syd," said Mr. Stryver. "I don't care about money. She is a charming creature, and I have made up my mind to please myself. On the whole, I think I can afford to please myself. She will have in me a man already pretty successful, and still climbing pretty quickly up the ladder of success, and a man of some distinction. It's really good luck for her, but she deserves good luck. Are you surprised?"

Carton, still drinking the punch, replied, "Why should I be surprised?"

"Do you approve?"

Carton, still drinking the punch, replied, "Why shouldn't I approve?"

"Well!" said his friend Stryver, "you're taking this better than I thought you would. Even though I have a strong will, I was worried that you'd argue with me. I'm tired of living this way—I've come to the point where I think it would be a good thing to have a home to go to when I wanted—and to stay away from if I didn't. Miss Manette would look good enough to do me credit in any station. As for you, Sydney, you need to take better care of yourself. You're living too hard—one of these days you're going to collapse. Have you thought about getting a nurse?" The condescension with which he said it, made him look twice as big as he was, and four times as offensive.

"Think about it," pursued Stryver, "in your own way. I have looked it in the face, in my own way. Marry. Provide somebody to take care of you. Never mind that you don't understand women, and can't stand to be in women's company. Find somebody. Find some respectable woman with a little property—maybe a landlady—and marry her as security against a rainy

Compare Stryver's notion of marriage to Lucie with Darnay's.

Note the irony: Stryver is thinking about getting himself a wife and suggests that Carton get himself a nurse.

day. That's the kind of thing for you. Think about it, Sydney."

"I'll think about it," Sydney replied.

THIS IS THE END OF THE
ELEVENTH WEEKLY INSTALLMENT.

Research Opportunity:

Look up eighteenth-century marriage attitudes and customs and compare them with nineteenth-century attitudes and customs.

A Tale of Two Cities

CHARLES DICKENS

CHAPTER XII

The Fellow of Delicacy

FIRMLY INTENT TO offer Miss Lucie Manette the benefits of marriage, he decided to tell her this grand news before the Long Vacation. He decided to get the preliminaries over with, and then they could decide whether to marry before Michaelmas, or during the Christmas recess between it and Hilary.

He could see the strong points of his case—all the way to the verdict. On worldly grounds—the only grounds really worth considering—it was a clear case, and had no weaknesses. He gave undeniable evidence as the plaintiff—the person pressing the suit. The counsel for the defense threw up his hands in utter defeat, and the jury did not even bother to deliberate. The case was settled and Lucie would undoubtedly be thrilled to marry Stryver. How could it happen any other way?

And so, Mr. Stryver asked for a formal date to take Miss Manette to Vauxhall Gardens, so he could tell her his plans. When Miss Manette declined, he suggested Ranelagh. When she declined again, he decided to go to Soho and tell her at her home.

Toward Soho, therefore, Mr. Stryver shouldered his way from the Temple. Anyone who had seen him practicing his opening and closing arguments while

✔ *The earlier note on page 157 explains these dates.*

✔ *Vauxhall Gardens was the most famous and popular "pleasure garden" of the eighteenth century. Originally opened in the 1660s and undergoing several renovations and expansions, the gardens provided tree-lined promenades for walks, covered shelters for picnic lunches, and places for listening to music. Eventually, Vauxhall began to be overrun by ladies of ill-repute and ruffians. Ranelagh Gardens briefly became the more fashionable and popular attraction. Stryver's second invitation, after Lucie's refusal to accompany him to Vauxhall, probably indicates that he thought she was simply hesitant to be seen in a public place of questionable reputation.*

❓ *What image is created by the use of the verb "shouldered"?*

he was still on Saint Dunstan's side of Temple Bar, bumping weaker people out of his way, would have seen how confident he was of his success.

Since he was going past Tellson's Bank, and he both banked there and knew that the Manettes banked there, he stopped in to tell Mr. Lorry what good news he was about to deliver to Lucie. So, he pushed open the door with the weak rattle in its throat, stumbled down the two steps, got past the two ancient cashiers, and shouldered himself into the musty back closet where Mr. Lorry sat in front of large books with lined paper for numbers, with perpendicular iron bars on his window as if that were also lined for numbers as well.

"Hello!" said Mr. Stryver. "How do you do? I hope you are well!"

It was an unusual characteristic of Stryver's that he always seemed too big for any place, or space where he found himself. He was so much too big for Tellson's, that even old clerks on the opposite side of the room looked up with displeasure, as though he were squeezing them against the wall. The manager himself, reading the paper off in the distance, looked displeased, as if Stryver's head had butted him in the stomach.

The discreet Mr. Lorry said, in a low voice that he hoped Stryver would imitate, "How do you do, Mr. Stryver? How do you do, sir?" and shook hands. Mr. Lorry had a manner of shaking hands that seemed to make himself less prominent and his partner more so. Any clerk at Tellson's who shook hands with a customer did so in this same manner.

"Can I do anything for you, Mr. Stryver?" asked Mr. Lorry, in his business character.

"Why, no, thank you. This is a private visit, Mr. Lorry. I have come for a private word."

"Oh indeed!" said Mr. Lorry, bending down his ear, while his eye strayed to the manager far off.

"I am going," said Mr. Stryver, leaning his arms confidentially on the desk, which seemed to disappear under them, "I am going to offer myself in marriage to your agreeable little friend, Miss Manette, Mr. Lorry."

Writing Opportunity:

As you read this scene, compare and contrast Mr. Lorry and Mr. Stryver. Write an essay in which you explain how the contrast of their characters and the description of Stryver in the bank creates humor.

"Oh dear me!" cried Mr. Lorry, rubbing his chin, and looking at his visitor dubiously.

"Oh dear me, sir?" repeated Stryver, drawing back. "Oh dear you, sir? What do you mean, Mr. Lorry?"

"My meaning," answered the man of business, "is, of course, friendly and appreciative. That it is very noble of you. In short, my meaning is everything you could desire. But—really, you know, Mr. Stryver—" Mr. Lorry paused, and shook his head at him in the oddest manner, as if he were compelled against his will to add, "you know there really is so much too much of you!"

"Well!" said Stryver, slapping the desk with his argumentative hand, opening his eyes wider, and taking a long breath, "if I understand you, Mr. Lorry, I'll be hanged!"

Mr. Lorry adjusted his little wig at both ears in a nervous gesture, and bit the feather of a pen.

"D-n it all, sir!" said Stryver, staring at him, "am I not eligible?"

"Oh dear yes! Yes. Oh yes, you're eligible!" said Mr. Lorry. "If you say eligible, you are eligible."

"Am I not prosperous?" asked Stryver.

"Oh! yes, yes, you are prosperous," said Mr. Lorry.

"And coming up in the world?"

"If you come to coming up in the world, you know," said Mr. Lorry, delighted to be able to agree with Stryver once more, "nobody can doubt that."

"Then what on earth do you mean, Mr. Lorry?"

demanded Stryver, visibly disappointed.

"Well! I—Were you going there now?" asked Mr. Lorry.

"Straight!" said Stryver, with a plump of his fist on the desk.

"Then I think I wouldn't, if I was you."

"Why?" said Stryver, shaking a forefinger at him. "You are a man of business and bound to have a reason. State your reason. Why wouldn't you go?"

"Because," said Mr. Lorry, "I wouldn't go on such a mission unless I thought that I would succeed."

"D-n ME!" cried Stryver, "but this beats everything."

Mr. Lorry glanced at the distant manager, and then at the angry Stryver.

"Here's a man of business—a man of years—a man of experience—in a Bank," said Stryver, "and having listed three leading reasons for complete success, he says there's no reason at all!"

"When I speak of success, I speak of success with the young lady; and when I speak of causes and reasons to make success probable, I speak of causes and reasons that will work with the young lady. The young lady, my good sir," said Mr. Lorry, mildly tapping Stryver's arm, "the young lady. The young lady comes before anything else."

"Then do you mean to tell me, Mr. Lorry," said Stryver, squaring his elbows, "that it is your opinion that the young lady we are discussing is a Fool?"

"Not exactly so. I mean to tell you, Mr. Stryver," said Mr. Lorry, reddening, "that I will hear no disrespectful word spoken about that young lady, and that if I knew any man—which I hope I do not—whose temper was so overbearing, that he could not restrain himself from speaking disrespectfully about young lady at this desk, not even Tellson's should prevent my giving him a piece of my mind."

Mr. Stryver's blood-vessels began to feel the burden of keeping a lid on his anger. Mr. Lorry's veins, methodical as they could usually be, were in no better state now that it was his turn.

"That is what I mean to tell you, sir," said Mr. Lorry. "Let there be no mistake about it."

Mr. Stryver sucked the end of a ruler for a little while, and then smacked it against his teeth, which probably gave him a toothache. He broke the awkward silence by saying, "This is something new to me, Mr. Lorry. You deliberately advise me not to go up to Soho and offer myself—myself, Stryver of the King's Bench bar?"

"Do you ask me for my advice, Mr. Stryver?"

"Yes, I do."

"Very good. Then I give it, and you have repeated it correctly."

"And all I can say of it is," laughed Stryver with a vexed laugh, "that this—ha, ha!—beats everything past, present, and future."

"Now understand me," pursued Mr. Lorry. "As a man of business, I am not justified in saying anything about this matter, for, as a man of business, I know nothing about it. But, I am speaking as an old man, who has known Lucie Manette and her father since he carried her in his arms. You asked me for my advice. Now, do you think I may not be right?"

"Not I!" said Stryver, whistling. "It's hard to find common-sense in your fellow-men. I can perceive sense in certain situations—all you can do is sell me the foolishness you think to be true."

"What I think, Mr. Stryver, I can describe for myself. And understand me, sir," said Mr. Lorry, quickly flushing again, "I will not—not even at Tellson's—allow anyone else to try to tell me what I think."

"There! I beg your pardon!" said Stryver.

"Granted. Thank you. Well, Mr. Stryver, I was about to say—it might be more painful to you to find yourself mistaken, especially from the lips of Doctor Manette or Miss Manette—and it might be difficult for them to have to be plain with you. If you like, I am willing to see if I am correct, by going to their house,

❷ *What has Mr. Lorry offered to do?*

and presenting your case to them. Afterwards, I will come to you and give you my findings—if you don't agree with them at that point, you can test them for yourself. What do you say?"

"How long would this take?"

"Oh! It is only a question of a few hours. I could go to Soho in the evening, and come to your chambers afterwardss."

"Then I say yes," said Stryver: "I won't go up there now, I am not as impatient as I was. I say yes, and I shall expect you to come by tonight. Good morning."

Then Mr. Stryver turned and burst out of the Bank, causing such a breeze that the ancient clerks had to brace themselves to remain standing.

The attorney was sharp enough to tell that the banker would not have been as forceful as he had, if he did not think that he was correct. Unprepared as he was for anyone to doubt his success in this matter, he accepted Lorry's concern. "And now," said Mr. Stryver, shaking his forefinger at the Temple in general, "I'm going to prove all of you wrong."

He found a good bit of relief in his talent as a courtroom showman, and declared to himself in his best, booming defense-lawyer voice, "You shall not get the better of me, young lady. I'll have the better of you."

Accordingly, when Mr. Lorry called that night as late as ten o'clock, Mr. Stryver, had surrounded himself with books and papers, so as he might look as if he had forgotten Miss Manette entirely. He even showed surprise when he saw Mr. Lorry, and seemed completely preoccupied.

"Well!" said Mr. Lorry, after a full half-hour of fruitless attempts to bring Stryver around to the matter. "I have been to Soho."

"To Soho?" repeated Mr. Stryver, coldly. "Oh, my goodness, yes! What am I thinking of!"

"And I have no doubt," said Mr. Lorry, "that I was correct in the views I expressed this morning. My opinion is confirmed, and I repeat my advice."

"I assure you," returned Mr. Stryver, in the friendliest way, "that I am sorry for your disappointment, and sorry for her poor father's disappointment. I know this will always be a cause for regret for him. Let us say no more about it."

"I don't understand you," said Mr. Lorry.

"I am not surprised," replied Stryver, nodding his head in a smoothing and final way; "no matter, no matter."

"But it does matter," Mr. Lorry urged.

"No it doesn't. I assure you, it doesn't. I thought there might be common sense and ambition where there are none. Young women have made these sorts of decisions before, and have ended in poverty and obscurity. To be honest, I'm glad it didn't work out, because it would not have benefited me in a worldly way—I could have gained nothing by marrying her. There is no harm done. I never proposed to the young lady; after thinking about it, I'm not sure that I would have committed myself to that extent. Mr. Lorry, there is no way to control the giddiness of girls—if you try, you will always be disappointed. Please say no more about it—I regret it for you, and for them, but not for me. I must thank you for letting me use you to hear her opinion; you know her much better than I do—it would not have been good for me to have gone."

Mr. Lorry was so surprised, that he looked quite stupidly at Mr. Stryver shouldering him toward the door, with an expression of generosity, forbearance, and goodwill, on his face. "Make the best of it, my dear sir," said Stryver; "say no more about it. Thank you again for allowing me to hear your advice. Good night!"

Mr. Lorry was out in the night before he knew where he was. Mr. Stryver was lying back on his sofa, winking at his ceiling.

❷ *Who is the "Fellow of Delicacy" identified in the title of this chapter?*

A Tale of Two Cities

CHARLES DICKENS

CHAPTER XIII
The Fellow of No Delicacy

IF SYDNEY CARTON ever shone anywhere, he certainly never shone in the house of Doctor Manette. He had been there often, during a whole year, and had always been the same moody and morose lounger there. When he cared to talk, he talked well; but, the cloud of apathy, which covered him with such a fatal darkness, was very rarely pierced by the light within him.

And yet he did have some affection for the streets around that house, and for the senseless stones that made their pavements. Many a night he vaguely and unhappily wandered there—when wine had failed to make him happier—for a few hours. Many a dreary daybreak revealed his solitary figure lingering there, and still lingering there when the first beams of the sun showed the beauty in the architecture of churches and tall buildings. It may have been that the quiet time brought some sense of better things, into his mind. Recently, his neglected bed had been occupied less and less—there were many nights when he would only throw himself down there for an hour or two, then rise up to head to Soho.

On a day in August, when Mr. Stryver had headed off for his vacation, Sydney found himself pacing

❷ *Look up the words "morose" and "apathy." What is the main characteristic of Carton's personality?*

on those Soho streets. He suddenly snapped out of indecision and formed the specific intention to walk straight to the Doctor's door.

He was shown upstairs, and found Lucie sewing, alone. She had never been very comfortable with him, and so she found herself somewhat embarrassed as he seated himself near her table. However, this time she noticed a change in his face, and wondered about it.

"I fear you are not well, Mr. Carton!"

"I'm not. But the life I lead, Miss Manette, is not conducive to good health."

"Is it not a pity—forgive me for speaking this aloud—not to live a better life?"

"God knows it is a shame!"

"Then why not change it?"

Looking gently at him again, she was surprised and saddened to see that there were tears in his eyes. There were tears in his voice too, as he answered, "It is too late for that. I shall never be better than I am. In fact, in time, I shall only sink lower and be worse."

He leaned an elbow on her table, and covered his eyes with his hand. The table trembled in the silence that followed.

She had never seen him this way, and was quite distressed. He knew her to be so, without looking at her, and said, "Please forgive me, Miss Manette. What I want to say to you has made me weak. Will you hear me?"

"If it will do you any good, Mr. Carton, if it would make you happier, it would make me very glad!"

"God bless you for your sweet compassion!"

He uncovered his face after a little while, and spoke steadily. "Don't be afraid to hear me. Don't shrink from anything I say. I am like someone who died young, leaving all of my potential still ahead of me."

"No, Mr. Carton. I am sure that the best part of your life is yet to come. I am sure that you might be much, much worthier of yourself."

"Even though I know that can never be, I shall never forget that you said it!"

She was pale and trembling.

"If you could have loved such a man as me— wasted, drunken, misused—he would have known that he would only have dragged you down with him, to sorrow and repentance. I know that you do not love me. I am thankful that it cannot be."

"Even without loving you, can I not save you, Mr. Carton? Can I not steer you— forgive me again!—to a better course? Can I in no way repay your confidence? I know this is a confidence," she modestly said, after a little hesitation, and in earnest tears, "I know you would say this to no one else. Can I not help you to make good with your life, Mr. Carton?"

He shook his head.

"No, Miss Manette. If you will hear me through a very little more, that is all I could ever ask you to do. I wish you to know that you have been the last dream of my soul. Since I met you, I have been troubled by a regret that I didn't think I'd ever feel again. I have heard whispers from old voices, that I thought were silent forever, inspiring me to improve. I have had unformed ideas of starting fresh, beginning anew, shaking off my laziness, and picking up abandoned ambitions. But it's a dream—all a dream, that ends in nothing, and leaves me exactly where I was, but I wish you to know that you inspired it."

"Will nothing of it remain? O Mr. Carton, think again! Try again!"

"No, Miss Manette. All through it, I have known myself to be quite undeserving. And yet I have had the weakness—still *have* the weakness—to want you to know how quickly and masterfully you kindled me—heap of ashes that I am—into fire. But a useless fire, doing no service, idly burning away."

"Since it is my misfortune, Mr. Carton, to have made you more unhappy than you were before you knew me—"

"Don't say that, Miss Manette, for, if anything could have saved me, you would have. You could never be the cause of my becoming worse."

"Have I no power to help at all?"

"Right now you are seeing me at my best. Let me simply live the rest of my misguided life."

"A life which I have told you is capable of better and finer things, Mr. Carton!"

"Please don't ask me again to believe that, Miss Manette. I have proved myself, and I know better. But I am making you unhappy. I will come to my point soon. Will you let me believe, when I look back to this day, that I confided the last secret of my life to you, and that it is safe in your heart and will never be revealed?"

"If that will give you any peace, yes."

"Not even to the person who should become closest to your heart?"

"Mr. Carton," she answered, after an agitated pause, "the secret is yours, not mine. I promise to respect it."

"Thank you. And again, God bless you."

He kissed her hand lightly and moved toward the door.

"Do not worry, Miss Manette. I will never bring up this topic again. In the hour of my death, I will smile to hold this one good memory—and I will thank and bless you for the fact that my last true statement of myself was made to you, and that my name, and faults, and miseries were gently carried in your heart."

His behavior was so different from the manner in which he usually acted, and it was so sad to think how much he had thrown away, and how much he every day kept down and perverted, that Lucie Manette wept mournfully for him as he stood looking back at her.

"Be comforted!" he said, "I am not worth your tears, Miss Manette. An hour or two from now, I will again find myself among my low companions, indulging in my base habits. Be comforted! In my deepest heart of hearts, I will always feel toward you, what I am now, even though outwardly I will remain lost. The next-to-last request I make of you is that you honestly believe that this is my true inward self."

"I will, Mr. Carton."

"My last request of all, is this. After this, I will leave. I know there's no use in my saying it, but it rises out of my soul. For you—and for anyone dear to you—I would do anything. If my career were one that invited self-sacrifice, I would do anything to help you or anyone you loved. Try to think of me, from time to time, as impassioned and sincere in this one thing. The time will come, not too far in the future, when you will form new ties and new loves—ties that will change your home and family, make it all the happier and more dear to you. O Miss Manette, when the image of a happy father's face looks up at you, when you see your own beautiful child playing at your feet, think now and then that there is a man who would give his life, to save the life of someone you loved!"

He said, "Farewell!" said a last "God bless you!" and left her.

THIS IS THE END OF THE
TWELFTH WEEKLY INSTALLMENT.

Writing Opportunity:

How does this conversation between Carton and Lucie foreshadow the novel's ending? Gather evidence from the previous chapters and speculate what is likely to develop in future chapters.

A Tale of Two Cities

CHARLES DICKENS

CHAPTER XIV
The Honest Tradesman

MR. JEREMIAH CRUNCHER, sitting on his stool in Fleet Street with his grisly child beside him, saw a great many things of different types and sorts. Who wouldn't be amazed at the tide of humanity—heading east into the sun, then west with the sun, then eventually beyond the reach of the sun—that passed before him every day?

Because a small part of his income came from rowing stout women from the Tellson's side of the River Thames to the other side, Jerry would never wish for this "tide" of moving humanity to stop. Although his encounter with each individual woman was quite brief, Mr. Cruncher always grew to like the woman so much that he had a strong desire to drink to her health. It was from the gifts bestowed upon him toward this benevolent purpose, that he made some of his finances.

There was a time when a poet sat on a stool in a public place, and contemplated while passersby stared at him. Mr. Cruncher, sitting on a stool in a public place, but not being a poet, contemplated as little as possible, and looked around him. It so happened that there were very few women who needed a quick trip across the river, there were very small crowds

London Bridge had been the only bridge spanning the Thames River until the building of the Putney Bridge in 1729 and Westminster Bridge in 1740. Even then, it was fastest and safest to travel from one bank of the Thames to the other by boat than to try to cross one of the bridges. Great numbers of Watermen were employed to row people and goods up, down, and around the Thames. Apparently Jerry is, in addition to being a Porter, at least a part-time Waterman.

Remember that we've already noted the custom of toasting to a woman's health. What is the clear implication here?

In his biography of the Italian poet Dante, the poet Boccaccio relates a tale in which Dante sat on a bench for several hours reading a book while a riotous festival was taking place. Afterwards, he was asked how he could have concentrated during the uproar, to which he responded that he heard nothing. Dickens is most likely alluding to this episode in his description of Jerry Cruncher, who is not a poet, and sits on his stool looking around.

to look at—even to the point where Jerry suspected Mrs. Cruncher of "flopping" against him—and then a procession came down Fleet Street that grabbed his attention. Looking in that direction, Mr. Cruncher could tell that some kind of funeral was coming along, and that there was a sort of protest to this funeral, which created an uproar.

Young Jerry," said Mr. Cruncher, turning to his offspring, "it's a buryin'."

"Hooray, father!" cried Young Jerry.

The young gentleman shouted his exultant reply in a tone that suggested he had some secret knowledge or other. The father was so offended, that he watched for an opportunity, and slapped his son on the ear.

"Wadaya mean? What are you cheering at? What are you tellin' your own father, you young Rip? This boy is getting to be too much for me!" said Mr. Cruncher, watching him closely. "Him and his hoorays! Don't let me hear no more out of you, or you'll feel some more of me. D'ya hear?"

"I wasn't doing no harm," Young Jerry protested, rubbing his cheek.

"Drop it then," said Mr. Cruncher; "I won't have none of your 'no harms.' Get up on top of that there seat, and look at the crowd."

His son obeyed, and the funeral procession approached; they were bawling and hissing around a dingy hearse and dingy mourning coach. In this mourning coach, there was only one mourner, dressed in the dingy accessories that were considered necessary to the "dignity" of the position of chief mourner. The position did not appear to please him at all, however, with an increasing mob of rabble surrounding the coach, deriding him, making grimaces at him, and incessantly groaning and calling out: "Yah! Spies! Tst! Yaha! Spies!" with curses too numerous and obscene to repeat.

Funerals always had a remarkable attraction for Mr. Cruncher. He always pricked up his senses, and became excited when a funeral passed Tellson's.

❷ *Remember, what does Jerry mean by Mrs. Cruncher's "flopping"?*

Naturally, therefore, a funeral with this uncommon interest excited him greatly, and he asked the first man who ran into him: "What is it, brother? What's going on?"

"I don't know," said the man. "Spies! Yaha! Tst! Spies!"

He asked another man. "Who is it?"

"I don't know," returned the man, clapping his hands to his mouth nevertheless, and yelling in a surprising heat and with the greatest passion, "Spies! Yaha! Tst, tst! Spi-ies!"

Finally, a person better informed on the matter, tumbled against Jerry, and from this person he learned that the funeral was the funeral of one Roger Cly.

"Was he a spy?" asked Mr. Cruncher.

"Old Bailey spy," returned his informant. "Yaha! Tst! Yah! Old Bailey Spi-i-ies!"

"Why, to be sure!" exclaimed Jerry, recalling the Trial at which he had assisted. "I've seen him. Dead, is he?"

"Dead as mutton," returned the other, "and can't be too dead. Pull 'em out, there! Spies! Drag 'em out of there! Spies!"

Since the crowd didn't have anything to yell, they made up for it with eagerness, and loudly repeating the suggestion to pull 'em out, and to drag 'em out, mobbed the hearse and the coach so closely that they had to stop. When the crowd opened the coach doors, the single mourner hurried out and was in their hands for a moment; but he was so alert that in another moment he was scurrying away up a side street, leaving his cloak, hat, long hatband, white pocket-handkerchief, and other articles behind.

The people tore these things to pieces and scattered them far and wide with great enjoyment, while the local merchants quickly shut up their shops. In those days, a riotous mob stopped at nothing, and was a much-dreaded monster. They had already opened the hearse to take the coffin out, when some brighter genius suggested that they stay with it to the funeral

❷ *Who was Roger Cly and where have we seen him before?"*

❷ *Compare this mob scene with others we have already seen in the book. What is Dickens's point?*

❷ *Bearbaiting was a very popular spectacle in England from Roman times until it was outlawed in 1835 because of its cruelty to the bear and the dogs. A bear, often blinded, was chained to a stake by one hind leg or by the neck and attacked by bull dogs. The bear would strike out with its claws and the dogs were also mauled and often killed as they tortured the bear. This bear leader is a man whose job is to tend the bear. In this scene, he is apparently at the funeral/protest with his bear in tow.*

❷ *Saint Pancras was a Roman citizen who converted to Christianity and was beheaded for his faith at the age of 14 around the year 304. In the Borough of Camden in London, there are actually two St. Pancras Churches, "Old St Pancras" and "New St. Pancras." The churchyard of Old St. Pancras Church was the original burial site of the parents of Mary Shelley, who wrote Frankenstein, and other notables such as Johann Christian Bach, youngest son of the famous composer Johann Sebastian Bach. St. Pancras is usually prayed to in order to prevent or remedy— among other things—cases of false witness and perjury. This is a likely reason why Dickens chose the churchyard of this particular church as the destination of this particular funeral procession.*

instead. The coach was immediately filled with eight inside and a dozen out, while as many people as could possibly fit and hang on got on the roof of the hearse. One of the first of these volunteers was Jerry Cruncher himself, who hid in the far corner of the mourning coach so that no one from Tellson's would see him.

The undertakers in charge of the procession protested weakly against these changes in the ceremonies, but, realizing that these new passengers might actually throw them in the river, quickly agreed to the new plan. The rearranged procession started, with a chimney-sweep driving the hearse—assisted by the regular driver, who was perched beside him and watching him very closely—and with a pieman, also assisted by the regular driver, driving the mourning coach. A bear-leader—a popular street character of the time—was drafted to add to the spectacle, before the parade had gone far down the Strand, and his bear—who was black and very mangy—gave an air of solemn sadness to the part of the procession in which he walked.

Thus, with a good deal of beer drinking, pipe smoking, lusty singing—and a neverending pretense of grief—the riotous procession went its way, adding members at every step. All the shops shut up, as it moved along, before it got to them. Its destination was the old church of Saint Pancras, far off in the fields. Eventually the procession arrived, insisted on pouring into the burial-ground, and finally, accomplished the burial of the deceased Roger Cly.

The dead man gotten rid of, and the crowd now needed some other source of entertainment, another brighter genius (or perhaps the same one who had thought to join the funeral procession rather than protest it) got the idea to identify people who just happened to be walking by as Old Bailey spies, and wreak vengeance on them. Scores of innocent people were thus chased and beaten. The crowd became bored again, and decided to switch to the sport of window-breaking, and from that to looting. At last, after several hours, a rumor started that the Guards were coming. The crowd gradually melted away, and perhaps the Guards came, and perhaps not, but this was the usual course of events of a mob.

Mr. Cruncher did not participate in the "games" that followed the burial of Mr. Cly, but had remained behind in the churchyard, to talk with the undertakers. The place had a soothing influence on him. He bought a pipe from a neighboring public-house, and smoked it, looking in at the railings and intensely considering the spot.

"Jerry," said Mr. Cruncher, speaking to himself in his usual way, "you see that there Cly that day, and you see with your own eyes that he was a young 'un and a healthy 'un."

He finished his pipe and thought a little longer. Then he hurried away so that he might be seen sitting on his stool in front of Tellson's—where he was supposed to be—at closing time when all of the clerks and bankers left. For some reason, he stopped at the office of a well-known surgeon on his way back.

Young Jerry was dutifully awaiting his father's return to the bank, and reported "no job" in his absence. The bank closed, the ancient clerks came out, the usual watch was set, and Mr. Cruncher and his son went home to tea.

"Now, I tell you how it is!" said Mr. Cruncher to his wife, on entering. "If, as an honest tradesman, my project goes wrong tonight, I'll know for sure that you've been praying against me, and I'll pay you back just the same as if I seen you do it."

The dejected Mrs. Cruncher shook her head.

"Why, you're at it right in front of me!" said Mr. Cruncher.

"I am saying nothing."

"Well, then, don't think nothing. You might as well flop as meditate. It doesn't matter how you go against me. One way is as bad as another. Drop it altogether."

"Yes, Jerry."

"Yes, Jerry," repeated Mr. Cruncher sitting down

❂ Here is a clue to Jerry's mystery, the reason his wife prays for him to fail at his work, the reason he has rust on his hands, and the secret his son seems to know but will not reveal.

"Not infrequently" is an example of litotes.

Consider the clues we have been given and speculate where Jerry is going tonight.

to tea. "Ah! It is yes, Jerry. That's all you have to say—*yes, Jerry.*"

Mr. Cruncher meant nothing by all of this, but simply wanted—as people not infrequently do—to express general sarcastic dissatisfaction.

"You and your *yes, Jerry,*" said Mr. Cruncher, taking a bite out of his bread-and-butter. "Ah! I think so. I believe you."

"You are going out tonight?" asked his decent wife, when he took another bite.

"Yes, I am."

"May I go with you, father?" asked his son, eagerly.

"No, you may not. I'm going—as your mother knows—fishing. That's where I'm going. Going fishing."

"Your fishing rod gets rather rusty; don't it, father?"

"That's none of your business."

"Will you bring any fish home, father?"

"If I don't, you'll have little to eat tomorrow," returned the father, shaking his head. "Now that's questions enough from you. I ain't a' goin' out, till you've been long in bed."

He spent the rest of the evening keeping his wife in conversation, so she would have no time to meditate. When he was not speaking to her, he had his son keep the conversation going. Unfortunately, his only topic of conversation was the reasons for his dissatisfaction with her. It was ironic, that someone who claimed not to believe in God would fear her prayers, just as it would be ironic that an unbeliever in ghosts should be frightened by a ghost story.

"And mind you!" said Mr. Cruncher. "No games tomorrow! If I—as a honest tradesman—succeed in providing a little meat for the breakfast table, you will not refuse it, and eat only bread. If I—as a honest tradesman—am able to provide a little beer, none of your drinking only water. When you go to Rome, do as Rome does. Rome will be a' ugly customer to you, if you don't. I'm your Rome, you know."

Then he began grumbling again. "Look how skinny your boy is! How are you going to pray agin' vittles and drink, when it's a mother's duty to help her son get big?"

This was clearly a sensitive area for young Jerry, who urged his mother to pray her hardest for his father's success.

And so the evening passed in the Cruncher household. Young Jerry was soon ordered to bed, as was his mother. After sitting and smoking alone for a few hours, around one o'clock, Jerry rose up from his chair, took a key out of his pocket, opened a locked cupboard, and brought forth a sack, a crowbar, a rope and chain, and other fishing tackle of that nature. Gathering these articles around him skillfully, he muttered a parting curse toward Mrs. Cruncher, put out the light, and left the little house.

❷ Note the irony. The items listed are not typical "fishing tackle," but Jerry has insisted that he is going fishing.

Young Jerry, who had only pretended to undress when he went to bed, followed his father out. Under cover of the darkness he followed his father out of the room, followed him down the stairs, followed him down the court, followed him out into the streets. He was not worried about getting into the house again, for it was full of lodgers, and the door stood ajar all night.

Curious to observe his father's mysterious occupation, young Jerry clung to the shadows along the buildings in the streets. They were going north, when the father was joined by another disciple of Izaak Walton, and the two trudged on together.

❷ Who is Izaak Walton? Why is this allusion ironic?

Within half an hour, they had gone beyond the flickering lanterns, and the sleeping watchmen. At the last gate, another "fisherman" joined them—so silently, that if Young Jerry had been superstitious, he might have thought the second man to have split himself into two.

The three went on, and Young Jerry went on, until the three stopped under a bank overhanging the road. Upon the top of the bank was a low brick wall, topped by an iron railing. In the shadow of bank and wall, the three men left of the road and went up a dark lane. Here the brick wall rose to a height of some eight or ten feet. Crouching down in a corner, peeping up the lane, Young Jerry watched as the form of his father—pretty well defined against a watery and clouded moon—nimbly climbed an iron gate. He was quickly over, and then the second fisherman got over, and then the third. They all dropped softly on the ground inside the gate, and lay there a little—listening perhaps. Then, they crawled away on their hands and knees.

It was now Young Jerry's turn to approach the gate, which he did, holding his breath. Crouching down again in a corner, and looking in, he made out the three fishermen creeping through patches of weeds and grass! All the gravestones in the churchyard—it was a large churchyard that they were in—looked like ghosts in white, while the church tower itself looked like the ghost of a monstrous giant. They did not creep far before they stopped and stood up. And then they began to fish.

First they fished with a shovelt. Next, Jerry appeared to be turning some instrument like a giant corkscrew. Whatever tools they worked with, they worked hard, until the awful clanging of the church clock terrified Young Jerry so much that he ran off, with his hair as stiff as his father's.

❷ *What does Young Jerry see that frightens him so?*

But, his long-cherished desire to know more about his father's "honest business," not only stopped him from running away, but lured him back again. The three men were still "fishing" with great perseverance, when he peeped in at the gate for the second time, but, now they seemed to have a "bite." There was a screwing and complaining sound down below, and their bent figures were strained, as if by a weight. Slowly, the weight below emerged into the moonlight. Young Jerry very well knew what it would be, but, when he saw it, and saw his father about to wrench it open, he was so frightened—being new to the sight—

that he ran off again, and never stopped until he had run a mile or more.

He would not have stopped then, but he desperately needed to catch his breath. He imagined that the coffin he had seen was chasing him, hopping behind him on its narrow end, always just ready to catch him and grab his arm. It was an inescapable fiend too. It made the whole night behind him dreadful, and he darted out into the main roadway to avoid dark alleys, afraid that it would pop out at him. It hid in doorways too, shaking and bouncing as if it were laughing at him. It got into shadows on the road, and lay cleverly on its back to trip him. Yet all this time it never stopped chasing him from behind and gaining on him, so that when the boy got to his own door, he was half dead. And even then the coffin would not leave him alone, but followed him upstairs with a bump on every step. It climbed into bed with him, and lay down—dead and heavy—on his chest when he fell asleep.

From his oppressed slumber, Young Jerry was awakened after daybreak and before sunrise, by the presence of his father in the family room. Something had gone wrong with him; at least, so Young Jerry could tell, because he was holding Mrs. Cruncher by the ears, and knocking the back of her head against the head-board of the bed.

"I told you I would," said Mr. Cruncher, "and I did."

"Jerry, Jerry, Jerry!" his wife implored.

"You oppose yourself to the profit of the business," said Jerry, "and me and my partners suffer. You was to honor and obey; why the devil don't you?"

"I try to be a good wife, Jerry," the poor woman protested, with tears.

"Is it being a good wife to oppose your husband's business? Is it honoring your husband to dishonor his business? Is it obeying your husband to disobey him on the vital subject of his business?"

"You hadn't started the dreadful business then, Jerry."

Jerry is referring to the old wedding vows in which the bride promised to "love, honor, and obey" her husband. The groom promised to "love, honor, and cherish" his wife.

"It's enough for you," retorted Mr. Cruncher, "to be the wife of a honest tradesman. You don't need to fill your female mind worrying about when he took to his trade or when he didn't. A' honorin' and obeyin' wife would leave his trade alone altogether. Call yourself a religious woman? If you're a religious woman, then give me a' irreligious one! You have no more nat'ral sense of duty than this here Thames River."

This argument was conducted in a low tone of voice, and ended with the "honest tradesman's" kicking off his clay-soiled boots, and lying down on the floor. After taking a timid peep at him lying on his back, with his rusty hands under his head for a pillow, his son lay down too, and fell asleep again.

There was no fish for breakfast, and not much of anything else. Mr. Cruncher was out of temper, and kept an iron pot-lid by him to throw at Mrs. Cruncher, in case he saw any sign of her saying Grace. He was brushed and washed at the usual hour, and set off with his son toward his acknowledged job.

❷ *What does Dickens mean by Jerry's "acknowledged job"?*

This Young Jerry, walking with the stool under his arm at his father's side along sunny and crowded Fleet Street, had recovered his wits—a far cry from the Young Jerry of the night before, running home through darkness and solitude from his Grim Pursuer.

"Father," said Young Jerry, as they walked along, being careful to keep at arm's length and to have the stool well between them, "what's a Resurrection-Man?" Mr. Cruncher came to a stop on the pavement before he answered, "How should I know?"

✔ *The theme of Resurrection has already been introduced and begun to be developed. Dr. Manette was "recalled to life" when he was released from prison and restored to his daughter, and Charles Darnay was essentially brought back to life when he was acquitted of the capital crime of treason.*

"I thought you knowed everything, Father," said the boy.

"Hem! Well," returned Mr. Cruncher, going on again, and lifting his hat to give his spikes free play, "he's a tradesman."

"What's his goods, father?" asked the brisk Young Jerry.

"His goods," said Mr. Cruncher, after turning it over in his mind, "is a branch of scientific goods."

"Persons' bodies, ain't it, father?" asked the lively boy.

"I believe it is something like that," said Mr. Cruncher.

"Oh, father, I should so like to be a Resurrection-Man when I'm quite growed up!"

Mr. Cruncher was soothed, but shook his head like a doubtful schoolmaster about to teach a grave moral lesson. "It depends upon how you develop your talents. Be careful to develop your talents, and never to say more than you need to anybody. There's no way to tell today what you may grow up fit for." As Young Jerry, thus encouraged, walked on ahead a few yards to set the stool in the shadow of the Bar, Mr. Cruncher added to himself, "Jerry, you honest tradesman, there's still hope that that boy will be a blessing to you, and make up for his disappointing and interfering his mother!"

THIS IS THE END OF
THE THIRTEENTH WEEKLY INSTALLMENT.

Writing Opportunity:

Explain the extended metaphor of fishing, as it is used for a euphemism for Cruncher's late-night escapades in this chapter.

Writing Opportunity:

Examine and discuss the joke Dickens might be making by having this grave-robbing scene take place in the cemetery where the parents of the author of Frankenstein were originally buried.

A Tale of Two Cities

CHARLES DICKENS

CHAPTER XIV
Knitting

THE DRINKING HAD begun earlier than usual in the wine shop of Monsieur Defarge. As early as six o'clock in the morning, thin faces peeping through its barred windows had seen other faces inside, bending over small measures of wine. Monsieur Defarge sold a very thin wine at the best of times, but this wine was unusually thin—and apparently sour, or going sour, for it seemed to make those who drank it quite gloomy. No lively, wild flame leaped out of the pressed grape of Monsieur Defarge, but, a smoldering fire that burnt in the dark, lay hidden in the dregs of it.

This had been the third morning in a row, on which there had been unusually early drinking at the wine shop of Monsieur Defarge. It had begun on Monday, and now it was Wednesday. There had been more early-morning worrying than drinking. Many men, who had no money to pay the price of even a tiny drop of wine, had listened and whispered and slunk around the shop from the time of its opening. These were just as interested in the place, however, as if they could have afforded whole barrels, and they slid from seat to seat, and from corner to corner, swallowing talk instead of drink, with greedy looks. Even though the crowd was unusually large, the owner was not

Notice how, again, a new weekly installment begins with a shift in scene from London to Paris.

Examine the metaphor of fire for wine and its impact on its drinkers.

The use of a single verb— "swallowing"—in connection with two direct objects (one figurative and one literal)—"talk and drink"—is an example of a zeugma or syllepsis.

visible. No one missed him for, nobody who entered the shop bothered to look for him. Nobody asked for him. Nobody thought it was odd to see only Madame Defarge in her seat, presiding over the distribution of wine, with a bowl of battered, small coins before her, as much defaced and scarred from their original mint condition as the specimens of humanity who gave them to her.

Explain the simile comparing the coins to the customers in the wine shop.

The spies would have noticed a bored, distracted crowd. Card games slowed and were abandoned, domino players only built towers with them, drinkers drew figures on the tables with spilt drops of wine. Madame Defarge herself picked out the pattern on her sleeve with her toothpick, and tilted her head as if she saw and heard something inaudible and invisible a long way off.

This was the state of Saint Antoine, until midday. It was high noon, when two dusty men passed through the neighborhood's streets and under its swinging lamps. One of these men was Monsieur Defarge, the other a mender of roads in a blue cap. Dusty and thirsty, the two entered the wine shop. Their arrival had lit a kind of fire in the breast of Saint Antoine, fast spreading as they walked along. The flames of this flickering and spreading fire were the fierce faces that appeared at the windows to watch the men's arrival. Yet, no one followed them, and no man spoke when they entered the wine shop, even though the eyes of every man there were turned upon them.

Here's the fire metaphor again.

"Good day, gentlemen!" said Monsieur Defarge.

It may have been a signal for a general easing of the tension. Defarge was answered with a general chorus of, "Good day!"

"It is bad weather, gentlemen," said Defarge, shaking his head.

At this, every man looked at his neighbor, and then all cast down their eyes and sat silent. Except one man, who got up and left.

"My wife," said Defarge aloud, addressing Madame

Defarge, "I have traveled a good number of leagues with this good mender of roads, called Jacques. I met him—by accident—a day and half's journey out of Paris. He is a good child, this mender of roads, called Jacques. Give him a drink, my wife!"

A second man got up and went out. Madame Defarge set wine before the mender of roads named Jacques, who tipped his blue cap to the company, and drank. In the breast of his blouse he carried some coarse dark bread; he chewed on this from time to time, and sat munching and drinking near Madame Defarge's counter. A third man got up and went out.

Defarge refreshed himself with a long drink of wine, but, he took less than he had given to the stranger, since he could have wine whenever he wanted. He stood, waiting until the countryman had made his breakfast. He looked at no one in the room, and no one looked at him, not even Madame Defarge, who had taken up her knitting, and was busily at work.

"Have you finished your meal, friend?" he asked after a time.

"Yes, thank you."

"Come, then! You shall see the apartment that you will occupy. It will suit you marvelously."

Out of the wine shop into the street, out of the street into a courtyard, out of the courtyard up a steep staircase, out of the staircase into an attic,— the same attic where once a white-haired man had sat on a low bench, stooping forward and very busy, making shoes. No white-haired man was there now; but, the three men were there who had left the wine shop earlier. Between them and the white-haired man in England, was the one small link, that they had once looked in at him through the chinks in the wall.

❷ *To what attic has Defarge taken the mender of roads?*

Defarge closed the door carefully, and spoke in a subdued voice, "Jacques One, Jacques Two, Jacques Three! This is the witness I, Jacques Four, arranged to meet. He will tell you all. Speak, Jacques Five!"

The mender of roads, blue cap in hand, wiped his dark forehead with it, and said, "Where shall I begin, Monsieur?"

"Begin at the beginning," was Monsieur Defarge's reasonable reply.

"I saw him then, Messieurs," began the mender of roads, "a year ago this summer, underneath the carriage of the Marquis, hanging by the chain. Behold the manner of it. I left my work on the road, the sun going down, the carriage of the Marquis slowly climbing the hill, he hanging by the chain—like this."

Again the mender of roads went through the whole performance. He should have been perfect at it by that time, as it had been the main source of entertainment in his village for a whole year.

Jacques One broke in, and asked if he had ever seen the man before?

"Never," answered the mender of roads, standing back up.

Jacques Three demanded how he afterwardss recognized him then?

"By his tall figure," said the mender of roads, softly, and with his finger at his nose. "When Monsieur the Marquis demands that evening, 'Say, what is he like?' I tell him, 'Tall as a ghost.'" "You should have said, short as a dwarf," returned Jacques Two.

"But what did I know? The deed was not then accomplished, and he didn't confide in me. Under those circumstances even, I would not have said anything. But Monsieur the Marquis points at me with his finger and says, 'Bring me that rascal!' I swear, Messieurs, I offer nothing."

"He is right there, Jacques," murmured Defarge, to him who had interrupted. "Go on!"

"Good!" said the mender of roads, with an air of mystery. "The tall man is lost, and he is sought—how many months? Nine, ten, eleven?"

"No matter, the number," said Defarge. "He is

❷ *Who is the tall man riding under the Marquis' carriage that we are talking about?*

well hidden, but unfortunately he is finally found. Go on!"

"I am again at work upon the hillside, and the sun is again about to go to bed. I am collecting my tools to go back down to my cottage down in the village below, where it is already dark, when I raise my eyes, and see coming over the hill six soldiers. In the midst of them is a tall man with his arms bound—tied to his sides—like this!"

With the aid of his indispensable cap, he represented a man with his elbows bound fast at his hips, with cords that were knotted behind him.

"I stand aside, Messieurs, by my heap of stones, to see the soldiers and their prisoner pass (for it is a lonely road, anything out of the ordinary is worth pausing to look at), and at first, as they approach, I see no more than that they are six soldiers with a tall man bound, and that they are almost black to my sight— except on the side of the sun going to bed, where they have a red edge, Messieurs. Also, I see that their long shadows are on the hollow ridge on the opposite side of the road, and are on the hill above it, and are like the shadows of giants. Also, I see that they are covered with dust, and that the dust moves with them as they approach, *tramp, tramp!* But when they arrive near to me, I recognize the tall man, and he recognizes me. Ah, but he would be happy to throw himself down the hillside once again, as on the evening when he and I first met, not far from the same spot!"

He described it as if he were there, and it was evident that he saw it vividly. He probably had not seen much in his life.

"I do not show the soldiers that I recognize the tall man. He does not show the soldiers that he recognizes me. We do it, and we know it, with our eyes. 'Come on!' says the chief of that company, pointing to the village, 'bring him fast to his tomb!' and they bring him faster. I follow. His arms are swollen because of being bound so tight, his wooden shoes are large and

Note the vivid imagery of the marching men, silhouetted against the setting sun, the side toward the sun glowing red, long shadows marching beside them.

clumsy, and he limps. Because he limps, and is slow, and they shove at him with their guns—like this!"

He imitated the action of a man's being pushed forward by the butt-ends of muskets.

"As they descend the hill like madmen running a race, he falls. They laugh and pick him up again. His face is bleeding and covered with dust, but he cannot touch it; and so they laugh again. They bring him into the village. Everyone comes out to watch. They take him past the mill, and up to the prison. We all see the prison gate open in the darkness of the night, and swallow him—like this!"

He opened his mouth as wide as he could, and shut it with a sounding snap of his teeth. Seeing that he was not wanting to ruin the effect by opening his mouth again, Defarge said, "Go on, Jacques."

"The whole village withdraws," the mender of roads continued, standing on his tip-toes and speaking in a low voice, "the whole village whispers by the fountain. The whole village sleeps, and the whole village dreams of that poor fellow, within the locks and bars of the prison on the hill, never to come out of it, except to die. In the morning, with my tools on my shoulder, eating my crust of black bread as I go, I pass by the prison, on my way to my work. There I see him, high up, behind the bars of a lofty iron cage, bloody and dusty as the night before, looking through. His hands are bound, and he cannot wave to me. I dare not call to him. He looks at me like a dead man."

Defarge and the three glanced darkly at one another. The expressions on all their faces were dark, repressed, and revengeful, as they listened to the countryman's story. Their attitude, while it was secret, was authoritative too. They had the manner of a rough tribunal, Jacques One and Two sitting on the old bed, each with his chin resting on his hand, and his eyes intent on the road-mender, Jacques Three, equally intent, on one knee behind them, nervously stoking his chin. Defarge stood between them and the narrator, whom he had stationed in the light of the window, by turns looking first at him, and then at the other Jacques, and then at the speaker again.

"Go on, Jacques," said Defarge.

"He remains up there in his iron cage some days. Everyone in the village looks at him secretly, for we are all afraid. But we always look up, from a distance, at the prison on the hill. And in the evening, when the work of the day is done and we gather to gossip at the fountain, our faces are all turned toward the prison. Before this, they were turned toward the posting-house. Now, they are turned toward the prison. They whisper at the fountain, that—even though he has been condemned to death—he will not be executed. They say that petitions have been presented in Paris, showing that he was enraged and made mad by the death of his child. They say that a petition has been presented to the King himself. What do I know? It is possible. Perhaps yes, perhaps no."

"Listen then, Jacques," Jacques Number One interrupted sternly. "Know that a petition was indeed presented to the King and Queen. Everyone here—except you—saw the King take it. He was in his carriage in the street, sitting beside the Queen. It is Defarge here, who—risking his own life—darted out before the horses, with the petition in his hand."

"And once again listen, Jacques!" said Number Three, kneeling, his fingers constantly massaging his chin and jaw. His face was set with a greedy, hungry look, but it was not food and drink that he hungered for. "The guard, the horsemen and footmen all surrounded the petitioner, and beat him. You hear?"

"I hear, Messieurs."

"Go on then," said Defarge.

"Still, everyone in the village whispers at the fountain," resumed the countryman, "that he was brought to our village to be executed on the spot, and that he will very certainly be executed. We even whisper that—because he has slain Monseigneur, and because Monseigneur was the father of his tenants—serfs—whatever you call them—he will be executed

❷ *Parricide is the murder of
one's father. In the feudal
system of Medieval Europe,
serfs were little more than
slaves, owned by the lord on
whose land they'd been born.
The Church taught these serfs
to regard their lords as their
fathers since they relied on
him for every aspect of their
existence.*

for parricide. One old man says at the fountain, that
his right hand, armed with the knife, will be burnt off
before his face; that, into wounds which will be cut
into his arms, his chest, and his legs, they will pour
boiling oil, melted lead, hot resin, wax, and sulphur;
and finally, that he will be torn limb from limb by four
strong horses. That old man says, all this was actually
done to a prisoner who made an attempt on the life of
the late King, Louis XV. But how do I know if he lies?
I am not a scholar."

"Listen once again then, Jacques!" said the
man with the restless hand and the hungry look.
"The name of that prisoner was Damiens, and the
execution—just as you describe it—was all done in
broad daylight, right here in the streets of Paris, in
front of a crowd of well-dressed women who watched
the 'entertainment,' drawn out until nightfall, when
poor Damiens had lost two legs and an arm, but was
still alive! And why was he punished like this? How
old are you?"

"Thirty-five," said the mender of roads, who
looked closer to sixty.

"Ah. This happened when you were more than
ten years old. You might have seen it."

"Enough!" said Defarge, with grim impatience.
"Long live the Devil! Go on."

"Well! Some whisper this, some whisper that.
They speak of nothing else. Even the sound of the
fountain appears to carry the same tune. Finally, on
Sunday night when everyone is asleep, soldiers come,
winding down from the prison, and their guns ring on
the stones of the little street. Workmen dig, workmen
hammer, soldiers laugh and sing; in the morning, by
the fountain, there is raised a gallows forty feet high,
poisoning the water."

The mender of roads appeared to look through
the low ceiling, rather than at it. He pointed as if he
saw the gallows somewhere in the sky.

"All work is stopped. Everyone assembles there.
Nobody leads the cows out, the cows are there with

the rest. At midday, we hear the roll of drums. Soldiers have marched into the prison in the night, and the prisoner is in the midst of many soldiers. He is bound like before, and in his mouth there is a gag—tied like this, with a tight string, making him look almost as if he were laughing." He imitated it, by creasing his face with his two thumbs, from the corners of his mouth to his ears. "On the top of the gallows is fastened the knife, blade upwards, with its point in the air. He is hanged there forty feet high—and is left hanging—poisoning the water."

The three Jacques looked at one another, as he used his blue cap to wipe his face, which had started to perspire again while he described the scene.

"It is frightening, Messieurs. How can the women and the children draw water from the fountain? Who can gossip in the evening, under that shadow? Under it, have I said? When I left the village, Monday evening as the sun was going to bed, and looked back from the hill, the dead man's shadow struck across the church, across the mill, across the prison. It actually seemed to strike across the earth, Messieurs, all the way to the horizon!"

The hungry-looking man gnawed one of his fingers as he looked at the other three, and his finger trembled with the craving that was on him.

"That's all, Messieurs. I left at sunset (as I had been warned to do), and I walked on, that night and half next day, until I met (as I was told I would) this comrade. With him, I came here, sometimes riding and sometimes walking, through the rest of yesterday and through last night. And here you see me!"

After a gloomy silence, the first Jacques said, "Good! You have acted and retold faithfully. Will you wait for us a little, outside the door?"

"Very willingly," said the mender of roads, whom Defarge escorted to the top of the stairs. The mender of roads sat wearily on the top step, and Defarge returned to the room.

The three were standing, and their heads leaning

together in conversation when he returned to the attic.

"How say you, Jacques?" demanded Number One. "Should we register this offense?"

"Yes, registered as doomed to destruction," returned Defarge.

"Magnificent!" croaked the man with the craving.

"The chateau, and all the race?" inquired the first.

"The chateau and all the race," returned Defarge. "Extermination." The hungry-looking man repeated, in a rapturous croak, "Magnificent!" and began gnawing another finger.

"Are you sure," Jacques Two asked Defarge, "that no embarrassment can arise from how we keep the register? No doubt it is safe, for no one beyond ourselves can read it, but will we *always* be able to decipher it—or, I ought to say, will *she*?"

"Jacques," returned Defarge, drawing himself up, "if Madame my wife had decided to keep the register in her *memory* alone, she would not lose a word of it—not a *syllable* of it. Knitted—in her own stitches and her own symbols—it will always be as plain to her as the sun. Confide in Madame Defarge. It would be easier for the weakest coward that lives, to erase himself from existence, than to erase one letter of his name or crimes from the knitted register of Madame Defarge."

There was a murmur of confidence and approval, and then the hungry-looking man asked, "Is this county bumpkin to be sent back soon? I hope so. He's not very bright and probably a little dangerous."

"He knows nothing," said Defarge, "at least nothing more than would easily send him to the gallows . Let him stay with me. I will be in charge of him. I will take care of him, and set him on his road. He wishes to see something of the fine world—the King, the Queen, and Court. I'll let him see them on Sunday." "What?" exclaimed the hungry man, staring. "Is it a good sign,

❷ *If they register the whole of the Marquis' "race" to extermination, whom would this include?*

❷ *What sort of register are they talking about?*

that he wishes to see Royalty and Aristocracy?"

"Jacques," said Defarge, "If you want a cat to desire milk, you must carefully show her some. You should carefully show a dog his natural prey, if you wish him to hunt it down one day." Nothing more was said, and the mender of roads, having already fallen asleep on the top step, was invited to lie down on the pallet-bed and rest. He needed no persuasion, and was soon asleep.

Worse quarters than Defarge's wine shop, could easily have been found in Paris for a provincial slave of that degree. Except for a mysterious fear of Madame, sitting and knitting, his life was new and wonderful. But, Madame sat all day at her counter, so completely unaware of him, and so absolutely determined not to notice that his being there had any connection with anything more than that he was a man in a wine shop, that he trembled with fright whenever she so much as glanced at him.

Therefore, when Sunday came, the mender of roads was not very pleased (though he said he was) to find that Madame was to accompany monsieur and himself to Versailles. It was additionally disturbing to have Madame knitting all the way there, in a public coach. It was likewise disturbing, to have Madame still knitting as the crowd waited to see the carriage of the King and Queen.

"You work hard, Madame," said a man near her.

"Yes," answered Madame Defarge. "I have a good deal to do."

"What do you make, Madame?"

"Many things."

"For instance—"

"For instance," returned Madame Defarge, calmly, "shrouds."

The man moved a little farther away, as soon as he could, and the mender of roads fanned himself with his blue cap, feeling the day to be extremely hot and humid. Fortunately, he did not have long to wait for his glimpse of royalty, for, in just a few minutes, the

❷ *What is Defarge saying here?*

✔ *Versailles was the royal residence of France from 1682 until 1789 when the French Revolution began. Started as a small hunting lodge in a village outside of Paris, it would eventually become one of the most costly and extravagant buildings in the world.*

✔ *A shroud is a cloth used to cover a dead body.*

✔ *Although he inherited enormous debts and a nearly-
bankrupt governor, Louis XVI
(the King with the large face
in this novel) spent a huge
sum of money redesigning
and replanting the gardens
at Versailles almost immediately after he became King.
These are the spectacular
gardens that so overwhelm
the mender of roads.*

❷ *Who are "these fools" and
what is "it"? What is Defarge
predicting?*

✔ *Remember what you learned
about the Three Estates.*

large-faced King and the fair-faced Queen came in their golden coach, attended by a glittering multitude of laughing ladies and fine lords, all in jewels and silks and powder and splendor. In the grand procession were elegantly snobbish figures and handsomely scornful faces of both sexes, and the mender of roads was so caught up in the moment, that he cried *Long live the King, Long live the Queen, Long live everybody and everything!* as if he had never heard of ever-present Jacques. Then, there were gardens, courtyards, terraces, fountains, green banks, more King and Queen, more lords and ladies, more *Long live they all!* until he was absolutely overcome with sentiment and wept. During this entire scene, which lasted about three hours, he had plenty of shouting and weeping and sentimental company, and throughout Defarge held him by the collar, as if to restrain him from flying at the objects of his brief devotion and tearing them to pieces.

"Bravo!" said Defarge, clapping him on the back when it was over, like a mentor, "You are a good boy!"

The mender of roads was now coming to himself, and was nervous about having made a mistake in his reaction to the spectacle, but Defarge insisted he had nothing to worry about.

"You are the fellow we want," said Defarge, in his ear. "You make these fools believe that it will last for ever. Then, they are the more insolent, and it is the sooner ended."

"Yes!" cried the mender of roads, reflectively; "That's true."

"These fools know nothing. While they despise you, and every breath you and a hundred like you take—they actually regard their horses and dogs higher than you—they only know what your breath tells them. Let it deceive a little longer. It cannot deceive them too much."

Madame Defarge looked condescendingly at the man, and nodded in confirmation.

"As to you," said she, "you would shout and shed

tears for anything, if it made a show and a noise. Tell me! Wouldn't you?"

"Yes, Madame, I think I would. For the moment, anyway."

"If you were shown a great heap of dolls, and were told to tear them to pieces and rob them—for your own advantage—you would pick out the richest and gayest. Admit it! Wouldn't you?"

"Oh yes, Madame."

"Yes. And if you were shown a flock of birds that couldn't fly, and were told to strip them of their feathers—for your own advantage—you would pick the birds of the finest feathers, wouldn't you?"

"I would indeed, Madame."

"You have seen both dolls and birds today," said Madame Defarge, with a wave of her hand toward the place where the aristocracy had just been. "Now, go home!"

❷ *Explain the significance of this exchange. Who or what are the "dolls" and the "birds"?*

THIS IS THE END OF THE FOURTEENTH WEEKLY INSTALLMENT.

Writing Opportunity:

Imagine that you are a resident of the town whose water supply is now threatened by debris from the dead body hanging over your well. Write a letter to Monsieur Gabelle, the town administrator, expressing your concerns..

Research Opportunity:

Collect photographs of the Palace of Versailles and compare them with the image of the Saint Antoine neighborhood of Paris that Dickens gives us.

A Tale of Two Cities
CHARLES DICKENS

CHAPTER XVI
Still Knitting

MADAME DEFARGE and her husband returned happily to the heart of Saint Antoine, while a speck in a blue cap wandered back to where the chateau of Monsieur the Marquis—now in his grave— stood among the whispering trees. There was a rumor that the expressions of the stone faces on the chateau were altered. There was another rumor in the village that when the knife was plunged into the Marquis's sleeping body, the faces changed, from expressions of pride to expressions of anger and pain. It was also whispered that when that dangling figure was hauled up forty feet above the fountain, the faces changed again, and now bore a cruel look of being avenged. This was the expression they would have forever. In the stone face over the great window of the bedroom where the murder was committed, two tiny chinks were pointed out in the sculptured nose, which everybody recognized as the face of the Marquis himself. Nobody had noticed the resemblance before the murder. On the rare occasion when two or three ragged peasants emerged from the crowd to take a hurried peep at this petrified image of Monsieur the Marquis, they didn't dare look at the face for long, before they ran away.

Marquis's chateau and peasant hut, stone face and

❷ *What is the narrator saying
in this philosophical passage?*

dangling figure, the blood-red stain on the stone floor,
and the pure water in the village well—thousands of
acres of land—a whole province of France—all France
itself—lay under the night sky, concentrated into a
faint hair-breadth line. So does a whole world—with
all its greatnesses and littlenesses—lie in a twinkling
star. And just as mere science can split a ray of light
and analyze it, so can more wonderful minds see
beyond the feeble shining of this earth of ours, into
every individual thought and act, every vice and
virtue, of every thinking creature on it.

The Defarges, husband and wife, came plodding
under the starlight, in their public vehicle, to that
gate of Paris where their journey led them. There was
the usual delay at the barrier guardhouse, and the
usual lanterns were shone in their faces for the usual
examination and inquiry. Monsieur Defarge climbed
down, knowing one or two of the soldiers there, and
one of the police. He knew the police officer especially
well and hugged him warmly.

❷ *What is being implied here?*

When Saint Antoine had again enfolded the
Defarges in his dusky wings, and they, having finally
gotten down near the Saint's boundaries, were picking
their way on foot through the black mud and garbage
of his streets, Madame Defarge spoke to her husband,
"Say then, my friend, what did Jacques of the police
tell you?"

"He told me everything he knows, but that was
very little. Another spy has been assigned to our
quarter. There may be many more, for all that he can
say, but he knows of one."

❷ *Notice the personification and
the imagery: the neighborhood of Saint Antoine as a
winged angel enfolding his
residents in his wings, etc.*

"Eh well!" said Madame Defarge, raising her
eyebrows with a cool business air. "It is necessary to
register him. What is his name?"

"He is English."

"So much the better. His name?"

"Barsad," said Defarge, making it French by pro-
nunciation. But, he had been so careful to get it accurately, that he then spelled it for his wife.

"Barsad," repeated Madame. "Good. Christian name?"

"John."

"John Barsad," repeated Madame, after murmuring it once to herself. "Good. What does he look like? Is that known?"

"About forty years old, about five feet nine, black hair, dark complexion. He's got a rather handsome face—dark eyes, thin face, well-defined nose, but not straight. It bends toward the left cheek, giving him a rather sinister expression."

"That is a fine description!" said Madame, laughing. "He shall be registered tomorrow."

They turned into the wine shop, which was closed (for it was midnight), and where Madame Defarge immediately took her post at her desk. She counted the small change that had been taken during her absence, examined the stock, and went through the entries in the book, making a few entries of her own. She asked the serving man every possible question about who was in the shop, what had been said, what had happened. Finally, she dismissed him to bed. Then she turned out the contents of the bowl of money for the second time, and began knotting them up in her handkerchief, in a chain of separate knots, for safe keeping through the night. All this while, Defarge, with his pipe in his mouth, walked up and down, watching her in a satisfied manner, but never interfering. This is how he handled most of the affairs of his life.

The night was hot, and the shop, close shut and surrounded by so foul a neighborhood, smelled foul. Monsieur Defarge did not have a very sensitive sense of smell, but the stock of wine smelt much stronger than it ever tasted, and so did the stock of rum and brandy and aniseed. He whiffed the mixture of scents away, as he put down his smoked-out pipe.

"You are tired," said Madame, raising her glance as she knotted the money. "There are only the usual odors."

Historians estimate that there may have been anywhere from 300 to 3,000 spies, commissioned by the police, working at any given time in pre-Revolutionary Paris.

❷ *What is the significance of this exchange? What is Defarge's point? Madame Defarge's?*

"I am a little tired," her husband acknowledged.

"You are a little depressed, too," said Madame, who was never so busy with the accounts that she didn't have attention for him as well. "You men!"

"But my dear!" began Defarge.

"But my dear!" repeated Madame sarcastically, "but my dear! You are discouraged tonight, my dear!"

"Well," said Defarge, with a deep sigh, as if a thought had been twisted out of his heart, "it has been a long time."

"It *has* been a long time," repeated his wife. "And when has it *not* been a long time? Vengeance and retribution require a long time. That is the rule."

"It does not take a long time to strike a man with lightning," said Defarge.

"How long," demanded Madame, calmly, "does it take to make and store the lightning? Tell me."

Defarge raised his head thoughtfully, as if there were something in that too.

"It does not take a long time," said Madame, "for an earthquake to swallow a town. Eh well! Tell me how long it takes to prepare the earthquake?"

"A long time, I suppose," said Defarge.

"But when it is ready, it happens, and grinds to pieces everything in front of it. In the meantime, it is always preparing, though it is not seen or heard. That is your consolation. Keep it."

She tied a knot with flashing eyes, as if she were strangling a foe. "I tell you," said Madame, extending her right hand, for emphasis, "that although it is a long time coming, it is on the road and coming. It never retreats. It never stops. I tell you it is always marching forward. Look around and consider the lives of all the world that we know, consider the faces of all the world that we know, consider the rage and discontent to which the Jacquerie addresses itself with more and more certainty every hour. Can this situation last? Bah! I mock your discouragement."

"My brave wife," replied Defarge, standing before

her with his head a little bent, and his hands clasped behind his back, like a timid and attentive pupil before his teacher, "I do not question all this. But it has lasted a long time, and it is possible—you know well, my wife, it is possible—that it may not come, during our lives."

"Well! So what if it doesn't?" demanded Madame, tying another knot, as if there were another enemy strangled.

"Well!" said Defarge, with a half-complaining and half-apologetic shrug. "We won't see the triumph."

"We will have helped it," returned Madame, with her extended hand in strong action. "Nothing that we do is done in vain. I believe, with all my soul, that we shall see the triumph. But even if not, even if I absolutely knew that I would not, show me the neck of an aristocrat and tyrant, and still I would—" Then Madame, with her teeth set, tied a very terrible knot indeed.

"Hold!" cried Defarge, reddening a little as if he felt accused of cowardice; "I too, my dear, will stop at nothing."

"Yes! But it is your weakness that you sometimes need to see your victim and your opportunity—to keep you going, to encourage you. Encourage yourself without that. When the time comes, let loose a tiger and a devil, but wait for the time with the tiger and the devil chained—not shown—yet always ready."

Madame emphasized the conclusion of this piece of advice by striking her little counter with her chain of money as if she knocked its brains out, and then gathering the heavy handkerchief under her arm in a quiet manner, observing that it was time to go to bed.

The next day at noon, the admirable woman stood in her usual place in the wine shop, knitting away diligently. A rose lay beside her, and if she now and then glanced at the flower, it was not in a suspicious way. There were a few customers, drinking or not drinking, standing or seated, sprinkled about. The

Again, the subtle hint of a positive by the use of a negative is litotes.

❷ *What effect is Dickens creating by noticing the flies?*

day was very hot, and heaps of flies fell dead into the glasses around Madame. Their death did not influence the other flies, who also flew into the residue, and likewise died. Curious to consider how heedless flies are!—perhaps they thought the same thing at Court that sunny summer day.

A figure entering at the door threw a shadow on Madame Defarge which she felt to be a new one. She laid down her knitting, and began to pin her rose in her head-dress, before she looked at the figure.

It was interesting. The moment Madame Defarge took up the rose, the customers ceased talking, and began gradually to drop out of the wine shop.

"Good day, Madame," said the newcomer.

"Good day, Monsieur."

❷ *Why do the customers leave when Madame Defarge puts the rose in her hair?*

She said it aloud, but added to herself, as she resumed her knitting, "Hah! Good day"—about forty years old, five feet nine, black hair, dark complexion, rather handsome face—dark eyes, thin face, well-defined nose, but not straight—bending toward the left cheek, giving him a rather sinister expression! "Good day, one and all!" "May I have a little glass of old cognac, and a mouthful of cool fresh water, Madame?"

❷ *Who is this newcomer?*

Madame politely fulfilled his request.

"This is marvelous cognac, Madame!"

It was the first time the poor stock had ever been complimented like that, and Madame Defarge knew better. She replied, however, that the cognac was flattered, and again picked up her knitting. The visitor watched her fingers for a few moments, and took the opportunity to look around.

"You knit with great skill, Madame."

"I am used to it."

"A pretty pattern too!"

"You think so?" said Madame, looking at him with a smile.

"Decidedly. May I ask what it is for?"

"A hobby," said Madame, still looking at him with a smile while her fingers moved nimbly.

"Not for use?"

"That depends. I may find a use for it one day. If I do—Well," said Madame, drawing a breath and nodding her head with a stern kind of flirtatiousness, "I'll use it!"

It was remarkable, but, the rose on Madame Defarge's headdress seemed to be driving all of her customers away. Two men had entered separately, and had been about to order a drink, when they saw the flower, hesitated, pretended to look around as if for some friend who was not there, and went away. Nor, was there a single man left of those who had been there when this visitor entered. They had all walked out. The spy had kept his eyes open, but had been able to detect no sign. They had shuffled away in a poverty-stricken, purposeless, accidental manner, quite natural and unquestionable.

"JOHN," thought Madame, checking off her work as her fingers knitted, and her eyes looked at the stranger. "Stay long enough, and I shall knit 'BARSAD' before you go." "You have a husband, Madame?"

"I have."

"Children?"

"No children."

"Business seems bad?"

"Business is very bad. The people are so poor."

"Ah, the unfortunate, miserable people! So oppressed, too—as you say."

"As *you* say," Madame corrected him, and skillfully knitting an extra something into his name that meant him no good.

"Pardon me. Certainly it was I who *said* so, but you naturally *think* so. Of course."

"I *think*?" returned Madame, in a high voice. "I and my husband have enough to do to keep this wine shop open, without thinking. All we think, here, is how to live. That is the subject we think of, and it gives us enough to think about from morning to night, without worrying ourselves with others' concerns. Do I think for others? I don't *think* so."

❷ *What is Madame Defarge knitting?*

❷ *Who is Gaspard? How do we know about him?*

The spy—who was there to pick up any rumors he could find or make—did not show his confusion on his face, but stood, leaning his elbow on Madame Defarge's little counter, occasionally sipping his cognac.

"This was a bad business, Madame, Gaspard's execution. Ah! the poor Gaspard!" He said this with a sigh of great compassion.

"My faith!" returned Madame, coolly and lightly, "If people use knives to murder the aristocracy, they have to pay for it. He knew beforehand what the penalty would be for the luxury of killing the Marquis; he has paid the price."

"I believe," said the spy, looking every bit like an angry rebel himself, "I believe there is much compassion and anger in this neighborhood for the poor fellow? Just between you and me."

"Is there?" asked Madame, innocently.

"Isn't there?"

"Here is my husband!" said Madame Defarge.

As the keeper of the wine shop entered, the spy saluted him by touching his hat, and saying, with a warm smile, "Good day, Jacques!"

Defarge stopped short, and stared at him.

"Good day, Jacques!" the spy repeated, not quite as confidently under Defarge's stare.

"You are mistaken, *Monsieur*," replied the keeper of the wine shop. "You confuse me with someone else. My name is not Jacques. I am Ernest Defarge."

"It doesn't matter," said the spy, struggling to act at ease, "good day!"

"Good day!" answered Defarge, dryly.

"I was saying to your wife, with whom I had the pleasure of chatting when you entered, that they tell me there is much sympathy and anger in Saint Antoine, concerning the unhappy fate of poor Gaspard. It's no wonder there is!"

"No one has told me so," said Defarge, shaking his head. "I know nothing about it."

Having said this, he passed behind the little

counter, and stood with his hand on the back of his wife's chair, looking at their enemy. Husband or wife, either one of them would have enjoyed shooting him.

The spy, very good at his job, did not change his outward expression, but drained his little glass of cognac, took a sip of fresh water, and asked for another glass of cognac. Madame Defarge poured it for him, started her knitting again, and hummed a little song.

"You seem to know this neighborhood well; even better than I do," observed Defarge.

"Not at all, but I do hope to know it better. I am extremely interested in the poor souls who live here."

"Hah!" muttered Defarge.

"The pleasure of speaking with you, Monsieur Defarge," continued the spy, "reminds me that I have some connection with your name."

"Have you?" said Defarge, with little interest.

"Yes, indeed. When Doctor Manette was released, you, his old servant, took care of him, I know. He was brought here to you."

"That is true, yes," said Defarge. His wife touched him gently, as if by accident, with her shoulder; and this was a signal to him that it would be best for him to answer the spy's questions, but to answer them as briefly as possible.

"His daughter came here—to you. And she took him from here—from your care. She was, I believe, accompanied by a neat, brown gentleman in a little wig. What was his name? Ah, Lorry—of the bank of Tellson and Company. They took Doctor Manette over to England, I believe."

"That is true," repeated Defarge.

"Very interesting memories!" said the spy. "I have known Doctor Manette and his daughter, in England."

"Is that so?" said Defarge.

"You don't hear much about them now?" said the spy.

"No," said Defarge.

"The truth is," Madame interrupted, pausing in her

work and her little song, "we never hear about them. We received the news of their safe arrival in England, and perhaps another letter, or two. But, since then, they have gone their way, and we have gone ours. We have not communicated with one another."

"I see, Madame," replied the spy. "Well, as it turns out, Miss Manette is going to be married."

"Going?" echoed Madame. "She was pretty enough to have been married long ago. You English are emotionless, it seems to me."

"Oh! You know I am English."

"Your accent is," replied Madame. "And what the accent is, I suppose the man is."

He did not seem to like the fact that he had been so easily identified as English, but he offered a quick laugh as if to show that it didn't matter that she knew he was not French. After sipping his cognac to the bottom, he added, "Yes, Miss Manette is going to be married. But not to an Englishman. She is marrying someone who—like herself—is French by birth. And speaking of Gaspard—ah, poor Gaspard! It was so cruel what they did to him!—what a strange coincidence that she is going to marry the nephew of Monsieur the Marquis! Of course, since poor Gaspard killed Monsieur the Marquis, this nephew *is* the present Marquis. But they do not know him as the Marquis in England. There, he is Mr. Charles Darnay. D'Aulnais is the name of his mother's family."

Madame Defarge knitted steadily, but the information had a visible effect upon her husband. No matter what he did, behind the little counter—striking a match and lighting his pipe, he was upset and had to fight to keep his hand from shaking. The spy noticed the shopkeeper's reaction and made a mental note of it.

Since he found success with his one hit—whatever it was worth—and since no customers seemed to be coming in to help him discover any more information, Mr. Barsad paid for what he had drunk, and left. He did say—very politely—before he left, that he looked

Stop and review all of the various connections of the various characters so far. Update the chart you began earlier.

Note again Dickens' mildly sarcastic tone. Barsad is speaking with forced and exaggerated politeness. Why is Defarge so visibly upset by this information about Lucie Manette?

forward to the pleasure of seeing Monsieur and Madame Defarge again. For some minutes after he had left, the husband and wife remained exactly as he had left them, in case he came back.

"Can it be true," whispered Defarge, looking down at his wife as he stood smoking with his hand on the back of her chair, "what he has said of Ma'amselle Manette?"

"Since *he* has said it," she replied, raising her eyebrows a little, "it is probably false. But it may be true."

"If it is—" Defarge began, and stopped.

"If it is?" repeated his wife.

"—and if the Revolution does come, while we are alive to see it, I hope—for *her* sake—that Destiny will keep her husband out of France."

"Her husband's destiny," said Madame Defarge, with her usual calm, "will take him where he is to go, and will lead him to the end that is to end him. That is all I know."

"But it is very strange—isn't it very strange," said Defarge, almost as if he were pleading with his wife to admit what he was saying, "that—after all our sympathy for Monsieur her father, and herself—her husband's name should be knitted under your hand at this moment, by the side of that spy's?"

"Stranger things than that will happen when the Revolution does come," answered Madame. "I have them both here, and they both deserve to be here."

She rolled up her knitting when she had said those words, and eventually took the rose out of the kerchief that was wound about her head. Either the residents of Saint Antoine instinctively knew that the object was gone, or they had been on the watch for its removal. Either way, the neighbors started to wander into the wine shop, very shortly afterwards, and the wine shop returned to its usual atmosphere. In the evening, during the height of summer, Saint Antoine turned himself inside out, and residents sat on doorsteps and windowsills, stood on filthy street corners, for a breath

❷ *What is Defarge struggling to suggest is "strange"? What is the significance of what Madame Defarge is knitting?*

❷ *What two secret codes of the Revolution have we now been introduced to?*

✔ *Note the personification. The residents of the neighborhood coming outside in the heat of summer is the neighborhood "turning himself inside out."*

of air. On these evenings, Madame Defarge—always carrying her knitting—would walk from place to place and from group to group. She was a Missionary. There were many like her, and it would be a good thing for the world if such people as they never appeared again. All the women knitted. They knitted worthless things; but, the thoughtless work was a thoughtless substitute for eating and drinking. The hands moved for the jaws and the stomach. If the bony fingers had been still, the minds would have remembered that the stomachs were empty.

As Madame Defarge moved from group to group, the women's fingers worked more quickly, with a fierceness that seemed to increase with every little knot of women she spoke with.

Her husband smoked at his door, looking after her with admiration. "A great woman," he said. "A strong woman, a grand woman. A *frightfully* grand woman!"

Darkness closed around, and then came the ringing of church bells and the distant beating of the military drums in the Palace Courtyard. Still, the women sat knitting. Darkness surrounded them. Another sort of darkness was also closing in. Soon, the church bells— that rang pleasantly on this summer night from every church steeple in France—would be pulled down from their steeples and melted into thundering cannons. Soon the military drums would be beating to drown the wretched voices of fighting peasants. So much was closing in about the women who sat knitting. Their very selves were closing in around a system that had not yet been built, where they would sit knitting, knitting, and dropping heads.

THIS IS THE END OF THE FIFTEENTH WEEKLY INSTALLMENT.

❷ *We know why Madame Defarge knits. Why do the other women knit?*

❷ *On what note of foreshadowing does this installment end?*

Research Opportunity:

Report on the religious beliefs of the French Republic. How is it appropriate that Mme. Defarge is described as a missionary, based on these beliefs?

Writing Opportunity:

Explain the metaphors Mme. Defarge uses to describe the building anger of the French peasantry—the lightning and the earthquake. Assess their validity, giving evidence from the text.

A Tale of Two Cities

CHARLES DICKENS

CHAPTER XVII

One Night

T HE SUN HAD never gone down with a brighter glory in that corner of Soho, than on one memorable evening when the Doctor and his daughter sat under the plane tree together. The moon had never risen with a milder radiance over London, than on that night when it found them still seated under the tree, and shone upon their faces through its leaves.

Lucie was to be married tomorrow. She had reserved this last evening for her father, and they sat alone under the plane tree.

"You are happy, my dear father?"

"Quite, my child."

They had said little, though they had been there a long time. When it was still light enough to work and read, she did not sew as she usually did, nor did she read to him. Many times in the past she had both of these things, but, this time was not quite like any other, and nothing could make it so.

"And I am very happy tonight, dear father. I am deeply happy in the love that Heaven has given me— my love for Charles, and Charles's love for me. But, if my life were not to be still dedicated to you, or if my marriage made it necessary for us to live separately— even only a few streets away from each other—I would

Notice how the previous chapter ends with the approach of night, and this chapter begins with the approach of night.

❷ *What is the narrator saying here?*

be more unhappy than I could explain. Even now—"

Even then, she could not control her voice.

In the sad moonlight, she hugged him around his neck, and laid her face upon his chest. Moonlight is always sad, just as sunlight is, and just as the light called human life is—when it comes, and when it leaves. "Father! Can you promise me, one last time, that you are absolutely certain that my love for my husband and my family, and my duties as Charles's wife will never come between us? I know it, but do *you* know it? In your own heart, are you absolutely confident of my undying love?"

Her father answered, with a cheerful confidence he could not have pretended, "I am sure, my darling! More than that," he added, as he tenderly kissed her, "my future is brighter because of your marriage, than it could have been—than it ever was—without it."

"If only I could believe that, Father!"

"Believe it! It is the truth. This is the way life should be, my dear. You are young and so totally devoted to me that you cannot understand how worried I have been that your life would be wasted caring only for me."

She moved her hand toward his lips, but he held it and continued, "Wasted, my child. I worried that your life would be wasted, turned aside from the natural order of things—for my sake. You are so unselfish, that you cannot fully understand how much I have thought about this. Simply ask yourself how *I* could be truly happy if you weren't?"

"If I had never met Charles, I would have been quite happy with you."

He smiled at her unconscious admission that—having met Charles— she would have been unhappy without him, and replied, "You *did* see him, and it is Charles. If it had not been Charles, it would have been someone else. And if you had never met someone, I know I would have been the cause, and then that dark episode of my life would have ruined not only my life, but yours."

It was the first time, except at the trial, that she had ever heard him refer to his period of his suffering. It gave her a strange and new feeling to hear it, and she remembered it long afterwards.

"See!" said the Doctor of Beauvais, raising his hand toward the moon. "I have looked at the moon from my prison window. I have looked at her when it has been such torture to me to think of her shining upon the world I had lost, that I have beaten my head against my prison walls. I have looked at her, feeling so dull and lifeless, that I have thought of nothing but the number of horizontal lines I could draw across her when she was full, and the number of perpendicular lines with which I could intersect them." He added in his quiet, thoughtful manner, as he looked at the moon, "It was twenty lines each direction, I remember, and the twentieth was difficult to squeeze in."

The strange thrill with which she heard him recall that time deepened as he continued, but there was nothing shocking in the way he spoke of it. He only seemed to contrast his present cheerfulness with the torture that was over.

"I have looked at her, thousands of times thinking about the unborn child from whom I had been torn. Whether it was alive. Whether it had been born alive, or the poor mother's shock had killed it. Whether it was a son who would one day avenge his father—There was a time in my imprisonment, when my desire for vengeance was unbearable. Whether it was a son who would never know his father's story, who might even live to consider the possibility of his father's having disappeared of his own free will. Whether it was a daughter who would grow to be a woman."

She drew closer to him, and kissed his cheek and his hand.

"I have imagined that my daughter would forget me—or even, because she never knew me, would never even think about me. I have imagined her at every age, year after year. I have seen her married to a man who knew nothing of my fate. I imagined myself

❷ *Why do you suppose the author chooses to bring up Doctor Manette's home town at this point?*

❓ *What does Manette mean by being "worse than dead"?*

being worse than dead because no one remembered that I was alive."

"Father! It hurts me to think that you even *had* such thoughts about such a daughter. Surely you don't think that *I* was that daughter?"

"You, Lucie? It is only because of the relief you have brought to me, that I am able to remember these thoughts and share them with you. What was I just saying?"

"She knew nothing about you. She cared nothing about you."

"So! But on other moonlit nights, when the sadness and the silence touched me in a different way, with something like a sad sense of peace, I imagined her visiting me in my cell, and leading me to freedom beyond the Bastille. I have seen her image in the moonlight often, just as I now see you. But I never held that imaginary daughter in my arms. You understand that you are not the child I am speaking of?"

❓ *What do you suppose Manette is recollecting here? How can there be two imaginary Lucies, neither of whom was the real Lucie?*

"I was not the daughter who led you to freedom?"

"No. She was another person completely. The imaginary girl that my mind fixed on, was another child, almost more real. I had no idea what she would look like, except that she had to be like her mother. The forgetful daughter looked like her mother—just as you do—but was not *you*. Can you follow me, Lucie? Probably not. It would take years as a solitary prisoner to understand the confused working of my mind back then."

His calm manner could not prevent her blood from running cold, as he tried to describe his old condition.

"In that more peaceful mood, I used to imagine her, coming to me and taking me in the moonlight, and taking me out to show me her married home. It was full of her loving memory of her lost father. My portrait was in her room, and I was in her prayers. Her life was active, cheerful, useful, but she never forgot me or my sad, sad story."

"I was that child, my father, I was not half so good, but in my love that was I."

"And she showed me her children," said the Doctor of Beauvais, "and she had told them about me, and had been taught to pity me. When they passed a prison of the State, they kept far from its frowning walls, and looked up at its bars, and spoke in whispers. She could never rescue me. I imagined that she always brought me back to my cell after showing me those things. But I would be grateful and happy, blessed by her kindness to her poor father. And I would bless her for her faithful love."

"I hope *I am* that child, father. Will you bless me like that tomorrow?"

"Lucie, I speak of these awful memories only to assure you that I love you more than words can tell. And I am thankful to God for my great happiness. Even my wildest, happiest thoughts back then never came near the happiness that I have known with you, and that we can look forward to." He embraced her, blessed her to Heaven, and thanked Heaven for having given her to him. After a while, they went into the house.

No one was invited to the next day's wedding ceremony but Mr. Lorry. There would be no bridesmaid but the raw-boned Miss Pross. The marriage was to make no change in their place of residence. They had been able to enlarge it, by taking the upper rooms formerly rented to someone else. This was all they needed or wanted.

Doctor Manette was very cheerful at the little supper they ate after coming inside. Just the three of them—Lucie, the Doctor, and Miss Pross—sat at the table. The Doctor regretted that Charles was not there. He was tempted to the loving little plot that kept him away; and toasted his health and happiness affectionately.

Eventually, the time came for him to bid Lucie good night, and they separated. But, in the stillness of

✔ *Note the irony. Dickens has laid many clues to suggest that something in France, something in Charles Darnay's family history, Doctor Manette's story, and the Defarges' past is going to threaten the idyllic happiness that Lucie and the Doctor have—as well as their future happiness.*

3:00 in the morning, Lucie came nervously downstairs again, and stole into his room. She was haunted by a vague fear she could not name.

Everything was, however, in its place. Everything was quiet, and her father lay asleep, his white hair on the untroubled pillow, and his hands lying quiet on the coverlet. She hid her candle in a shadow far from him, crept up to his bed, and put her lips to his. She then leaned over and looked at him.

His face was still handsome, but his bitter years of captivity had left deep lines and creases. He kept his expression calm with a determination so strong, that he controlled it even in his sleep. There wasn't a more remarkable face in its quiet, resolute, and guarded struggle with an unseen enemy, in all the world of sleep, that night.

Lucie timidly set her hand on his breast, and whispered a prayer that she would always be as true to him as she truly wanted to be, and as he deserved. Then, she removed her hand, and kissed his lips once again, and went away. The sunrise came, and the shadows of the leaves of the plane tree fell upon his face, as softly as her lips had.

Writing Opportunity:

Analyze the imagery of this chapter. How is it appropriate, given the mental and emotional state of the Manettes? How is it ironic, given the coming events in the story? Use evidence from the text to support your answer.

A Tale of Two Cities

CHARLES DICKENS

CHAPTER XVIII
Nine Days

LUCIE'S WEDDING DAY was shining brightly, and the party was ready outside the closed door of the Doctor's room, where he was speaking with Charles Darnay. They were ready to go to church—the beautiful bride, Mr. Lorry, and Miss Pross—to whom the event was almost perfect and would have *been* perfect, if only her brother Solomon could have been the bridegroom.

"And so," said Mr. Lorry, who could not stop telling the bride how beautiful she was, and who had been moving round her as if to memorize every detail of her simple yet pretty dress, "and so it was for this day that I brought you across the Channel, when you were such a baby! Lord bless me! How little I thought what I was doing! How lightly I valued the obligation I was placing on my friend Mr. Charles!"

"You didn't mean it," remarked the matter-of-fact Miss Pross, "so how could you know it? Nonsense!"

"Really? Well, don't cry," said the gentle Mr. Lorry.

"I am not crying," said Miss Pross. "You are."

"I, my Pross?" (By this time, Mr. Lorry dared to be pleasant with her, once in a while.)

"You were, just now; I saw you, and I am not

Mr. Lorry was the agent who brought Lucie and her mother out of France and to England after Dr. Manette's imprisonment. Years later, Mr. Lorry again brought Lucie from France to England with the newly-released Doctor.

Charles Darnay wanted to tell the Doctor something about his family, but the Doctor had told him to wait and tell it on the morning of his wedding to Lucie.

surprised. Such a beautiful gift as the silverware you gave them, is enough to bring tears into anybody's eyes."

"It is so nice of you to say," said Mr. Lorry. "This is an event that makes a man think about all he has lost. Dear, dear, dear! To think that there might have been a Mrs. Lorry, any time in these almost fifty years!"

"Never!" cried Miss Pross.

"You think there never might have been a Mrs. Lorry?"

"Pooh!" rejoined Miss Pross. "You were a bachelor from the day you were born."

"Well!" observed Mr. Lorry, smiling broadly and adjusting his little wig, "That seems likely, too."

"And you were made to be a bachelor," pursued Miss Pross, "before you were even born."

"Then, I think," said Mr. Lorry, "that I was dealt a very unlucky hand, and that I should have had some say in choosing my fate. But, enough about me! Now, dear Lucie," drawing his arm soothingly round her waist, "I hear them moving around in the next room, and Miss Pross and I—as two formal folks of business—are anxious not to miss the last chance to say something to you that I know you wish to hear. You leave your good father in excellent hands. We will take the best possible care of him during the next two weeks, while you are on your wedding trip in Warwickshire. Even the bank will not be as important to me as he will. And when, at the end of the two weeks, he comes to join you and your beloved husband, on your next two-week's trip in Wales, you will agree that we have sent him to you in perfect health and completely happy. Now, I hear somebody's step coming to the door. Let me kiss my dear girl with an old-fashioned bachelor blessing, before your husband comes to claim his bride."

For a moment, he held her at arm's length to look at the familiar expression on her forehead, and then pulled her close and laid her bright golden hair

❷ *What is the purpose of this conversation?*

against his little brown wig with genuine tenderness and affection.

The door of the Doctor's room opened, and the Doctor came out with Charles Darnay. The Doctor was deathly pale—which he had not been when he and Charles went in together. He was as calm as he had been before they went in, but the look he gave Mr. Lorry indicated that a cold wind was blowing through his heart. He gave his arm to his daughter, and took her downstairs to the carriage that Mr. Lorry had hired in honor of the day. The rest followed in another carriage, and soon, in a nearby church, with no strange eyes looking on, Charles Darnay and Lucie Manette were happily married.

❷ *What do you suppose Charles told him that has caused this reaction?*

In addition to the tears that glistened among the smiles of the little group when the ceremony was done, some diamonds—very bright and sparkling, which had been kept securely in Mr. Lorry's pocket— sparkled on the bride's hand. They returned home to breakfast. Everything was happy, and the golden hair that had mingled with the poor shoemaker's white locks in the Paris attic, were mingled with them again in the morning sunlight, when Lucie embraced her father in parting.

❷ *Why, again, the references to Lucie and Manette's reunion in Paris?*

It was a hard parting, but not for long. Her father cheered her up, and said at last, gently freeing himself from her arms, "Take her, Charles! She is yours!"

Her nervous hand waved to them from a carriage window, and she was gone.

The Doctor, Mr. Lorry, and Miss Pross were alone. It was only when they returned to the welcome shade of the cool old hall, that Mr. Lorry noticed that a great change had come over the Doctor.

He had, of course, repressed much in the years Lucie had cared for him. And some reaction should have been expected when he no longer had a reason to repress all that he had. But, it was that scared, lost look—the same expression he had when Mr. Lorry and Lucie first saw him in the Defarges' attic—that worried Mr. Lorry. And the Doctor's unconscious habit of holding his head and drearily wandering away into his own room when they got upstairs, reminded Mr. Lorry of Defarge, the wine shop keeper, and the midnight carriage ride to get the newly-released Doctor out of Paris and out of France.

"I don't think," he whispered to Miss Pross, after some serious thought, "I think don't think we should speak to him just now—not disturb him at all. I must check in with the Bank, so I will go there right now and come back soon. Then, we will take him on a ride into the country, have dinner, and everything will be all right."

It was easier for Mr. Lorry to go into Tellson's, than to leave Tellson's. He was detained two hours. When he came back, he climbed the old staircase alone. Entering the Doctor's apartment, he was stopped by a low sound of knocking.

"Good God!" he said, with a start. "What's that?"

Miss Pross, with a terrified face, was at his ear. "O me, O me! All is lost!" she cried, wringing her hands. "What do we tell Ladybird? He doesn't know me, and *he's making shoes!*"

Mr. Lorry tried to calm her, and went himself into the Doctor's room. The bench was turned toward the light, as it had been when he had seen the shoemaker at his work before. His head was bent down, and he was very busy. "Doctor Manette. My dear friend, Doctor Manette!"

The Doctor looked at him for a moment, half-curiously, half angrily at being spoken to, and bent over his work again.

He had taken off his coat and vest. His shirt was open at the throat, as it used to be when he did that work, and even the lines and creases in his face had come back to him. He worked hard—impatiently—as if he had some sense that he'd been interrupted.

Mr. Lorry glanced at the work in his hand, and observed that it was a shoe of the old size and shape.

Notice how in the previous chapter he was "the Doctor" and now he's "the shoe-maker."

He took up another that was lying by him, and asked what it was.

"A young lady's walking shoe," he muttered, without looking up. "It ought to have been finished long ago. Leave it alone."

"But, Doctor Manette. Look at me!"

He obeyed, in the old thoughtless, submissive manner, without pausing in his work.

"Don't you know me, my dear friend? Think again. This is not your proper occupation. Think, dear friend!"

Nothing could force the Doctor to speak more. He looked up, for a moment at a time, when Mr. Lorry asked him to, but, nothing the banker said could get the Doctor to utter another word. He worked, and worked, and worked, in silence, and speaking to him was like speaking to a wall, or on the air. The only sign of hope that Mr. Lorry could make out, was that the Doctor sometimes quickly looked up without being asked to. When he did, there seemed to be a faint expression of curiosity or puzzlement in his face— as if he were trying to sort through some doubts in his mind.

Two things were clear to Mr. Lorry, as more important than anything else. The first was that this must be kept secret from Lucie. The second was that it must be kept secret from everyone who knew the Doctor. Together with Miss Pross, he took immediate steps toward the second precaution, by letting everyone know that the Doctor was not well, and required a few days of complete rest. To help keep the news from Lucie, Miss Pross was to write and say that the Doctor had been called away professionally. In her letter, Miss Pross would make mention of an imaginary letter, supposedly written hastily by the Doctor himself and mail it with the real one Miss Pross would write.

Although these steps were wise to avoid causing any alarm, Mr. Lorry took them seriously hoping the Doctor would quickly come to himself. If recovery was quick, Mr. Lorry had then decided to discover the cause of this relapse and thus maybe prevent another.

Toward the end of returning the Doctor quickly to his senses and forming an opinion as to what had caused this episode, Mr. Lorry took a leave of absence from Tellson's—the first of his entire career—and set up a post at the window of the Doctor's room to observe him.

He quickly found that it was worse than useless to speak to him, since, if Mr. Lorry pressed him for a response, he became worried. Mr. Lorry therefore gave up trying to engage the Doctor in conversation on the very first day, and decided simply to stay with him, as a silent protest against the delusion into which he had fallen, or was falling. He remained, therefore, in his seat near the window, reading and writing, and occasionally remarking to the shoemaker that the room was not a prison.

Doctor Manette took what was given him to eat and drink, and continued working, until it was too dark to see—actually continued working half an hour after it was too dark for Mr. Lorry to read or write. When the Doctor put his tools aside until morning, Mr. Lorry rose and said to him, "Would you like to go out?"

The Doctor looked down at the floor on either side of him as he had done in the tiny room in the Defarge's attic, looked up at Mr. Lorry as he had done, and repeated in the old low voice, "Out?"

"Yes, for a walk with me. Why not?"

The Doctor made no effort to answer, and said not a word more. But, Mr. Lorry thought he saw something in the way the Doctor leaned forward on his bench with his elbows on his knees and his head in his hands that suggested he was, in some vague way, asking himself, "Why not?" The wise man of business saw an opportunity here, and decided to hold it.

Miss Pross and he divided the night into two shifts, and looked in on the Doctor from time to time from the next room. He paced up and down for a long time

Mr. Lorry apparently believes that—since he does not fit in the Doctor's illusion of being again in the Bastille—his presence in the room will somehow help the Doctor leave the illusion and return to his normal self.

before he lay down. When he did finally lie down, he fell asleep. In the morning, he was up early, and went straight to his bench and to work.

On this second day, Mr. Lorry greeted him cheerfully by his name, and spoke to him on topics that had recently been important to them. The Doctor offered no reply, but it was evident that he heard what was said, and that he thought about it. This encouraged Mr. Lorry to have Miss Pross come in with her sewing, several times during the day. At those times, Miss Pross and Mr. Lorry quietly spoke of Lucie, and of her father—sitting and working in the room with them— just as they would have if there had been nothing wrong. They did not do this long enough, or often enough to trouble him, and it made Mr. Lorry happy to believe that the Doctor looked up more often, and that he seemed to notice some inconsistencies between his illusions and his actual surroundings.

When it fell dark again, Mr. Lorry asked him as he had the evening before, "Dear Doctor, will you go out?"

As he had the evening before, the Doctor repeated, "Out?"

"Yes, for a walk with me. Why not?"

This time, Mr. Lorry pretended to leave when the Doctor did not answer, but, after staying out of the room for a full hour, he returned. In the meanwhile, the Doctor had moved to the seat in the window, and sat there looking down at the plane tree. When Mr. Lorry returned, he returned to his bench.

The time passed very slowly, and Mr. Lorry's hope faded. His heart grew heavier and heavier and heavier every day. The third day came and went...the fourth... the fifth. Five days...six days...seven days...eight days...nine days.

With a hope ever darkening, and with a heart always growing heavier and heavier, Mr. Lorry passed through this anxious time. The secret was well kept, and Lucie was unaware and happy; but Mr. Lorry could not fail to notice that the shoemaker, whose hand had been a little out of practice on the first day, was growing dreadfully skillful, and that he had never concentrated on his work, and never exhibited such skill, as he did in the dusk of the ninth evening.

❷ *On what note of suspense does Dickens end this weekly installment?*

THIS IS THE END OF THE
SIXTEENTH WEEKLY INSTALLMENT.

Research Opportunity:

Research the various types of mental shock. Prepare a report for your class in which you diagnose the ailment which seems to have stricken Dr. Manette.

A Tale of Two Cities

CHARLES DICKENS

CHAPTER XIX
An Opinion

EXHAUSTED BY HIS VIGIL, Mr. Lorry fell asleep at his post. On the tenth morning, he was startled awake by the shining of the sun into the room, and he realized that he had fallen into a heavy slumber some time during the dark night.

He rubbed his eyes and stood, but he wondered whether he might still be asleep. Going to the door of the Doctor's room and looking in, he saw that the shoemaker's bench and tools were set aside again, and that the Doctor himself sat reading at the window. He was in his usual morning clothes, and his face (which Mr. Lorry could see clearly), was still very pale but plainly attentive on the book he was studying.

Even when he had convinced himself that he was awake, Mr. Lorry felt uncertain for few moments whether the days of shoemaking might have been a disturbed dream of his own. After all, didn't he plainly see his friend before him in his usual clothing, and performing his usual morning activity? And was there any sign that he could see, that the episode he so clearly remembered had actually happened?

But the answer was obvious. If he'd simply been dreaming, then why was he, Mr. Jarvis Lorry, waking up in the Doctor's house? How did he fall asleep, in his clothes, on the sofa in Doctor Manette's consulting room? And why was he debating these points outside the Doctor's bedroom door in the early morning?

Within a few minutes, Miss Pross stood whispering at his side. He now had no doubt that the Doctor had indeed gone through an episode where he believed himself to be in his cell in the Bastille, and that now he seemed to be recovered. Mr. Lorry suggested that they should wait until the regular breakfast time, and meet the Doctor as if nothing unusual had happened. If he appeared to be in his normal state of mind, Mr. Lorry would then cautiously ask the Doctor himself about what the strange episode may have meant and what may have caused it.

Miss Pross agreed, and they worked out a plan. After getting ready, Mr. Lorry presented himself at breakfast in his usual white linen. The Doctor was summoned as usual, and came to breakfast.

As far as it was possible to understand without giving the Doctor too much information too quickly and alarming him, the Doctor at first thought that his daughter's marriage had taken place yesterday. Mr. Lorry casually mentioned what day of the week it was, and what day of the month. This set the Doctor thinking and counting, and evidently made him uneasy. In all other respects, however, he was so calm and so fully himself, that Mr. Lorry decided it would be safe to ask for the information he needed.

Therefore, when breakfast was finished and cleared away, and he and the Doctor were left together, Mr. Lorry said, with sincere feeling, "My dear Manette, I am eager to have your confidential opinion on a very strange case in which I am very interested. What I mean is, it is very strange to me. With your knowledge and experience, you may not find it strange at all."

Glancing at his hands, which were stained by the shoe leather he'd been handling the past nine days, the Doctor looked troubled, and listened attentively. He had already glanced at his hands more than once.

"Doctor Manette," said Mr. Lorry, touching him

affectionately on the arm, "the case is the case of a particularly dear friend of mine. Please consider it, and tell me what to do. For his sake, Doctor Manette and for his daughter's."

"If I understand," said the Doctor quietly, "some mental shock—?"

"Yes!"

"Be clear," said the Doctor. "Spare no detail."

Mr. Lorry saw that they understood one another, and continued. "My dear Manette, it is the case of an old and a prolonged shock, one that had a great effect on my friend's emotions and on his mind. His mind. It is the case of a shock under which my friend was beaten down—it's hard to say how long because even he cannot recall exactly how long he suffered—and there is no other way to find out. It is the case of a shock from which my friend did recover—but I heard him once admit that even he did not know how it was that he recovered. He recovered so completely from this shock, in fact, he has been a brilliant man, has been able to push his mind to learn more, has gained impressive strength in his body. In short, it was a total recovery, and he has been a most healthy man. Unfortunately, however, there has been," he paused and took a deep breath, "a slight relapse."

The Doctor, in a low voice, asked, "How long did this relapse last?"

"Nine days and nights."

"How did it show itself? I assume," glancing at his hands again, "he was doing something he used to do when he was in shock?"

"That is the fact."

"Now, did you ever see him," asked the Doctor, distinctly and collectedly, though in the same low voice, "doing that originally?"

"Once."

"And when the relapse fell on him, was he partially—or completely—the same as he was before?"

"I think completely."

"You spoke of his daughter. Does his daughter know of the relapse?"

"No. It has been kept from her, and I hope will always be kept from her. It is known only to myself, and to one other who may be trusted."

The Doctor grasped Mr. Lorry's hand, and murmured, "That was very kind. That was very thoughtful!" Mr. Lorry grasped the Doctor's hand in return, and neither of them spoke for a while.

"Now, my dear Manette," said Mr. Lorry eventually, as kindly and affectionately as he could, "I am a mere man of business, and unfit to cope with matters like this. I do not have the necessary knowledge. I am simply not intelligent enough. I need guidance. And there is no one for me to turn to but you. Tell me, how did this relapse come about? Is there danger of another? Could another one be prevented? How should another relapse be treated? How does it happen at all? What can I do for my friend? No man ever wanted to help a friend more than I want to help mine, if only I knew how. But I don't know how to even start. If your knowledge and experience could put me on the right track, I might be able to do much. However, knowing nothing, I can do nothing. Please discuss it with me. Please help me to understand it, and teach me how to be a little more helpful."

Doctor Manette sat meditating after these sincere words were spoken, and Mr. Lorry did not press him. "I think it probable," said the Doctor, breaking silence with an effort, "that the person saw his relapse coming."

"Did he dread it?" Mr. Lorry dared to ask.

"Very much." The Doctor said it with an involuntary shudder.

"You have no idea how heavily this worry weighs on the sufferer's mind, and how difficult—how almost impossible—it is for him to force himself to speak about it."

"Would it help him," asked Mr. Lorry, "if he

could talk about what is happening to him, while it is happening?"

"I think so. But it is, as I have told you, next to impossible. I even believe it—in some cases—to be absolutely impossible."

"Now," said Mr. Lorry, gently laying his hand on the Doctor's arm again, after a short silence on both sides, "what caused this attack?"

"I believe," returned Doctor Manette, "that there had been an extremely strong reminder of what had caused the mental shock in the first place. Some intense memories of that time were brought to mind, I think. It is probable that he had worried about those memories surfacing in his mind. He tried to prepare himself, but it was useless. Maybe the effort to prepare himself even made him *less* able to bear it."

"Would he remember what took place during the relapse?" asked Mr. Lorry, with natural hesitation.

The Doctor looked sadly round the room, shook his head, and answered, in a low voice, "Not at all."

"Now, as to the future," hinted Mr. Lorry.

"As to the future," said the Doctor, recovering firmness, "I would be very optimistic. Since this first relapse was so relatively short, I would have great hope. He had long seen this storm coming, and he recovered quickly. I do not think that another relapse is likely."

"Well, well! That's good news. I am thankful!" said Mr. Lorry.

"*I* am thankful!" repeated the Doctor, bending his head with reverence.

"There are two other points," said Mr. Lorry, "about which I have a few questions. May I go on?"

"You couldn't do your friend a better service." The Doctor gave him his hand.

"My friend studies quite a bit. He works hard to gain new knowledge, to conduct experiments. Now, does he work too hard?"

"I do not think so. His mind may be one of those

that *needs* to be kept busy. That might be its natural tendency. But it might also be partly the result of his affliction. The less his mind was occupied with healthy things, the more it would be in danger of turning in the unhealthy direction. He may have noticed that about himself."

"You are sure that he is not under too great a strain?"

"I think I am quite sure of it."

"My dear Manette, if he were overworked now—"

"My dear Lorry, I doubt if that could easily be. The pull toward his madness is very strong, and it needs an equal pull in the healthy direction."

"Excuse me, as a persistent man of business. Assuming for a moment, that he was overworked, would this show itself in some relapse?"

"I do not think so," said Doctor Manette firmly, "I think that one memory is the only thing that can bring on a relapse. And since your friend has had one and recovered, I doubt there is anything else connected with that memory to harm him. I am fairly confident that there is nothing that would bring about another one."

The Doctor spoke timidly, like a man who knew how minor a thing could confuse the delicate organization of the mind, and yet confidently, like a man who had gained his knowledge through his own endurance and suffering. It would have been unkind for Mr. Lorry to destroy that confidence, so he said that he was more relieved and encouraged than he really was. Then he asked his second question. He felt this one to be the most difficult of all, but, remembering that he and Miss Pross had once discussed the Doctor's mental unease and to what extent he thought about his past suffering and, remembering what he had seen in the last nine days, he knew that he must face it.

"The job he started doing again," said Mr. Lorry, clearing his throat. "Let's call it—Blacksmith's work. Blacksmith's work. Let's say—merely as an illustration—that during his bad time, he used to work

❷ *So far, this chapter has not advanced the plot or revealed a significant amount of exposition. What is the "one memory" that Manette refers to that brought on his relapse?*

❷ ***Irony alert***: *What do you suppose is likely to happen when a character asserts that "nothing" can cause something to happen?*

at a little forge. And let's say that he was unexpectedly found at his forge again. Isn't it sad that he still keeps this forge around?"

The Doctor shaded his forehead with his hand, and tapped his foot nervously on the floor.

"He has always kept it by him," said Mr. Lorry, with an anxious look at his friend. "Wouldn't it be better if he simply got rid of it?"

Still, the Doctor, with shaded forehead, tapped his foot nervously on the floor.

"You do not find it easy to advise me?" said Mr. Lorry. "I quite understand it to be a difficult question. And yet I think—"

"You see," Doctor Manette interrupted him, "it is very hard to explain the inner workings of this poor man's mind. He once longed so painfully for that work, and it was so welcome when it came. I have no doubt that it greatly relieved him. By keeping the hands busy, he allowed his brain to rest. As he became more skilled, the ability of his hands made up for the feeling that he was losing his mind. The work was his salvation when he had no other hope, and he has never been able to bear the thought of completely getting rid of it. Even now, when I believe he is more confident about his condition than he has ever been. He is even able to talk about himself with confidence. Still the idea that he might need that old employment, and not find it, terrifies him."

He looked like that lost child, as he raised his eyes to Mr. Lorry's face.

"But isn't it possible—and remember that I am nothing more than a dull man of business and am more used to dealing in bank notes, coins, and other material objects—isn't it possible that the tools themselves *remind* my friend of his past suffering and his current mental difficulties? If the thing were gone, my dear Manette, might not the fear go with it? In short, isn't keeping the forge actually a sign that he is giving in to his fear?"

There was another silence.

❷ *What is Mr. Lorry asking Manette to do?*

"You must also realize," said the Doctor, tremulously, "that the forge is like an old friend."

"I would not keep it," said Mr. Lorry, shaking his head, for he grew firmer in his opinion as he saw the Doctor grow more upset. "I would recommend him to sacrifice it. I only want your authority. I am sure it does no good. Come! Give me your authority, like a dear good man. For his daughter's sake, my dear Manette!" The Doctor's internal struggle was strange for Mr. Lorry to watch.

"For the daughter, then, yes, let it be done. I will allow it. But, I would not take it away while he was present. Let it be removed when he is not there. Let him miss his old companion after he has gone out."

Mr. Lorry readily agreed to that, and the conversation was ended. They passed the day in the country, and the Doctor was quite restored. On the three following days he remained perfectly well, and on the fourteenth day, he went away to join Lucie and her husband. Mr. Lorry explained to the Doctor the trick they had used to keep Lucie from worrying, and the Doctor wrote to Lucie the letter Miss Pross had alluded to. Thus, Lucie had no suspicions.

The night after the Doctor left home to begin his trip with Lucie and Darnay, Mr. Lorry went into his room with an axe, a saw, a chisel, and a hammer. Behind the closed door, while Miss Pross held a light for him, Mr. Lorry hacked the shoemaker's bench to pieces, feeling strangely guilty. Even Miss Pross held the candle as if she were assisting at a murder, and her thin grimness certainly gave her the appropriate appearance. The burning of the body—that they'd chopped up in pieces small enough—was started without delay in the kitchen fire, and the tools, shoes, and leather, were buried in the garden. Such destruction and secrecy make honest minds feel so guilty, that Mr. Lorry and Miss Pross almost felt—and almost looked—like accomplices in a horrible crime.

✔ *Note the extended metaphor. Destroying the bench and tools is compared to a murder. Burning them in the stove is the "burning of the body."*

A Tale of Two Cities

CHARLES DICKENS

CHAPTER XX
A Plea

WHEN THE NEWLYWEDS came home, the first person who came to offer his congratulations, was Sydney Carton. They had not been at home many hours, when he presented himself. He still looked and acted the same; but there was a certain strength of confidence about him, which Charles Darnay had never noticed before.

Sydney took Darnay aside into a window, and spoke to him quietly so that no one could hear.

"Mr. Darnay," said Carton, "I wish we could be friends."

"We are already friends, I hope."

"You're being polite. You're supposed to say that. But, I mean something beyond mere politeness. Indeed, when I say I wish we might be friends, I don't really mean that, either."

Charles Darnay—as would be expected—asked him, in a polite and friendly manner, what he *did* mean?

"Upon my life," said Carton, smiling, "I understand in my mind what I mean, but I'm finding it very difficult to explain it to you. But let me try. You remember a certain famous occasion when I was more

❂ *Sydney is referring to the evening after Darnay's trial.*

drunk than—than usual?"

"I remember a certain famous occasion when you forced me to accuse you of drinking."

"I remember it too. The worst part of those occasions is that I always remember them. I hope that might be taken into consideration when I stand at my final Judgement. Don't worry, I'm not going to preach."

"I'm not at all worried. Seriousness in you, is not at all worrisome to me."

"Ah!" said Carton, with a careless wave of his hand, as if he waved that away. "On this particular drunken occasion (one of many, as you know), I was quite rude about liking you, and not liking you. I wish you would forget it."

"I forgot it long ago."

"Manners again! But, Mr. Darnay, forgetting is not as easy for me, as you pretend it is for you. I have by no means forgotten it, and a flippant answer like that does not help me to forget it."

"If it was a flippant answer," returned Darnay, "I apologize for it. I did not intend to do anything but turn a petty thing, which seems to trouble you too much, aside. I give you my word as a gentleman, that I have long ago forgotten that conversation. Good Heaven, what was there to forget? Don't you think the thing I would remember about that day would be the way you saved my life?"

"As far as that goes," said Carton, "I must tell you—when you make such a big deal of it—that it was mere professional trickery. I doubt I really cared what became of you, when I performed it. Listen! I say *when I performed it*. I am speaking of the past."

"You make light of my obligation to you," returned Darnay, "but I won't argue with you about it."

"Absolute truth, Mr. Darnay, trust me! But we're missing the point. I was speaking about our being friends. Now, you know me. You know I have absolutely no aspirations, dreams, or goals. I'm not capable of having such goals. If you doubt it, ask Stryver, and he'll tell you so."

"I prefer to form my own opinion."

"Well! At any rate you know me as a wicked dog, who has never done any good, and never will."

"I don't know that you 'never will.'"

"But I do, and you must take my word for it. Well! If you could allow such a worthless fellow, and a fellow of such indifferent reputation, coming and going at odd times, I would ask to have the privilege to come and go whenever I wanted. You could consider me nothing more than a useless piece of furniture that you tolerate because you've always had it around, but that you never even notice anymore. I wouldn't abuse the permission. Chances are I wouldn't use it even four times in a year. It would satisfy me simply to know that I had it."

"But would you *try* to be a familiar visitor?"

"That is another way of saying that I have the permission I wanted. I thank you, Darnay. I may use that freedom with your name?"

"I think so, Carton, by now."

They shook hands on it, and Sydney turned away. Within a minute afterwards, he was, to all outward appearance, as shallow as ever.

When he was gone, and in the course of the evening spent with Miss Pross, the Doctor, and Mr. Lorry, Charles Darnay briefly mentioned this conversation, and suggested that Sydney Carton's problem was simple carelessness and recklessness. There was no bitterness in the way he spoke about Sydney Carton, and he was not making fun of the man. He simply recognized how the man made himself appear to others.

He had no idea that his comments would linger in the thoughts of his fair young wife, but, when he later joined her in their own rooms, he found her waiting for him with her forehead wrinkled in thought as it often did.

Remember the promise Sydney once made to Lucie.

"You are thoughtful tonight!" said Darnay, drawing his arm about her.

"Yes, Charles," with her hands on his breast, staring at him with eyes that were full of question. "I am rather thoughtful tonight, for I have something on my mind."

"What is it, my Lucie?"

"Will you promise not to ask me one question, if I beg you not to?"

"Of course."

He brushed her golden hair from her cheek, and lay his other hand against the heart that beat for him!

"I think, Charles, poor Mr. Carton deserves more consideration and respect than you showed him tonight."

"Indeed? Why?"

"That is what you are not to ask me. But I think—I *know*—he does."

"If you know it, it is enough. What would you have me do, Lucie my dear?"

"I would ask you to always be very generous with him. Be very lenient of his faults when he is not here. I would ask you to believe that he has a heart he very, very seldom reveals, and that there are deep wounds in it. My dear, I have seen it bleeding."

"It bothers me to think that I have done him any wrong," said Charles Darnay, quite surprised. "I never thought of him as soulful and wounded."

"It is the truth. I fear he will never recognize his own worth and potential. There is barely any potential that he hasn't already thrown away. But, I am sure that he is capable of good things, gentle things, even magnanimous things."

She looked so beautiful in the purity of her faith in this lost man, that her husband could have looked at her as she was for hours.

"And, O my dearest Love!" she urged, clinging nearer to him, laying her head upon his breast, and raising her eyes to his, "remember how strong we are

❷ *Why does Lucie believe Sydney deserves more consideration than Charles has shown him? What is she remembering?*

✒ *Look up the word "magnanimous" in the dictionary.*

in our happiness, and how weak he is in his misery!"

The request touched him. "I will always remember it, dear Heart! I will remember it as long as I live."

He bent over the golden head, and put the rosy lips to his, and folded her in his arms.

THIS IS THE END OF THE
SEVENTEENTH WEEKLY INSTALLMENT.

A Tale of Two Cities

CHARLES DICKENS

CHAPTER XXI

Echoing Footsteps

IT HAS ALREADY BEEN mentioned that the corner where the Doctor lived is a fine one for hearing echoes. Always winding the golden thread which bound her husband, and her father, and herself, and Miss Pross, in a life of quiet bliss, Lucie sat in the still house in the calmly echoing corner, listening to the echoing footsteps of years.

At first, there were times—though she was a perfectly happy young wife—when her sewing would slowly fall from her hands, and her eyes would fill with tears. She could sense something coming in the echoes, something that would cause her heart to stop. She wavered between hope and fear—hopes of a new love that she did not yet know, and fear that she would not be alive on earth to enjoy this new love. Among the echoes then, she imagined that she heard the sound of footsteps at her own early grave. Her thoughts about the husband who would be left in grief, and who would mourn for her so much, swelled to her eyes, and broke like waves of tears.

That time passed, and her little Lucie was born.

Then, among the echoes, there was the tread of the baby's tiny feet and the sound of her babbling first words. Lucie, the mother, paid no attention to

❷ *What type of passage begins this new weekly installment?*

the greater echoes growing louder in their corner. Her ears were dedicated to the sounds made by her beloved daughter. The shady house was sunny with a child's laugh, and the Divine friend of children seemed to take her child in His arms and made it a sacred joy to her.

Always winding the golden thread that bound them all together, weaving her happy influence through the fabric of all their lives, Lucie heard only friendly and soothing sounds in the echoes of years. Her husband's footstep was strong and prosperous. Her father's firm and equal. Miss Pross was the undisciplined war-horse, snorting and pawing the earth under the plane tree in the garden!

Even when there were sorrowful sounds among the happy ones, they were not harsh or cruel. Even when golden hair, like her own, lay in a halo on a pillow round the sick and weary face of a little boy, and he said, with a radiant smile, "Dear papa and mamma, I am very sorry to leave you both, and to leave my pretty sister; but I am called, and I must go!" Those were not tears all of agony that wetted his young mother's cheek, as the spirit departed from her embrace that had been entrusted to it. Suffer them and forbid them not. They see my Father's face. O Father, blessed words!

Thus, the rustling of an Angel's wings joined with the other echoes. The wind's sigh as it blew over the lost son's little garden tomb were mingled with them also. Lucie heard them both in a hushed murmur—like the breathing of a summer sea sleeping on the sandy shore—as the little Lucie, comically watching her mother perform her morning chores, or dressing a doll at her mother's footstool, chattered in the languages of the Two Cities that were blended in her life.

The Echoes rarely represented the actual footstep of Sydney Carton. Only about six times a year, at most, he claimed his privilege of coming in uninvited, and would sit among them through the evening, as he had

❷ Who is this "Divine friend of children" alluded to here?

❷ What is happening in this episode?

✔ Note that the child is not saying this. The parents are "hearing" it in the baby's smile.

✔ Explain the allusion in this sentence.

❷ What are the Two Cities? What are the two languages?

once done often. He never came there intoxicated with wine. And one other significant thought regarding him was whispered in the echoes, which has been whispered by all true echoes for ages and ages.

Every man who has ever loved a woman, lost her, and yet continued to think of her kindly and lovingly, has found that her children felt an unusual strange sympathy with him—an instinctive pity for him. How the children can sense the man's continued devotion to their mother, no echoes tell, but it is true, and it was true in this case. Sydney Carton was the first stranger to whom little Lucie held out her chubby arms, and he remained her favorite as she grew. The little boy had spoken of him, with almost his last breath. "Poor Carton! Kiss him for me!"

Mr. Stryver shouldered his way through the law, like some great engine forcing itself through dirty water, and dragged his useful friend along with him like a boat being towed behind him. As the boat towed like this is usually in a bad way, and mostly under water, so, Sydney's life seemed "swamped." But he was used to his life and had come to accept that this was the life he was to lead. Thus, he no more thought of rising from his state of lion's jackal, than any real jackal might hope to become a lion.

Stryver was rich; had married a pretty widow with property and three boys, who had nothing particularly remarkable about them except the straight hair of their dumpling-shaped and soft heads.

These three young gentlemen walked into the quiet corner in Soho like three lambs, followed by Mr. Stryver who was as puffed up and pompous as he could be. Stryver offered the boys as pupils to Lucie's husband, delicately saying "So! here's some bread and butter to help you put food on your table, Darnay!" Darnay politely rejected the offered "bread and butter." Stryver puffed himself larger with indignation, and carefully taught the young gentlemen to be cautious of the pride of Beggars, like that tutor-fellow. He also began to tell Mrs. Stryver—over his full-bodied

❶ King's Bench was at one time the highest court of common law in England—called "King's Bench" (or "Queen's Bench") because the king (or queen) used to sit there in person. It consisted of a chief justice and four junior justices. Mr. Stryver's "King's Bench colleagues" would most likely be other lawyers who try cases in this court.

❷ Why do you suppose Dickens is emphasizing how happy these years are and how perfect a wife, daughter, and mother Lucie is?

❸ Note the date: July 1789.

wine—how Mrs. Darnay had once actually pursued *him*, and how he had successfully warded off her advances. Some of his King's Bench colleagues, who occasionally drank with Mr. Stryver and told the lie, forgave him for it by saying that he had told it so often, he believed it himself.

These were among the echoes to which Lucie— sometimes quiet and thoughtful, sometimes happy and laughing—listened in her little corner of Soho, until her little daughter was six years old. We need not tell how dear to her heart were the echoes of her child's footsteps, and those of her father's, always strong and confident, and those of her dear husband's. It was also clear that the sounds of her home, under her housekeeping, were music to her. There were echoes from her father, who often told her that he found her to be even more devoted to him married—if that were possible—than single. Echoes too came from her husband, who had said to her that she truly made him feel as though he were indeed the most important care in her life. "What is the magic secret, my darling? You manage to be *everything* to all of us, yet you never seem to be hurried, or too much busy?"

But, throughout these happy years, there were menacing echoes as well, rumbling from a distance. It was now, near little Lucie's sixth birthday, that these began to have an awful sound, like a great storm in France with a dreadful sea rising.

On a night in mid-July, one thousand seven hundred and eighty-nine, Mr. Lorry came in late, from Tellson's, and sat down by Lucie and her husband in the dark window. It was a hot, windy night, and all three of them remembered that long-ago Sunday night when they had watched the lightning from the same place.

"I was beginning to think," said Mr. Lorry, pushing his brown wig back, "that I would have to spend the entire night at Tellson's. We have been so busy all day, that we didn't know what to do first, or which way to turn. There so much trouble in Paris, that we have actually a "run of confidence" upon us! Our customers over there, don't seem able to trust their property to us fast enough. They are absolutely frantic about sending it to England."

"That doesn't look good," said Darnay.

"Not good, you say, my dear Darnay? Yes, but we don't know why they're doing it. People are so unreasonable! Some of us at Tellson's are getting old, and we really can't be troubled with extraordinary business without a sound reason."

"You know how gloomy and threatening the sky is."

"I know that, of course," agreed Mr. Lorry, trying to believe that his sweet temper was soured, and that he was grumbling, "but I just feel like being peevish after my long difficult day. Where is Manette?"

"Here he is," said the Doctor, just then entering the dark room.

"I'm glad you're home, for the frenzy that has surrounded me all day, has made me nervous without reason. You are not going out, I hope?"

"No. I am going to play backgammon with you, if you want," said the Doctor.

"I don't think I do want to, if I may speak my mind. I am not fit to be pitted against you tonight. Is the tea tray still there, Lucie? I can't see."

"Of course, we've left it set up just for you."

"Thank you, my dear. Your child is safe in bed?"

"And sleeping soundly."

"That's good. Everything safe and well! I don't know why anything would be otherwise here, thank God, but I have been so put out all day, and I'm not as young as I used to be!" Lucie handed him a cup of tea. "Ah, thank you, my dear. Now, come and take your place in the circle, and let us sit quiet, and hear the echoes about which you have your theory."

"Not a theory; it was merely a daydream."

"A daydream, then, my wise pet," said Mr. Lorry,

❷ Usually, a "run" on a bank is the occasion of too many depositors trying to withdraw too much money at one time. The "run of confidence" that Mr. Lorry is talking about, however, seems to be the opposite event. Depositors in Paris are rushing to put their money into the bank where it will be protected, and available to them should they have to leave France for England.

❷ Is Darnay talking about the weather here?

patting her hand. "There is indeed a great number of these echoes, isn't there? And they are loud, aren't they? Just listen to them!"

They sat and listened to the footsteps of London, hurrying to safety before the coming storm broke. They listened to reckless, angry, and dangerous footsteps strong enough to force their way into anybody's life, footsteps not easily cleaned once they were stained red, the footsteps raging in far off Saint Antoine, as the little circle sat in the dark London window.

What is the image Dickens is creating here?

That very morning, Saint Antoine had been a vast dusky mass of scarecrows heaving back and forth, with frequent gleams of light above their heads, where steel blades and bayonets shone in the sun. A tremendous roar arose from the throat of Saint Antoine, and a forest of naked arms struggled in the air like shriveled branches of trees in a winter wind, all the fingers clutching at every weapon—or anything that could pass for a weapon—that was tossed up from below.

Note the continued personification.

Research Opportunity:

What is the date, and what is happening?

Not one person in the mob had any idea where the weapons had come from, how they'd come into the hands of the Revolution, or who had commanded that today be the day they were distributed, but, muskets *were* being distributed—so were cartridges, powder, and balls, bars of iron and wood, knives, axes, pikes, every weapon that could be imagined. People who could find nothing else, used their own bleeding hands to pry stones and bricks out of their walls . Every pulse and heart in Saint Antoine was on high-fever strain and at high-fever heat. Every living creature there considered his life to be worthless, and was driven mad with a passionate willingness to sacrifice it.

Just as a whirlpool has a center point, so did all

this raging circle round Defarge's wine shop, and every human drop in the bucket couldn't help but be drawn toward the vortex where Defarge himself—already dirty with gunpowder and sweat—issued orders, passed out weapons, pushed this man back, dragged this man forward, disarmed one to arm another, labored and strove in the thickest of the uproar.

"Keep near to me, Jacques Three," cried Defarge. "Jacques One and Two, separate and put yourselves at the head of as many of these patriots as you can. Where is my wife?"

"Eh, well! Here you see me!" said Madame, calm as ever, but not knitting today. Madame's firm right hand held an axe, instead of her knitting needles, and in her belt were a pistol and a cruel knife.

"Where are you going, my wife?"

"I am going with you," said Madame. "You will see me at the head of the women, very soon."

"Come, then!" cried Defarge, in a resounding voice. "Patriots and friends, we are ready! The Bastille!"

❷ *What does the Bastille represent to the French peasantry?*

With a roar that sounded as if all the breath in France had been funneled into the detested word, the living sea rose, wave on wave, depth on depth, and overflowed the city to that point. Alarm-bells ringing, drums beating, the sea raging and thundering on its new beach, the attack begun. Deep ditches, double drawbridge, massive stone walls, eight great towers, cannon, muskets, fire and smoke all separated this human sea from its goal. Through the fire and through the smoke—*in* the fire and smoke, for the sea of rebelling peasants pressed him up against a cannon, and, at that moment, he became a cannonier—Defarge of the wine shop worked like a manful soldier, two fierce hours.

✔ *Describe the hyperbole and the metaphor in this sentence.*

Another deep ditch, one remaining drawbridge, still the massive stone walls, eight great towers, cannon, muskets, fire and smoke. One drawbridge lowered! "Work, comrades all, work! Work, Jacques One, Jacques Two, Jacques One Thousand, Jacques Two Thousand, Jacques, Jacques Twenty-Five Thousand! In the names of all the Angels or the Devils—whichever you prefer—work!" called Defarge of the wine shop, still at his canon, which had long grown too hot to fire.

"To me, women!" cried Madame his wife. "We can kill as well as the men once we're inside!" And to her, with a shrill thirsty cry, the women ran. They were "armed" with an odd assortment of things that could be called weapons only because they could be used to injure and kill, but they were all armed by their hunger for revenge.

More cannon, muskets, fire and smoke—and, there was still the deep ditch to be crossed, the one remaining drawbridge to be lowered, the massive stone walls to be breached, and the eight great towers to be conquered. The sea started to show some gaps, made by the falling wounded. Flashing weapons, blazing torches, smoking wagonloads of wet straw, hard work at neighboring barricades in all directions, shrieks, volleys, shouts of hatred, bravery without hesitation, boom, smash and rattle, and the furious sounding of the living sea—but, still the ditch, and the drawbridge, and the massive stone walls, and the eight great towers, and still Defarge of the wine shop at his cannon, now twice as hot as it was before.

A white flag from within the fortress, and a conference—this the residents of Saint Antoine could see but not hear through the raging storm. Suddenly the sea rose wider and higher, and swept Defarge of the wine shop over the now-lowered drawbridge, past the massive stone outer walls, and in among the eight great towers. The defenders of the Bastille had surrendered!

The force of the ocean carrying Defarge was so irresistible, that it was impossible for him even to breathe or turn his head—just as if he had been struggling in the surf at the South Sea—until he was set down in the outer courtyard of the Bastille. There, pressed into a corner, he struggled to look around. Jacques Three was nearly at his side. He could see

✔ Dickens is maintaining his metaphor, comparing the mass of peasants to a rising sea.

❷ What effect is Dickens creating by merely listing the sights and sounds of the battle rather than trying to describe the actions?

Madame Defarge, further inside the conquered fortress, still leading some of her women. Her knife was in her hand. Everywhere was tumult, exultation, deafening and maniacal bewilderment, astounding noise, and furious chaos.

"The Prisoners!"

"The Records!"

"The secret cells!"

"The instruments of torture!"

"The Prisoners!"

Of all these cries, and ten thousand confused roars, "The Prisoners!" was the cry most repeated by the sea that rushed in, as if there were an eternity of people, as well as of time and space. When the front waves rolled past, dragging the overtaken prison officers with them, and threatening them all with instant death if they failed to lead the mob to any secret place, Defarge grabbed one of these men—a gray-haired old man who had a lighted torch in his hand—separated him from the rest, and shoved him up against the wall.

"Show me the North Tower!" said Defarge. "Quick!"

"I will," replied the man, "follow me. But there is no one there."

"What is the meaning of One Hundred and Five, North Tower?" asked Defarge. "Quick!"

"The *meaning*, Monsieur?" "Is it the identification of a prisoner, or a place—a cell? Or does it mean that I must kill you now?"

"Kill him!" croaked Jacques Three, who had come nearby.

"Monsieur, it is a cell."

"Show it to me!"

"Come this way, then."

Jacques Three, craving bloodshed as usual, and disappointed by the fact that this jailer was probably going to be spared, held onto Defarge's arm as Defarge held onto the jailer's. The noise of the ocean of rebels was so loud as it flooded into the fallen Fortress, that the three men could barely hear one another

❷ *Where have we heard "One Hundred Five, North Tower" before?*

during this brief conversation, even though their three heads had leaned very closely in toward one another. Everywhere outside, too, the angry sea beat the walls with a deep, hoarse roar. Occasionally, some partial shouts of tumult broke and leaped into the air like spray.

Defarge, the jailer, and Jacques Three—still holding one another's arms—ran as fast as they could through gloomy vaults where the light of day had never shone, past hideous doors of dark dens and cages, down cavernous flights of steps, and again up steep rugged staircases of stone and brick—more like dry waterfalls than staircases. Here and there—especially at first—the sea of men came toward them and swept by. But when they had descended as far as they could, and were winding and climbing up a tower, they were alone. Surrounded by the massive thickness of walls and arches, the storm raging both inside and outside of the Fortress was dull and subdued, as if they'd been made deaf by the noise they'd just left.

The jailer stopped at a low door, put a key in a clashing lock, swung the door slowly open, and said, as they all bent their heads and went in, "One hundred and five, North Tower!"

There was a small, heavily-grated window—without glass—high in the wall, with a stone wall in front of it, so that the sky could be only seen by stooping low and looking up. There was a small chimney, also heavily barred, a few feet within the cell. There was a heap of old feathery wood ashes on the hearth. There was a stool, and a table, and a straw bed. There were the four blackened walls, with a rusted iron ring in one of them.

"Pass that torch slowly along these walls, so I can see them," said Defarge to the jailer.

The man obeyed, and Defarge followed the light closely with his eyes.

"Stop! Look here, Jacques!"

"A. M.!" croaked Jacques Three, as he read greedily. "Alexandre Manette," said Defarge in his ear,

❷ What is the significance of this cell?

tracing the letters with his blackened forefinger, deeply stained with gunpowder. "And here he wrote 'a poor physician.' And it was most likely he who scratched a calendar on this stone. What is that in your hand? A crowbar? Give it to me!"

He knocked the worm-eaten stool and table over, and easily beat them to pieces.

"Hold the light higher!" he said, angrily, to the jailer. "Examine those pieces carefully, Jacques. And look! Here is my knife," throwing it to him; "rip open that bed, and search the straw. Hold the light higher, you!" With a menacing look at the jailer, he climbed onto the hearth, and, peering up the chimney, struck and pried at its sides with the crowbar. He worked at the iron grating across it. In a few minutes, some mortar and dust came dropping down, and he turned his face to avoid it. He groped furiously through the fallen mortar and dust. He groped through the wood ashes. He groped in a crack in the chimney that his crowbar had either discovered or made.

"Nothing in the wood, and nothing in the straw, Jacques?"

"Nothing."

"Let us collect them together, in the middle of the cell. So! Light them, you!"

The jailer lit the little pile, which blazed high and hot. Stooping again to exit through the low-arched door, they left the fire burning, and retraced their way to the courtyard. Their hearing seemed to return, and soon they were in the raging flood once more.

They found it surging and tossing, looking for Defarge himself. Saint Antoine demanded to have its wine shop keeper leading the force that was watching the governor who had defended the Bastille and shot at the people. Without Defarge, the governor could not be marched to the Hôtel de Ville for judgment. He might escape, and the people's blood—which all of a sudden seemed to have some value, after many years of being worthless—would go unavenged.

In the swirling mass of confusion that surrounded

❷ *What do you suppose they are looking for?*

❷ *Notice how the language used in this long episode reflects the rhythm of the mob.*

this grim-faced officer, looking extremely out of place in his gray coat and red decoration, there was only one calm figure—a woman. "See, there is my husband!" she cried, pointing him out. "See Defarge!" She stood immovable, close to the grim, old officer and remained immovable, close to him. She remained immovable and close to him as they marched through the streets, and as Defarge and the rest dragged him along. She remained immovable, close to him when the mob approached its destination, and began to hit him from behind. She remained immovable, close to him when the growing rain of stabs and punches fell heavy on him, and was so close to him when he dropped dead under it. Then, as if suddenly coming to life, she put her foot on his neck, and—with her cruel knife—cut off his head.

The time had finally come when Saint Antoine was to carry out his horrible plan of hanging men in place of the lamps that swung over the streets of the neighborhood and show his power and his true character. Saint Antoine's passion was afire, and the Reign of Terror had begun, on the steps of the Hotel de Ville where the governor's body lay, and on the sole of the shoe of Madame Defarge where she had stepped on the body to keep it steady for her knife.

"Lower the lamp over there!" cried the people of Saint Antoine, after searching for a new means of death to satisfy their lust, "Here is one of the governor's soldiers!" The lamp was lowered. The governor's soldier was hanged, and the sea rushed on.

This was a sea of dark and threatening waters, wave after wave of uncontrolled destruction, whose depth and force were not yet known. This sea of violently swaying shapes, voices of vengeance, and faces so hardened by suffering that they offered no hint of pity and felt no shame or guilt at their actions.

But, in this ocean of fierce and furious faces, there were two groups of faces—each seven in number—so completely different from the rest. The first seven were the faces of prisoners, suddenly released by the

Remember how Dickens personifies Saint Antoine when talking about the residents of the neighborhood.

storm that had burst open their prison. These were carried high overhead like champions—all frightened, lost, and amazed. For them it was as if the Last Day had come, and those who rejoiced around them were lost spirits.

The other seven faces there were seven dead faces, whose drooping eyelids and half-closed eyes now awaited the Last Day. They were impassive faces, but not expressionless. Instead, they lay in a fearful pause, as if they would jump to life at any moment and accuse the angry mob of their unjust murders.

Seven prisoners were released. Seven gory heads were stuck on pikes. The keys of the accursed Fortress with the eight strong towers, along with some discovered letters and other memorials of prisoners were carried triumphantly through the streets of Paris on this day in mid July of 1789. Heaven protect Lucie Darnay and those she loves, and keep her frightful dream about footsteps entering her life from coming true. These people are mad and the blood they spill, unlike the word written on the muddy wall of Defarge's wine shop so many years ago, will not be so easily cleaned up.

✔ *Note the discovery of prisoners' letters, and remember how Defarge was searching for something in Doctor Manette's old cell.*

THIS IS THE END OF THE EIGHTEENTH WEEKLY INSTALLMENT.

Writing Opportunity:

Explain how the imagery of the weather in the first part of the chapter foreshadows the building political storm across the English Channel.

Research Opportunity:

Research and report on the actual events surrounding the storming of the Bastille on July 14, 1789. How "accurate" is Dickens's account? What purpose would Dickens have for making the changes he made?

A Tale of Two Cities

CHARLES DICKENS

CHAPTER XXII
The Sea Still Rises

ONE WEEK AFTER Saint Antoine's unbelievable triumph, Madame Defarge sat at her counter, as usual, watching her customers. Madame Defarge wore no rose in her head, for the great brotherhood of Spies had learned—even in one short week—to stay out of this neighborhood. The lamps across the streets had a dangerously elastic swing with them.

Madame Defarge, with her arms folded, sat in the morning light and heat, studying the wine shop and the street outside. In both, there were several groups of loiterers—poor, filthy, and miserable—but now with a visible sense of power enthroned on their suffering. The most ragged nightcap, sitting crookedly on the most wretched head, seemed to say, "I know how hard it is for me to sustain my life, but do you know how easy it is for me to destroy your life?" Every thin, bare arm that had been without work before, could always take up the work of killing. The fingers of the knitting women were vicious, knowing that they now also had the power to destroy. The anger long below the surface of Saint Antoine could now safely be shown on his face.

Madame Defarge sat observing it. She approved so fully of the change in her people's understanding

❤ *Explain this vague reference to the swinging of the lamps in connection with the spies.*

❷ *What has changed in the hearts and minds of the residents of Saint Antoine?*

of themselves that it was hard for her to suppress a devilish smile as she stood in her shop, knitting. One of her sisterhood knitted beside her. The short, rather plump wife of a starved grocer, and the mother of two children, this companion had already earned the nickname of *the Vengeance*.

"Listen!" said the Vengeance. "Listen, then! Who's coming?"

A murmur flew through Saint Antoine to the wine shop, much like a flame along a trail of gunpowder.

"It is Defarge," said Madame. "Silence, patriots!" Defarge came in breathless, pulled off a red cap he wore, and looked around him! "Listen, everyone!" said Madame again. "Listen to him!"

Panting, Defarge stood against a background of eager eyes and open mouths that formed outside the door. All those within the wine shop had sprung to their feet.

"Say then, my husband. What is it?"

"News from the other world!"

"What are you talking about?" cried Madame, contemptuously. "The other world?"

"Does everybody here recall old Foulon, who told the famished people that they might eat grass, and who died, and went to Hell?"

"Everybody!" from all throats.

"The news is of him. He is among us!"

"Among us!" from the universal throat again. "And dead?"

"Not dead! He feared us so much—and with reason—that he had his people *say* that he was dead. They even had a grand mock funeral. But they have found him alive, hiding in the country, and have brought him in. I have just seen him on his way to the Hotel de Ville, a prisoner. I have said that he had reason to fear us. Say all! Had he reason?"

Wretched old sinner of more than seventy years— if he did not know his sin, he certainly knew of it now.

A moment of profound silence followed. Defarge

and his wife looked steadily at one another. The Vengeance stooped, and the beat of a drum was heard as she moved it at her feet behind the counter.

"Patriots!" said Defarge, in a determined voice, "Are we ready?"

Instantly Madame Defarge's knife was in her girdle; the drum was beating in the streets. The Vengeance, uttering terrific shrieks, and flinging her arms about her head like all the forty Furies at once, was tearing from house to house, rousing the women.

The men were terrible, in the bloody-minded anger with which they looked from windows, took up any weapons they had and came pouring down into the streets. The women, however, would freeze blood that had already been chilled. They jumped up from their household work, from their infants and their sick, and poured out into the streets, shrieking and gnashing their teeth.

Villain Foulon captured, my sister! Old Foulon arrested, my mother!

Criminal Foulon caught, my daughter!

Then, twenty more women joined these, beating their breasts, tearing their hair, and screaming.

Foulon alive!

Foulon who told the starving people they might eat grass!

Foulon who told my old father that he might eat grass, when I had no bread to give him!

Foulon who told my baby it might suck grass, when these breasts where dry!

O mother of God, this Foulon!

O Heaven our suffering! Hear me, my dead baby and my withered father: I swear on my knees, on these stones, to avenge you on Foulon!

Husbands, and brothers, and young men, Give us the blood of Foulon, Give us the head of Foulon, Give us the heart of Foulon, Give us the body and soul of Foulon, Shred Foulon to pieces, and dig him into the ground, that grass may grow from him!

With these cries, great numbers of women whirled

In Greek mythology, the Furies or Erynies were the goddesses of vengeance: Tisiphone (avenger of murder), Megaera (the jealous) and Alecto (constant anger). Their role was to be merciless in punishing all crime including the violating of basic social principles. When the state failed to uphold its own law or protect all of its citizens from wrong, the Furies would avenge the wrongs done to the powerless. They would protect beggars and strangers, even helpless animals. They are depicted with snakes for hair and blood dripping from their eyes. (But, they are not to be confused with the Gorgons who also had snakes growing from their heads.) From them come the words "furious" and "infuriated."

about, hitting and scratching their own friends until they dropped into a passionate faint, and were saved from being trampled only by the men.

Nevertheless, not a moment was lost. Not a moment! This Foulon was at the Hôtel de Ville, and might be set free. Armed men and women flocked out of the Quarter so fast that they created almost a suction so that, a mere fifteen minutes later, not a human creature remained in Saint Antoine except for a few old crones and crying children.

No. They were all by that time cramming into the Hall of Examination where this old man—ugly and wicked—was. When the Hall could simply hold no more, the bloodthirsty "patriots" overflowed into the street. The Defarges, husband and wife, the Vengeance, and Jacques Three, were in the first group to arrive, and stood very close to Foulon in the Hall.

"See!" cried Madame, pointing with her knife. "See the old villain bound with ropes. That was a nice touch to tie a bunch of grass upon his back. Ha, ha! That was well done. Let him eat it now!" Madame put her knife under her arm, and clapped her hands just as if she were at a play.

Once the crowd began to notice the grass in Foulon's hands, the applause throughout the Hall grew. Eventually, the sun rose so high that it shone directly down on the old prisoner's head, as if to offer some sign of blessing or protection. Such a sign was too much to bear, and Saint Antoine immediately mobbed him!

Everyone—even those at the farthest rear of the crowd—heard the news immediately—that Defarge had but sprung over a railing and a table, and grabbed the hated villain in a deadly embrace. Madame Defarge followed close behind and cut one of the ropes with which he was tied—the Vengeance and Jacques Three had not yet caught up with them, and the men at the windows had not yet swooped into the Hall, like vultures, when the cry seemed to resound throughout the city, "Bring him out! Bring him to the lamp!"

They dragged him down, and then up, and then head first on the steps of the building. They dropped him onto his knees. Then they dragged him up onto his feet, and then threw him down on his back again. He was dragged, and hit, and choked by the bunches of grass and straw that were shoved into his mouth by hundreds of hands. He was torn, bruised, panting, bleeding—always begging for mercy. At one moment, there was a frenzy of action. Next there was a lull as the people pulled each other away from his so they could see. Then, he was pulled—like a log of dead wood dragged through a forest of legs—to the nearest street corner where one of the fatal lamps swung. There Madame Defarge let him go—just as a cat might have done to a mouse—and silently and calmly looked at him while they got ready, and while he begged her, begged all of the women who were furiously screeching at him the whole time. The men sternly shouted to have him killed with grass in his mouth. Once, he was hoisted up, but the rope broke, and they caught him as he fell—shrieking. They pulled him up a second time, and the rope broke, and they caught him again—shrieking. Finally the rope was merciful and held him. He was no sooner dead, than they cut off his head and stuck it on a high pike, with enough grass in its mouth to delight all of Saint Antoine.

This was not the end of Saint Antoine's wrath that day—Foulon's son-in-law soon swayed beside the old man, and then the crowd found out that another of the people's enemies and insulters, was coming into Paris under a guard five hundred strong, in cavalry alone. Saint Antoine wrote his crimes on flaring sheets of paper, seized him—indeed, they would have torn him out of the heart of an army to keep Foulon company— set his head and heart on pikes, and carried the three spoils of the day, in a parade through the streets.

Not until long after dark night had fallen did the men and women come back to the children, wailing and breadless. Then, the miserable bakers' shops were beset by long lines of hungry Frenchmen, patiently

Notice how Dickens emphasizes the crowd's poverty by comparing them to strings, and pointing out the smallness of their lights and fires because they could not afford fuel.

Note Madame Defarge's response. She is still not completely satisfied.

What is the "voice of the drum" that has not changed?

waiting to buy bad bread. While they waited with stomachs so empty they were near fainting, they passed the time by congratulating each other on the triumphs of the day, replaying them over and over again in their conversations. Gradually, these strings of ragged people shortened and frayed away, and then poor lights began to shine in high windows, and slender fires were made in the streets, at which neighbors cooked in common, afterwardss supping at their doors.

These suppers were just as insufficient as before—no meat and little sauce to accompany the bread. Yet, the bread was made a little more enjoyable by being shared with loved ones, and there was an air of cheerfulness throughout the district. Fathers and mothers—who had been tearing at their enemies throughout the day—played gently with their children. Lovers still lived in a world of poverty, hunger, and disease, but this night they were able to love and hope.

It was almost morning, when the last customers left Defarge's wine shop. While fastening the door, Monsieur Defarge said to his wife, in husky tones, "Our triumph has come at last, my dear!"

"Eh well!" returned Madame. "Almost."

Saint Antoine slept. The Defarges slept. Even the Vengeance slept with her husband, the starved grocer, and the drum was at rest. The drum's voice was the only one in Saint Antoine that the violence had not changed. The Vengeance, as custodian of the drum, could have wakened it up and it would have sounded exactly as it did before the Bastille fell, or old Foulon was seized. But the voice of Saint Antoine had changed forever.

Writing Opportunity:

Consider the mood of the residents of Saint Antoine at the end of this chapter. In what ways is this mood ironic? Use evidence from the text to support your answer.

A Tale of Two Cities

CHARLES DICKENS

CHAPTER XXIII
Fire Rises

THE VILLAGE WHERE the fountain had been poisoned by Gaspard's corpse was different in these days. The prison on the crag was not so dominant. There were still soldiers to guard it, but not many. There were still officers to guard the soldiers, but not one of them knew what his men would do, except that they would not follow orders.

Far and wide lay a ruined country. Every green leaf, every blade of grass and blade of grain, was as shriveled and poor as the miserable people. Everything was bowed down, dejected, oppressed, and broken. Homes, fences, farm animals, men, women, children, and the soil that fed them—all worn out.

The noble class in France often had worthy individuals in it. It was a national blessing, gave a noble tone to things, was a polite example of what a luxurious and shining life could be. Nevertheless, the Aristocracy were the class that had, somehow or other, brought things to this desperate extreme. As they believed Creation had been designed entirely for their enjoyment, it was strange that It should be completely used up so soon! God must surely be shortsighted! But the best that France could produce did indeed seem to be used up. And now that the last drop of blood had

> ✔ Remember, this is the village of the Marquis St. Evremonde, who was murdered by Gaspard. His nephew, Charles Darnay, is now the Marquis.

> ✔ Many historians note that the winter of 1787-1788 had been brutal with heavy snows and freezing temperatures. The muddy spring that flooded acres of farmland and made it impossible for farmers to plant, was followed by a severe drought the summer of 1789. The devastation of this drought is what Dickens is describing here.

> ✔ Don't miss the sarcasm here.

A "score" equals twenty—as in Lincoln's famous "Four score and seven years ago…"

Explain the allusion of "returning to dust."

also been squeezed from the classes below, and their anger had begun to threaten his life, the aristocracy began to run away.

However, the aristocracy's absence was not the change seen now. For scores of years gone by, whoever happened to hold the land had squeezed it and wrung it, but had seldom actually *visited* it except for his hunting vacations. No, the change consisted in the appearance of strange faces of low class, rather than in the disappearance of the high class.

For, in these times, as the mender of roads worked, alone, in the dust, seldom bothering to think that *dust he was and to dust he must return*, because he was too busy thinking how little he had for supper and how much more he would eat if he had it. In these times, as he raised his eyes from his lonely labor, and studied the view, he would see some rough figure approaching on foot. In earlier times, such strangers were rare, but now one saw them all the time. As the figure approached, the mender of roads was not surprised to see that it was a shaggy-haired man, looking like a barbarian, tall. He wore wooden shoes that even the mender of roads could tell were clumsy. The stranger was grim, rough, dark-skinned, caked in the mud and dust of many highways, damp with the moisture of many low marshes, sprinkled with the thorns and leaves and moss of many shortcuts through woods.

A man like this came upon him, like a ghost, at noon in the July weather, as he sat on his heap of stones under a bank, hiding from a shower of hail.

The man looked at him, looked at the village in the hollow, at the mill, and at the prison on the crag. When he had identified these objects, he said, in a dialect that was just understandable:

"How goes it, Jacques?"

"All well, Jacques."

"Shake hands, then!"

They shook hands, and the man sat down on the heap of stones.

"No dinner?"

"Nothing but supper now," said the mender of roads, with a hungry face.

"It is the same everywhere," growled the man. "I meet no dinner anywhere."

He took out a blackened pipe, filled it, lighted it with flint and steel, inhaled on it until it was in a bright glow. He then, suddenly held it away from him and dropped something into it from between his finger and thumb, that blazed and went out in a puff of smoke.

"Shake hands, then." The mender of roads said it this time, after watching these operations. They again shook hands.

"Tonight?" said the mender of roads.

"Tonight," said the man, putting the pipe in his mouth.

"Where?"

"Here."

He and the mender of roads sat on the heap of stones looking silently at one another, with the hail driving in between them, until the sky began to clear over the village.

"Show me!" said the traveler then, moving to the top of the hill.

"See!" returned the mender of roads, with extended finger. "You go down here, and straight through the street, and past the fountain—"

"Forget all that!" interrupted the traveler, rolling his eye over the landscape. "I won't go through any streets or past any fountains. So?"

"About two miles beyond the top of that hill above the village."

"Good. When do you finish work?"

"At sunset."

"Will you wake me, before you leave? I have walked two nights without resting. Let me finish my pipe, and I'll sleep like a child. Will you wake me?"

"Of course."

"Dinner" refers to the midday meal while "supper" refers to the evening meal. The mender of roads is saying there is not enough food for what we would call "lunch."

The wayfarer smoked his pipe out, put it in his breast pocket, slipped off his great wooden shoes, and lay down on his back on the heap of stones. He was fast asleep almost immediately.

As the road-mender did his dusty labor, and the hail-clouds, rolling away, revealed bright bars and streaks of sky, he was fascinated by the figure on the heap of stones. His eyes were so often turned toward him, that he used his tools without thinking, and very poorly. The bronze face, the shaggy black hair and beard, the coarse woolen red cap, the rough mixed dress of homemade stuff and hairy skins of beasts, the powerful frame thinned by spare living, and the sullen and desperate tightness of the lips in sleep, filled the mender of roads with awe. The traveler had traveled far, and his feet were sore, and his ankles chafed and bleeding. His huge shoes, stuffed with leaves and grass, had been heavy to drag over the many long miles, and his clothes had worn into holes, just as he himself had worn into sores. Stooping down beside him, the road-mender tried to get a peek at secret weapons in his pockets. But his attempt failed, for the traveler slept with his arms crossed upon him, and set as firmly as his lips. Fortified towns with their stockades, guard-houses, gates, trenches, and drawbridges, seemed to be nothing more than air against this figure. And when he lifted his eyes from him to the horizon and looked around, he imagined similar men—which no obstacle could stop—heading to danger and adventure all over France.

The man slept on—through hail, sunshine, and shadow, until the sun was low in the west, and the sky was glowing. Then, the mender of roads got his tools together and, ready to go down into the village, awoke him.

"Good!" said the sleeper, rising on his elbow. "Two miles beyond the top of the hill?"

"Approximately."

"Approximately. Good!"

The mender of roads went home—the strong wind

pushing the dust on ahead of him—and was soon at the fountain, squeezing himself in among the scrawny cows that had been brought there to drink. After the village had eaten its meager supper, it did not creep to bed, as it usually did, but came outdoors again, and remained there. Whispering spread through them all, and then they all turned and stared off in the same direction. Monsieur Gabelle, chief official of the place, became uneasy; went out on his housetop alone, and looked in that direction too. He glanced down from behind his chimneys at the darkening faces by the fountain below, and sent word to the sexton who kept the keys of the church, that there might be need to ring the bell before long.

The night darkened. The trees that surrounded the old chateau—keeping it isolated—swayed in the rising wind, as if to threaten the tremendous building—massive and dark in the gloom. Up the two terrace flights of steps the rain ran wildly, and beat at the great door, like a swift messenger awakening everyone inside. Uneasy gusts of wind went through the hall, among the old spears and knives, and passed, lamenting, up the stairs, and shook the curtains of the bed where the last Marquis had slept. Through the woods, from East, West, North, and South, came four heavy-footed, disheveled figures, walking boldly yet cautiously into the courtyard. Four lights broke out there, and moved away in different directions, and all was black again.

But, not for long. Presently, the chateau began to be visible by some light of its own, as though it were glowing. Then, a flickering streak played behind the architecture of the front, picking out transparent places, and showing where balconies, arches, and windows were. Then it soared higher, and grew broader and brighter. Soon, from twenty of the great windows, flames burst forth, and the stone faces awakened, staring out from the fire.

The few people who still resided in the house sprung to what little action they could take. One

❷ *Notice that these men are very similar to the man who spent the afternoon napping while the mender of roads worked. We were told earlier in this chapter that such men used to be rare but had become familiar sights in recent days.*

❷ *What have the four men done to the chateau?*

man quickly saddled a horse and rode away. The horse, foaming at the mouth from a hard ride, arrived at Monsieur Gabelle's door. "Help, Gabelle! Help, every one!"

The alarm bell rang impatiently, but no other help appeared. The mender of roads and two hundred and fifty of his friends stood at the fountain, with their arms folded, staring at the pillar of fire in the sky. "It must be forty feet high," they said grimly. But they never moved.

The rider from the chateau, and the foaming horse, clattered away through the village, and galloped up the steep and stony hillside, to the prison on the crag. At the gate, a group of officers were looking at the fire. Standing a little way from them was a group of soldiers, also staring idly at the fire.

"Help, gentlemen—officers! The chateau is on fire, but we might still be in time to save some valuable objects from the flames ! Help, help!"

The officers looked at the soldiers, and the soldiers looked at the fire. The officers gave no orders, instead answering the rider with shrugs and biting their lips, "It'll have to burn."

As the rider rattled down the hill again and through the street, the village was lighting its lamps. The mender of roads, and his two hundred and fifty friends, acting as if they'd been inspired all at the same moment, had rushed into their houses, and were putting candles in every pane of glass in every window. Because *everything* was in short supply, the villagers had to "borrow" the candles from Monsieur Gabelle. When he hesitated to lend them out, the mender of roads—once so meek and humble—remarked that carriages would burn quite well, and that post horses would roast. The chateau was left to burn. In the roaring and raging of the inferno, a red-hot wind, driving straight from the depths of hell, seemed to be blowing the building away. With the rising and falling of the blaze, the stone faces looked as if they were in torment. When great masses of stone and timber fell, the face with the two dints in the nose was clouded in smoke. It soon struggled out of the smoke again, as if it were the face of the cruel Marquis, burning at the stake and fighting with the fire.

The chateau burned. The nearest trees, touched by the fire, scorched and shriveled. Trees at a distance, set on fire by the four fierce figures, surrounded the blazing building with a new forest of smoke. Molten lead and iron boiled in the marble basin of the fountain. The water ran dry. The water in the tops of the towers vanished like ice before the heat, and trickled down into four rugged wells of flame. The stone walls seemed to shatter in slow motion. Confused birds wheeled about and dropped into the furnace. The four fierce figures trudged away, East, West, North, and South, along the night-darkened roads, guided by the beacon they had lighted, toward their next destination. The illuminated village had seized hold of the bell, and, firing the lawful ringer, rang for joy.

Note how the bell was rung at first as a signal of distress, and now it is ringing as a signal of triumph.

Not only that, but the village, light-headed with hunger and the excitement of the fire, remembered that it was Monsieur Gabelle who collected taxes and rent. They did *not* remember that he had collected only a small portion of the taxes due and *no* rent since the death of the previous Marquis. The mob of villagers nonetheless suddenly desired to have an interview with him. They surrounded his house and shouted for him to come out. At that point, Monsieur Gabelle heavily barred his doors and went up to his roof, behind his stack of chimneys. This time he decided that—if his door were broken in—he'd toss himself head first over the wall, and crush a man or two below.

It was probably a long night for Monsieur Gabelle up on the roof, with the distant chateau for a lamp, the beating at his door, bell-clanging for music. Not to mention the fact that there was a street lamp slung across the road before his gatehouse, and the village was most eager to replace the lamp with him. The suspense was indeed difficult for Gabelle, spending an entire summer night on the brink of a black ocean, ready to take a deadly plunge into it if necessary as Monsieur Gabelle had resolved! However, the friendly dawn finally appeared. The candles went out, and the people scattered. Monsieur Gabelle came down, bringing his life with him for a short time longer.

Within a hundred miles, and in the light of other fires, there were other officials less fortunate that night and other nights, whom the rising sun found hanging across once-peaceful streets—where they had been born and lived their entire lives.

And there were other villagers and townspeople less fortunate than the mender of roads and his friends. In other villages and towns the officials and soldiers defended their government with success, and hanged the rebellious peasantry. The fierce figures, however, were steadily moving East, West, North, and South, and whether it was peasants or officials who hung, fire burned. It was impossible to figure out what sort of gallows would stop this crowd.

❷ *What gruesome invention is foreshadowed at the end of this weekly installment?*

THIS IS THE END OF THE
NINETEENTH WEEKLY INSTALLMENT.

Writing Opportunity:

Is Monsieur Gabelle the proper target of the villagers' anger? Why or why not? Use evidence from the text to support your answer.

Research Opportunity:

How did the French military respond to the growing Revolution? Research what actually happened in history, and report on how the monarchy was (or was not) supported by its soldiers.

A Tale of Two Cities

CHARLES DICKENS

CHAPTER XXIV
Drawn to the Loadstone Rock

THREE YEARS PASSED, filled with many similar risings of fire and risings of sea. For three years the firm earth was shaken by the rush of an angry ocean that now had no low tide, but was always pounding shore, higher and higher, to the terror and wonder of the people who witnessed it. Three more birthdays of little Lucie had been woven by the golden thread into the peaceful fabric of the life of her home.

For many nights and many days the residents of the little corner in Soho listened to the echoes. When the echoes were the sounds of marching feet, the residents grew afraid, for they imagined the footsteps to be the footsteps of an angry mob, under a red flag. With their country in danger, the mob had descended from humans into wild beasts.

Because the Aristocracy was not only not wanted in France, but stood a great chance of being killed in France, they had fled as best they could. Just like the farmer who spent years trying to summon the Devil, and—once he succeeded—was so frightened that he immediately ran away, the Aristocracy had done everything that could be done to raise up the "devil" of the oppressed peasantry only to be terrified by the risen peasants in their Hellish strength.

✪ *A loadstone, or lodestone (from the Old English word for "way," "journey," or "course") is a magnet, something that attracts. Here, of course, the reference is that the Manette-Darnay family will be irresistibly drawn into the situation in France.*

✪ *Explain the two key metaphors in this paragraph.*

✪ *This is possibly an allusion to one of Aesop's fables "The Old Man and Death":*
An old laborer, bent double with age and toil, was gathering sticks in a forest. He eventually grew so tired that he threw the bundle of sticks to the ground and cried out: "I can no longer stand this life. I wish Death would come and take me!"
As he spoke, Death—a skeleton in a black robe, carrying a scythe—appeared and demanded, "What do you want, Mortal?"
"Please, sir," replied the terrified woodcutter, "would you kindly help me to lift this bundle of sticks on to my shoulder?"
The moral of the story is that we should be careful what we wish for, for we just might get it.

◐ Note the metaphor here. Dickens is comparing the "circles" of the French Court: "from that exclusive inner circle to its outermost rotten ring..." to a bull's eye, which would be the target for the French revolutionaries.

◐ This brief passage is jammed full of allusions. The "mote" in the "eye" is an allusion to Matthew 7:3-5 in which Jesus criticizes hypocrites by telling them they cannot remove specks (imperfections) from their brothers' eyes until they remove huge chunks of imperfections from their own eyes.
"Lucifer's pride" is an allusion to a few debated passages in the Old Testament. Essentially, Lucifer was the brightest, most beautiful angel in Heaven—God's favorite—but he presumed to be equal to God and was cast out of Heaven—along with 144,000 of his followers. Thus, Pride is the first deadly sin, the sin of angels. These fallen angels became Satan and his demons in Hell. The allusion here is that the "shining circles" of the French court were blinded by their pride, overestimated their position and their worth, and ended up being cast out of France.

The shining Bull's Eye of the Court was gone, or it would have been the target for a hurricane of national bullets. It had never been a good eye to see with—had always been as blind as a mole with the "mote" Lucifer's pride in it. But the members of the various circles had all run away and were gone. The entire Court—from that exclusive inner circle to its outermost rotten ring of intrigue, corruption, and lies—was gone. Royalty was gone. It had been imprisoned in its Palace and "suspended."

August of the year 1792 had arrived, and the aristocracy was by this time scattered far and wide.

Of course, the headquarters and gathering place of the outcast French aristocracy in London was Tellson's Bank. Ghosts are supposed to haunt the places with which they were most familiar in life, and this now-penniless French aristocracy haunted the spot where their pennies used to be. Also, it was the place to which any reliable information about what was happening in France was likely to arrive first. Tellson's was a generous house, and was most lenient with old customers who had fallen from their high estate. Those nobles who had seen the coming storm in time, and—anticipating the mob's plundering their homes or confiscating their money—had wisely deposited their money with Tellson's, were always used as credit references by their poor brothers. As far as French information was concerned, Tellson's was—at that time—a kind of High Exchange. Because this was so well known to the public, and there were so many requests for news—any news—that Tellson's sometimes wrote a line or two about the latest news and posted it in the Bank's windows. That way anyone who ran through Temple Bar could read it.

On a hazy, humid afternoon, Mr. Lorry sat at his desk, and Charles Darnay stood leaning on it, talking with him in a low voice. The prison-like closet that had once been reserved for interviews with the manager, was now the News-Exchange, and was filled to overflowing. It was about half an hour or so before closing time.

"But, although you are the youngest man that ever lived," said Charles Darnay, hesitating a little before continuing, "I must still suggest to you—"

"I understand. You think I am too old?" said Mr. Lorry.

"Unsettled weather, a long journey, uncertain means of traveling, a disorganized country, a city that may not be even safe for you."

"My dear Charles," said Mr. Lorry, with cheerful confidence, "these are reasons to go, not to stay away. It is safe enough for me. Nobody will care to trouble an old man of nearly eighty when there are so many other people there more worth troubling. As far as its being a disorganized city, well...if it were *not* a disorganized city, there would be no reason to send anyone there, someone who knows the city and the business, someone Tellson's can trust. And, as for the uncertain traveling, the long journey, and the winter weather, well...if *I* can't inconvenience myself for the sake of Tellson's Bank, after all these years, then who can?"

"I wish I were going myself," said Charles Darnay, somewhat restlessly, as if he were thinking aloud.

"Well then! You're someone to give advice!" exclaimed Mr. Lorry. "You wish you were going yourself? You...a born Frenchman? You're a wise counselor."

"My dear Mr. Lorry, it is because I am a Frenchman, that the thought—which I really did not mean to say out loud—has occurred to me often. I can't help but think that—since I once had sympathy for them, and since I abandoned my property to them—that they might listen to me. I might be able to convince them to show some restraint. Only last night, after you had left us, when I was talking to Lucie—"

"When you were talking to Lucie," Mr. Lorry repeated. "Yes. I wonder you are not ashamed to even

❷ *Is Charles at all realistic in his thinking? Why or why not?*

mention her name! Wishing you were going to France at a time like this!"

"However, I am not going," said Charles Darnay, with a smile. "It is more to the purpose that you say you are."

"And, the truth is, I am going. The truth is, my dear Charles," Mr. Lorry glanced at the distant House, and lowered his voice, "you have no idea how difficult banking in France has become, and of the serious threat to our books and papers over there. The Lord above knows what would happen to any number of people, if some of our documents were seized or destroyed. And they might be, at any time, you know. For who can say that Paris won't be burned to the ground at any time! Now, I may be the only one who can go through those old records, decide what should be removed, and hurry back! And should I not volunteer when Tellson's admits this need?—Tellson's, whose bread I have eaten for sixty years—simply because my joints are a little stiff? Why, I am a mere boy compared to half a dozen old codgers here!"

"I do admire the gallantry of your youthful spirit, Mr. Lorry."

"Tut! Nonsense, sir!—And, my dear Charles," said Mr. Lorry, glancing at the House again, "you must remember, that getting things out of Paris—no matter what they are—is next to impossible right now. Just today, papers and precious matters were brought to us here by the strangest means you could imagine.—I speak in strict confidence. It is not business-like to whisper it, even to you.—And these unusual, unbelievable couriers—each and every one of them—barely made it safely through the Barriers. At any other time, our documents could come and go, just as easily as here in business-like Old England. But now, everything is stopped."

"And are you really going tonight?"

"I really go tonight. The business has simply become too important to put it off any longer."

"And no one is going with you?"

Used like this, the word "House" does not mean the banking establishment itself (Tellson's Banking House) but an officer of the bank— its president or chief officer.

The Barriers were gates in the city walls as well as along certain roads which had been constructed to collect tolls and taxes for people passing through them. After the Revolution, they were used as checkpoints to allow or deny travelers the right to pass through.

"All sorts of people have been suggested to me, but I won't have any of them. I intend to take Jerry. Jerry has been my bodyguard on Sunday nights for a long time, and I am used to him. Nobody will suspect Jerry of being anything but an English bull-dog, or of having any design in his head but to fly at anybody who touches his master."

"I must say again that I admire your bravery and youthfulness."

"And I must say again, nonsense, nonsense! When I have completed this small duty, then maybe I'll accept Tellson's proposal to retire and live a life of leisure. Then there will be time to think about growing old."

This conversation took place at Mr. Lorry's usual desk, with the exiled French aristocracy swarming within a yard or two of it, bragging about what they were going to do to get even with the "dishonest, disloyal, and ungrateful" French peasantry that had chased them out of the country. The former nobles were famous for insisting that this Revolution was not something that had been "brewing" for years. Their own delusions, combined with the ridiculous plots of the displaced aristocracy to restore France to a condition that had utterly worn itself out—and had worn out Heaven and earth as well—was hard for any sane man who knew the truth to endure without speaking up. And it was this kind of nonsense all around him—like an annoying ringing in his ears— that added to Charles Darnay's troubled mind, and made him so restless.

Among the talkers was Stryver of the King's Bench Bar. He had been very successful and was well on his way to state promotion. Promotion was therefore his favorite subject of conversation. He suggested to the complaining aristocracy an idea for blowing the French people up and exterminating them from the face of the earth. France could do without them. Darnay heard him, strongly moved to object. He stood, undecided whether he wanted to leave and hear no more of the man's stupidity, or stay and argue with him.

☑ Here's another of those
Dickensian coincidences: that
the letter should appear just
when Darnay is at Lorry's
desk to see the envelope.

The House approached Mr. Lorry, and laying a soiled and unopened letter before him, asked if he had yet discovered any traces of the person to whom it was addressed? The House laid the letter down so close to Darnay that he could read the address, fairly easily, in fact, because it was his own right name—his official name. Translated into English, the address read:

> Very Important. To the gentleman formerly known as the Marquis St. Evremonde, of France. Trusted into the care of Messrs. Tellson and Co., Bankers, London, England.

On the morning of his daughter's wedding, Doctor Manette had made it his one urgent and specific request of Charles Darnay—that the secret of this name be kept strictly between the two of them—unless he, the Doctor, freed Darnay from the promise. Nobody else knew this to be his name. Lucie herself had no suspicion of the fact. Neither had Mr. Lorry.

☑ Remember that Darnay is the
Marquis following the assassination of his uncle.

❷ Why do you suppose Charles
and the Doctor have insisted
on keeping Charles' true
identity a secret?

"No," said Mr. Lorry. "I think I have shown it to everybody now here, and no one can tell me where this gentleman is to be found."

Since it was almost closing time, many of the talkers began to walk past Mr. Lorry's desk. He held out the letter, and the aristocrats looked at it. Each and every dispossessed French nobleman had some unpleasant comment—either in French or in English—to make about the Marquis St. Evremonde.

"He's the nephew, I believe, of the Marquis who was murdered. Whatever the relationship, he's the Marquis' corrupt heir." said one. "I'm happy to say that I never knew him."

"A coward who abandoned his post," said another. This particular exiled noblemen had been—"a few years ago"—smuggled out of Paris, legs pointing up and half suffocated, in a load of hay.

"Infected with those new philosophies," said a third, eyeing the direction through his glass in passing;

"openly defied the last Marquis, abandoned his estates when he inherited them, and left them to the rabble peasants. But they'll give him what he deserves. I hope, anyway."

"Hey?" cried the blatant Stryver. "Did he though? Is that the sort of fellow? Let us look at his infamous name. Damn the fellow!"

Darnay, unable to restrain himself any longer, touched Mr. Stryver on the shoulder, and said, "I know him."

"Do you, by Jupiter?" said Stryver. "That is a shame."

"Why is it a shame?" Darnay asked, barely hiding his growing anger.

"Didn't you just hear what he did, Mr. Darnay? Don't ask, why, in these times."

"But I do ask why."

"Well, I'll say it again, Mr. Darnay, I am sorry to hear that you know him. I am sorry to hear that you don't seem to understand why I am sorry. Here is a fellow, who—infected by the most ridiculous and sinful ideas ever to be written about—has abandoned his property to the lowest scum of the earth. And you ask me why I am sorry that a man—a *teacher* no less—knows him? Well, I'll tell you why I'm sorry. I am sorry because I believe this scoundrel might be able to contaminate you. That's why."

Remembering his secret and his promise to Dr. Manette, Darnay—with great difficulty—controlled his anger and said, "You may not understand the gentleman."

"I understand how to put you in a corner, Mr. Darnay," said Stryver, the bully, "and I'll do it. If you call this fellow is a gentleman, then I *don't* understand him. And you may tell him so, with my compliments. You may also tell him—from me—that after abandoning his worldly goods and position to this mob of butchers, it's a wonder that he's not their chief and leader. But, no, gentlemen," said Stryver, looking all around, and snapping his fingers, "I know a little something about

In terms of philosophy, the eighteenth century is called "The Age of Reason," or "The Enlightenment." Thinkers and writers like Voltaire, Jean Jacques Rousseau, Thomas Paine, Thomas Jefferson, etc., wrote about the rights of human beings, the idea that all humans are equal, that governments exist to serve the people, and so forth. The American Revolutionary War was founded on Enlightenment philosophies and was an inspiration to many nations, including France. We have already seen that Charles Darnay agrees with many Enlightenment ideals. These are the "new philosophies" the other men criticized him for having.

Where is the irony in this exchange?

According to the Oxford English Dictionary, to "drive [someone] into a corner" is to put him or her into a difficult situation from which it will be difficult to escape.

human nature, and I tell you that you'll never find a person like this…this *Evremonde*, trusting himself to the mercies of the people he claims to love so much. No, gentlemen, he'll always show them a clean pair of heels very early in the fight, and sneak away."

"With those words, and one last snap of his fingers, Mr. Stryver shouldered himself into Fleet Street, amidst the applause and cheers of the crowd of exiles. Mr. Lorry and Charles Darnay were left alone at Lorry's desk, as the crowd made its way from the Bank.

"Will you take charge of the letter?" asked Mr. Lorry. "You know where to deliver it?"

"I do."

"Try to explain to him, that we imagine the letter was addressed here because the sender probably thought we would know where to forward it. It has been here quite a while."

"I will do so. Do you start for Paris from here?"

"From here, at eight."

"I will come back, to see you off."

Very upset with himself, and with Stryver and most other men, Darnay made his way into the quiet of the Temple, opened the letter, and read it. These were its contents:

Prison of the Abbaye, Paris.
June 21, 1792.

TO THE GENTLEMAN FORMERLY KNOWN
AS THE MARQUIS,

After having long been in danger of my life at the hands of the village, I have been seized, with great violence and indignity, and brought a long journey on foot to Paris. On the road I have suffered a great deal. Nor is that all; my house has been destroyed—razed to the ground.

The crime for which I am imprisoned, Sir, and for which I will be called before the Tribunal, and for which I will lose my life—without your so generous help)—is, they tell me, Treason against the Majesty of the People. They say I have acted *against* them for an emigrant.

It has been useless, but I have tried to tell them that I have acted *for* them, and not against, just as you commanded.

It has been useless, but I have tried to tell them that, even *before* the Republic seized the property of emigrants, I returned to them the taxes they had already stopped paying, that I had collected no rent, that I opposed no punishments. Their only response is, that I acted on behalf of an emigrant, and *where is that emigrant?* Ah! most gracious Sir, *where is that emigrant?* I cry in my sleep *where is he?* I demand of Heaven, will he not come to save me? But I receive no answer. Ah, Sir, I send my desperate cry across the sea, hoping it may perhaps reach your ears through the great bank of Tellson.

For the love of Heaven…for the love of justice … for the love of generosity…for the honor of your noble name, I beg you, Sir, to help me and set me free.

My only crime is that I have been true to you. Oh, Sir, I pray that you will now be true to me!

From this horrible, horrible prison, where every passing hour brings me closer to my execution, I send you, kind Sir, the assurance of my sad service.

> Your afflicted,
> GABELLE.

An emigrant is a person who leaves his or her country to live in another. In the "republic" that was formed during the French Revolution, it was a capital crime to emigrate from France. All emigrants (most of the aristocracy) lost all property they left behind, and faced execution if they returned.

The uneasiness that lay hidden in the back of Darnay's mind was brought front and center by this letter. He felt such shame and guilt at the thought of an old servant—a *faithful,* old servant—being in trouble for no crime other than loyalty to him that he paced back and forth in the Temple, trying to decide what to do. He was so ashamed of himself that he almost hid his face from people who passed by where he paced.

He knew very well that he had acted imperfectly— in his horror of the deed which had established his family's bad reputation—in his resentment and distrust of his uncle—and in the hatred he felt for the crumbling social system he was supposed to enforce. He knew very well that he had acted too impulsively— in his love for Lucie and his desire to turn his back on

Note the reference to a single deed that set the family's reputation.

his social "rank and privilege." Disowning his family and surrendering his estates had not been a *new* idea to him, but he knew that he should have been more systematic in how he did it. He should have supervised transferring ownership of the land to the peasants who lived on it. At one time he had *intended* to do it, but it had never been done.

He had been so happy his own chosen English home. Having refused his inheritance, he'd *always* had to work, and the condition in France had deteriorated so *quickly*. Truly, the events of this week completely wiped from memory the events of last week, and the events of next week would simply be a repeat of last week's. He knew very well that he had simply given in to circumstances, rather than taking control of the situation as he should have. He had been troubled by the way he'd handled matters, but he had done nothing to fix it. He had looked for a good time to act, but everything happened so quickly and, all of a sudden, it was already too late. The aristocracy were fleeing France by every highway and byway, and their property was being confiscated and destroyed. Their very names were being blotted out. He knew all this as well as any new authority in France who might criticize him for it.

But, he had oppressed no man. He had imprisoned no man. He was so unwilling to demand the legal rents and dues to which he was entitled, that he had freely given them up. He had thrown himself into the world with no privilege of rank or family. He had established his own life for himself, and earned his own bread. Monsieur Gabelle had run the poor, debt-ridden estate—on written instructions—to spare the people, to give them what little there was to give—whatever fuel the heavy creditors would let them have in the winter—whatever fruits and vegetables the creditors would allow in the summer. No doubt Gabelle had tried to explain these facts, for his own safety, but the appearance of harshness was too clear. Gabelle would need proof.

❷ *Why is it important for us to know that the estate is "debt-ridden"?*

And so Charles Darnay decided that he would go to Paris.

Yes. Like the seaman in the old story, the winds and currents drove him within reach of the Loadstone Rock, and now it was pulling him to itself. He could not resist. Every single thought in his mind led him undeniably to that terrible attraction. His inner discomfort had always been that evil people with evil intentions were performing evil actions in his native country of France, and that he, Charles Darnay—who knew that he was far better than they—was not there. Surely he could do *something* to lessen the bloodshed, and encourage the angry, vengeful mob to be merciful and humane.

Half ignoring his sense of what he had to do and half tortured by it, he had to compare himself with Mr. Lorry, an eighty-year-old gentleman who fulfilled his sense of duty without question. In that comparison, he, Darnay, was the lesser man. Then the sneers of the other exiled noblemen and Stryver's accusation that he'd turned his back on his duty stung him bitterly. Then came Gabelle's letter—the plea of an innocent man, imprisoned and in danger of being sentenced to death—asking him to live up to his sense of honor and do his duty.

His resolution was made. He must go to Paris.

Yes. The Loadstone Rock was drawing him, and he must sail on, until he landed. He knew of no rock. He saw hardly any danger. Since everything he had done—even though he had only half-done it—was motivated by good intentions, surely the rebelling peasants in France would be grateful to him when he arrived and listen to his testimony on behalf of Gabelle.

Then, that glorious vision of doing good—which is so often the cheerful delusion of so many good minds—arose before him. He even saw himself as something of a hero, arriving home to guide this raging Revolution that was running so fearfully wild.

As he paced back and forth with his resolution

In "The Tale of the Third Calendar, a King's Son," from The Arabian Nights, *the narrator is shipwrecked on the "Black Mountain," an island-sized loadstone rock. The attraction of this magnet is so strong that it pulls all of the nails out of the ship's boards, and the ship sinks, leaving the narrator as the sole survivor. The point is that Charles Darnay is being pulled irresistibly to disaster in France, just as the narrator's ship was destroyed as it was pulled to the Black Mountain.*

made, he considered that neither Lucie nor her father must know of it until he was gone. Lucie should be spared the pain of separation, and her father—who was always reluctant to remember his own troubled past—should know about it as something *already done* and not have to anticipate it with dread. He did not consider how much his refusal to settle his affairs in France had to do with his unwillingness to frighten the Doctor. But, that circumstance too, had had its influence in his course. He continued to pace back and forth, busy in his thoughts, until it was time to return to Tellson's and say good-bye to Mr. Lorry. As soon as he arrived in Paris, he would present himself to this old friend, but he wouldn't mention his plan now.

Note, again, the hint that Charles's family history might have something to do with Dr. Manette's imprisonment.

A carriage with post horses was ready at the Bank door, and Jerry was booted and equipped.

"I have delivered that letter," said Charles Darnay to Mr. Lorry. "I would not consent to your being charged with any written answer, but perhaps you will take a verbal one?"

"I will," said Mr. Lorry, "if it is not dangerous."

"Not at all. Though it is to a prisoner in the Abbaye."

"What is his name?" said Mr. Lorry, with his open notepad in his hand.

"Gabelle."

"Gabelle. And what is the message to the unfortunate Gabelle in prison?"

"Simply, that he has received the letter, and will come."

"Any time mentioned?"

"He will start upon his journey tomorrow night."

"Any person mentioned?"

"No."

He helped Mr. Lorry to wrap himself in a number of coats and cloaks, and went out with him from the warm atmosphere of the old Bank, into the misty air of Fleet Street. "My love to Lucie, and to little Lucie," said Mr. Lorry at parting, "and take precious care of them till I come back." Charles Darnay shook his head and doubtfully smiled, as the carriage rolled away.

That night—it was the fourteenth of August—he sat up late, and wrote two emotional letters. One was to Lucie, explaining the strong obligation he was under to go to Paris, and explaining to her, in great detail, why he was so confident that he would be in no personal danger while there. The other letter was to the Doctor, entrusting Lucie and their dear child to his care, and also expressing his confidence in his safety. To both, he wrote that he would send letters as proof of his safety, immediately after his arrival.

It was a hard day, that last day among them, with this first separation of their lives together on his mind. It was hard to maintain the innocent lie of which they were profoundly unsuspicious. But, an affectionate glance at his wife, so happy and busy, made him resolute not to tell her what was coming. Indeed, it was so strange for him to do *anything* without her knowledge and assistance that he had considered telling her. Still, the day passed quickly. Early in the evening he embraced his wife and daughter, pretending that he had an appointment and would be home very soon. He'd already hidden a suitcase of clothing, and so he stepped out into the heavy mist of the heavy streets, with a heavier heart.

The unseen force was drawing him tightly to itself now, and all the tides and winds were setting straight and strong toward it. He left his two letters with a reliable messenger, to be delivered half an hour before midnight, and no sooner, and began his journey. "For the love of Heaven...for the love of justice...for the love of generosity...for the honor of your noble name!" was the poor prisoner's cry with which he strengthened his sinking heart, as he left all that was dear on earth behind him, and floated away for the Loadstone Rock.

THIS IS THE END OF THE
TWENTIETH WEEKLY INSTALLMENT.

THE END OF THE SECOND BOOK.

Research Opportunity:

Research some of the writers of the Enlightenment and report on their ideas, their sources, and the effects of their ideas.

Writing Opportunity:

Write an essay in which you discuss the suspenseful note on which this second book ends, and what you predict might happen in the remaining book.

A Tale of Two Cities

CHARLES DICKENS

BOOK THE THIRD. THE TRACK OF A STORM

CHAPTER I

In Secret

IT WAS SLOW going for travelers journeying from England to Paris in the autumn of 1792. There would have been more than enough of bad roads, bad carriages, and bad horses to delay him, even if there had been no revolution in France, but, the changed times brought other obstacles as well. Every town gate and village taxing house had its band of citizen-patriots, with their muskets—loaded and ready. Their role was to stop everyone who passed, cross-question them, inspect their papers, look for their names in lists of their own, turn them back, or send them on, or stop them and arrest them, as they pleased. All this was supposedly for the good of the new Republic—One and Indivisible—of Liberty, Equality, Fraternity, *or Death.* Charles Darnay had not traveled very far into France before he realized that he had no hope of leaving and returning to England until he was declared a "good citizen" at Paris. Whatever might happen, there was no turning back. Well he knew that every shabby village through which he passed, every gate on every road that closed behind him might as well have one more iron door in the long line of barriers between him and England.

He was so closely and carefully watched, that—if

The motto "Liberté, Egalité, Fraternité" (Liberty, Equality, Fraternity) is an expression of Enlightenment ideals and first appeared during the French Revolution as one of many mottoes stating the "goals" of the Revolution. It was written into the 1958 French Constitution. Here, Dickens is actually pointing out the hypocrisy of the Revolution in that the ideals of Liberty, Equality, and Fraternity applied only to those who agreed with the Revolution. Those who disagreed were simply executed.

he'd been caught in a net, or were being carried to Paris in a cage—he could not have felt his freedom more completely gone.

Travel restrictions were so tight that, not only was he stopped twenty times in every stage of his journey, but he was delayed even more by being followed, stopped, and taken back to the previous checkpoint at least twenty times a day. He was also met at certain check points and *accompanied* by "citizens" who said it was their responsibility to keep track of him.

He had already been several days in France, when he went to bed tired out, in a little town on the high road, still a long way from Paris.

And the only thing that had gotten him even that far had been his ability to produce the letter from poor Gabelle, in a prison in Paris, begging for his master the Marquis to come and save his life. He had had so much trouble at the guardhouse of this tiny village that he felt he really might be in trouble. It was, therefore, no surprise at all to find himself awakened in the middle of the night—awakened by a timid local clerk and three armed patriots in their rough red caps and with pipes in their mouths, who sat down on the bed.

"Emigrant," said the clerk, "I am going to send you on to Paris, with an escort."

"Citizen, I would like nothing more than to get to Paris, though I do not need the escort."

"Silence!" growled a red-cap, hitting the bedspread with the butt-end of his musket. "Peace, aristocrat!"

"It is as the good patriot says," observed the timid clerk. "You are an aristocrat, and must have an escort. And must pay for it."

"I have no choice?" asked Charles Darnay.

"Choice! Listen to him!" cried the same scowling red-cap. "As if it was not a favor to be protected from the lamp iron!"

"It is always as the good patriot says," observed the clerk. "Rise and dress yourself, emigrant."

Darnay obeyed, and was taken back to the guard house, where other patriots in rough red caps were

In revolutionary France, passports were required for travel even between places within France. The country was threatened with foreign invasion and suspicious of returned emigrants (like Darnay), many of whom had joined forces with foreign invaders and were suspected of mounting a counter-revolution.

French patriots during the Revolution adopted red caps called "Phrygian caps" as part of their informal uniform. The Phrygians were an ancient Asian people, living in what is now Turkey. Their cone-shaped caps became "caps of liberty" when the style was adopted by freed Roman slaves. The red Phrygian cap, or bonnet rouge, was soft and made of wool, with the peak bent over at the top.

The lamp iron is probably a reference to the rebels' tendency to hang their enemies from city lampposts.

smoking, drinking, and sleeping by a watch fire. Here he paid a large sum of money for his escort, and then started on his way—with the escort—on the wet, wet roads at three o'clock in the morning.

The escort consisted of two mounted patriots in red caps and tri-colored cockades, armed with national muskets and sabers. They rode on either side of Darnay.

Darnay controlled his own horse, but a loose line was attached to Darnay's bridle, the end of which one of the patriots kept tied around his wrist. And so they started out, with a sharp rain driving in their faces, riding like cavalry officers over the uneven town pavement, and out upon the muddy roads. And so they traveled all the muddy miles that lay between them and Paris.

They traveled at night, halting an hour or two after daybreak, and resting until twilight. The escorts were so scantily clothed, that they used straw to cover their legs and to fill tears in their tattered coats to keep themselves dry.

Charles Darnay did not let the fact that he was "under escort" worry him. It did make him slightly uneasy to be attended by such impoverished men—and one of the escorts was fairly drunk, waving his musket carelessly—but these were personal discomforts. Darnay figured that the escort was for no other reason than that he had not yet had a chance to plead his case and speak to Gabelle.

But when they came to the town of Beauvais—which they did at evening when the streets were filled with people—he could not deny that the state of affairs was very alarming. A frightening crowd gathered to see him dismount at the posting yard, and many voices called out loudly, "Down with the emigrant!"

He stopped in the act of swinging himself out of his saddle and resumed it as his safest place. "Emigrant, my friends?" he called. "Do you not see me here, in France, of my own will?"

"You are a cursed emigrant," cried a man who

A cockade is a knot of ribbons worn in the hat as a badge of one's office or political party. This particular tricolor cockade was introduced in 1789 as a sign of opposition to the white flag of the French royal family. The three colors were red, white, and blue, which eventually became the colors of the French flag.

Where have we heard the name of this town before?

❷ *What is surprising about what the townspeople of Beauvais reveal?*"

shod horses for a living, charging him angrily, hammer in hand. "And you are a cursed aristocrat!"

As it was obvious the man intended to grab the bridle of Darnay's horse, the postmaster threw himself between this man and the Darnay's bridle. In a soothing voice, he said to the farrier, "Leave him alone! He will be judged at Paris."

"Judged!" repeated the farrier, swinging his hammer. "Ay! and condemned as a traitor." At this the crowd roared approval.

The postmaster was just beginning to lead the horse into the yard. The drunken patriot sat calmly in his saddle watching. As soon as he could make his voice heard, Darnay said, "Friends, you are fooling yourselves, or you have been lied to. I am not a traitor."

"He lies!" cried the smith. "He is a traitor since the decree. His life is surrendered to the people. His cursed life is not his own!"

At the instant Darnay saw a frenzy in the eyes of the crowd. They surely would have attacked him in another moment, when the postmaster turned his horse into the yard, the escort rode in close on his horse's flanks, and the postmaster shut and barred the double gates. The farrier pounded the gates with his hammer, and the crowd groaned, but no more was done.

"What is this decree that the smith spoke of?" Darnay asked the postmaster, when he had thanked him, and stood beside him in the yard.

"A decree allowing for the property of emigrants to be confiscated and sold."

"When was it passed?"

"On the fourteenth."

"The day I left England!"

"Everybody says it is just the first one, and that there will be others—if there aren't already—banishing all emigrants, and condemning them to death if they return. That is what he meant when he said your life was not your own."

"But such a decree has not been passed yet?"

"What do I know!" said the postmaster, shrugging his shoulders. "It may already have been passed, or it will soon be passed. It makes no difference."

They rested on some straw in a loft until the middle of the night, and then rode forward again when the town was asleep. Among the many wild changes Darnay saw, not the least was how rare sleep had apparently become. After a long and lonely ride over dreary roads, they would come to a cluster of poor cottages, not steeped in darkness, but all glittering with lights. They would find the people, like ghosts in the dead of the night, dancing hand in hand around a shriveled tree of Liberty, or standing together singing a Liberty song.

Happily, however, there was sleep in Beauvais that night so that they could leave, and they passed on once more into solitude and loneliness, jingling through the unseasonable cold and wet. They passed barren fields that had yielded no crops that year, broken up by the blackened remains of burnt houses. They were surprised by the sudden appearance—as if from out of ambush—of patriot patrols keeping watch on all the roads.

By daylight, they were before the wall of Paris. The barrier was closed and strongly guarded when they rode up to it.

"Where are the papers of this prisoner?" demanded a determined-looking man in authority, who was summoned out by the guard.

To protest being called "prisoner," Charles Darnay requested the speaker to take notice that he was a free traveler and French citizen, accompanied by an escort which had been imposed on him because of the troubled state of affairs, and which he had paid for.

"Where," repeated the same person, without listening to him at all, "are the papers of this prisoner?"

The drunken patriot had them in his cap, and produced them. Casting his eyes over Gabelle's letter,

✔ *According to the Oxford English Dictionary, a "tree of liberty" is a tree or a pole planted in celebration of a revolution or victory securing liberty. The term is used chiefly in reference to the French Revolution. In France, they were most often tall poles with Phrygian caps at the top. It is estimated that by May, 1792, there were about 60,000 trees of liberty planted in France.*

✔ *Notice how earlier Darnay was "emigrant" and now he is "the prisoner."*

the same person in authority showed some surprise, and studied Darnay closely.

He left them without saying a word, and went into the guard-room. Meanwhile, they sat on their horses outside the gate. Looking around while waiting, Charles Darnay saw that the gate was held by a mixed guard of soldiers and patriots, the patriots far outnumbering the soldiers; and that—while it seemed easy enough for peasants' carts bringing in supplies to *enter* the city—*leaving* the city was very difficult for even the poorest people. A long line of men and women—not to mention animals and all sorts of vehicles—was waiting to leave. But, the process of checking identification and travel permits was so strict, that they filtered through the barrier very slowly. Some of these people knew their turn for examination was a long way off, and they lay down on the ground to sleep or smoke. Others talked to each other, or simply wandered around. Everyone— man and woman alike—was wearing the red cap and tricolor cockade.

After sitting on his horse a full half hour, Darnay saw the man in authority return from the guard house. He commanded the attendant to open the gate, gave the two escorts a receipt for delivery of the prisoner, and told Darnay to dismount. Darnay obeyed, and his own tired horse was led away while the escorts rode off back the way they had come.

Darnay followed the person in authority into a guard room, smelling of common wine and tobacco, where soldiers and patriots, asleep and awake, drunk and sober, and in various states in between, were standing and lying around. The light in the guard house—half originating in the dim oil-lamps of the night, and half from the overcast day—was likewise uncertain. A few record books were lying open on a desk, and an officer with a dark and angry face, seemed to be in charge of these.

"Citizen Defarge," said this man to Darnay's

conductor, as he took a slip of paper to write on. "Is this the emigrant Evremonde?"

"This is the man."

"Your age, Evremonde?"

"Thirty-seven."

"Married, Evremonde?"

"Yes."

"Where married?"

"In England."

"Without doubt. Where is your wife, Evremonde?"

"In England."

"Without doubt. You are assigned, Evremonde, to the prison of La Force."

"Just a minute!" exclaimed Darnay. "Under what law, and for what crime?"

The officer looked up from his slip of paper for a moment.

"We have new laws, Evremonde, and new offenses, since you were here." He said it with a sarcastic smile, and went on writing.

"I beg you to notice that I have come here voluntarily, in response to that letter from a fellow countryman that you have right there. I demand no more than the chance to assist my friend. Is that not my right?"

"Emigrants have no rights, Evremonde," was the harsh reply. The officer wrote until he had finished, read over to himself what he had written, sanded it, and handed it to Defarge, with the words "In secret."

Defarge motioned to Darnay that he must accompany him. Darnay obeyed, and a guard of two armed patriots attended them.

"Is it you," said Defarge, in a low voice, as they went down the guardhouse steps and turned into Paris, "who married the daughter of Doctor Manette, once a prisoner in the Bastille?"

"Yes," replied Darnay, looking at him with surprise.

✔ *To be imprisoned "in secret" (en secret in French) was to be placed in solitary confinement, completely isolated from the other prisoners.*

❷ What do you suppose is troubling Defarge?

✔ Joseph Guillotine, a French physician, invented the guillotine in 1789. At the time, it was hailed as a more humanitarian form of execution than the executioner's axe, which often took several blows to sever the head.

❷ To whom is Defarge referring?

"My name is Defarge, and I keep a wine shop in the Quarter of Saint Antoine. Possibly you have heard of me."

"My wife came to your house to reclaim her father! Yes!"

The word "wife" seemed to remind Defarge of something painful, and he blurted out, "In the name of that sharp female newly born, and called *La Guillotine*, why did you come to France?"

"You heard me say why, a minute ago. Do you not believe it is the truth?"

"A bad truth for you," said Defarge, speaking with knitted brows, and looking straight before him.

"Indeed I am lost here. All here is so unfamiliar, so changed, so sudden and unfair, that I am absolutely lost. Can you offer me a little help?"

"None." Defarge spoke, always looking straight before him.

"Will you answer me a single question?"

"Perhaps. Depending on the question. You can ask."

"In this prison that I am going to so unjustly, will I have any contact with the outside world?"

"You will see."

"I am not to be simply buried there, prejudged, and without the chance to present my case?"

"You will see. But, what then? Other people have been similarly buried in worse prisons before now."

"But never by me, Citizen Defarge."

The only answer Defarge offered was to glance darkly at him. They walked on in a steady and set silence. The deeper they sank into this silence, the less hope there was— or so Darnay thought—of Defarge's softening in any slight degree. He, therefore, broke the silence and said, "It is extremely important to me that I be able to get word to Mr. Lorry of Tellson's Bank, that I have been thrown into the prison of La Force. You know, Citizen, even better than I, exactly how important this is. Will you see that that is done for me?"

"I will do nothing for you," Defarge replied stubbornly. "My duty is to my country and the People. I am the sworn servant of both, against you. I will do *nothing* for you."

Darnay felt it hopeless to ask him further questions, and his pride was irritated besides. As they walked on in silence, he couldn't help but see how used the people were to the sight of prisoners passing along the streets. Children hardly noticed him. A few people turned their heads, and a few shook their fingers at him because he was an aristocrat. Beyond that, the fact that a man in good clothes should be going to prison, was no more remarkable to them than that a laborer in working clothes should be going to work. In one narrow, dark, and dirty street through which they passed, an excited speaker, standing on a stool, was preaching to an excited audience about the crimes against the People, of the king and the royal family. The few words that Darnay caught from this man's lips, informed him that the king was in prison, and that every one of the foreign ambassadors had left Paris. On the road (except at Beauvais) he had heard absolutely nothing. He had been completely isolated.

He knew that he was in much more danger than he had been when he left England. He knew that danger had multiplied around him fast, and might increase even faster and faster yet. He had to admit to himself that he might not have made this journey, if he had had any inkling of the events of these past few days. Yet, his doubts were not really as dark as they seemed. As troubled as the future was, it was the *unknown* future. In its uncertainty was still a naïve hope.

There was no way he could have foreseen the horrible massacre that would begin in a few short days and would last for nine long months. He had never heard of the "sharp female newly-born, and called *La Guillotine*." Probably those who were soon to commit the deeds of terror had not yet formed an idea of what they were about to do. How, then, could a man of peace have conceived of them?

✅ *With the establishment of the First Republic (September 20, 1792), the monarchy was abolished (September 21, 1792), and Louis XVI and his family were imprisoned. The King was beheaded on the guillotine on January 21, 1793.*

✅ *Do not be confused: The "foreign ambassadors" who have left Paris are not French aristocracy; they are the representatives of other nations. What this essentially means is that the First Republic is not recognized by other nations as a legitimate government.*

✅ *While historians debate the exact date, all agree that the Reign of Terror began in September 1793 and lasted for nine months until June/July 1794 when its leader, Maximilien Robespierre, was executed on the guillotine as some 250,000 had been before him.*

❷ What do you suppose the narrator is foreshadowing here?

✔ Don't miss the subtle reference to the vast numbers of people imprisoned during this Reign of Terror.

He dreaded a harsh imprisonment, and separation from his wife. He did not know enough to dread anything else yet. With this on his mind, which was enough to carry into a dreary prison courtyard, he arrived at the prison of La Force.

A man with a bloated face opened the strong gate, and Defarge announced, "The Emigrant Evremonde."

"What the Devil! How many more of them will there be?" exclaimed the man with the bloated face.

Ignoring the complaint, Defarge took his receipt and withdrew with his two fellow patriots.

"What the Devil, I say again!" exclaimed the jailer, left with his wife. "How many more will there be?"

The jailer's wife, having no way of answering, merely replied, "You've got to be patient, my dear!" She rang a bell and three turnkeys entered in response. They echoed the sentiment, one added, "For the love of Liberty;" but that conclusion sounded terribly out of place in the prison.

The prison of La Force was a gloomy prison, dark and filthy, and with a horrible, foul smell.

"*In secret*, too," grumbled the jailer, looking at the written paper. "As if I was not already full to bursting!"

He angrily stuck the paper in a file, and Charles Darnay waited for him for half an hour. Sometimes he paced back and forth in the room. Sometimes he rested on a stone seat. Whatever he did, he was always aware that he was in prison and had no choice but to wait until the jailer or someone remembered he was there.

"Come!" said the chief, finally picking up his keys, "Come with me, Emigrant."

Through the dismal prison twilight, Darnay followed him through corridors and up and down staircases. Many doors clanged shut and locked behind them, until they came into a large, low-ceilinged chamber, crowded with prisoners—both men and women. The women were seated at a long table, reading and writing, knitting, sewing, and embroidering. The men were—for the most part—standing behind their chairs, or lingering up and down the room.

It is natural to associate prisoners with crime, and shame, and disgrace; and Charles Darnay found himself instinctively drawing away from his fellow prisoners in the room. But the most astonishing aspect of this experience—that had seemed completely unreal since the night of his arrest and the beginning of his ride to Paris under escort—was that the prisoners in the room all rose at once when he entered and bowed or curtseyed to him as if he were indeed a nobleman entering a room in his grand chateau.

These gestures of social politeness were so clouded by the gloom of the prison and the filth and misery of the prisoners that Charles Darnay almost thought he was being greeted by ghosts instead of living human beings. Everything was ghostlike here. There was no beauty, only the ghost of beauty. No stateliness, but the ghost of stateliness. No elegance or pride, only the ghosts of elegance and pride. The ghost of frivolity, the ghost of wit, the ghost of youth, the ghost of age—all waiting a release from prison as if they were awaiting their ride on Charon's boat, all looking at him with eyes that were filled with the death they had already died when they entered the hopeless prison.

Explain the significance of the allusion to Charon.

The sight of the ghosts paying him respect paralyzed him. The jailers in the room would have fit in a normal prison, but they looked bloated and grotesque in the control of beautiful, refined women and their beautiful daughters—surely, ghosts all. Surely, some awful disease had brought him to these gloomy shades!

Who are these prisoners?

"On behalf of myself and my unlucky companions," said a gentleman of courtly appearance and manners, coming forward, "I have the honor of welcoming you to La Force. We all sympathize with your ill fortune. May it soon end happily! It would be extremely rude to ask your name and position in society if we were anywhere else, but here it is not."

Charles Darnay shook himself out of his daydream,

and explained who he was, being careful to be as polite to his new acquaintance as the man had been to him.

"I hope," said the gentleman, following the chief jailer with his eyes, who moved across the room, "that you are not in secret?"

"I do not understand what that means, but I have heard them say so."

"Ah, what a pity! We are so sorry! But do not be afraid. Several members of our little society here have started out in secret, but then it did not last for long." Then he turned to his fellow prisoners and announced, "I am sorry to inform the society that our friend is *in secret*."

There was a murmur of pity as Charles Darnay crossed the room to a grated door where the jailer was waiting for him. Many voices offered him good wishes and encouragement. Among these, the soft and compassionate voices of women were conspicuous. At the door, he turned to thank them for their kindness, but it was closed under the jailer's hand, and the ghosts vanished from his sight forever.

The gate opened on a stone staircase, leading upward. When they had climbed forty steps (Darnay counted them), the jailer opened a low black door, and they passed into a solitary cell. It was extremely cold and damp, but was not dark.

"Yours," said the jailer.

"Why am I confined alone?"

"How do I know!"

"I can buy pen, ink, and paper?"

"Those are not my orders. You will be visited, and can ask then. At present, you may buy your food and nothing more."

In the cell were a chair, a table, and a straw mattress. While the jailer glanced over these objects, and the four walls, before leaving, it occurred to Darnay that this jailer was so sickly bloated that he looked like a man who had been drowned and filled with water. When the jailer was gone, he thought in the same wandering way, "So now I am left as if I were dead." Stopping then, to look down at the mattress, he looked away with a sick feeling, and thought, "And in disgusting insects crawling in that straw is the first decay of the body after death."

"Five paces by four and a half, five paces by four and a half, five paces by four and a half." Darnay walked back and forth in his cell, counting its measurement. Through the tiny window, he could hear the roar of the city, and the muffled sound soon haunted his mind with random thoughts:

He made shoes, he made shoes, he made shoes.

The prisoner counted the measurement again, and paced faster, to draw his mind with him from that latter repetition.

❷ *What is happening here?*

"The ghosts that vanished when the door closed. There was one among them, the appearance of a lady dressed in black, who was leaning in the recess of a window, and she had a light shining upon her golden hair, and she looked like * * * * Let us ride on again, for God's sake, through the illuminated villages with the people all awake! * * * * He made shoes, he made shoes, he made shoes. * * * * Five paces by four and a half."

With such scraps tossing and rolling upward from the depths of his mind, the prisoner walked faster and faster, stubbornly counting and counting, while the roar of the city changed so that he heard voices he knew along with the voices of all of the prisoners who'd ever been unjustly imprisoned.

THIS IS THE END OF THE
TWENTY-FIRST WEEKLY INSTALLMENT.

Writing Opportunity:

Discuss three examples of situational irony in this chapter. Use evidence from the text to support your essay.

A Tale of Two Cities

CHARLES DICKENS

CHAPTER II
The Grindstone

TELLSON'S BANK, in the Saint Germain Quarter of Paris, was in a wing of a large house that was protected from the street by a high wall and a strong gate that led to a courtyard. The house belonged to a great nobleman who had lived in it until he ran away, disguised in his cook's dress so that he would be allowed to pass the borders. While he was really no more than a mere beast fleeing its hunters, he believed himself to be no other than the same nobleman who required three strong men and his cook to prepare and deliver his chocolate in the morning.

But with the aristocracy gone, and the same three strong men ready and willing to cut their former employer's throat in order to absolve themselves of ever having worked for him—and accepting the high wages he paid them—the house has been cordoned off, and then confiscated. For, all things moved so fast, and decree followed decree with that cruel speed, that now upon the third night of the autumn month of September, patriot agents of the law were in possession of Monseigneur's house, and had marked it with the three colors of the Republic, and were drinking brandy in its state apartments.

A place of business in London like Tellson's in

Remember that the Defarges live in the Saint Antoine Quarter.

Some historians give September 5, 1793, as the beginning of the Reign of Terror.

Paris would soon have driven the Chief Officer out of his mind. For proper and sober British responsibility and respectability would never have allowed potted orange trees in the Bank courtyard. Or a Cupid over the counter. Yet that's how things were in Tellson's-Paris. Tellson's had painted over the Cupid, but he was still visible on the ceiling, in his linen frock, aiming his arrows (as he very often does) at money from morning to night. Having such a painting in the branch at Lombardy Street in London would certainly have driven the bank into bankruptcy. So would the curtained alcove behind the picture of the god. And so would a mirror hanging on the wall. And so would the staff of clerks—who were not old—and who actually took part in social activities and even sometimes danced in public.

Don't miss the small sarcastic joke here that Cupid's target (a reason for falling in love) is often not personal charm but money.

Yet, a *French* Tellson's could get by with these things extremely well—and, as long as the times held together—no man had been so frightened by these unbusinesslike ornaments that he withdrew his money.

Now, with events in Paris so drastically changed, no one knew what money would be withdrawn from Tellson's—what silver would be taken—what silver would be left to tarnish—what documents would be saved and what documents would be left to rot in vaults. No one could have said, that night, any more than Mr. Jarvis Lorry could, although he thought about it constantly. He sat by a newly-lighted wood fire (this year of drought and famine now promised an early winter), and on his brave and honest face was a look so dark that the brightest lamp could not lighten it—a look of horror.

He was living in rooms in the Bank, and it was an unexpected benefit that they received a small degree of security from the Revolutionary occupation of the main building. But the loyal old gentleman never gave a thought to his own personal safety. Danger, security—they were all the same to him, as long as he did his duty. On the opposite side of the courtyard, under the portico, was a large area for the parking of carriages. Indeed, some carriages of the runaway nobleman were still there. Fastened to two of the portico's columns were two enormous, lighted torches. Visible in the light of these torches, standing out in the open air, was a large sharpening stone. It was carelessly mounted and seemed to have been brought there—and hastily—from some nearby blacksmith shop, or other workshop. Rising and looking out of window at these harmless objects, Mr. Lorry shivered, and returned to his seat by the fire. He had opened, not only the glass window, but the lattice blind outside it, and he had closed both again, and he shivered through his frame.

From the streets beyond the high wall and the strong gate, there came the usual night hum of the city, with now and then an indescribable ring in it, weird and unearthly.

"Thank God," said Mr. Lorry, clasping his hands, "that no one near and dear to me is in this dreadful town tonight. May He have mercy on all who are in danger!"

❷ Where is the irony in this passage?

Soon afterwards, the bell at the great gate sounded, and he thought, "They have come back!" and sat listening. But, there was no loud parade into the courtyard, as he had expected, and he heard the gate clash again, and all was quiet.

❷ Who are "they"?

His overall nervousness and sense of dread eventually became worry about the bank. It was well guarded, and he once more got up to make an informal visit to the guards, when his door suddenly opened, and two figures rushed in. When he recognized them, he fell back into his chair in amazement.

Lucie and her father! Lucie stretching her arms out to embrace him. She looked so earnest, so intent, that it seemed as though her expression of resolve had been painted on her face to give it the strength to make it through her current ordeal.

"What is this?" cried Mr. Lorry, breathless and

confused. "What is the matter? Lucie! Manette! What has happened? What has brought you here? What is it?"

Her determined expression failed her, and she cried out in Lorry's arms, "Oh my dear friend! My husband!"

"Your husband, Lucie?"

"Charles."

"What about Charles?"

"He's here."

"Here? In Paris?"

"Has been here a few days—three or four—I don't know how many—I can't collect my thoughts. He came on a mission of generosity. He was stopped at the barrier, and sent to prison."

The old man could not stifle the cry that rose in his throat. Almost at the same moment, the bell of the great gate rang again, and a loud noise of feet and voices came pouring into the courtyard.

"What is that noise?" said the Doctor, turning toward the window.

"Don't look!" cried Mr. Lorry. "Don't look out! Manette, for your life, don't touch the blind!"

The Doctor turned, his hand resting on the window latch. With a cool, bold smile, he said, "My dear friend, I have a charmed life in this city. I have been a Bastille prisoner. There is no patriot in Paris— in all of *France*—who would lay a finger on me except maybe to hug me and carry me on his shoulders like a hero, once he knew that I had been a prisoner in the Bastille. My old pain has given me power. That is what got us through the barrier. That is what got us the news about Charles, and brought us here. I knew it would be like that. I knew I could help Charles. I told Lucie so." He looked again toward the still-closed window. "What is that noise?"

"Don't look!" cried Mr. Lorry, absolutely desperate. "No, Lucie, my dear, nor you!" He placed his arm round her, and held her. "Don't be so terrified, my love. I solemnly swear to you that I know of no harm

❷ *How influential do you think Dr. Manette will truly be?*

having happened to Charles. That I had no suspicion even of his being here. What prison is he in?"

"La Force!"

"La Force! Lucie, my child, if you have ever been brave and helpful in your life—and you have always been both—you will calm yourself now, and do exactly as I say. This is more important than I can tell you. First of all, there is nothing you can do tonight. I say this, because what I must ask you to do—for Charles's sake—is the hardest thing of all to do. You must let me put you in a room at the back here. You must leave your father and me alone for two minutes. This really is a matter of life and death."

"I will obey you and trust you."

The old man kissed her, and hurried her into his room. He locked her in and then came hurrying back to the Doctor. He opened the window and partly opened the blind. Laying his hand upon the Doctor's arm, he looked out with him into the courtyard.

The light from the blazing torches revealed a throng of men and women—not nearly enough to fill the courtyard—no more than forty or fifty in all. The patriots occupying the house had let them in at the gate, and they had rushed in to work at the sharpening stone. Since the walled courtyard was a convenient and secure spot, the sharpening stone had evidently been set up there for this use.

But, such awful workers, and such awful work!

The sharpening stone had a double handle. The two men turning the handles had faces that were more horrible and cruel than the wildest barbarians dressed for war. They wore false eyebrows and moustaches, and their hideous faces were bloody and sweaty. Their eyes were wide and vacant from bloodlust and lack of sleep.

As these hoodlums turned and turned the handles, their long and matted hair flew forward over their eyes, and then backwards over their necks. Some women held wine to their mouths for them to drink. The horrible combination of dripping blood, and dripping wine, and the stream of sparks flying from metal against stone, the entire scene was hellish. Manette and Lorry could not see a single creature in the group not smeared with blood. Men stripped to the waist shoved one another to be the next at the sharpening stone. Blood stained their limbs and bodies. Men in all sorts of rags, with blood stains on those rags, men dancing wildly, waving women's lace and silk and ribbon they had stolen from ransacked mansions smeared their blood stains on their dainty trophies. Hatchets, knives, bayonets, swords were all brought to be sharpened, and were all red with blood. Some of the dulled swords were tied to the wrists of those who carried them, with strips of linen and bits of clothing, all sorts of ties, but all deep in the one color. And as the men who frantically wielded these weapons snatched them from the stream of sparks and tore away into the streets, their frenzied eyes were the same red color. They were eyes which anyone who saw them would have gladly given up twenty years of his life to close them with a well-aimed gun.

They saw the entire scene in a moment, not daring to risk exposing themselves to the angry mob any longer. They drew back from the window, and the Doctor looked for explanation in his friend's ashy face.

"They are murdering the prisoners," Mr. Lorry whispered, glancing fearfully around the locked room. "If you are sure of what you say; if you really have the power you think you have—and as I believe you have—make yourself known to these devils, and get taken to La Force. It may already be too late, I don't know, but certainly don't waste any time."

Doctor Manette shook Lorry's hand firmly and hurried from the room without even putting on his hat. He was already in the courtyard by the time Mr. Lorry returned to the window.

His streaming white hair, his remarkable face, and his naïve confidence, as he put the weapons aside like water, carried him instantly to the stone and center of everyone's attention. For a few moments there was a pause, and then a flurry of activity and a murmur. Mr. Lorry heard the old doctor speak, but he could not tell what was said. Then he saw Manette—surrounded by the frenzied mob—placed in the middle of a line twenty men long, all linked shoulder to shoulder, and hand to shoulder. They marched out of the courtyard shouting, "Long live the Bastille prisoner! Help for the Bastille prisoner's family in La Force! Make room for the Bastille prisoner in front there! Save the prisoner Evremonde at La Force!" and a thousand similar shouts.

Mr. Lorry closed the lattice again with a fluttering heart, closed the window and the curtain, and hastened to Lucie. He told her that her father was being helped by the People, and gone in search of her husband. He found her child and Miss Pross in the room with her, but, it never occurred to him to be surprised by their appearance until a long time afterwardss.

Lucie had, by that time, fallen into a stupor on the floor at Lorry's feet, clinging to his hand. Miss Pross had laid the child down on Lorry's bed, and her head had gradually fallen on the pillow beside the child. It was indeed a long night!

Twice more in the darkness the bell at the great gate sounded, and the sharpening stone whirled and spluttered.

"What is it?" cried Lucie, frightened. "Hush! The soldiers' swords are sharpened there," said Mr. Lorry. "The place is national property now, and used as a kind of armory, my love."

Soon after that second scene at the sharpening stone, the day began to dawn, and Mr. Lorry softly detached himself from her clasping hand, and cautiously looked outside again. A man—so filthy that he could have been a badly wounded soldier creeping back to life on a field of corpses—was rising from the ground by the side of the grindstone, and looking around vacantly. Eventually, in the dim light of dawn, he noticed one of the abandoned carriages.

❷ *How would you character-ize Dickens' portrayal of the revolutionary mob?*

Explain the metaphor in this paragraph.

He staggered over to that gorgeous vehicle, climbed in at the door, and shut himself in to sleep on its dainty cushions.

The Great Sharpening Stone, Earth, had also turned when Mr. Lorry looked out again. The sun shone red on the courtyard. But, the smaller sharpening stone stood alone there in the calm morning air. It was indeed red, but not with the light of the morning sun.

Writing Opportunity:

Compare and contrast the scene of the rebels at the grindstone with the peasants drinking greedily from the spilled barrel of wine in the first book of the novel. How have diction and syntax changed in this description? How has the mood changed, if at all?

A Tale of Two Cities

CHARLES DICKENS

CHAPTER III
The Shadow

WHILE JARVIS LORRY would have risked everything he owned, including his own life, to protect Doctor Manette, Lucie, and their family, he did not feel he had any right to put Tellson's bank or its interests in any danger by sheltering the wife of an emigrant prisoner in Tellson's building. Personally, he would have loved to have Lucie and her daughter stay with him, but he had to think of business. He was, after all, a man of business.

He first thought of Defarge, and considered looking for the wine shop to consult with Manette's oldest and most loyal friend about the safest place for the Manettes to live so they would not be threatened by the confused violence in the city. But, the same thoughts that suggested him, disqualified him as well. He lived in the most violent Quarter of the city, and was most likely very influential there—deeply involved in its dangerous workings.

It was approaching noon, and the Doctor had not yet returned. Every minute's delay threatened to compromise Tellson's, so Mr. Lorry finally spoke with Lucie. She said that her father had spoken of renting rooms for a short term, in that Quarter, near the Bank. Lorry could think of no objection to this—on a strictly business level. He also realized that—even if everything were all right with Charles, and he were released from prison—he certainly would not be allowed to leave the city. Mr. Lorry, therefore, went out in search of an apartment and succeeded in finding one. It was on a deserted side street he could tell by all of the buildings' closed blinds that they were all deserted.

He immediately took Lucie and her child there, along with Miss Pross. He did the best he could to assure them of their safety—and tried to assure himself of this as well. He left Jerry with them, a big enough person to bar the door and survive a considerable fight before he would let anyone in to harm Lucie and the others. Still, the entire afternoon dragged as his mind was full of thoughts of the harm that could come to them while he was not there.

The constant worry made it an exhausting afternoon until the Bank finally closed. He was again alone in his room, considering what to do next, when be heard a footstep on the stairs. In a few moments, a man stood before him, studying him closely. "Mr. Lorry?" the man said quietly.

"I am Jarvis Lorry. Do you know me?"

The stranger was a strongly made man with dark, curling hair. He appeared to be from forty-five to fifty years of age. As an answer to Lorry's question, he merely repeated—without any change of emphasis, "Do you know me?"

"I have seen you somewhere."

"Perhaps at my wine shop?"

Considerably nervous, yet extremely curious, Mr. Lorry asked, "You come from Doctor Manette?"

"Yes. I come from Doctor Manette."

"What does he say? Does he send a message?"

Defarge handed him an open scrap of paper. It was in the Doctor's handwriting and said, "Charles is safe, but I cannot safely leave here yet. The man who is carrying this note is doing me the favor of bringing a note from Charles to Lucie. Please let him see Lucie."

It was dated from La Force, within an hour.

❷ *How is this situation getting complicated? What are some of the possible outcomes?*

Mr. Lorry was joyfully relieved after reading this note aloud and asked Defarge, "Will you go with me to where his wife is staying?"

"Yes," returned Defarge.

Mr. Lorry had not yet noticed how flat and unemotional Defarge's tone was. He put on his hat and they went down into the courtyard. There, they found two women—one, knitting.

"Madame Defarge, surely!" said Mr. Lorry, who had last seen her seventeen years ago doing exactly the same thing.

"Yes," replied her husband.

"Will she be going with us?" asked Mr. Lorry, seeing that she moved as they moved.

"Yes. She must be able to recognize their faces and know the persons. It is for their safety."

Beginning to be worried by Defarge's attitude, Mr. Lorry looked suspiciously at him, and led the way. Both the women followed. The second woman was the Vengeance.

They passed through the streets as quickly as they could, climbed the staircase of the new home, and were admitted by Jerry. Lucie sat in the front room, alone, weeping.

Mr. Lorry's news about Charles, however, excited her and she held Defarge's hand affectionately as he handed her the letter from Charles. Little did she consider what that same hand might have been ready to do to Charles had not the Doctor suddenly appeared at the prison the night before.

❷ *What is Dickens suggesting here?*

"My dear Lucie, be brave. I am well, and your father has influence around me. You cannot answer this. Kiss our child for me."

That was all the letter said. It brought such happiness to Lucie that she turned from Defarge to his wife and kissed her hands. It was a passionate, loving, thankful, womanly action. But Madame made no response. She merely dropped her cold and heavy hand and started knitting again.

Something in the older woman's touch frightened

Lucie. She stopped in the act of putting the note in her bosom and—with her hands still near her neck—looked terrified at Madame Defarge. Madame Defarge met the lifted eyebrows and forehead with a cold, impassive stare.

"My dear," said Mr. Lorry, attempting to explain, "there are frequent uprisings in the streets, and—although it is not likely they will ever trouble you—Madame Defarge wishes to see those whom she has the power to protect. That way, she may know them and identify them. I believe," said Mr. Lorry, himself a little hesitant in his reassuring words, as he grew increasingly alarmed at the stony manner of the three. "Is that correct, Citizen Defarge?"

Defarge looked gloomily at his wife, and gave no other answer than a gruff sound of agreement.

"Perhaps you should bring Little Lucie out here, and Miss Pross," suggested Lorry, doing whatever he could think of to make the meeting comfortable. "Our Miss Pross, Defarge, is an English lady, and knows no French."

Stubborn Miss Pross appeared. She had already boasted to Lorry and Lucie that she considered herself to be a match for any "foreigner" and would not be upset by any distress or danger. She strode boldly into the room with her arms crossed. When she first saw the Vengeance, she said—in English, "Well, Boldface, I see *you* eat well enough!" Her greeting to Madame Defarge was little more than a cough, and she barely glanced at Mr. Defarge. Neither of them paid her much attention, but Madame Defarge seemed very interested in the child.

"Is that his child?" said Madame Defarge, stopping in her work for the first time, and pointing her knitting-needle at little Lucie as if it were the finger of Fate.

"Yes, Madame," answered Mr. Lorry; "this is our poor prisoner's darling daughter—and only child."

Something in the way Madame Defarge and the Vengeance looked at Lucie's child moved Lucie to kneel beside her and hug her close. The shadow on

✔ *Notice that Madame Defarge does not say "the" child, but "his" child. She is thinking of Charles, a descendent of the Evremonde family.*

❷ *Why do you think Madame Defarge is so interested in the child?*

Madame Defarge and her party's faces then seemed to fall—threatening and dark—on both the mother and the child.

"That is enough, my husband," said Madame Defarge. "I have seen them. We may go."

Her manner was menacing enough—not in any visible and obvious way, but implied—to alarm Lucie. Laying her hand on Madame Defarge's arm, she pleaded, "You will be good to my poor husband, won't you? You won't harm him? You will help me to see him if you can?"

"Your husband is not my business here," returned Madame Defarge, looking down at her with perfect composure. "It is the *daughter of your father* who is my business here."

❷ *What is significant about Madame Defarge's subtle choice of words here?*

"For *my* sake, then, be merciful to my husband. For *my child's* sake! She will put her hands together and pray you to be merciful. We are more afraid of you than of these others."

Madame Defarge received this as a compliment. She looked at her husband with something like a smile. Defarge had been uneasily biting his fingernails and looked at her, setting his face into a sterner expression.

"What is it that your husband says in that little letter?" asked Madame Defarge, with a frown. "Influence. He says something about influence?"

"That my father," said Lucie, hurriedly taking the paper from her breast, but with her alarmed eyes on Madame Defarge and not on the letter, "has much influence around him."

"Surely that, then, will release him!" said Madame Defarge. "Let it."

"As a wife and mother," cried Lucie, most earnestly, "I implore you to have pity on me and not to exercise any power that you possess, against my innocent husband. Use it instead to help him. Oh, sister woman, think of me. As a wife and mother!"

Her expression as cold as ever, Madame Defarge looked at Lucie. Then, turning to her friend the

Note the strong bitterness at the heart of Madame Defarge's character.

Vengeance, she said, "No one seems to have cared much about the wives and mothers we have known our entire lives. Many *innocent husbands* of the wives and mothers we have known have been taken from them and imprisoned. All our lives we have seen our sister-women suffer. We have seen *them* suffer. We have seen *their children* suffer through poverty, hunger, nakedness, all sorts of oppression and neglect. Haven't we wives and mothers seen all of that?"

"We have seen nothing else," replied the Vengeance.

"We have endured this a long time," said Madame Defarge, turning her eyes again upon Lucie. "You be the judge! Is it likely that the trouble of one wife and mother would matter very much to us now?"

She resumed her knitting and went out. The Vengeance followed. Defarge went last, and closed the door.

"Have courage, my dear Lucie," said Mr. Lorry. "Courage, courage! So far everything is actually going well for us—much better than it has recently gone with many poor souls. Cheer up, and be grateful."

"I'm not ungrateful, but that dreadful woman seems to throw a shadow on me and on all my hopes."

"Tut, tut!" said Mr. Lorry, "What is this gloom? It is just that, a shadow, with no substance to it."

But he too had to admit that he sensed the shadow in the manner of these Defarges, and—in his secret mind—it troubled him greatly.

On what note of foreshadowing does this weekly installment end?

THIS IS THE END OF THE
TWENTY-SECOND WEEKLY INSTALLMENT.

A Tale of Two Cities
CHARLES DICKENS

CHAPTER IV
Calm in Storm

DOCTOR MANETTE DID not return until the morning of the fourth day of his absence. Such dreadful things had happened—he had witnessed—during his absence, that he was determined to keep Lucie unaware. In fact, it was not until long afterwards—when Lucie was far away from France—that she learned that eleven hundred innocent prisoners—both men and women—had been killed by the citizens of the Republic. At the time of her father's return, all she knew was that there had been an attack on the prisons and that the political prisoners had all been in danger. Some had been dragged from their cells by the mob and killed.

He did tell Mr. Lorry—and swore him to absolute secrecy—that, that first night, the mob guided him through a horrible scene of butchery and bloodshed to the prison of La Force. In the prison he had found a self-appointed Tribunal sitting. The prisoners were being brought before this Tribunal—one at a time— and this Tribunal then ordered the prisoner either to be taken out and massacred, or to be released, or (in a few cases) to be sent back to their cells. The men who led him from the courtyard with the sharpening stone took the Doctor to this Tribunal. He had told them

❷ *The days that Doctor Manette is gone are the days of the "September massacre" of September 2-6, 1792, in which Parisian mobs stormed the prisons of the Abbaye, La Force, Châtalet, and the Conciergerie, slaughtering over 1,000 prisoners. While Dickens does not speculate as to the reasons for this outburst of violence, the massacres were partly the result of a public panic over the Prussian invasion of France. Some historians believe the real targets of the massacres were prisoners suspected of being part of a counter-revolution. If this were the case, a returned emigrant like Darnay would truly be in trouble. What effect does Dickens's not offering a reason for the massacres have?*

316

A TALE OF TWO CITIES

his name and profession and that he had been—for eighteen years—a secret and unaccused prisoner in the Bastille. One of the members of the Tribunal stood and identified him. This man was Defarge.

The Doctor continued to tell Mr. Lorry of his experiences that first night. He learned through the record books on the table that Charles Darnay was among the living prisoners. Many members of this Tribunal were asleep. Some were bloody from recent murders. Some clean. Some sober and some drunk. He pleaded with this ragtag group for Charles's life and liberty. His first emotional pleas, and his own experiences as someone who had suffered under the government they'd just overthrown succeeded in convincing the Tribunal to send for Charles Darnay and examine him. It seemed that he was just about to be released when...*something*...something which the Doctor did not understand led to a private conversation among several members of the Tribunal. Then the man who sat as President informed Doctor Manette that the prisoner was to remain in custody, but should—for the Doctor's sake—be held in safe custody.

At that point, on some signal the Doctor did not see or hear, Charles Darnay was again taken back into the interior of the prison. The Doctor, however, pleaded for permission to stay and see for himself that Charles was all right and was being taken care of. He received this position and stayed in the Hall of Blood until the mad danger of the past four days was over.

The sights the Doctor had seen there! He'd only been able to grab brief bits of food and sleep. The mob's insane joy over prisoners who were saved were as astonishing as the insane ferocity against those who were cut to pieces. He described having seen one prisoner who had been set free. But as he left the prison, an ignorant savage ran him through with a pike. The Doctor was asked to dress the released man's wound. Leaving by the same gate, he found the poor man in the arms of a company of Samaritans, who

❷ *What does Doctor Manette manage to secure for Charles?*

❂ *Explain the allusion to Samaritans in the description of the Paris mob.*

were seated on the bodies of their victims. The Doctor was both shocked and sickened by the inconsistency of the mob—the way they helped him care for a man they themselves had nearly killed. These gentle nurses helped the Doctor make a litter to carry the injured man to safety, and then immediately picked up their weapons and threw themselves once again into the frenzied slaughter.

As Mr. Lorry heard these things, and as he watched the face of his friend—now sixty-two years old—he began to worry that such dreadful experiences might cause a relapse, and the Doctor might once again fall into his madness. Still, Lorry had to admit that he had never seen his friend like this. For the first time, the Doctor felt that his suffering was a source of strength and power. For the first time, he felt that in that sharp fire, he had slowly forged the iron which could break the prison door of his daughter's husband, and save him.

What madness is the author talking about?

Explain the metaphor of the iron in the forge.

"Everything works for the good, my friend," the Doctor reassured Mr. Lorry. "My time in prison was not a mere waste. As my daughter was so helpful restoring me to myself, I will now be helpful restoring her dearest loved one to her. And, with the help of Heaven, I will do it!"

And when Jarvis Lorry saw the bright and energetic eyes, the resolute face, the calm, strong look and posture of this man whose life always seemed to have been stopped—like a clock—for so many years, and then started again, he believed.

The Doctor had appeared to grow so strong in Lorry's eyes that the banker was confident that no obstacle would prove too great for the Doctor to overcome. He was a doctor, and he had business with all sorts and classes of humankind—slave and free, rich and poor, bad and good. He used the personal influence he gained by having been a famous prisoner of the Bastille to establish himself as the inspecting physician of three prisons, including La Force. Now he could now assure Lucie that her husband was no

The French monarchy had been abolished on September 21, 1792. The next day, the National Convention announced the beginning of the First Republic. On January 15, 1793, Louis XVI was found guilty of "crimes against the people." Six days later he was beheaded by the guillotine. Immediately before his beheading, he proclaimed to the mob of spectators, "I die innocent of all the crimes laid to my charge; I Pardon those who have occasioned my death; and I pray to God that the blood you are going to shed may never be visited on France."

As a part of the Revolution's attempt to do away with every remnant of the old regime, a new calendar was adopted. The French Revolutionary Calendar (or Republican Calendar) was officially adopted in France on October 24, 1793 and abolished on 1 January 1806, by Emperor Napoleon I. Years were counted from the beginning of the "Republican Era," September 22, 1792 (the day the French First Republic was proclaimed, one day after the Convention abolished the monarchy). Thus, the calendar is based on a date one year before it was actually adopted. The first day of each year included the autumnal equinox.

longer confined alone but held with the other prisoners. He saw Charles every week, and was able to deliver messages straight from his lips. Sometimes Charles sent Lucie a letter, but she was not allowed to write to him. Of the hundreds of suspected "enemies of the republic," the most suspected were those emigrants who had established permanent connections abroad.

This new role of the Doctor's was undoubtedly strenuous. Still, the wise Mr. Lorry saw that the Doctor took pride in his activities, and this pride was a source of strength for him. Nothing unbecoming tinged the pride; it was a natural and worthy one; but he observed it as a curiosity. The Doctor knew that—up until then—his imprisonment had been viewed by his daughter and friend as an affliction, a source of weakness. Now that this was changed, and the Doctor regarded himself as invested with a power that no one else possessed. And this was the power that would ultimately lead to Charles's release, maybe even his ability to return to England. This change in the Doctor's attitude eventually reached the point, that he took charge of the little trio, and required them—as the weaker and dependent—to rely on him. Now, he was taking care of Lucie, whereas in London, she had taken care of him.

"A surprising turn of events," thought Mr. Lorry, in his wise and friendly way, "but there is something… right…about it. So, take charge, my friend. We couldn't be in better hands."

But, although the Doctor tried hard—and never stopped trying—to get Charles Darnay freed—or at least get him brought to trial—the public current of the time was too strong and fast for him. The New Era began. The king was tried, doomed, and beheaded. The Republic of Liberty, Equality, Fraternity, or Death, declared for victory or death against the world in arms. The black flag waved night and day from the great towers of Notre Dame. Three hundred thousand men—called to arms against the tyrants of the earth—rose from all the parts of France. How could one man's private influence prevail against the floods of the Year One of Liberty—the flood of blood rising from below, not of rain falling from above!

There was no pause, no pity, no peace, no period of rest, no sense of the passing of time. Though days and nights circled as regularly as when time was young, and the evening and morning were the first day, there was no other measurement of time. It was lost in the raging fever of a nation, just as it is in the fever of one patient. Now, breaking the unnatural silence of a whole city, the executioner showed the people the head of the king—and now, it seemed almost in the same breath, the head of his fair wife—which had had eight weary months of imprisoned widowhood and misery, to turn it gray.

And yet, even as the time seemed to fly by, at the same time, it seemed to drag. A revolutionary Tribunal was established in the capital, and forty or fifty thousand revolutionary committees were set up all over the land. The land fell under a law of the Suspected, which took away all security for liberty or life, and delivered any good and innocent person into the hands of any bad and guilty one. Prisons were filled to bursting with people who had committed no crime, and could obtain no hearing. These things became the normal state of affairs, and seemed to become long-standing traditions before they were many weeks old. Above all, one hideous figure grew as familiar as if it had always been there—the figure of the sharp female called La Guillotine.

It was the popular topic for jokes—the best cure for a headache—it was guaranteed to prevent one's hair from turning gray—it made the skin gloriously pale—it was the National Razor which shaved close—those who "kissed" La Guillotine, looked through the little window and sneezed into the sack.

It became a sign of renewal and regeneration, even replacing the Cross. Models of it were worn on chains from which the Cross was thrown away. It was bowed down to and believed in while the Cross was denied.

✅ *Genesis 1: 3–5 reads, "God said, 'Let there be light.' And there was light. And God saw the light, that it was good. And God divided the light from the darkness. And God called the light Day, and the darkness he called Night. And the evening and the morning were the first day." In this fairly difficult passage, Dickens is emphasizing the chaos into which France has fallen with the execution of its King. He is also probably commenting on the Revolutionary calendar that was supposed to replace the traditional Christian one.*

✅ *The queen, Marie Antoinette, was executed eight months after her husband. However, Dickens is saying, in the Revolution's confused sense of the passage of time, the two executions seemed to come almost simultaneously.*

✅ *Pale skin was considered so beautiful that women of fashion would cover their faces with a plaster-like substance and then paint their make-up on. The joke is that, once the head is severed from the body, the skin of the face would, of course, be pale.*

❓ *What is significant about the Guillotine taking the place of the Cross in Revolution culture?*

It had cut off so many heads, that it was permanently stained a foul red, as was the ground it polluted. It was taken apart—like a toy-puzzle for a young Devil—and put together again when it was needed. It silenced the most eloquent speakers, struck down the powerful, and abolished the beautiful and good. In one morning, it lopped off the heads of twenty-two public officials in just as many minutes. The name of Samson, the strong man of Old Scripture, had been given to the chief operator who worked it. Armed with the guillotine instead of a donkey's jawbone, he was stronger than his namesake, and blinder, and killed his thousand Philistines every day.

Explain the use of the executioner to allude to Samson.

The Doctor walked past these horrors, and the bloodthirsty mob, careful to stare straight ahead and not show an expression of disgust. Still, he was confident in his power, cautiously persistent in his goal, and had no doubt that he would eventually be able to secure Charles's release. Yet the current of the time swept by, so strong and deep, and carried the time away so quickly, that Charles had been in prison one year and three months. The Revolution had become so much more wicked and unfocused in that December, that the rivers of the South were jammed with the bodies of innocent people who had been violently drowned by night. Prisoners were shot in lines and squares under the southern wintry sun. Still, the Doctor walked among the terrors looking neither left nor right. No man was better known than he, in Paris, yet no man was in a stranger situation. Silent and kind, he was indispensable both in the hospital and the prisons. He used his art to tend to murderers and their victims alike. He was a man apart. Practicing his medicine, the appearance and the story of the "Bastille Captive" put him in his own class of men. He was not suspected. He was never brought in for questioning. In many ways, it was almost as if he were more a spirit moving among living persons than a living person himself.

Charles arrived in France in September 1792. It is now December 1793.

Research Opportunity:

Research and report on the details of the calendar developed and adopted during the French Revolution.

A Tale of Two Cities

CHARLES DICKENS

CHAPTER V
The Woodcutter

ONE YEAR AND three months. During all that time Lucie was never sure, from hour to hour, that the Guillotine would not cut off her husband's head the next day. Every day, through the stony streets, the farmers' carts that once had brought scant amounts of food from the famished countryside into the famished city now rattled along, filled with Enemies of the Revolution who were condemned to die. Lovely girls, bright women of all ages and conditions, men—both young and old—gentlemen and peasants. All were destined to feed the neverending hunger of La Guillotine. Every day, cartloads of people were brought into light from the dark cellars of the filthy prisons, and carried to *Her* through the streets to satisfy her unquenchable thirst. Liberty, Equality, Fraternity, or Death—the last was absolutely the easiest to grant.

So, if the dangerous situation Lucie Manette Darnay had suddenly found herself in drew her into periods of despair, she was really no different from many women. But, from the hour when she first held the white head of her father in the garret of Saint Antoine, she had been true to her duties. She was truest to them during times of trial—as all quietly loyal and good persons have always been and will always be.

❷ *To whom does the "Her" refer?*

✔ *Note Dickens's sarcasm here. It is easier to kill people than to attempt to give them the ideals liberty, freedom, and brotherhood.*

As soon as they were established in their new home, and her father had begun his work, she arranged her little household exactly as if her husband were there. Everything had its appointed place and its appointed time. Little Lucie had her lessons as regularly as if they had all been at home in England. The little tricks Lucie used to allow herself to believe that she and Charles would soon be reunited, the little things she did to prepare for his return—setting aside his chair and his books—and the solemn prayers she whispered were just about the only ways she expressed how heavily her worries weighed on her mind.

Her appearance did not really change. The plain dark dresses that looked almost like mourning dresses, which she and her child wore, were as neat and as cared for as the brighter clothes of happy days. She did lose her color, and the old and intent expression on her forehead became her usual expression. Otherwise, she remained very pretty. Sometimes at night, when she kissed her father, she would burst into the grief she had kept inside all day, and would tell him that the only person she could rely on was him. He always answered firmly, "Nothing can happen to him without my knowledge, and I know that I can save him, Lucie."

Only a few weeks after they arrived in Paris, the Doctor came home one evening and said, "My dear, there is an upper window in the prison. Sometimes Charles is able to be there at three in the afternoon. When he can get to it, he thinks he might be able to see you in the street if you stood in a certain place that I can show you. But you will not be able to see him. Even if you could, it would not be safe for you to make any sign of recognition."

"O show me the place, father, and I will go there every day."

From that time, in every kind of weather, she waited there two hours every day. As the clock struck two, she was there, and at four she turned away. When it was not too wet or cold for her child to be with her, they went together. Otherwise, she went alone. But, she never missed a single day.

Her waiting spot was the dark and dirty corner of a small, winding street. A woodcutter's shack was the only house at that end. The rest of the street was wall. On the third day of her being there, the woodcutter noticed her.

"Good day, Citizeness."

"Good day, Citizen."

This form of address was now required by law. The more enthusiastic patriots had been using it for some time, but now it was law for everybody.

"Walking here again, Citizeness?"

"You see me, Citizen!"

The woodcutter, who was a little man (he had once been a mender of roads), glanced at the prison, pointed toward the prison, and—putting his ten fingers before his face to represent bars— peeped through them humorously. "But it's none of my business," he said and went on sawing his wood.

❷ *What are we being told here?*

The next day he was watching for her, and spoke to her the moment she appeared.

"What? Walking here again, Citizeness?"

"Yes, Citizen."

"Ah! A child too! Is this your mother, my little Citizeness?"

"Should I say yes, Mamma?" whispered little Lucie, drawing close to her mother.

"Yes, dear."

Little Lucie looked up at the woodcutter. "Yes, Citizen."

"Ah! But it's not my business. My work is my business. See my saw! I call it my Little Guillotine. La, la, la; La, la, la! And off his head comes!" The end of the log fell as he spoke, and he threw it into a basket.

"I call myself the Samson of the firewood guillotine. See here again! Loo, loo, loo; Loo, loo, loo! And off her head comes! Now, a child. Tickle, tickle; Pickle, pickle! And off its head comes. All the family!"

❷ *Notice that the woodcutter has cut off three "heads": a man's, a woman's, and a child's. What might he be suggesting?*

Lucie shuddered as he threw two more pieces of

firewood into his basket, but it was impossible to be there while the woodcutter was at work, and not be in his sight. From that point on, she always spoke to him first in an attempt to secure his good will. She often gave him drink-money, which he readily received.

He was an odd fellow, and sometimes when she forgot about him while she gazed at the prison roof and grates, lifting her heart up to her husband. But, when she came to herself, she would always find him looking at her, with his knee on his bench and his saw stopped in its work. "But it's not my business!" he would generally say at those times, and would briskly begin his sawing again.

In every kind of weather, in the snow and frost of winter, in the bitter winds of spring, in the hot sunshine of summer, in the rains of autumn, and again in the snow and frost of winter, Lucie passed two hours every day at this place. Every day when she left it, she kissed the prison wall. She learned from her father that her husband did see her. Perhaps it might be once in five or six times. Then it might be two or three times in a row. It might be not for a week or two. It was enough that he could and did see her when he had the chance, and—on that possibility—she would have gladly waited the entire day, seven days a week.

And so Lucie's year passed until the month of December 1793, while her father daily walked among the terrors, looking neither left nor right. One lightly-snowing afternoon she arrived at the usual corner. It was the day of some riotous rejoicing and a sort of festival. She saw the houses—as she walked along—decorated with little pikes, and with little red caps stuck upon them. They were also decorated with tricolored ribbons and with the standard inscription in tricolored letters, "Republic One and Indivisible. Liberty, Equality, Fraternity, or Death!"

The miserable shop of the woodcutter was so small, that its entire front furnished very little space for this motto. He did, nonetheless, find someone to scrawl the words wherever there was room. On his roof, he displayed the pike and cap, as a good citizen must, and in a window he set his saw, calling it his "Little Guillotine." His shop was closed, and he was not there—which was a relief to Lucie.

But, he was not far away, for soon she heard movement and shouting coming from down the street. The unusual noise frightened her. A moment later, a throng of people came pouring around the corner by the prison wall, in the midst of whom was the woodcutter hand in hand with the Vengeance. There were at least five hundred people, and they were dancing like five thousand demons. There was no other music than their own singing. They danced to the popular Revolution song, keeping a ferocious time that was like a gnashing of teeth in unison. Men and women danced together, women danced together, men danced together, as chance brought them together. At first, they were a mere storm of coarse red caps and coarse woolen rags; but, as they filled the place, and stopped to dance about Lucie, some ghostly figure of a lunatic dancer seemed to rise up among them. They advanced, retreated, slapped another's hands, clutched another's heads, spun around alone, grabbed one another and spun round in pairs, until many of them fell to the ground. While those were down, the rest linked hand in hand, and all spun round together. Then the ring broke, and in separate rings of two and four they turned and turned until they all stopped at once, began again, struck, clutched, and tore, and then reversed the spin, and all spun round the other way. Suddenly they stopped again, paused, began again, formed into lines the whole width of the narrow street, and—with their heads low down and their hands high up—swooped screaming off. No fight could have been half as terrible as this dance. It was so obviously a decayed sport—something that had once been innocent but had sunk into pure deviltry—a healthy pastime that had deteriorated into a means of angering the blood, bewildering the senses, and hardening the heart. Any actual dancing skill that

❓ *What important piece of information is being emphasized here?*

✅ *The dance Dickens is describing is the Carmagnole. Originally a peasant costume from the Piedmont region of Italy, it was brought to Paris by the revolutionaries in Marseilles, in 1789. The name also was given to a revolutionary song in 1792, as well as the wild dance that went with it. This song heaps scorn upon Marie Antoinette (Madame Veto), who was believed to be a traitor, and the aristocrats who supported her. The tune was simple enough that even the illiterate could learn the lyrics with which to proclaim their devotion to the Revolution. The lyrics to the song appear in the Teacher's Guide.*

may have been demonstrated only served to make the dance even uglier, showing how perverted everything that had once been good had become.

This was the Carmagnole. As it passed, leaving Lucie frightened and bewildered in the doorway of the woodcutter's house, the feathery snow fell as quietly and lay as white and soft, as if the dance had never passed.

She turned and saw her father standing beside her. "O father!" she said, "such a cruel sight."

"I know, my dear, I know. I have seen it many times. But don't be frightened! Not one of them would harm you."

"I am not frightened for myself, Father. But when I think of Charles and these cruel, cruel people."

"We will free him from their cruelty very soon. When I left him, he was climbing to the window, and I came to tell you. There is no one here to see. You may kiss your hand toward that highest shelving roof."

"I do, father, and I send him my soul with it!"

"Can you see him?"

"No, father," said Lucie, weeping as she kissed her hand.

They heard a muffled footstep in the snow. Madame Defarge. "I salute you, Citizeness," said the Doctor.

"I salute you, Citizen," she replied, passing. Nothing more. Madame Defarge was gone, like a shadow over the white road.

"Give me your arm. Let Charles see you walk away bravely and cheerfully." When they had left the spot, he paused and whispered to her, "Charles is summoned for tomorrow."

"For tomorrow!"

"There is no time to lose. I am well prepared, but there are some things I must do, that I could not do until he was actually summoned before the Tribunal. He has not received the notice yet, but I know that he will be summoned for tomorrow. You are not afraid?"

She could scarcely answer, "I trust in you."

❷ *Why do you suppose Dickens has Madame Defarge pass by on this particular day?*

"Do so, completely. Your suspense is nearly ended, my darling. He shall be restored to you within a few hours. I have secured for him every form of protection I can. I must see Mr. Lorry."

He stopped. They heard a heavy lumbering of wheels, and they both knew too well what it meant. One. Two. Three. Three tumbrels faring away with their dread loads over the hushing snow.

"I must see Lorry," the Doctor repeated, turning her away.

The loyal old gentleman was still in his important position in the bank. He and his books were frequently called for to examine which property had been confiscated and made national. What he could save for the owners, he saved. There was no better man alive to hold onto what Tellson's had secured for their clients before the confiscations, and to keep quiet about how much they still had.

A murky red and yellow sky, and a rising mist from the River Seine, signaled the approach of darkness. It was almost dark when they arrived at the Bank. The stately residence of the banished nobleman was completely deserted. Above a heap of dust and ashes in the court, ran the letters: *National Property. Republic One and Indivisible. Liberty, Equality, Fraternity, or Death!*

There was someone with Mr. Lorry—the owner of a riding coat sitting on a chair—who looked as if he did not want to be seen. When she saw him, Lucie stopped where she was and uttered a sharp cry. It couldn't be Charles, free and sitting, talking with Mr. Lorry. It was with a sharp pang of disappointment when the man turned fully toward her and smiled, and she recognized her sworn friend, Sydney Carton. "He has been taken to the Conciergerie, and summoned for tomorrow."

THIS IS THE END OF THE
TWENTY-THIRD WEEKLY INSTALLMENT.

> ✔ *The tumbrels are the farmers' carts that are now used to transport the condemned to the Guillotine.*

> ✔ *The Conciergerie was originally a part of the palace of King Philip IV and was named for the royal guards (Concierge) who protected it. It was converted into a prison after the French royal family established its royal residence in the Louvre Palace (now a famous art museum). During the Reign of Terror, the Conciergerie was known at the "ante-chamber of the Guillotine" because it was the place where prisoners waited for their "trials" and again waited to be executed (the only two possible outcomes of a trial before the Tribunal were to be set free or condemned to death). In the period between April 2, 1793 and May 31, 1795, 2,600 persons were driven in tumbrils from the Concierge to nearby Concorde Square and beheaded.*

Review and Predict:

What do we know about Sydney Carton, and what purpose might Dickens have to bring him back into the plot at this point?

A Tale of Two Cities
CHARLES DICKENS

CHAPTER VI
Triumph

THE TRIBUNAL OF five Judges, Public Prosecutor, and Jury, sat every day. Their lists were posted every evening, and were read out by the jailers of the various prisons to their prisoners. The standard jailer-joke was, "Come out and listen to the 'Evening Paper,' you inside there!"

"Charles Evremonde, called Darnay!"

So at last began the 'Evening Paper' at La Force.

When a name was called, its owner stepped forward into a spot reserved for those who were announced as appearing on the Tribunal's fatal list. Charles Evremonde, called Darnay, knew what the announcement of his name meant. He had seen hundreds called in exactly the same manner.

His bloated jailer glanced over his reading glasses to be certain that Charles had taken his place. Then he continued reading the list, making a similar pause at each name. There were twenty-three names, but only twenty were responded to. One of the summoned prisoners had died in jail and been forgotten. Two others had already been guillotined and forgotten. The list was read in the same vaulted chamber where Darnay had first seen the associated prisoners on the night of his arrival. Every one of those prisoners had

Note how casually Dickens mentions the callousness and inefficiency of the Republic's prison system.

been killed in the massacre. Every human creature he had since cared for and parted with, had died on the scaffold.

There were hurried words of farewell and kindness, but the parting was soon over. This parting of friends happened every day, and those who remained at La Force for another evening were planning some games of forfeits and a little concert. They all crowded to the grates and wept, but twenty places in the planned entertainments had to be refilled, and it was near the lock-up hour, when the common rooms and corridors would be delivered over to the great dogs who kept watch there through the night.

The prisoners were not unkind or unfeeling in their good-byes, but circumstances didn't encourage the formation of close attachments. Similarly—although with a subtle difference—a type of bravado that led some who would not have been condemned to demand execution, was not mere boastfulness, but a sign of the insanity of the times. It is a known fact that, during plagues, some people will develop a fondness for the disease and almost a desire to die by it.

The passage to the Conciergerie was short and dark. The night in the rat-infested cell was long and cold. The next day, fifteen prisoners were called to trial before Charles Darnay. The fifteen trials combined took no more than an hour and a half—and all fifteen prisoners were condemned.

"Charles Evremonde, called Darnay," was at last called.

His judges sat upon the Bench in feathered hats, but the rough red cap and tricolored cockade was the most common headdress in the room. Looking at the Jury and the riotous audience, Charles could almost believe that the usual order of things was reversed, and that the felons were trying the honest men. The lowest, cruelest, and worst of the people of Paris were in obvious control—shouting and jeering, applauding, booing and howling, with no authority even trying to

To play forfeits, one person is chosen to leave the room. The others each must "forfeit" an item to be placed in the middle of the room. The chosen person returns and "auctions" off each of the forfeited items—describing it as if it were for sale. The person whose item it is must claim it, and then perform some amusing or embarrassing dare (sing a song, dance barefoot, etc.) in order to win it back.

quiet them. Most of the men were armed in one way or another. Some of the women wore knives or daggers. Some ate and drank as they watched.

Many knitted.

Among the knitters was one who sat in a front row beside a man Charles recognized as Defarge. He noticed that once or twice this woman whispered in his ear, and that she seemed to be his wife. But, what he noticed most was that—although they sat as close to him as they could—they never looked toward him. They seemed to be waiting for something with a dogged determination. They looked at the Jury, and at nothing else. Under the President of the Court sat Doctor Manette. From what Charles could see, the Doctor and Mr. Lorry were the only men there—unconnected with the Tribunal—who wore their usual clothes instead of the grosser costume of the Carmagnole.

Charles Evremonde, called Darnay, was accused by the public prosecutor as an emigrant, whose life was forfeit to the Republic, under the decree which banished all emigrants on pain of Death. It did not matter that the decree was dated *after* his return to France. *There* he was, and there was the decree. He had been arrested in France, and his head was demanded.

"Take off his head!" cried the audience. "An enemy to the Republic!"

The President rang his bell to silence those cries, and asked the prisoner whether it was not true that he had lived many years in England?

It was true.

Was he not an emigrant then? What did he call himself?

Not an emigrant, he hoped, within the sense and spirit of the law. Why not? the President of the Court desired to know.

Because he had voluntarily given up a title he disliked, and a social rank he disliked, and had left his country *before* the word "emigrant" had gained its current meaning. In England, he lives by his own

❷ Consider all of the "clues" Dickens has dropped throughout the book that contribute to this scene's suspense.

❷ A law that makes an act committed before the law's passage illegal is called an ex post facto law (from Latin for "from a thing done afterwards," or "after the deed"). Because of their inherent unfairness—how can a person be justly punished for doing something that was not illegal when he did it?—ex post facto laws are expressly forbidden by the Constitution and are considered a violation of the "rule of law" in all free and democratic societies. The fact that Dickens points out that Charles is being tried under such a law indicates the essential unfairness and lawlessness of this First Republic.

❷ What distinction is Charles trying to make? Do you think the Court will make the same distinction?

❷ Remember that Dickens used this same narrative technique when describing Charles's earlier trial in Book II, Chapter III.

work, rather than on the work of the overburdened people of France.

What proof had he of this?

He handed in the names of two witnesses: Theophile Gabelle, and Alexandre Manette.

But he had married in England? the President reminded him.

True, but not an English woman.

A citizeness of France?

Yes. By birth.

Her name and family.

Lucie Manette, only daughter of Doctor Manette, the good physician who sits there.

This answer had a happy effect upon the audience. Cries in praise of the well-known good physician resounded throughout the hall. So easily were the people moved, that tears immediately rolled down several ferocious faces which had been glaring at the prisoner only a moment before, as if they were eager to drag him out into the street and kill him.

Answering this line of questioning in this way, Charles Darnay was carefully following Doctor Manette's instructions. The same advice directed every step that lay before him, and had prepared every inch of his road.

The President of the Court asked, why he returned to France when he did, and not sooner.

He had not returned sooner, he replied, simply because he had no means of living in France, except for those he had given up. In England, he lived by teaching the French language and literature. He returned when he did, on the urgent and written request of a French citizen, who claimed that his life was in danger. He had come back to save a citizen's life regardless of the personal risks. Was that illegal in the eyes of the Republic?

The audience shouted enthusiastically, "No!" and the President rang his bell to quiet them. Ignoring the bell, they continued to cry "No!" until they gradually settled down on their own.

The President asked the name of that citizen. The accused explained that the citizen was Theophile Gabelle, his first witness. He also mentioned Gabelle's letter, which had been taken from him at the Barrier, but which he did not doubt would be found among the papers then before the President.

The Doctor had taken care that it should be there—had assured him that it would be there. The President shuffled through the papers on his desk, found the letter, and read it aloud. Citizen Gabelle was called to confirm that he had, in fact, written that letter. Citizen Gabelle also hinted—very subtly and politely—that, given the heavy burden of work that faced the Tribunal as it prosecuted and tried the many enemies of the Republic, he had been forgotten in his prison of the Abbaye. In fact, the Tribunal seemed to have forgotten all about him until three days ago when he had been summoned before it, and set free. The Jury had claimed that he had earned his freedom by delivering to them the citizen Evremonde, called Darnay. Doctor Manette was questioned next. His high personal popularity, and the cleanness of his answers, made a great impression. He showed that the Accused had been his first friend on his release from his long imprisonment. He explained that the accused had remained in England, always faithful and devoted to his daughter and himself in their exile. He continued that—far from being a favorite of England's Aristocrat government, he had actually stood trial, accused of being a traitor to England and a friend of the United States. As the Doctor made all of these facts clear, with his typical honest simplicity, the Jury and the audience became one. When he appealed to Monsieur Lorry, an English gentleman present in the Court, who had also been a witness on that English trial and could confirm the truth of what the Doctor was claiming, the Jury declared that they had heard enough, and that they were ready with their votes.

At every vote—the Jurymen voted aloud and individually—the audience set up a shout of applause.

❷ *What is Dickens suggesting about Gabelle's imprisonment and the letter he wrote to Darnay?*

All the voices were in the prisoner's favor, and the President declared him free.

What followed was a spectacular scene that perfectly illustrated the fickleness of the mob. The tearful joy with which the entire courtroom received the news of the acquittal showed either that the mob had not lost all sense of humanity or that they wanted to ease the violent, bloodthirsty reputation which they had earned in other countries. Jurymen and audience members rushed to embrace each other and the Freed Prisoner. Charles Darnay was so thronged with people that, after his long and unhealthy imprisonment, he was actually in danger of fainting from exhaustion. With a slight chill, Darnay also acknowledged to himself that—had the Jury voted to execute him—the scene would look very much the same as the wild mob grabbed him and dragged him out into the street.

As there were still many more accused persons to be tried, Darnay was quickly removed from the courtroom, and this saved him from the dangerous clutches of the well-wishing crowd. The next called were five men who were to be tried together—accused of being enemies of the Republic because they had failed to "assist her by word or deed." Their trial was so quick—almost as if the Jury had regained its bloodthirstiness and wanted to make up for the opportunity they lost in acquitting Charles—that the five were condemned even before Charles, the Doctor, and Mr. Lorry managed to make their way out into the street. As these unfortunate five were being dragged from the room, the first of them looked over at Charles and raised his forefinger. This was the sign among the prisoners to indicate that they had been sentenced to death. The four companions whispered ironically, "Long live the Republic!"

The five had had, it is true, no audience to lengthen their trial. When Charles and Doctor Manette passed through the gate, there was a great crowd around. Charles thought he recognized every face he had seen in Court—except two, for which he looked in vain. As

❷ *What two faces are not with the celebrating crowd outside the court?*

he came out, the crowd mobbed him again, weeping, embracing, and shouting.

They put him into a great chair that they had taken either out of the Court itself, or one of its rooms or hallways. Over the chair they had thrown a red flag, and to the back of it they had tied a pike with a red cap on its top. In this car of triumph, he was carried to his home on men's shoulders. He was surrounded by a sea of red caps heaving about him, and more than once he suspected that he was dreaming, and that he was in a tumbrel on his way to the Guillotine.

They formed a wild, dreamlike parade. People embraced whomever they met and pointed him out. They carried him on, reddening the snowy streets with the popular color of the Republic, just as they had reddened the streets with a deeper color. They carried him into the courtyard of the building where he lived. Dr. Manette had gone on before, to prepare Lucie, and when her husband stood upon his feet, she fainted into his arms. As he held her close and kissed her, a few of the people began dancing. Immediately the rest all began dancing, and the courtyard overflowed with the Carmagnole. Then, they raised into the empty chair a young woman from the crowd to be carried as the Goddess of Liberty, and then swelling and overflowing out into the adjacent streets, and along the river's bank, and over the bridge, the Carmagnole absorbed them all and whirled them away.

Charles clutched the Doctor's hand, as he stood victorious and proud before him. He grasped the hand of Mr. Lorry, who came panting in breathless from his struggle against the tide of the Carmagnole. He kissed little Lucie, lifting her up so that she could clasp her arms round his neck. And he embraced the energetic and faithful Pross. Then he took his wife into his arms, and carried her up to their rooms.

"Lucie! I am safe."

"Oh Charles, let me thank God for this on my knees."

They all reverently bowed their heads and hearts.

❓ *How would you characterize the character of Lucie Darnay?*

✒ *According to French historian Louis Blanc, an actress, Mlle. Malliard was selected to personify the Goddess of Liberty. She was taken to Notre Dame Cathedral in Paris, seated on the altar and given a large candle to hold, signifying that Liberty was the light of the world.*

In Roman mythology, the goddess of freedom is Libertas. Originally a goddess of personal freedom, she evolved to become the goddess of the entire commonwealth. She was commonly depicted as a female figure wearing a pileus (a felt cap, worn by slaves when they were set free), a wreath of laurels, and carrying a spear. French sculptor Frederic-Auguste Bartholdi based his famous "Liberty Enlightening the World" on these figures of the goddess of Liberty, replacing Libertas's felt cap with a crown and her spear with a torch and carved tablet. We know this famous figure by her more common name, The Statue of Liberty.

When she was again in his arms, he said to her, "And now thank your father and congratulate him. No other man in France could have done what he has done for me."

She laid her head upon her father's breast, as she had laid his poor head on her own breast, long, long ago. He was happy that he had been able to repay her earlier devotion to him. He was rewarded for his suffering. He was proud of his strength. "You must not be weak, my darling," he told her. "Stop trembling. I have saved him."

Writing Opportunity:

Compare and contrast Darnay's two capital trials.

Writing Opportunity:

Examine the different contexts in which Dickens uses the color red. What effect does Dickens create in each of these cases.

Research Opportunity:

Research and report on the events of November 10, 1793 and/or December 10, 1793, especially the "transformation" of the Cathedral of Notre Dame into the "Temple of Reason," and the celebrations of the Goddess(es) of Liberty.

A Tale of Two Cities
CHARLES DICKENS

CHAPTER VII
A Knock at the Door

"I HAVE SAVED HIM."

It was not merely another dream from which the Doctor always awoke. Charles was really here. Yet, his wife trembled with a vague but heavy fear.

The atmosphere in the whole city was so thick and dark. The people were so passionately revengeful and fitful. The innocent were so often put to death on vague suspicion and simple malice. It was impossible to forget that many men and women—who were as innocent as her husband and as dear to others as he was to her—every day shared the fate which he had been spared. Her heart simply could not be as light and happy as she felt it should be. The shadows of the wintry afternoon were beginning to fall, and even now the dreadful carts were rolling through the streets. Her mind followed them, looking for him among the Condemned. And then she clung closer to his real presence and trembled more.

Her father, strong and confident in the face of Lucie's fear, was a remarkable sight. No attic, no shoemaking, no *One Hundred and Five, North Tower,* now! He had accomplished the task he had set for himself. His promise was redeemed. He had saved Charles. Let them all lean on him.

❷ *What evidence suggests that this is not yet the story's "happy ending"?*

They all ran a very thrifty household—not only because it was safest not to show off wealth in the face of the people's poverty, but also because they were not rich. Charles, throughout his imprisonment, had had to pay heavily for his bad food, and for his guard, and toward the living of the poorer prisoners. Partly for this reason, and partly to avoid having a spy among them, they kept no servant. The citizen and citizeness who acted as porters at the courtyard gate, performed occasional tasks for them, and Jerry (almost wholly transferred to them by Mr. Lorry) had become their daily employee, and slept there every night.

It was a law of the Republic One and Indivisible of Liberty, Equality, Fraternity, or Death, that the name of every resident of every house or apartment be legibly inscribed on the door or doorpost of that house. Mr. Jerry Cruncher's name, therefore, duly appeared on the doorpost down below; and—as the afternoon shadows deepened—Jerry Cruncher himself appeared. He had been supervising a painter whom Doctor Manette had hired to add the name of "Charles Evremonde, called Darnay" to the list of residents.

In the universal fear and distrust that darkened the time, all the usual harmless ways of life were changed. In the Doctor's little household—as in very many others—the articles of daily consumption that were wanted were purchased every evening, in small quantities and at various small shops. Their desire was not to attract any attention to themselves or to cause any envy among the poor shopkeepers by purchasing too much at one time.

For several months, Miss Pross and Mr. Cruncher had done the shopping, Pross carrying the money and Jerry the basket. Every afternoon at about the time when the street lamps were lighted, they ventured out and made their necessary purchases. Although Miss Pross—through her long association with a French family—might have been very comfortable with the French language, she had no desire to learn it and, therefore, knew no more of that "nonsense" (as she

❷ *Consider Miss Pross's refusal to learn French and her calling it "nonsense." How eager are Americans to learn a language other than their own?*

was pleased to call it) than Mr. Cruncher did. So her manner of marketing was to throw a noun at the head of a shopkeeper, and, if that were not the name of the item she wanted, to look round for that thing, take hold of it, and hold on to it until the bargain was concluded. She always made a bargain for it, by holding up, as a statement of its just price, one finger less than the merchant held up, whatever his number might be.

"Now, Mr. Cruncher," said Miss Pross, whose eyes were red from crying for joy, "if you are ready, I am."

Jerry hoarsely said that he was at Miss Pross' sservice. He had worn all his rust off long ago, but nothing would file his spiky head down.

"We need all sorts of things," said Miss Pross, "so we'll probably have a difficult time. We want wine, too. Nice toasts these Redheads will be drinking, wherever we buy it."

"It shouldn't make any difference to you," retorted Jerry, "whether they drink to your health or the Old Un's."

"Who's that?" said Miss Pross.

Mr. Cruncher, pretending an air of wise condescension, explained himself as meaning "Old Nick's."

"Ha!" said Miss Pross, "You don't need an interpreter to understand these French creatures. They have only one toast, and it's, 'To Midnight Murder and Mischief!'"

"Hush! Please be careful!" cried Lucie.

"Yes, yes, yes, I'll be careful," said Miss Pross; "but I may say in the privacy of our home, that I hope there won't be any onion-and tobacco-breathed hugging going on in the streets. Now, Ladybird, do not move from that fire till I come back! Take care of the dear husband you have recovered, and don't move your pretty head from his shoulder—as you have it now—until I come back. May I ask a question, Doctor Manette, before I go?"

❷ What is the purpose of this mildly humorous scene of Pross and Cruncher shopping?

❷ Remember that Jerry had been a "resurrectionist," digging up corpses from the cemetery and selling them for scientific experiments. He was also described as having thick, spiky hair.

❷ Why does Miss Pross refer to the French as "Redheads"?

❷ Old Nick was a common nickname for the Devil.

Miss Pross's motto is a quotation from the second stanza of the British national anthem, "God Save the King," or "God Save the Queen" (depending on the gender of the monarch ruling at the time). Americans borrowed the tune for our well-known "My Country, 'Tis of Thee." Full lyrics of the anthem are in the Teacher's Guide.

"I think you may take that liberty," the Doctor answered, smiling.

"For goodness sake, don't talk about *Liberty*. We've had quite enough of that," said Miss Pross.

"Hush, dear! Again?" Lucie remonstrated.

"Well, my sweet," said Miss Pross, nodding her head energetically, "the fact of the matter is that I am a subject of His Most Gracious Majesty King George the Third." Miss Pross curtseyed at the name and continued, "and as a British subject, my motto is, 'Confound their politics, Frustrate their knavish tricks, On him our hopes we fix, God save the King!'"

Mr. Cruncher, in a sudden surge of loyalty, growlingly repeated the words after Miss Pross, like somebody at church.

"I am glad you have so much of the Englishman in you, though I wish you had never taken that cold in your voice," said Miss Pross, approvingly. "But my question, Doctor Manette is...Is there..." Here she paused, trying to make light of a subject that was really a source of concern for all of them. "Is there any chance of our getting out of this place?"

"I'm afraid not yet. It would still be dangerous for Charles."

"Heigh-ho-hum!" said Miss Pross, cheerfully stifling a sigh as she glanced at Lucie's golden hair in the light of the fire. "Then we must have patience and wait, that's all. We must hold up our heads and fight low, as my brother Solomon used to say. Let's go, Mr. Cruncher! Don't you move, Ladybird!"

They went out, leaving Lucie, and her husband, her father, and the child, by a bright fire. Mr. Lorry was expected to arrive at any moment from the Banking House. Miss Pross had lighted the lamp, but had put it aside in a corner, so that they could enjoy the firelight undisturbed. Little Lucie sat by her grandfather with her hands clasped through his arm, while he—in a tone not rising much above a whisper—began to tell her a story of a great and powerful Fairy who opened a prison wall and let out a prisoner who had once done the Fairy a favor. All was subdued and quiet, and Lucie was more at ease than she had been.

"What is that?" she cried suddenly.

"My dear!" said her father, stopping in his story, and laying his hand on hers, "control yourself. You're so anxious that the smallest thing—nothing—startles you!"

"I thought I heard strange footsteps on the stairs," she said excusing herself, with a pale face and in a faltering voice.

"My love, the staircase is as still as Death."

As he said the word, a blow was struck upon the door.

Don't miss the irony in the Doctor's simile.

"Oh father, father. What can this be! Hide Charles. Save him!"

"My child," said the Doctor, rising, and laying his hand upon her shoulder, "I have already saved him. What weakness is this, my dear! Let me check."

He took the lamp in his hand, crossed the two outer rooms, and opened the door. A rude clattering of feet over the floor, and four rough men in red caps, armed with sabers and pistols, entered the room.

"The Citizen Evremonde, called Darnay," said the first.

"Who seeks him?" answered Darnay.

"I seek him. We seek him. I know you, Evremonde. I saw you before the Tribunal today. You are again the prisoner of the Republic."

The four surrounded him, where he stood with his wife and child clinging to him.

"Tell me how and why am I again a prisoner?"

"It is enough that you return straight to the Conciergerie, and will know tomorrow. You are summoned for tomorrow."

What is the literary term for this type of event in a story?

Doctor Manette was so shocked and alarmed by this intrusion that he seemed to be turned into stone. He stood with the lamp in his hand, as if he were a statue made to hold it. Finally, he managed to stir from his trance, put the lamp down, and confront the speaker. "You have said you know him. Do you know me?"

"Yes, I know you, Citizen Doctor."

"We all know you, Citizen Doctor," said the other three.

He looked absently from one to another, and said, in a lower voice, after a pause, "Will you answer his question for me then? How does it happen that he is again a prisoner of the Republic?"

"Citizen Doctor," said the first, reluctantly, "he has been denounced by the Section of Saint Antoine. This citizen," pointing out the second who had entered, "is from Saint Antoine."

The citizen he indicated nodded his head, and added, "He is accused by Saint Antoine."

"Accused of *what*?" asked the Doctor.

"Citizen Doctor," said the first, still reluctantly, "please ask no more. If the Republic demands sacrifices from you, we have no doubt that you—as a good patriot—will be happy to make them. The Republic is more important than any one of us. The People is supreme. Evremonde, we are in a hurry."

"One word," the Doctor pleaded. "Will you tell me who denounced him?"

"That is against the law," answered the first. "But you can ask this citizen from Saint Antoine."

The Doctor turned toward that man.

He moved uneasily on his feet, rubbed his beard a little, and at length said, "Well! Truly it is against law. But he is denounced—severely—by the Citizen and Citizeness Defarge. And by one other."

"What other?"

"Do you ask, Citizen Doctor?"

"Yes."

"Then," said he of Saint Antoine, with a strange look, "you will be answered tomorrow. Now, I will say no more!"

THIS IS THE END OF THE
TWENTY-FOURTH WEEKLY INSTALLMENT.

Review and Predict:

Look at all of the information we have and predict a possible outcome of the story. Specifically:

- Who is the third denouncer? Why do you suspect him or her?

- Will Charles be saved? How or by whom?

A Tale of Two Cities

C H A R L E S   D I C K E N S

C H A P T E R   V I I I
A Hand at Cards

HAPPILY UNAWARE OF the new crisis at home, Miss Pross wove her way through the narrow streets and crossed the river by the bridge of the Pont-Neuf, mulling over in her mind the number of important purchases she had to make. Mr. Cruncher, carrying the basket, walked beside her. They both looked to the right and to the left into most of the shops they passed, looked out for social crowds of people, and went out of their way to avoid any very excited group of talkers. It was a raw evening, and the misty river, blurred with blazing lights and harsh noises, showed where the barges were stationed in which the smiths worked, making guns for the Army of the Republic. Woe to the man who played tricks with that Army, or got an undeserved promotion in it! Better for him that his beard had never grown, for the National Razor shaved him close.

Having purchased a few small articles from the grocer, and a tiny bit of oil for the lamp, Miss Pross reminded herself of the wine they wanted. After peeping into several wine shops, she stopped at the sign of the *Good Republican Brutus of Antiquity*—not far from the National Palace—where she liked the appearance of things. This shop looked quieter than

❷ *What is the National Razor? What figure of speech is Dickens using?*

✅ *The name of the wine shop is probably an obscure allusion to Lucius Junius Brutus who rebelled against the last Roman king and helped establish the Roman Republic. References to the Roman Republic were popular during the French Revolution as the French fancied themselves as establishing something like a Roman Republic themselves.*

Remember that the Defarges' wine shop in the quarter of Saint Antoine was also a gathering place for the Revolution where outsiders were distrusted and not really welcome.

any other wine shop they had passed. And, though red with patriotic caps, it did not seem as red as the rest. She asked Mr. Cruncher what he thought, and he agreed that the wine shop of the *Good Republican Brutus of Antiquity* would be a safe place for them to enter. And so she did, accompanied by her companion and protector.

The two ill-fitting customers entered the shop and walked defiantly past the crowd of dirty, bearded, pipe-smoking men—some wearing weapons, others with their weapons ready at nearby tables—who were gathered around a shirtless man reading aloud from a magazine. At a few of the other tables, there were customers who looked like sleeping dogs or bears in their shaggy coats and pants. When they reached the counter, they showed the shopkeeper what they wanted.

While the shopkeeper was measuring out the wine they had requested, a man in a far corner of the shop stood, muttered a few words of good-bye to his companion, and turned to leave. He briefly faced Miss Pross, who uttered a scream and clapped her hands.

In a moment, everyone in the shop was on their feet. Clearly a fight had broken out and somebody had been murdered. Everybody looked to see the victim fall, but all they saw were a man and a woman standing and staring at each other. The man looked every inch a Frenchman—and a thorough Republican at that. The woman was clearly English.

"What is the matter?" said the man who had caused Miss Pross to scream, whispering angrily in English.

"Oh, Solomon, dear Solomon!" cried Miss Pross, clapping her hands again. "After not seeing you or hearing from you in so long, do I find you here?"

Remember that Solomon is Miss Pross's long-lost brother. In Book II, Chapter VI, we were told that he had "borrowed" money from Miss Pross, lost it in some bad investments, and then deserted her in poverty. She had not heard from him since, but still regarded him with admiration and affection.

"Don't call me Solomon. Do you want to be the death of me?" asked the man, in a secretive, frightened way.

"Brother, brother!" cried Miss Pross, bursting into

tears. "What have I done to you that you should ask me such a cruel question?"

"Then hold your meddlesome tongue," said Solomon, "and come outside, if you want to speak to me. Pay for your wine, and come outside. Who's this man?"

Miss Pross shook her head lovingly yet sadly at her brother, who showed no sign that he was happy to be reunited with her. Through her tears, she answered, "This is Mr. Cruncher."

"Bring him outside too," said Solomon. "Does he think I am a ghost?"

Apparently, Mr. Cruncher did, to judge from his looks. He said not a word, however, and Miss Pross, digging to the bottom of her purse through her tears with great difficulty, paid for her wine. As she did so, Solomon spoke to the other shop patrons—in French—and they all returned to what they had been doing before Miss Pross's outburst.

"Now," said Solomon, stopping at the dark street corner, "what do you want?"

"How dreadfully unkind, from a brother I never stopped loving," cried Miss Pross, "to give me such a greeting, and show me no affection!"

"There. Confound it! There!" Solomon jerked his head forward and made a dab at Miss Pross's lips with his own. "Now are you happy?"

Miss Pross only shook her head and wept in silence.

"If you expect me to be surprised," said her brother Solomon, "I'm not. I knew you were here. I know about most people who are here. If you really don't want to put me in danger—which I half believe you do—go away as soon as possible, and leave me alone. I am busy. I am an official."

"My English brother Solomon," mourned Miss Pross, casting up her tear-filled eyes, "who had the potential to be one of the best and greatest men in his native country, an official among foreigners! And *such* foreigners! I'd almost rather see him lying in his–"

"I knew it!" cried her brother, interrupting. "I knew it. You want me dead. I shall be placed under suspicion, by my own sister. Just as I'm beginning to make a 'go' of things!"

"Heaven forbid!" cried Miss Pross. "I'd rather never see you again than see you dead. For I have always loved you, and I always will. Just say one affectionate word to me—let me know that there is not anger or bitterness or hatred between us, and I'll let you go."

Good Miss Pross begged her brother if the trouble between them had been her fault. As if Mr. Lorry had not known it for a fact, years ago, in the quiet corner in Soho, that this precious brother had spent her money and left her!

He did mutter the affectionate word she desired, but he said it with more grudging condescension than would have been possible if he really had been the morally upright sibling and she the scoundrel. But this is how it is with all people all over the world. As he struggled to show his sister some affection, Mr. Cruncher tapped him on the shoulder and unexpectedly asked him, "Is your name possibly John Solomon, or Solomon John?"

The official turned toward Jerry with sudden distrust.

"Come!" said Mr. Cruncher. "Speak out, you know. John Solomon, or Solomon John? She calls you Solomon, and she must know, being your sister. And I know you're John, you know. Which of the two goes first? And regarding that name of Pross...That wasn't your name in England."

"What do you mean?"

"Well, I don't know exactly what I mean, for I can't quite remember *what* your name was back home."

"No?"

"No. But I'll swear it had two syllables."

"Really?"

"Yes. The other one was one syllable. I know you. You was a spy-witness at the Bailey. What, in the name of the Father of Lies, own father to yourself, was you called at that time?"

"Barsad," said another voice, joining into the conversation.

"That's the name!" cried Jerry.

The speaker who had interrupted, was Sydney Carton. He had his hands behind him under the tails of his riding coat, and he stood at Mr. Cruncher's elbow as casually as he might have stood on any street corner in London.

"Don't be alarmed, my dear Miss Pross. I arrived at Mr. Lorry's, to his surprise, yesterday evening; we agreed that I would not present myself anywhere else until everything was all right, or unless I could be useful. I am here, to beg a little talk with your brother. I wish you had a better-employed brother than Mr. Barsad. I wish—for your sake— that Mr. Barsad was not a 'Sheep of the Prisons.'"

"Sheep" was a slang word for spy. The spy, who was pale, turned even paler, and asked Sydney Carton how he dared to—

"I'll tell you," said Sydney. "I saw you, Mr. Barsad, coming out of the Conciergerie while I was studying the walls, an hour or more ago. You have a memorable face, and I remember faces well. Since I was curious to see you there, and since I have a reason—which I believe you know—for connecting you with a friend of mine who has been very unfortunate lately, I followed you here. I walked into the wine shop here, right behind you, and sat near you. It was not hard to guess your occupation from the way you were bragging in there, and from the many rumors all over Paris about you. So, what had started out as a mere chance meeting began to form itself into a plan. I have a proposal for you, Mr. Barsad."

"What proposal?" the spy asked.

"It might be dangerous to discuss it here in the

❷ *To what trial is Jerry referring? What did we learn about John Barsad at that time?*

✔ *According to the Oxford English Dictionary, a "Sheep of the Prisons" was "a spy quartered in a prison with an accused person with the aim of obtaining incriminating evidence." Historians estimate that there were between 300 to 1,000 "sheep" in the Paris prisons during the Reign of Terror. Most of them were imprisoned themselves, and turned spy in hopes of gaining their own freedom.*

street. Would you favor me—in confidence—a few minutes of your time? Say, at the office of Tellson's Bank?"

"Are you threatening me?"

"Oh! Did I say that?"

"Then, why should I go there?"

"Really, Mr. Barsad, I can't say, if you can't."

"Do you mean that you *won't* say, sir?" the spy irresolutely asked.

"You understand me very perfectly, Mr. Barsad. I won't say why it might be in your best interest to come and talk to me."

"I told you so," said the spy, looking angrily at his sister; "if any trouble comes from this, it's your fault."

"Come, come, Mr. Barsad!" exclaimed Sydney. "Don't be ungrateful. If it weren't for my great respect for your sister, I might not have approached this subject so pleasantly. And I do have a little proposal that I wish to make that will probably turn out well for both of us. Will you go with me to the Bank?"

"I'll hear what you have got to say. Yes, I'll go with you."

"First, I propose that we escort your sister safely to the corner of her own street. Let me take your arm, Miss Pross. This is not a good city, at this time, for you to be walking in, unprotected. And, since Mr. Cruncher seems also to know Mr. Barsad, I will invite him to Mr. Lorry's with us. Are we ready? Come then!"

Miss Pross placed her hands on Sydney Carton's arm and looked up into his eyes, begging him to do her brother no harm. But the confident and inspiring expression in the man's eyes and the purposeful strength in his arm seemed to change him into a different type of man. No longer could Miss Pross believe that Sydney Carton was the easy-going good-for-nothing that he pretended to be.

But she was too afraid for the brother who did not deserve her affection to comment on what she had noticed.

They left her at the corner of the street, and

Carton led the way to Mr. Lorry's, which was just a few minutes' walk away. John Barsad, or Solomon Pross, walked at his side.

Mr. Lorry had just finished his dinner, and was sitting before a cheerful little fire—perhaps looking into the blaze and imagining the night he had looked into the red coals at the Royal George at Dover at the beginning of this tale, many years ago. He turned his head as they entered, and showed the surprise with which he saw a stranger.

"Miss Pross's brother, sir," said Sydney. "Mr. Barsad."

"Barsad?" repeated the old gentleman, "Barsad? I vaguely remember that name and the face."

"I told you you had a memorable face, Mr. Barsad," observed Carton, coolly. "Please sit down."

As he took a chair himself, he supplied the link that Mr. Lorry wanted, by saying to him with a frown, "Witness at that trial." Mr. Lorry immediately remembered, and regarded his new visitor with an undisguised look of hatred.

"Mr. Barsad has been recognized by Miss Pross as the 'affectionate' brother you have heard of," said Sydney, "and has acknowledged the relationship. I move on to worse news. Darnay has been arrested again."

Looking as if he's been hit, the old gentleman exclaimed, "What are you saying? I left him safe and free not more than two hours ago. I'm about to return to him!"

Carton nodded solemnly. "Arrested. When was it done, Mr. Barsad?"

"Just now, if at all."

"Mr. Barsad is the best authority possible, sir," said Sydney, "I overheard Mr. Barsad talking to a fellow 'Sheep' over a bottle of wine that the arrest had indeed taken place. He left the messengers at the gate, and saw them admitted by the porter. There is no earthly doubt that he is again in prison."

Mr. Lorry's business eye could tell that it would

be a waste of time to dwell on the point. Confused, but aware that the situation might depend on his remaining calm and alert, he collected himself and paid close attention.

"Now, I trust," said Sydney to him, "that the name and influence of Doctor Manette may be as helpful to him tomorrow as it was today? You did say he would be before the Tribunal again tomorrow, Mr. Barsad?"

"Yes, I believe so."

"I have to admit, Mr. Lorry," Carton continued, "that I am alarmed by Doctor Manette's not having had the power to prevent this arrest."

"He may not have known of it beforehand," said Mr. Lorry.

Carton nodded. "And it would certainly alarm the Doctor that he did *not* know, that he had not been informed. Especially when we consider how closely the mob identified him with his son-in-law."

"That's true," Mr. Lorry agreed, stroking his chin, and staring at Carton.

"In short," said Sydney, "this is a desperate time, when desperate games are played for desperate stakes. Let the Doctor play the winning game; I will play the losing one. No man's life here is worth purchase. Anyone carried home today by the people may be condemned tomorrow. Now, the stake I have resolved to play for, should it come to the worst, is a friend in the Conciergerie. And the friend I purpose to myself to win, is Mr. Barsad."

"You'd better have some good cards, sir," said the spy.

"Let's review and see what I hold," Carton replied smugly. "Mr. Lorry, you know what a brute I am. I wish you'd give me a little brandy."

Lorry gave it to him, and he drank a glassful, drank a second glassful, and then pushed the bottle thoughtfully away.

"Mr. Barsad,…" he went on, in the tone of one who really was looking over a hand of cards: "…Sheep of the prisons…emissary of republican

---

✔ *One of the definitions in the Oxford English Dictionary for "purchase" is "the price at which anything is or may be purchased or bought." So, when Carton says that no man's life is "worth purchase," he is saying that the life is not worth what it costs. In other words, it's cheap or valueless.*

❷ *What three "cards" does Sydney have to play in his game to get Barsad to cooperate with him?*

committees...sometimes a jailer...sometimes a prisoner... always a spy and secret informer...because
he's English, he's much more useful here because he
is less likely to be suspected of being a spy...he con-
ducts his business under a false name...That's a very
good card. Mr. Barsad, *now* employed by the republican French government, *used to be* employed by the
aristocratic *English* government, the *enemy* of France
and freedom. That's an *excellent* card. It would not
take a political genius to guess that this Mr. Barsad,
is *still* employed by the aristocratic English government. In fact, this Mr. Basard is probably the spy of
Pitt, the treacherous foe of the Republic crouching in
its bosom, the English traitor so well-known and so
difficult to find. Now *that's* a truly unbeatable card.
Have you followed my hand, Mr. Barsad?"

"Not to understand your play," returned the spy,
somewhat uneasily.

"I play my Ace, to denounce Mr. Barsad to the
nearest Section Committee. Look over your hand, Mr.
Barsad, and see what you have. Don't hurry."

He drew the bottle near, poured out another
glassful of brandy, and drank it. He could tell that the
spy was afraid that he would drink enough to gain the
boldness to denounce him then and there. Seeing the
fear, he poured and drank another glassful.

"Look over your hand carefully, Mr. Barsad. Take
your time."

It was a worse hand than Carton suspected. Mr.
Barsad saw losing cards in it that Sydney Carton knew
nothing of. He'd been removed from his original
position in England because he failed too often in
his attempts to convict men on his falsely sworn
testimony. At first he'd been sent to France to spy on
his fellow Englishmen, attempting to draw them into
conversation and lead them to reveal their Republican
sympathies. Gradually, he came to fill the same roles
among the French. Under the overthrown monarchy,
he was to spy on the residents of Saint Antoine who
collected in Defarge's wine shop. His position had

Pitt, or William Pitt the Younger, was Prime Minister of England during the French Revolution. England had declared war on France after the execution of Louis XVI in 1793, so "Pitt" (representing the English government in general) was officially an enemy of the Republic. Dickens's use of "Pitt" to represent the entire English government or English nation is an example of metonymy.

What "card" is Carton going to "play"?

allowed him to gather information about Doctor Manette's history, his imprisonment and his release. He used this information to build a relationship with the Defarges, and eventually even gained something like their trust. Still, it frightened Barsad to think how— every time he was in Madame Defarge's presence—she knitted and knitted, staring with unblinking eyes at his face. He knew he was stitched into her register and that it would take only one unsupported accusation to bring him to the Guillotine. He knew—as did every spy—that he was never safe. It was impossible to leave. He was trapped under the shadow of the axe. And, in spite of everything he'd done in the service of the reigning terror, a single word could bring him down. Once denounced—especially if he were denounced as a spy for England—he knew that the dreadful woman would produce that fatal register against him, and destroy his last chance of life. In addition, all secret men are men easily frightened, and here were surely enough damning cards to cause the holder to grow increasingly angry as he considered them.

"You do not seem to like your hand," said Sydney, with the great calm. "Do you play?"

Barsad turned to Mr. Lorry. "I think, sir, that I may appeal to a gentleman of your years and kindness, to ask this other gentleman—so much younger than you—whether he thinks he will really be able to play that Ace of his. I admit that I am a spy, and that it is considered a contemptible occupation—even though it must be filled by somebody. But this gentleman is no spy. Why should he lower himself and make himself one?"

"I will play my Ace, Mr. Barsad," said Carton, looking at his watch, "with no hesitation, in a very few minutes."

"I should have hoped that both of you gentlemen… out of respect for my sister—"

"I could not better show my respect for your sister than by finally relieving her of her brother," said Sydney Carton.

"You believe that, sir?"

"I have thoroughly made up my mind about it."

Barsad was used to being able to act calm despite how he was dressed or how he was feeling, but he was unnerved by his complete inability to understand Sydney Carton, who was indeed a mystery to men far wiser and with more integrity than John Solomon Pross Barsad.

While he was at a loss, Carton continued speaking, as if examining a hand of cards. "Indeed, now that I think of it, I do believe that I have another good card here, not yet revealed. That friend and fellow Sheep, who spoke of himself as 'pasturing' in the country prisons; who was he?"

"French. You don't know him," said the spy, quickly.

"French, eh?" repeated Carton, musing, and not appearing to notice him at all, though he echoed his word. "Well, he *may* be."

"He is, I assure you," said the spy; "though it's not important."

"Though it's not important," repeated Carton, in the same mechanical way. "Though it's not important. No, it's *not* important. No. But I do know the face."

"I don't think so. I am sure you don't. You couldn't," said the spy.

"I—couldn't," muttered Sydney Carton, filling his glass again. "I—couldn't. Spoke good French. But spoke it like a foreigner, I thought."

"Provincial," said the spy.

"No. Foreign!" cried Carton, slapping the table as the companion's identity suddenly occurred to him. "Cly! Disguised, but the same man. We had that man before us at the Old Bailey."

"Now, there you are jumping to conclusions, sir," said Barsad, with a smile that made his thin nose lean toward one side. "Here you really do give me an advantage over you. Cly—who I will freely admit was a partner of mine—has been dead several years. I attended him in his last illness. He was buried

❷ *What do you remember about Roger Cly?*

in London, at the church of Saint Pancras-in-the-Fields. His unpopularity with the mob at the moment prevented my following his remains, but I helped to lay him in his coffin."

Here, Mr. Lorry noticed that Jerry Cruncher, who had been dozing in a corner, sat up and showed interest in the conversation.

"Let's be reasonable," said the spy, "and let's be fair. I will show you a certificate of Cly's burial, which I just happen to have with me." He hurriedly produced and opened his valise. "There it is. Oh, look at it, look at it! You may hold it in your hand. It's no forgery."

Here, Mr. Cruncher rose and stepped forward. His hair could not have been more violently on end, if it had been licked by the Cow with the crumpled horn in the house that Jack built.

Unseen by the spy, Mr. Cruncher stood at his side, and touched him lightly on the shoulder.

"That there Roger Cly, master," said Mr. Cruncher, with a quiet and determined face. "So you put him in his coffin?"

"I did."

"Who took him out of it?"

Barsad leaned back in his chair, and stammered, "What do you mean?"

"I mean," said Mr. Cruncher, "that he warn't never in it. No! Not he! I'll have my head took off, if he was ever in it."

The spy looked round at the two gentlemen; they both looked astonished at Jerry.

"I tell you," said Jerry, "that you buried paving stones and dirt in that there coffin. Don't go and tell me that you buried Cly. It was a hoax. Me and two more knows it."

"How do you know it?"

"What's that to you?" growled Mr. Cruncher. "It's *you* that *I've* got a' old grudge again'—you with your shameful tricks on honest tradesmen! I'd grab your throat and choke you for half a guinea."

Sydney Carton was as surprised by this unexpected

"The House that Jack Built" is a well-known children's poem. (The full poem appears in the Teachers Guide.) Hair standing on end, as Jerry's has been described, used to be called a "cow lick." Dickens is making a joke about the number of "cow licks" Jerry has in his hair.

turn of events as was Mr. Lorry. He requested Mr. Cruncher to explain himself.

"Some other time, sir," he returned, evasively. "Right now is not a convenient time for explaining. What I will swear to, though, is that he knows full well that Roger Cly was never in that coffin. Let him say he was—let him speak so much as one syllable, and I'll either grab his throat and choke him," Mr. Cruncher paused and looked at the three men who were listening to him, "Or *I'll* go and denounce him."

"Hmmm! I see one thing," said Carton. "I hold another card, Mr. Barsad. Impossible, here in raging Paris, with Suspicion filling the air, for you to outlive denunciation, when you are apparently working with another aristocratic spy with the same history as yourself. Furthermore, this partner has the mystery about him of having pretended death and come to life again! A plot in the prisons of the foreigner against the Republic. A strong card. A certain Guillotine card! Do you play?"

"No!" returned the spy. "I give up. I confess that we were so unpopular with the outrageous mob, that I barely escaped from England alive, and that Cly was so closely followed, that he would never have gotten away at all but for that sham. But I have no idea *how* this man knows it was a sham."

"Don't bother about that," replied the argumentative Mr. Cruncher. "You'll have enough trouble dealing with Mr. Carton."

The Sheep of the Prisons turned from him to Sydney Carton, and said, with more decision in his voice, "We must get to the point. I go on duty soon, and can't afford to be late. You told me you had a proposal. What is it? And don't bother asking too much. If you ask me to do anything that would put me into unnecessary danger, I might be better off risking the consequences of refusing you as face the danger of complying with your demand. You talk of desperation. Well, we're *all* desperate here. Remember! I could denounce *you* if I wanted. I do have considerable influence. Now, what do you want?"

"Not much. You are a jailer at the Conciergerie?"

"I tell you once and for all, there is no such thing as an escape possible," said the spy, firmly.

"Simply answer the question I have asked. You are a jailer at the Conciergerie?"

"I am sometimes."

"You can be when you choose?"

"I can come and go when I choose."

Sydney Carton filled another glass with brandy and poured it slowly out onto the hearth, watching it as it dropped. When the glass was empty, he rose from his chair and said, "So far, we've talked in front of witnesses, because it was best that some others besides you and me knew the 'cards' we both had to play. Come into the dark room here, and let us have one final word alone."

THIS IS THE END OF THE
TWENTY-FIFTH WEEKLY INSTALLMENT.

❷ *This chapter has not advanced the plot at all. What two purposes has Dickens achieved here?*

A Tale of Two Cities

CHARLES DICKENS

CHAPTER IX

The Game Made

WHILE SYDNEY CARTON and the Sheep of the Prisons were in the adjoining dark room, speaking so low that Mr. Lorry and Jerry could not hear what was being said, the old banker looked at Jerry, his expression revealing a good deal of doubt and mistrust. The honest tradesman's reaction to Mr. Lorry's suspicion, made the old man distrust him even more. He squirmed in his seat, examined his fingernails very closely, and—whenever his eyes happened to meet Mr. Lorry's—he found it necessary to cough that kind of hollow cough that usually indicates that the cougher is hiding something.

❷ *Why does Dickens choose to refer to Jerry as an "honest tradesman" here?*

"Jerry," said Mr. Lorry. "Come here."

Mr. Cruncher sheepishly approached his employer.

"What have you been, besides a messenger?"

After some thought, accompanied with an intent look at the old man, Mr. Cruncher conceived the bright idea of replying, "Something of a'…agricultooral nature."

"My mind is very troubled right now," said Mr. Lorry, angrily shaking a forefinger at him, "I suspect that you have used the respectable and great house of Tellson's as a front, and that you have had an unlawful occupation of a … despicable nature. If you have, don't expect me to befriend you when you get back to England. If you have, don't expect me to keep your secret. Tellson's shall not be used."

"I hope, sir," pleaded the repentant Mr. Cruncher, "that a gentleman like yourself—who I've had the honor of doing odd jobs for till I'm old and gray, would think twice about harming me, even if it was true—and I don't say it is—but even if it was. And I hope a gentleman such as yourself would take into account that—if it was true—even still there'd be two sides to it. There might be medical doctors right this minute, a' pickin' up their *guineas* where a' honest tradesman don't pick up his *fardens*—fardens! no, nor yet his *half fardens*—half fardens! no, nor yet his *quarter*—a' bankin' away at Tellson's, and winking their eyes at that tradesman on the sly, a going in and going out to their own carriages. Well, that 'ud be imposing, too, on Tellson's. For you cannot sarse the goose and not the gander. And here's Mrs. Cruncher—or at least she was in the old days, a'-floppin' again' the business to that degree as is ruinating—completely ruinating! But you can bet them medical doctors' wives don't flop. Just try and catch 'em at it! Or, if they do flop, their floppings goes in favor of more patients, and how can you rightly have one without t'other? Then, what with undertakers, and what with parish clerks, and what with sextons, and what with private watchmen (all avaricious and all in it), a man wouldn't make much by it—even if it was so. And what little a man *did* make, would never do him any good, Mr. Lorry. He'd want nothing more than to quit, if he could see how, but,—once being in—even if it wos so."

"Ugh!" cried Mr. Lorry, softening in his harsh opinion of Jerry. "I am shocked at the sight of you."

"Now, what I would humbly offer to you, sir," pursued Mr. Cruncher, "even if it was so—which I don't say it is—"

"Don't lie," said Mr. Lorry.

"No, I will not, sir," returned Mr. Cruncher, as if

nothing were further from his mind—"which I don't say it is—what I would humbly offer to you, sir, would be this. Upon that there stool, at that there Bar, sets that there boy of mine, brought up and growed up to be a man, what will do your errands, run your messages, handle your light jobs, till you're dead and buried, if you wanted. If it was so—which I still don't say it is (for I will not lie to you, sir)—let that there boy keep his father's place, and take care of his mother. Don't blow the whistle on that boy's father—do not do it, sir—and let that father go into the line of the diggin' graves, and make amends for what he undigged—if it was so—by diggin'. That, Mr. Lorry," said Mr. Cruncher, wiping his forehead with his arm, as an announcement that he had arrived at the climax of his speech, "is what I would respectfully offer to you, sir. A man don't see all this here a goin' on dreadful round him, in the way of Subjects without heads. Dear me, plentiful enough to bring the price down to shipping costs and hardly that, without havin' his serious thoughts of things. And these here would be mine, if it was so, beggin' of you to bear in mind that what I said just now, I up and said in the good cause when I might have kep' quiet."

Finally, Jerry reminds Mr. Lorry that the only reason Lorry has to suspect him of resurrectionism is that he spoke up in order to help in Carton's quest to save Darnay.

"That at least is true," said Mr. Lorry. "Say no more now. It may be that I shall yet remain your friend, if you deserve it, and repent in action—not in words. I want no more words."

Mr. Cruncher rubbed his forehead, as Sydney Carton and the spy returned from the dark room. "Good-bye, Mr. Barsad," Carton said. "If you keep your end of our agreement, you have nothing to fear from me."

He sat down in a chair on the hearth, near Mr. Lorry. After Barsad left, Mr. Lorry asked him what "agreement" he and Barsad had reached.

"Not much. If the Tribunal condemns Darnay tomorrow, I have ensured access to him one time."

Mr. Lorry's face fell.

"It is all I could do," said Carton. "To ask for too much, would be to put Barsad in danger, and—as he himself said—nothing worse could happen to him if he were denounced. That was his card to play. There's no help for it."

"But access to him," said Mr. Lorry, "*after* he's condemned will not save him."

"I never said it would."

Mr. Lorry's eyes gradually rested on the fire. His heart was breaking for his darling Lucie, and the heavy disappointment of Charles's second arrest made them fill with tears. He was an old man now, overcome with anxiety, and he openly wept.

"You are a good man and a true friend," said Carton, in a strangely sad voice. "Forgive me if I notice that you are upset. I couldn't watch my father weep and do or say nothing. And I am moved by your sorrow as much as if you *were* my father. You, however, were not unlucky enough to have to claim a son like me."

Although he spoke with his usual flippant manner, there was also a sincerity in his tone and in the way he touched Mr. Lorry's hand that completely surprised the old man.

"To return to poor Darnay," said Carton. "Do not tell Lucie about this meeting with Barsad or our agreement. She might think it was set up to allow her to give Darnay the dreadful news when it won't give her access to him at all."

Mr. Lorry had not thought of that, and he looked quickly at Carton to see if it were in his mind. It seemed to be. Carton returned the look, and evidently understood it.

"She might think a thousand things," Carton said, "and any of them would only break her heart. Don't even tell her you've seen me. As I said to you when I first came, I'd better not see her. I don't need to see her to find some little favor I might do to help. You are going to her, I hope? She must be very depressed tonight."

"I am going now, right away."

"I am glad. She relies on you for so much and

truly loves you. How does she look?"

"Anxious and unhappy, but very beautiful."

"Ah!"

It was a long and grieving sound, like a sigh—almost like a sob. It made Mr. Lorry study Carton's face, which was turned to the fire. A shadow crossed the face and was gone almost the way a cloud will pass over the top of a hill on a windy day. He lifted his foot to put back one of the little flaming logs, which had rolled forward.

He wore the white riding coat and high boots, that were fashionable then, and the light of the fire reflecting off of their light surfaces made him look very pale. His long brown hair hung loose around his shoulders. He seemed to be ignoring the fire, and so Mr. Lorry pointed out that his boot was still on the hot embers of the flaming log.

"I forgot about it," Carton said.

Mr. Lorry again looked into the younger man's face. He noted the worn-out mood that clouded the naturally handsome features. In fact, he thought how Carton's expression reminded him of the expressions of prisoners who had given up hope.

"And your duties here have come to an end, sir?" said Carton, turning to him.

"Yes. As I was telling you last night when Lucie came in so unexpectedly, I have finally done all that I can do here. I *had* hoped to leave Lucie and Manette in perfect safety, but...I have my Leave to Pass. I was ready to go."

They were both silent.

"Yours is a long life to look back on, sir." said Carton, wistfully.

"I am seventy-eight years old."

"And you have been useful your entire life, always working, trusted, respected, and looked up to?"

"I have been a man of business, ever since I have been a man. Indeed, I may say that I was a man of business when I was still a boy."

"See what a place you fill at seventy-eight.

❷ *How would you describe Carton's mood and behavior in this chapter and Mr. Lorry's reaction to it?*

How many people will miss you when you leave it empty!"

"I am just a lonely, old bachelor," answered Mr. Lorry, shaking his head. "There is nobody to weep for me."

"How can you say that? Wouldn't *She* weep for you? Wouldn't Her child?"

"Yes, yes, thank God. I didn't quite mean what I said."

"It *is* a thing to thank God for isn't it?"

"Surely, surely."

"But...if you could honestly say that you had never found love, had earned no person's gratitude or respect, that no other person on earth had a tender place in his or her heart for you, that you had never done any good thing for which you might be remembered, your seventy-eight years would be seventy-eight heavy curses. Wouldn't they?"

"That is the truth, Mr. Carton; I think they would be."

Sydney turned his eyes again toward the fire, and, after a silence of a few moments, said, "Does your childhood seem far off? Do the days when you sat at your mother's knee, seem very long ago?"

Responding to his softened manner, Mr. Lorry answered, "Twenty years ago, they did. But as I come closer and closer to the end of my life, I travel in the circle, nearer and nearer to the beginning. It seems to be one of the ways we are prepared for death. I suddenly remember things I thought I'd forgotten a long time ago—my pretty young mother, and an innocence when I was not so aware of my own faults or the awful, awful faults of the World."

"I understand that feeling!" exclaimed Carton, with a bright flush. "And you are better off because of it?"

"I hope so."

Carton ended the conversation here, by standing to help Lorry on with his outer coat. "But you,"

❷ *Why do you suppose Carton is being so contemplative on this night? What is motivating this conversation and these questions?*

said Mr. Lorry, returning to the conversation, "you are young."

"Yes," said Carton. "I am not old, but I don't think I was born to grow old and contented like you. But enough about me."

"And about me as well," said Mr. Lorry. "Are you leaving?"

"I'll walk with you to her gate. You know my restless habits. If I should prowl about the streets a long time, don't be uneasy; I shall reappear in the morning. You go to the Court tomorrow?"

"Yes, unhappily."

"I shall be there, but only as one of the crowd. My Spy will find a place for me. Take my arm, sir."

Mr. Lorry did so, and they went downstairs and out to the streets. A few minute's walk brought them to the house where Lucie and her father were lodging. Carton left him there, but lingered a short distance away. He turned back to the gate again when it was shut and touched it. He had heard of Lucie's going to the prison every day. "She came out here," he said, looking about him, "turned this way, must have walked on these stones often. Let me follow in her steps."

It was ten o'clock at night when he stood before the prison of La Force, where she had stood hundreds of times. A little woodcutter had closed his shop and was smoking his pipe at his shop door.

"Good night, Citizen," said Sydney Carton. He paused before passing the shop for, the man eyed him inquisitively.

"Good night, Citizen."

"How goes the Republic?"

"You mean the Guillotine. Not bad. Sixty-three today. We shall reach a hundred a day soon. Samson and his men complain sometimes, of being exhausted. Ha, ha, ha! He is so funny, that Samson. Such a Barber!"

"Do you often go to see him—"

❷ *Why does the former mender of roads equate the Republic with the Guillotine?*

At the height of the Reign of Terror, so many persons were condemned by the Tribunals that a new and faster Guillotine had to be developed to keep up with all of the demanded executions.

"Shave? Always. Every day. What a barber! You have seen him at work?"

"Never."

"Go and see him when he has a good batch. Figure this to yourself, Citizen—she shaved the sixty-three today, in less time than it took to smoke two pipes! Less than two pipes. Word of honor!"

As the grinning little man held out the pipe he was smoking, to explain how he timed the executioner, Carton felt an almost irresistible urge to beat the life out of him. Instead, he turned away.

"You are not English," said the woodcutter, "even though you're dressed like an Englishman?"

"Yes," said Carton, pausing again, and answering over his shoulder.

"You speak like a Frenchman."

"I am an old student here."

"Aha, a perfect Frenchman! Good night, Englishman."

"Good night, Citizen."

"But do go and see the spectacle of the Guillotine," the little man persisted, calling after him. "And take a pipe with you!"

Sydney had not gone far out of sight, when he stopped in the middle of the street under a glimmering lamp, and wrote on a scrap of paper with his pencil. Then, crossing several dark and dirty streets—that were even dirtier than usual, for even the best public roads remained filthy in those times of terror—he stopped at a chemist's shop, which the owner was just closing.

He approached the counter and wished this citizen a good night. Then he laid the scrap of paper on the counter. "Whew!" the chemist whistled softly, as he read it. "Well, well, well!"

Sydney Carton paid no attention, and the chemist said, "For you, Citizen?"

"For me."

"You will be careful to keep them separate, Citizen? You know the consequences of mixing them?"

"Perfectly."

The chemist prepared two small packets and handed them to Carton. He put them, one by one, in the breast pocket of his inner coat, counted out the money to pay for them, and slowly left the shop. "There is nothing more to do until tomorrow," he said, glancing upward at the moon. "Still, I cannot sleep."

He did not say this in the tone of a restless man who refused to miss anything by wasting time asleep. Nor did he say it defiantly. Instead, he said it like a tired man who had wandered, lost and alone, but finally found his path and knew where he needed to go.

Long ago—when he still had the reputation among his friends as a youth of great promise—he lost his father. His mother had already died years before. The solemn words—which had been read at his father's grave—came to his mind as he wandered the dark streets, and lingered in the heavy shadows, with the moon and the clouds sailing on high above him:

> "I am the resurrection and the life," said the Lord. "Anyone who believes in me will live even if he dies, and everyone who lives and believes in me will never die."

In a city dominated by the axe, alone at night, with sorrow for the sixty-three who that day had been put to death, and sorrow for tomorrow's victims awaiting their doom that very moment in the prisons, Carton repeated these words and went on.

He walked, intensely interested in the lighted windows where people were going to bed. For a few hours of sleep, they could forget horrors that surrounded them while they were awake. He paused and studied the towers of the churches, where no prayers were said. The Republic had long ago rejected the Church because of years of priestly hypocrites, thieves, and scoundrels. He thought of the crowded cemeteries where talk of Heaven was no longer

These verses, John 11:25-6, are the opening lines of the Burial Service in the Anglican Book of Common Prayer. In the Gospel, Jesus's friend Lazarus has died. Before Jesus raises him from the dead, he says these words to Martha, Lazarus's sister.

Consider the various ways in which Dickens has mentioned the resurrection theme in this story. What final "resurrection" is foreshadowed?

allowed, only promises of "Eternal Sleep." He thought of the even more crowded jails and the streets through which the tumbrels carried their passengers to a death. And this death had become so common, that no one associated with the working of the Guillotine ever uttered a sorrowful story of a haunting Spirit. As Sydney Carton spent the entire night walking the streets of Paris, he found himself intensely interested in the whole life and death of the city that was settling down for a few hours of rest from its increasing fury.

There were few coaches out, for riders of coaches were likely to be suspected. Instead, the remaining nobles hid their heads under red nightcaps, put on heavy shoes, and trudged. But, the theatres were all well filled, and the people poured cheerfully out as he walked by. At one of the theatre doors, there was a little girl with her mother, looking for a way across the street through the mud. He carried the child over, and, before he set her down on the other side, he asked her for a kiss.

"I am the resurrection and the life," said the Lord. "Anyone who believes in me will live even if he dies, and everyone who lives and believes in me will never die."

Now that the streets were quiet, and the night wore on, the words were in the echoes of his feet, and in the air. Perfectly calm and steady, he sometimes repeated them to himself as he walked. But he heard them always.

The night slowly brightened. As he stood on the bridge listening to the water as it splashed against its walls, the beautiful mixture of houses and cathedrals shone brightly in the light of the moon, and the day dawned coldly, looking like a dead face out of the sky. Then, the night—with the moon and the stars—turned pale and died, and for a little while it seemed as if Creation had surrendered to Death's control.

But, the glorious sun, rising, seemed to erase that

thought—that burden of the night—from his heart. Looking at the sun's rays, he reverently shaded his eyes, and thought he saw a bridge of light appear between him and the sun, and the river sparkled under it.

The strong tide—so fast, so deep, and certain— was like a friend in the morning stillness. He walked beside the river, far from the houses, and in the light and warmth of the sun, fell asleep on the bank. When he awoke and was walking again, he stayed by the water just a little longer, watching a small whirlpool that turned and turned purposelessly, until the stream absorbed it, and carried it on to the sea. "Just like me!"

A trading boat, with a sail the color of a dead leaf glided into his view, floated by him, and faded away. As its silent wake disappeared, the prayer that had broken up out of his heart for forgiveness of his errors, ended in the words, *"I am the resurrection and the life."*

Mr. Lorry was already gone when he got back, and it was easy to guess where the good old man had gone. Sydney Carton drank nothing but a little coffee and ate some bread. He washed and changed to refresh himself, and then went to the place of trial.

The court was all abuzz, when Barsad, the Sheep of the Prisons, who was so feared that many called him "the black sheep," pressed Carton into a dark corner among the crowd. Mr. Lorry was there, and Doctor Manette was there. *She* was also there, sitting beside her father.

When her husband was brought in, she turned to look at him. Her own gaze was so encouraging, so full of love and tenderness, yet so courageous, that Darnay actually smiled briefly. No one noticed that the intensity of Lucie's look brought a similar smile to Sydney Carton's face.

The unjust Tribunal of the First Republic, had no order of procedure, to guarantee any reasonable hearing. If the laws and customs of France had been justly made and justly administered before the Revolution, there would have been none of the angry

❷ *What do the rising sun, the bridge, and the sparkling river symbolize here?*

revenge that threatened to destroy the country now.

Every eye was turned to the jury. They were the same determined patriots and good republicans as yesterday and the day before, and were the same as would sit tomorrow and the day after. Eager and outstanding among them was one man with a hungry face, and his fingers always hovering around his lips. His appearance gave great satisfaction to the spectators. He was a life-thirsting, cannibal-looking, bloody-minded juryman—the Jacques Three of St. Antoine. The whole jury looked like a jury of hounds chosen to try a deer.

Every eye then turned to the five judges and the public prosecutor. There was no favorable mood there today. Instead, an undeniably murderous air of seriousness there. Every eye then found some other eye in the crowd, and gleamed at it approvingly. Heads nodded at one another, before bending forward with a strained attention.

Charles Evremonde, called Darnay. Released yesterday. Reaccused and then re-arrested yesterday. Indictment delivered to him last night. Suspected and Denounced enemy of the Republic, Aristocrat, one of a family of tyrants, one of a race condemned, for using their privileges—which the Revolution so justly abolished—to oppress the People. Charles Evremonde, called Darnay—by virtue of this condemnation, absolutely Dead in Law.

This was the announcement with which the Public Prosecutor opened Darnay's trial.

The President of the Court asked whether the Accused was openly denounced or secretly.

"Openly, President."

"By whom?"

"Three voices. Ernest Defarge, wine merchant of St. Antoine."

"Good."

"Therese Defarge, his wife."

"Good."

"Alexandre Manette, physician."

✔ *Here is the name of the third person that the guards arresting Darnay would not give to Doctor Manette last night.*

A great uproar followed the final announcement. In the middle of it, Doctor Manette stood where he had been sitting, pale and trembling.

"President, I protest to you that this is a forgery and a fraud. You know the accused to be the husband of my daughter. My daughter, and those dear to her, are far dearer to me than my own life. Who and where is the liar who says that I denounce the husband of my own child?"

"Citizen Manette, be quiet. To fail to absolutely obey the Tribunal would be to break the Law. As to valuing your loved ones even more than your own life, *nothing* can be as valuable to a good citizen as the Republic."

The fickle audience applauded and cheered the President's words. The President rang his bell, and warmly continued, "If the Republic should demand that you sacrifice your child herself, you would have no choice but to sacrifice her. Listen to the evidence that will be presented. In the meanwhile, be silent!"

Frantic shouts were again raised. Doctor Manette sat down, with his wide eyes wandering around the noisy room, his lips trembling. Lucie drew closer to him. The hungry-looking man on the jury rubbed his hands together, and again placed his hand in his mouth.

Defarge was called, when the court was quiet enough so that his testimony could be heard, and he told the story of the Doctor's imprisonment, and of his having been a mere boy in the Doctor's service. He told the court about the Doctor's release, and his absent, unaware state of mind when he had been taken to Defarge's wine shop after the release. Toward the end of the very brief examination—because the Tribunal did its work very quickly and did not want to explore any subject that came before it too deeply—the President asked Defarge, "You did good service at the taking of the Bastille, Citizen?"

"I believe so."

Here, an excited woman screeched from the crowd,

❷ *What clues has Dickens provided throughout the book to suggest the source of Doctor Manette's denunciation?*

"You were one of the best patriots there. Admit it! You handled a cannon that day, and you were among the first to enter that accursed fortress when it fell. Patriots, I speak the truth!"

It was the Vengeance who stood and bowed to the Court and the audience. The President rang his bell, but the Vengeance, fed by the cheers and applause of the audience and shrieked, "I defy that bell!" This was met with even louder cheers and more thunderous applause.

"Inform the Tribunal of what you did that day within the Bastille, citizen."

"I knew," said Defarge, looking down at his wife, who stood at the bottom of the steps and stared fiercely up at him, "I knew that this prisoner, Doctor Alexandre Manette, had been imprisoned in a cell known as One Hundred and Five, North Tower. He told me himself. When he was first released, he could not remember his name and knew himself only as 'One Hundred and Five, North Tower.' As I manned my gun at the Bastille that day, I swore that I would examine that cell when the place fell. It fell. Led by a jailer, I climbed to the cell with a fellow citizen who is a member of this Jury. I searched the cell, very closely. In a hole in the chimney there was a stone that had been worked out and replaced. I found a written paper." Here he paused and held up a tattered, yellow scrap. "This is that written paper. I have made it my business to examine some other samples of Doctor Manette's handwriting. The handwriting on this piece of paper is identical. I place this paper—in Doctor Manette's own handwriting—into the hands of the President."

"Let it be read."

A dead silence waited for the reading of the letter. Charles looked lovingly at his wife, but Lucie felt torn whether to return her husband's gaze or look with concern toward her father. Doctor Manette kept his eyes fixed on the reader of his document. Madame Defarge stared at Darnay, never blinking. Defarge

So now we know what Defarge was looking for in Dr. Manette's cell.

stared at his exultant wife. All other eyes in the Court were intent upon the Doctor. Finally, the paper was read.

THIS IS THE END OF THE
TWENTY-SIXTH WEEKLY INSTALLMENT.

Writing Opportunity:

Write the letter that is about to be read, that Doctor Manette wrote while he was imprisoned in the Bastille.

A Tale of Two Cities

CHARLES DICKENS

CHAPTER X

The Substance of the Shadow

❓ *What does the title of this chapter mean?*

"I, ALEXANDRE MANETTE, unlucky and unhappy physician, native of Beauvais, and later a resident in Paris, write this sad paper in my cell in the Bastille, during the last month of the year, 1767. I write it in secret. I plan to hide it in the wall of the chimney, where I have slowly made a safe hiding place for it. Years from now, when I have died and turned to dust, some person may find this, read my tale, and pity me.

"These words are written by a rusty iron point in scrapings of soot and charcoal from the chimney, mixed with my own blood. I am in the tenth year of my captivity, and I have lost all hope. I know from terrible signs I have noticed in myself that I am going insane. I solemnly declare, however, that I am at this time in the possession of my right mind—that my memory is exact—and that I write the truth. I know that I shall answer for these, my last recorded words—whether anyone ever finds and reads them or not—at the Final Judgement.

"One cloudy, but moonlit night, in the third week of December (I think the twenty-second of the month) in the year 1757, I was walking on a quiet part of the pier by the Seine River, when a carriage came up behind me, driven very fast. As I moved aside to let it

❓ *Why would Dr. Manette explain in this document how he is creating it?*

✔ *The hidden and discovered letter was a popular literary convention for providing necessary plot information, unraveling mysteries, helping plots reach their resolutions.*

pass, a head stuck out the window, and a voice called to the driver to stop.

"The carriage stopped, and the same voice called to me by my name. I answered. The carriage was then so far ahead of me that two gentlemen had time to open the door and get out before I caught up with it. I noticed that they were both wrapped in cloaks, as if they were trying to hide their identities. As they stood next to each other, I also noticed that they both looked about my own age—maybe a little younger—and that they were very much alike, in height, mannerisms, voice, and (as far as I could tell) appearance.

"'You are Doctor Manette?' one of them asked me.

"'I am.'

"'Doctor Manette, formerly of Beauvais,' asked the other; 'the young physician, originally an expert surgeon, who has recently begun to establish a fine reputation in Paris?'

"'Gentlemen,' I replied, 'I am that Doctor Manette, whom you flatter.'

"'We've been to your home,' said the first, 'where we were told that you were probably walking in this direction. We followed, hoping to catch up with you. Will you please enter the carriage?'

"The manner of both was bossy, and they both moved to corner me between themselves and the carriage door. They were armed. I was not.

"'Gentlemen,' I said, 'I beg your pardon; but I usually ask who it is who seeks my help, and to what type of medical emergency I am called.'

"The man who had spoken second answered me. 'Doctor, we are people of noble class. As to the nature of the case, you will probably figure it out for yourself better than we could describe it. But enough delay. Will you please enter the carriage?'

"I had no choice but to obey, and I entered it in silence. They both entered after me. The carriage turned around, and drove on as fast as it had approached me.

❷ *Does Manette ask reasonable questions? Is the "gentlemen's" reply reasonable?*

"I repeat this conversation exactly as I remember it. I have no doubt that it is, word for word, the same. I describe everything exactly as it took place, forcing my mind not to wander from the task. Where I make the broken marks that follow here, I am stopping for now, and put my paper in its hiding-place. * * * *

"The carriage left the streets behind, passed the North Barrier, and emerged upon the country road. At two-thirds of a league from the Barrier, I had no idea how far we traveled, but eventually we stopped at a solitary house. We climbed out of the carriage and walked along a damp footpath in a garden where a neglected fountain had overflowed to the door of the house. It was not opened immediately—in answer to the ringing of the bell—and one of the gentlemen hit the man who opened it across the face with his heavy riding glove.

"There was nothing unusual about this action. I had seen common people struck more often than dogs. But, the other gentleman was also angry and struck the man with his arm. In that action, I noticed that the brothers were so exactly alike, that I realized they had to be twins.

"From the time we left the carriage at the outer gate—which had been locked, and which one of the brothers had opened and then relocked—I had heard cries coming from an upper room. I was immediately taken to this room. The cries grew louder as we ascended the stairs, and I found a patient in a high fever of the brain, lying on a bed.

"The patient was a remarkably beautiful, young woman—not much past twenty years old. Her hair was torn and ragged, and her arms were bound to her sides with sashes and handkerchiefs. I noticed that these bonds were all parts of a gentleman's clothes. On one of them, a fringed scarf, I saw the crest of a Noble, and the letter "E."

"In her writhing, the woman had sucked the end of the scarf into her mouth, and was in danger of suffocating. The first thing I did was pull the scarf

✔ *Remember that there were tax and toll barriers throughout France. These were among the issues that led to the Revolution.*

❷ *What do you suppose the "E" stands for?*

❷ *Who are the two brothers?*

from her mouth so that she could breathe. That is when I saw the crest and the initial.

"I turned her over gently, placed my hands on her breast to calm her and keep her down, and looked into her face. Her pupils were dilated and wild, and she constantly uttered piercing shrieks, and repeated the words, 'My husband, my father, and my brother!' and then counted up to twelve, and said, 'Hush!' For an instant, and no more, she would pause to listen, and then the piercing shrieks would begin again, and she would repeat the cry, 'My husband, my father, and my brother!' and would count up to twelve, and say, 'Hush!'

"'How long,' I asked, 'has this lasted?'

"To distinguish between the brothers, I will call them the elder and the younger. The elder was the one who seemed most to be in charge. It was the elder who replied, 'Since about this hour last night.'

"'She has a husband, a father, and a brother?'

"'A brother.'

"'And I assume you are not her brother?'

"He answered with great contempt, 'I am not.'

"'She has some recent association with the number twelve?'

"The younger brother impatiently answered, 'With twelve o'clock?'

"'See, gentlemen,' I said, still keeping my hands upon her breast, 'how useless I am! If I had known what I was coming to see, I could have come prepared. As it is, time must be lost. There are no medicines in this lonely place.'

"The elder brother looked to the younger, who said haughtily, 'There is a case of medicines here;' and brought it from a closet, and put it on the table. ****

"I opened some of the bottles, smelt them, and put the stoppers to my lips. They were all narcotics—opiates.

"'Do you doubt them?' asked the younger brother.

"'You see, Monsieur, that I am going to use them,' I replied, and said no more.

"With great difficulty—and after many attempts—I succeeded in making the patient swallow the dose that I wanted to give. I intended to repeat the dose after a while, and I also wanted to watch what effect the narcotic would have on the woman. So I sat down by the side of the bed. There was also a timid and abused woman present, and I guessed her to be the wife of the man downstairs who had been so slow to answer the bell. This woman had retreated into a corner. The house was damp and decayed, and oddly furnished. It had evidently been occupied recently, but seemed to be used only on a temporary basis. Some thick, old hangings had been nailed up at the windows, to deaden the sound of the shrieks. They continued in their regular pattern: 'My husband, my father, and my brother!' counting up twelve, and then, 'Hush!' Her frenzy was so violent, that I had not untied the bandages binding her arms. But I had looked at them to make certain that they were not hurting her. The only positive sign was that my hand on her breast calmed her enough that she could lie calmly for several minutes. It had no effect on the cries. You could have set your clock by their regularity.

"Because my hand did seem to be calming the young woman, I sat there for about a half an hour with the two brothers watching me. Finally, the elder brother said, 'There is another patient.'

"I was startled, and asked, 'Is it important?'

"'You had better see for yourself,' he answered carelessly and picked up a candle. * * * *

"The other patient lay in a back room which was sort of a loft over a stable. There was a low plastered ceiling over a part of it. The rest was open all the way to the ridge of the tiled roof, and there were beams across. Hay and straw were stored there, kindling for fires, and a heap of apples in sand. I had to pass through the storage part to get to the more finished

❷ *Why is the Doctor going into such painstaking detail about the setting of this episode?*

room where the new patient lay. I remember it clearly. I see them all, in this my cell in the Bastille—near the end of the tenth year of my captivity—as I saw them all that night.

"On some hay on the ground, with a cushion thrown under his head, lay a handsome peasant boy— a boy of not more than seventeen at the most. He lay on his back, with his teeth set, his right hand clenched on his breast, and his glaring eyes looking straight upward. I could not see where his wound was, as I knelt on one knee over him, but I could see that he was dying from a deep puncture.

"'I am a doctor, my poor fellow,' I said. 'Let me examine it.'

"'I do not want it examined,' he answered. 'Let it be.'

"The wound was under his hand, and I persuaded him to let me move his hand away. It was a sword-thrust, received from twenty to twenty-four hours earlier, but no skill could have saved him even if it had been looked to right away. By the time I saw him, he was already very close to death. As I looked at the elder brother, I saw him looking down at this handsome boy—whose life was fading quickly—as if he were a wounded bird, or a rabbit, but not at all as if he were a fellow human.

"'How did this happen, Monsieur?' I asked.

"'A crazy, young, common dog! A *serf*! He *forced* my brother to draw upon him, and has fallen by my brother's sword—as if he were a *gentleman*.'

"There was no pity or sorrow in this answer. The speaker seemed to feel that it was a tremendous inconvenience to have that lower order of creature dying there. It would have been better if he had died in some obscure way—the way vermin should die. He was absolutely incapable of any compassion toward the boy or his fate.

"The boy's eyes had slowly moved to him as he had spoken, and they now slowly moved to me.

"'Doctor, they are very proud, these Nobles; but

In medieval feudal society, the serf was the lowest class— essentially a slave owned by the noble who owned the land. Serfs had no rights and could do nothing without the noble's permission—usually accompanied by some fee or tax. While most of Europe slowly evolved away from feudalism in the sixteenth and seventeenth centuries— especially ending serfdom and affording the basic rights of citizenship to all persons— remnants of this archaic social order remained in France until the French Revolution. The treatment of the peasants—serfs—by the nobility was one of the chief reasons for the Revolution's anger and desire for vengeance. In fact, what is the elder brother's main concern in the death of this peasant youth?

we *common dogs* are proud too, sometimes. They plunder us, outrage us, beat us, kill us, but we have a little pride left, sometimes. She—have you seen her, Doctor?'

"The shrieks and the cries were audible there, though muffled by the distance.

"'Yes,' I said, 'I have seen her.'

"'She is my sister, Doctor. They have had their shameful rights, these Nobles, ruining the modesty and virtue of our sisters for many years. But we have had good girls among us. I know it, and have heard my father say so. She was a good girl. She was engaged to a good young man, too—a tenant of *his*. We were all tenants of *his*—that man's who stands there. The other is his brother, the worst of a bad race.'

"It was with the greatest difficulty that the boy gathered bodily force to speak; but, his spirit spoke with a dreadful emphasis.

"'We were so robbed by that man who stands there, as all we common dogs are by those superior Beings—taxed by him without mercy—obligated to work for him without pay—obligated to grind our corn at his mill, obligated to feed his tame birds with our tiny crops, and forbidden for our lives to keep a single tame bird of our own—plundered so greedily that when we happened to have a bit of meat, we ate it in fear, with the door barred and the shutters closed, so that his people would not see it and take it from us. I say, we were so robbed, and hunted, and were made so poor, that our father told us it was a dreadful thing to bring a child into the world, and that what we should most pray for, was, that our women might be barren and our miserable race die out!'

"I had never before seen this type of anger, breaking out like a fire. I'd supposed the people must have an anger hidden deep within them, but, I had never seen it break out until I saw it in the dying boy.

"'My sister married. Her husband was ill at that time, poor fellow. She married him so that she could take care of him in our cottage—our *dog hut*, as *that*

❤ *Here the boy is referring to the attitudes and behaviors that, over generations, bred the anger that eventually erupted into the French Revolution.*

❤ *Under feudalism, all of the serfs were bound to the land on which they were born. They had no rights to the land, however, as everything was owned by the nobility. The peasants were "tenants" in the sense that they were allowed to live on and work the land in exchange for fees, taxes, and rents. But they could not leave the land and seek to live elsewhere without the permission of their landlord.*

❷ *What subtle warning might Dickens be offering here?*

○ *If this were a true story, the brothers certainly would not let Manette stand there and listen to this boy's entire story. But Dickens needs the convention of the boy's story in order to get the information to Manette and then to the reader.*

○ *Certainly during the height of the Middle Ages, the nobility did enjoy "rights" like the ones described here. It is, however, something of an exaggeration to suggest that eighteenth-century noblemen still treated their peasants this harshly. Dickens, however, is trying to establish the horrid conditions of the country that resulted in the Revolution and illustrate the extreme cruelty of the Evremonde family.*

○ *According to the Oxford English Dictionary, medieval nobility enjoyed a privilege called* droit du seigneur *"by which the feudal lord might have sexual intercourse with the bride of a vassal on the wedding-night, before she cohabited with her husband." Certainly this privilege was no longer practiced by the eighteenth century, but the* droit du seigneur *was a popular convention of eighteenth- and nineteenth-century fiction.*

man would call it. She had not been married many weeks, when *that man's* brother saw her and admired her. He asked *that man* to lend her to him—for what does it matter that she was married? She was only a peasant! Her husband was only a peasant! *This man* was willing enough, but my sister was good and virtuous, and hated his brother as much as I do. So what do you suppose the two did, to persuade her husband to use his influence with her, to make her willing?'

"The boy's eyes, which had been fixed on mine, slowly turned to the watching brother, and I could tell by the expressions in both their faces that everything he said was true. The two opposing kinds of pride confronted one another. I can see it still—even in this Bastille—the gentleman's expression was all indifference, while the peasant's was all sentiment, and revenge.

"'Did you know, Doctor, that these Nobles have the right to harness us *common dogs* to carts, and drive us? They harnessed him and drove her husband. Did you know that they have the right to keep us on their grounds all night, quieting the frogs, so that their noble sleep will not be disturbed? They kept him out in the unhealthy mists at night, and ordered him back into his harness the next day. But he was not persuaded. No! Taken out of harness one day at noon, to eat—if he could find food—he sobbed twelve times, once for every stroke of the bell, and died on her bosom.'

"No human power could have kept that boy alive, but his determination to reveal all this wrongdoing strengthened him. He forced back the gathering shadows of death, just as he forced his clenched right hand to remain clenched, and to cover his wound.

"'Then, with *that man's* permission and even with his aid, his brother took her away. In spite of what I know she must have told his brother—and what that is, you will know soon, Doctor, if you don't know already—his brother took her away—for his pleasure and entertainment, for a little while. I saw her pass me on the road. When I took the news home, our father's heart broke. He never expressed any of the thoughts and emotions that must have overwhelmed him. I took my younger sister (for I have another) to a place where *this man* will never be able to find her, and where she will never be his property. Then, I tracked the brother here, and last night climbed in—a common dog, but sword in hand—Where is the loft window? It was somewhere here?'

"The room was fading from his sight. The world was narrowing around him. I glanced about me, and saw that the hay and straw were trampled over the floor, as if there had been a struggle.

"'She heard me, and ran in. I told her not to come near us until he was dead. He came in and first tossed me some pieces of money; then hit me with a whip. But I—though a *common dog*—struck at him so hard that he drew his sword. I don't care how humiliating it might be to him to admit, but the sword that he stained with my *common* blood he drew to defend himself! He thrust at me with all his skill to save his life.'

"Only a few moments earlier I had seen the pieces of a broken sword, lying in the hay on the floor. That weapon was a gentleman's. In another place, lay an old sword that seemed to have been a soldier's.

"'Now, lift me up, Doctor, lift me up. Where is he?'

"'He is not here,' I said, supporting the boy, and thinking that he referred to the brother.

"'He! Proud as these nobles are, he is afraid to see me. Where is the man who was here? Turn my face to him.'

"I did so, raising the boy's head against my knee. But the boy was superhumanly strong, and he raised himself completely so that I had to rise too or I would not have been able to support him.

"'Marquis,' said the boy, staring him, his eyes wide, and his right hand raised, 'in the days when all these things are to be answered for, I summon you and yours—to the last of your bad race—to answer for

❷ *This younger brother is the same man who killed the young boy with his carriage in Book I, Chapter VIII.*

❷ *Pay close attention to the boy's wording: "in the days when all these things are to be answered for…" What two characters in this story are included in the boy's curse, "to the last of your bad race…"?*

them. I mark this cross of blood upon you, as a sign that I do it. *In the days when all these things are to be answered for*, I summon your brother, the worst of the bad race, to answer for them individually. I mark this cross of blood upon him, as a sign that I do it.'

"Twice, he put his hand to the wound in his breast, and with his forefinger drew a cross in the air. He stood for an instant with the finger yet raised, and as it dropped, he dropped with it, and I laid him down—dead. * * * *

"When I returned to the bedside of the young woman, I found her raving precisely as she had been. I knew that this might last for many hours, and that it would probably end in her death.

"I repeated the medicines I had given her, and I sat at the side of the bed until very late in the night. She never stopped shrieking, never stumbled in the distinctness or the order of her words. They were always 'My husband, my father, and my brother! One, two, three, four, five, six, seven, eight, nine, ten, eleven, twelve. Hush!'

"This lasted twenty-six hours from the time when I first saw her. I had come and gone twice, and was again sitting by her, when she began to falter. I did everything that could be done to assist her—but that was not much. After a while, she sank into a drug-like stupor, and lay like the dead.

"It was almost like the calm after a long and fearful storm. I untied her arms, and called the woman to help me to arrange her body and the dress she had torn. It was then that I noticed that she was in the early stages of pregnancy. And I gave up all hope of being able to save her life.

"'Is she dead?' asked the Marquis, whom I will still describe as the elder brother, coming booted into the room from his horse.

"'Not dead,' I answered 'but about to die.'

"'These commoners are really quite strong!' he said, looking down at her with some curiosity.

"'There is amazing strength,' I answered him, 'in sorrow and despair.'

"He first laughed at my words, and then frowned at them. He moved a chair with his foot near to mine, ordered the woman away, and said in a subdued voice, "'Doctor, when I found the trouble my brother was in with these...*animals*, I recommended that you should be summoned. You have a strong reputation, and—as a young man with your fortune to make—you are probably aware that you have a career ahead of you. You are never to speak of the things you have seen here.'

"I listened to the patient's breathing, and avoided answering.

"'Are you listening to me, Doctor?'

"'Monsieur,' said I, 'professional ethics require that anything a patient tells me remain private between us.' It was a guarded answer, because I was troubled by what I had heard and seen.

❷ *What is the Marquis hinting to Manette?*

"Her breathing was so difficult to trace, that I carefully felt the pulse and the heart. There was still life, but only barely. Looking around as I returned to my seat, I found both of the brothers staring at me.****

"It is so difficult to write. The cold is so severe. I am so afraid of being discovered and taken to an underground cell and total darkness that I must cut this narrative short. My memory is clear and strong. I am not at all confused or doubtful. I can remember, and could repeat in exact detail, every word that was ever spoken between me and those brothers.

"She lingered for a week. Toward the end, I could understand a few syllables that she muttered to me. She asked me where she was, and I told her. She asked me who I was, and I told her. It was useless, but I asked her for her family name. She merely shook her head upon the pillow and kept her secret as the boy had done.

"I had no chance to ask her a question until I

❷ *Since you have developed a sense of how Dickens relies on coincidence and likes to tie all of the threads of his plotlines and characters together, who do you think is the girl and boy's family?*

had told the brothers that she was dying, and could not live another day. Until then—although neither of them ever actually dared to face her—one or other of them had always sat behind a curtain at the head of the bed when I was there. They didn't seem to care what I said to her, almost as if—the thought actually passed through my mind—I were dying too.

"It was obvious that their pride bitterly resented the younger brother's having crossed swords with a peasant and a mere boy at that. The only thought that seemed to have any effect on either of them was that this whole experience was *highly degrading to their family*, and was ridiculous. Whenever I caught the younger brother's eyes, their expression reminded me that he disliked me intensely because I knew what the boy had told me. He was smoother and more polite to me than the elder, but I could still see his dislike and distrust. I also saw that the elder also considered me something of a problem.

"My patient died, two hours before midnight. I was alone with her when her pathetic, young head drooped gently on one side, and all of her earthly sorrows ended.

"The brothers were waiting in a room downstairs, impatient to ride away. I had heard them, alone at the bedside, striking their boots with their riding-whips, and pacing up and down.

"'Is she finally dead?' asked the elder, when I entered.

"'She is dead,' I said.

"'I congratulate you, my brother,' were his words as he turned round.

"He had already offered me money, which I had postponed taking. He now gave me a roll of gold coins. I took it from his hand, but laid it on the table. I had thought about it and had decided not to take anything from these men.

"'Please excuse me,' I said, 'but under the circumstances, no.'

"They looked at each other, but bowed their heads

❷ *What legal means did the French nobility have for making persons who were the source of family problems disappear?*

to me as I bowed mine to them, and we parted without either of us saying another word. * * * *

"I am weary, weary, weary—worn down by misery. I cannot even read what I have written with this weak and tired hand.

"Early in the morning, the roll of coins was left at the door of my home in a little box with my name written on it. From the beginning, I had anxiously worried about what I should do. I decided on that day to write privately to the Minister, stating the nature of the two cases, and the place to which I had gone. I wrote to him all of the details of the case. I knew what Court influence was, and that the Nobles were immune from most forms of legal prosecution, and I expected that my letter would simply be ignored, but I wished to relieve my own mind. I had kept the matter absolutely secret—even from my wife—and this I also stated in my letter. I had no idea whatsoever of my real danger. But I was aware that I might be putting others in danger by sharing with them this information.

"I was very busy that day, and could not complete my letter that night. I awoke very early the next morning to finish it. It was the last day of the year. I just finished the letter, when I was told that a lady wished to see me. * * * *

"It is growing more and more difficult to write this. It is so cold and so dark that I am drowsy and numb. The gloom upon me is so dreadful.

"The lady was young, warm, and handsome. She was very upset. She introduced herself to me as the wife of the Marquis St. Evremonde. I recognized this as the title by which the boy had addressed the elder brother. It was fairly obvious that the initial embroidered on the scarf that had tied the poor girl's arms stood for *Evremonde*.

"I remember every word of my conversation with this Lady, but I cannot write them. I suspect that I am watched more closely now than I was when I first came to this prison. I never know when I am being watched. But this Lady—the wife of the Marquis—had partly

✆ *Remember, in Book II, Chapter IX, Charles alludes to the fact that the Evremonde family is probably the most hated and feared in all of France.*

suspected, and partly discovered, the main facts of the cruel story and of her husband's share in it. She did not know that the girl was dead. Her hope had been— she told me very sadly—to secretly show her some sympathy. She feared that her husband and brother-in-law had sinned so severely against Heaven that they must truly be cursed. Her hope had been to undo that curse, to turn the anger of Heaven away from a family that had long been hateful to the suffering people.

❷ *Who is the sister?*

"She had reason to believe that there was a young sister living, and her greatest desire was to help that sister. I could tell her nothing but that there was indeed a sister. Beyond that, I knew nothing. She told me that she had come to me and opened her heart to me because she hoped that I could tell her the name and where they lived. However, to this wretched hour I am ignorant of both. * * * *

"These scraps of paper are running out. One was taken from me, with a warning, yesterday. I must finish my record today.

"She was a good, compassionate lady, very unhappy in her marriage. How could she be happy? The brother distrusted and disliked her, and used his influence to work against her. She feared him. She feared her husband too. When I led her to the door, there was a child, a pretty boy some two to three years old, in her carriage.

"'For his sake, Doctor,' she said, pointing to him in tears, 'I will do whatever I can to repay the wrongs my husband and his brother have done. My son will never prosper in his inheritance otherwise. I sense that—if nothing is done to make up for this—my son will pay the price. There is not much that I can call my own—a few jewels—but I will make it my son's first and most important responsibility to give all of it to this injured family. To give it to them with compassion and begging their forgiveness. *If* he can ever find out who this sister is and where she might be.

"She kissed the boy, and, caressing him, said 'It is for your own sake. Will you be faithful, little Charles?'

The child answered her bravely, 'Yes!' I kissed her hand, and she took him in her arms, and went away caressing him. I never saw her again.

"Even though she had mentioned her husband's name, assuming that I already knew it, I did not mention it in my letter. I did not want to cause trouble for her for revealing to me what her husband had kept secret. I sealed my letter, and delivered it myself that day.

"That night—the last night of the year—around nine o'clock—a man in a black cloak rang at my gate and demanded to see me. He secretly followed my servant, Ernest Defarge upstairs. When my servant came into the room where I sat with my wife—O my wife, beloved of my heart! My fair, young English wife!—we saw the man, who was supposed to be at the gate, standing silently behind him.

"An urgent case in the Rue St. Honore, he said. It would not keep me late, he had a coach in waiting.

"That coach brought me here. It brought me to my grave. When we had gotten away from the house, a black scarf was pulled tightly over my mouth from behind, and my arms were pinned. The two brothers crossed the road from a dark corner, and identified me with a quick nod. The Marquis took from his pocket the letter I had written, showed it to me, burnt it in the light of a lantern he was holding, and extinguished the ashes with his foot. Not a word was spoken. I was brought here, I was brought to my living grave.

"Surely these brothers are Godless. If God had been able to move either of them to grant me any news of my dear, dear wife—even just a word to let me know whether she were alive or dead—I might have thought that He had not completely abandoned them. But, now I believe that the boy's curse—sealed with the mark of the red cross—is indeed fatal to them, and that they have no place in Heaven.

"Therefore, I, Alexandre Manette, unhappy prisoner, do on this last night of the year 1767, in my unbearable agony, denounce *them and their*

✔ *Note what we now know of the identities of the two brothers, the lady, and this child.*

❷ *Pause and Reflect: What does this document of Dr. Manette's mean?*

✓ *Explain the ambiguity in the phrase, "to the times when all these things shall be answered for."*

descendants, to the last of their race, to the times when all these things shall be answered for. *I denounce them to Heaven and to earth."*

A terrible sound arose when the reading of this document was finished, a bloodthirsty sound, calling for vengeance. The Doctor's story rekindled the angry and hateful passions of the time. There was not a single representative of the old order they would not gladly have sliced off with the guillotine.

It was clear that the Defarges had kept this paper until this very day, biding their time. It was also clear that there was no man on earth who had the power to save Charles Darnay.

It was all the worse for the doomed man that the denouncer was a well-known citizen, someone he loved and trusted, the father of his wife. One of the fanatical desires of the people was to return to the passions of the past when frenzied people would sacrifice everything—even their own lives or the lives of their loved ones—to the Cause. Therefore, there was nothing to stop the President from speaking directly to the Doctor. His own head would have been the next for the guillotine if he did not.

He rang his bell and announced that the good physician would earn even more of the Republic's admiration by exposing this hateful family of aristocrats to their just and final punishment. He would undoubtedly feel an intense satisfaction in making his daughter a widow and her child an orphan. The courtroom rang with wild excitement, patriotic fervor, but not a single touch of human sympathy.

"So, our Doctor is very influential and has many influential friends, has he?" murmured Madame Defarge, smiling to The Vengeance. "Save him now, my Doctor, save him now!"

At every juryman's vote, there was a roar of approval. Another and another. Roar after roar.

The vote was unanimous. Charles Evremonde, called Darnay was proclaimed an aristocrat at heart and by descent, an enemy of the Republic, a notorious oppressor of the People.

Back to the Conciergerie, and Death within twenty-four hours!

THIS IS THE END OF THE
TWENTY-SEVENTH WEEKLY INSTALLMENT.

Writing Opportunity:

Review the circumstances of Charles's arrest in England, his stated reasons for his frequent trips to France. Also reread his conversation with his uncle in Book Two, Chapter 9. Then write an essay in which you discuss the justice or injustice of Madame Defarge's hatred and of Charles's sentence.

A Tale of Two Cities
CHARLES DICKENS

CHAPTER XI
Dusk

LUCIE, THE PITIFUL wife of the innocent man thus
doomed to die, collapsed, as if she had been fatally
wounded. But she uttered no sound; and the voice
within her was so strong, telling her that she was the
one who needed to help Charles in his crisis, not add
to it, that she quickly got back up again and gave her
husband a comforting look.

The Judges had to participate in a public
demonstration outdoors, so the Tribunal adjourned.
The courtroom emptied quickly and noisily. Lucie
stood where she had been and stretched her arms
toward her husband. Her face glowed with love and
consolation.

"If only I could touch him! If only I could embrace
him just once! Oh, good citizens, if you would have
even that much compassion for us!"

There was only a jailer left in the courtroom, along
with two of the four men who had arrested Charles
the night before, and Barsad. The people had all
rushed outside to see the show in the streets. Barsad
suggested to the rest, "Let her embrace him then. It's
only a moment." It was silently agreed, and they lifted
her over the seats in the hall to a raised place where

he—by leaning over the dock—could fold her in his arms.

"Farewell, dear darling of my soul. My final blessing rests on you. We shall meet again, in the land of Eternal Rest!"

They were her husband's words, as he held her close.

"I can bear it, dear Charles. I am supported from above. Don't suffer for me. A parting blessing for our child."

"I send it to her through you. I kiss her through you. I say farewell to her through you."

He started to leave her. "Charles! Just one more moment!" He paused and looked sadly into her eyes. "We will not be separated long. I feel that this will break my heart very soon, but I will do my duty while I can. And when I leave her, God will give her friends, as He gave me."

Remember that Lucie's mother died soon after Manette's imprisonment, and Mr. Lorry took Lucie to England to be raised by Miss Pross.

Research Opportunity:

Look up the literary terms "Pathos" and "Bathos" and then write an essay in which you argue which applies to this scene. Be certain to support your argument with evidence from the text.

Her father had followed her, and would have fallen on his knees to both of them, but that Darnay put out a hand and stopped him, crying, "No, no! You have done nothing that requires you to kneel before us, asking for forgiveness. Now we know what a struggle you had all those years ago. Now we know what you thought when you first suspected my true family name, and then when you actually knew it. Now we know the natural hatred you struggled against—and conquered—for her dear sake. We thank you with all our hearts, and all our love, and all our duty. Heaven be with you!"

Her father's only answer was to draw his hands

through his white hair, and wring them with a shriek of anguish.

"This was inevitable," said the prisoner. "Destiny has been at work from the very beginning. It was while unsuccessfully trying to fulfill my poor mother's mission that I first met you. Good could never have come out of that evil. A happy ending was not possible to such an unhappy beginning. Be comforted, and forgive me. Heaven bless you!"

As the jailer pulled him away, Lucie released him, and stood looking after him with her hands touching one another as if she were praying, with a radiant look upon her face, and a comforting smile. As he went out at the prisoners' door, she turned, laid her head lovingly on her father's breast, tried to speak to him, and collapsed again at his feet.

Suddenly appearing from the hidden corner in which he had been hidden the entire time, Sydney Carton came and picked her up. Only her father and Mr. Lorry were with her. His arm trembled as it raised her and supported her head. There was an air about him that was not all of pity—that had a touch of pride in it.

"Shall I take her to a coach? I shall never feel her weight."

He carried her lightly to the door, and laid her tenderly down in a coach. Her father and their old friend got into it, and he took his seat beside the driver.

When they arrived at the gateway where he had paused in the dark not many hours before, he lifted her again, and carried her up the staircase to their rooms. There, he laid her down on a couch, where her child and Miss Pross wept over her.

"Don't wake her up," he said, softly, to Miss Pross, "she is better off unconscious."

"Oh, Carton, Carton, Carton!" cried little Lucie, jumping up and throwing her arms passionately around him, in a burst of grief. "Now that you have come, I think you will do something to help mamma,

Remember what Charles's mother said about Charles being doomed if they did not succeed in making some sort of restitution to the injured family.

✔ *It was a fairly common convention in Victorian novels for children—especially good children—to be especially sensitive to other people's moods and to have almost the ability to predict the future.*

❓ *What is the significance of that phrase?*

something to save papa! Oh, look at her, dear Carton! Can you, of all the people who love her, bear to see her like this?"

He bent over the child, and laid her cheek against his face. He stood up, and looked at her unconscious mother.

"Before I go," he said, and paused—"May I kiss her?"

Afterwards they all remembered that, when he bent down and touched her face with his lips, he murmured some words. The child, who was nearest to him, told them afterwards, and told her grandchildren when she was a handsome old lady, that she heard him say, "The life of someone you love."

When he had gone into the next room, he turned suddenly toward Mr. Lorry and her father, who were following, and said to the Doctor, "You had great influence only yesterday, Doctor Manette. These judges—and all the men in power—are very friendly to you, and very aware of your services, aren't they?"

"They hid nothing connected with Charles from me. I had every reason to believe that I would be able save him—and I did." He answered very slowly and with a great deal of apparent difficulty.

"Try your influence again. We certainly do not have a lot of time, but you must at least try."

"I intend to try. I will not rest a moment."

"That's good. I have known energy like yours to work miracles."

"I will go immediately," said Doctor Manette, "to the Prosecutor and the President. And I will go to others whom it is better that I not name. I will write too, and—But wait! There's that celebration in the streets, and no one will be available until dark."

"That's true. Well! It's a weak hope at the best, and it certainly isn't weakened any by having to wait till dark. I'd like to be kept informed how things go. Though I don't expect you'll meet with much success. When are you likely to have seen these powerful men, Doctor Manette?"

"Immediately after dark, I should hope. An hour or two from now."

"It will be dark soon after four. Let us stretch the hour or two. If I go to Mr. Lorry's at nine, can I expect to hear what you have done, either from him or from you?"

"Yes."

"Good luck, then."

Mr. Lorry followed Sydney to the outer door. "I have no hope," he said in a low and sorrowful whisper.

"Nor have I."

"Even if any of these men wanted to spare him— even if they *all* wanted to spare him—I doubt they'd dare to try after that demonstration in the court."

"I agree."

Mr. Lorry leaned his arm upon the doorpost, and bowed his face upon it.

"Don't despair," said Carton, very gently; "don't grieve. I encouraged Doctor Manette in this idea, only because I felt that it might one day be a comfort to *her*. Otherwise, she might think 'his life was recklessly thrown away or wasted,' and that would trouble her."

"Yes, yes, yes," returned Mr. Lorry, drying his eyes, "you are right." He paused. "But he will die, won't he? There is no real hope."

"Yes." answered Carton. "He will die. There is no real hope." And he walked with a settled step, down the stairs.

A Tale of Two Cities

CHARLES DICKENS

CHAPTER **XII**

Darkness

SYDNEY CARTON PAUSED in the street, not quite sure where to go. "At Tellson's banking house at nine," he said. "In the mean time, would it be a good idea for me to be seen in public? I think so. It is best that these people know that someone like me is in town. It is a wise precaution, and may be a necessary preparation. But I'd better be careful. Let me think it out!"

He walked back and forth in the already darkening street, and traced the thought in his mind to its possible consequences. His first impulse was confirmed. "It is best," he said, finally resolved, "that these people should know there is someone like me here." And he turned his face toward Saint Antoine.

Defarge had described himself, that day, as the keeper of a wine shop in the Saint Antoine suburb. It was not difficult for someone who knew the city well to find the wine shop without having to ask directions. When he found it, Carton left the narrower streets, dined at a small cafe and fell sound asleep after dinner. For the first time in many years, he had no strong drink. Since the night before, he had drunk nothing but a little light, thin wine, and last night he had poured the brandy slowly down on Mr. Lorry's

❷ *What do you suppose Sydney means by "someone like me"?*

❷ *What is Dickens establishing by saying, "He turned his face"? Why would Sydney go to Saint Antoine?*

hearth like a man who was done with it.

It was as late as seven o'clock when he awoke refreshed, and went out into the streets again. As he made his way toward Saint Antoine, he stopped at a shop window where there was a mirror, and slightly adjusted his tie, and his coat collar, and his wild hair. This done, he went on straight to Defarge's, and went in.

There happened to be no customer in the shop but Jacques Three, the man with the restless fingers and the croaking voice. This man, whom Carton had seen on the Jury, stood drinking at the little counter, talking with the Defarges. The Vengeance also participated in the conversation, like a regular member of the establishment.

Carton walked in, took his seat and asked—in very imperfect French—for a small glass of wine. Madame Defarge cast a careless glance at him. Then she looked at him more closely. Finally she walked up to the table herself and asked him what it was he had ordered.

He repeated what he had already said.

"English?" asked Madame Defarge, raising her dark eyebrows.

After looking at her, as if trying to figure out what she had said, he answered, in his former strong foreign accent, "Yes, Madame, yes. I am English!"

Madame Defarge returned to her counter to get the wine. As he picked up a Jacobin journal and pretended to try to figure out its meaning, he heard her say, "I swear to you, just like Evremonde!"

Defarge brought him the wine, and bid him a good evening.

"Excuse me?"

"Good evening."

"Oh! Good evening, Citizen." He filled his glass. "Ah! and good wine. I drink to the Republic."

Defarge went back to the counter, and said, "There is a faint similarity."

Madame sternly retorted, "I tell you a remarkable

There were two parties involved in the French Revolution. The Girondins were the moderate republicans and controlled the Legislative Assembly from late 1791 to late 1792. They were ultimately ousted by the radical Jacobins, led by the infamous Maximilien Robespierre. The Jacobins were the party responsible for the Reign of Terror. Clearly, the Defarges are members of this radical party.

resemblance." Jacques Three pacifically remarked, "He's just so much on your mind, you see, Madame." The jolly Vengeance added, with a laugh, "Yes, my friend! And you are so looking forward to seeing him again tomorrow!"

Carton followed the lines and words of his paper with a slow forefinger and with a studious and absorbed face. They were all leaning their arms on the counter close together, speaking low. After a few moments' silence, during which they all watched him without disturbing his attention from the Jacobin editor—they resumed their conversation.

"It is true what Madame says," observed Jacques Three. "Why stop? That is an excellent question. Why stop?"

"Well, well," reasoned Defarge, "but one must stop somewhere. Still, the question is still where?"

"At extermination," said Madame.

"Magnificent!" croaked Jacques Three. The Vengeance, also, highly approved.

"Extermination is good doctrine in general, my wife," said Defarge, rather troubled. "But this Doctor has suffered a great deal already. You saw him today. You saw his face when his paper was read."

"I saw his face!" repeated Madame, contemptuously and angrily. "Yes. I saw his face. I have seen his face to be *not* the face of a true friend of the Republic. Let him take care of his face!"

"And you have seen, my wife," said Defarge, in a tone of voice a father might use scolding a misbehaved child, "the anguish of his daughter, which must be a dreadful anguish to him!"

"I have seen his daughter," repeated Madame; "yes, I have seen his daughter, more times than one. I saw her today, and I saw her other days. I have seen her in the Court, and I have seen her in the street by the prison. Let me but lift my finger—!" She seemed to raise it (the listener's eyes were always on his paper), and to let it fall with a rattle on the counter in front of her, as if the axe had dropped.

❷ What do you suppose they are talking about?

✔ Note the tone of a subtle threat. Now Madame Defarge is turning her attention to the Doctor himself.

Notice how Dickens is beginning to soften Defarge and make Madame Defarge more angry and hateful than before.

"The citizeness is superb!" croaked the Juryman.

"She is an Angel!" said The Vengeance, and embraced her.

"As to you," continued Madame, speaking to her husband, "if it depended on you—which, happily, it does not—you would rescue this man even now."

"No I would not!" protested Defarge. "Not even if it were no harder than to lift this glass! But I would leave the matter there. I say, stop there."

"There you have it, Jacques," said Madame Defarge, furiously, "and there you have it, my little Vengeance! For *other* crimes as tyrants and oppressors, I have this noble class a long time on my register, marked for destruction and total extermination. Ask my husband, is that not so?"

"It is so," agreed Defarge.

"In the beginning of the great days, when the Bastille falls, he finds this paper of today. And he brings it home. And in the middle of the night when this place is empty, we read it—here on this very spot, by the light of this very lamp. Ask him, is that not so?"

"It is so," agreed Defarge.

"That night, I tell him—when we've read and re-read the paper, and the lamp is burnt out, and the day is beginning to dawn through those shutters and between those iron bars—I tell him that I have a secret I must tell him. Ask him, is that not so?"

"It is so," agreed Defarge again.

"And I tell him that secret. I tell him that I was brought up among the fishermen of the seashore. I tell him that that peasant family so injured by the two Evremonde brothers—as that Bastille paper describes—was *my* family. That the sister of the mortally wounded boy was *my* sister, that husband was *my* sister's husband, that unborn child was their child, that brother was *my* brother, that father was *my* father, those dead are *my* dead, and that summons to answer for those things descends to me!' Ask him, is that so."

According to the wording of both her brother's and the Doctor's denunciations, does the summons fall to Madame Defarge? What sin is she committing here?

"It is so," agreed Defarge once more.

"Then tell Wind and Fire where to stop," returned Madame, "but don't tell me."

Both her hearers derived a horrible enjoyment from the deadly nature of her fury—the listener could *feel* how white with rage she was—without seeing her. Defarge, a weak minority, said a few words for the memory of the compassionate wife of the Marquis, but only received from his own wife a repetition of her last reply. "Tell the Wind and the Fire where to stop—not me!"

Customers entered, and the group was broken up. The English customer paid for his wine, counted his change with some difficulty, and asked—as a stranger would—to be directed toward the National Palace. Madame Defarge took him to the door, and put her arm on his, in pointing out the road. The English customer thought that it might be a good deed to grab her arm, lift it over her head, and stab under it sharp and deep.

But, he went his way, and was soon swallowed up in the shadow of the prison wall. At nine o'clock, he emerged from the shadow to present himself in Mr. Lorry's room again, where he found the old gentleman walking back and forth in restless anxiety. He said he had been with Lucie until just now, and had only left her for a few minutes, to come and keep his appointment. No one had seen her father since he left the banking-house around four o'clock. Lucie had some faint hope that her father's intervention might again save Charles, but even her hope was slight. He had been gone more than five hours. Where could he be?

Mr. Lorry waited until ten. But Doctor Manette had not yet returned, and he did not want to leave Lucie any longer. It was, therefore, arranged that he should go back to her, and come to the banking-house again at midnight. In the meanwhile, Carton would wait alone by the fire for the Doctor.

He waited and waited, and the clock struck twelve. But Doctor Manette did not come back. Mr. Lorry

Again, she asserts that she is at least as strong as forces of nature that are not obedient to human will.

returned. Still no news of Doctor Manette. Where could he be?

They were discussing this question, and were almost building up some hope because of his long absence, when they heard him on the stairs. The instant he entered the room, it was plain that all was lost.

Whether he had really seen anyone, or had simply spent the evening wandering the streets, no one ever knew. As he stood staring at them, they asked him no questions, for his face told them everything.

"I cannot find it," said he, "and I must have it. Where is it?"

His head and throat were bare, and, as he spoke helplessly looking all around him. He took his coat off, and let it drop to the floor.

"Where is my bench? I have been looking everywhere for my bench, and I can't find it. What have they done with my work? Time presses. I must finish those shoes."

Carton and Lorry looked at one another, and their hearts died within them.

"Come, come!" the Doctor said, in a whimpering miserable way. "Let me get to work. Give me my work."

Receiving no answer, he tore his hair, and beat his feet upon the ground, like an angry child.

"Don't torture a poor forlorn wretch," he implored them, with a dreadful cry. "Give me my work! What is to become of us, if those shoes are not done tonight?"

Lost, utterly lost!

It was clearly beyond hope to reason with him, or try to restore him. As if they'd planned to, they each put a hand upon the Doctor's shoulder, and soothed him to sit down before the fire. They promised that he would have his work soon. He sank into the chair, and brooded over the embers, crying. As if everything that had happened since the attic time was a dream,

❷ *What has happened to Doctor Manette?*

Mr. Lorry saw him shrink into the exact figure that Defarge had protected.

They were both terrified by this image of ruin, but they also knew that there was no time to succumb to terror. Their beloved Lucie—who had lost husband and now father in a single day—needed them too much now for them to wallow in their own fear. Again, as if they'd planned it, they looked at one another with one meaning in their faces. Carton was the first to speak.

"The last chance is gone. It was not much. You had better take him to her. But, before you go, you must listen to me. Don't ask me why I make the stipulations I am going to make, and demand the promise I am going to demand. I have a reason—a good one."

"I do not doubt it," answered Mr. Lorry. "Say on."

The figure in the chair between them, was all the time rocking itself back and forth, and moaning. They spoke lowly, as if they were watching by a sickbed.

Carton stooped to pick up the Doctor's coat, and the small case in which the Doctor carried the lists of his day's duties fell onto the floor. Carton picked it up and found a folded paper in it. "We should look at this!" he said. Mr. Lorry nodded his consent. He opened it, and exclaimed, "Thank GOD!"

"What is it?" asked Mr. Lorry.

"Just a moment! Let's take everything one step at a time. First," he put his hand in his coat, and took another paper from it, "this is the certificate that allows me to pass out of this city. Look at it. You see—Sydney Carton, an Englishman?"

Mr. Lorry held it open in his hand, gazing in his earnest face.

"Keep it for me until tomorrow. I'll be seeing Darnay tomorrow, you remember, and I had better not take this into the prison."

"Why not?"

"I don't know; I just prefer not to. Now, take this paper of Doctor Manette's. It is a similar certificate, enabling him and his daughter and her child—*at any*

❷ *What has Carton given to Lorry? What does this suggest?*

time—to pass the barrier and the frontier! You see?"

"Yes!"

"Perhaps he obtained it as his last and final precaution against danger. Put it carefully with mine and your own. Now, look! I always suspected that he had this paper. It is good, until revoked, but it might soon be revoked. I have reason to think it will be."

"They are not in danger?"

"They are in great danger. They are in danger of denunciation by Madame Defarge. I know it from her own lips. I have overheard her tonight, and I am absolutely certain of their danger. I have lost no time, and since then, I have seen the spy. He agrees with me. He knows that a woodcutter who lives by the prison wall is under the control of the Defarges, and has been coached by Madame Defarge to testify to having seen Her"—he never mentioned Lucie's name—"making signs and signals to prisoners. It is easy to guess what they will accuse her of, a prison plot. It will involve her life—and perhaps her child's—and perhaps even the Doctor's—for both have been seen with her at the prison. Don't look so horrified. You will save them all."

"I pray that I may, Carton! But how?"

"I am going to tell you how. It will depend solely on you, and it could depend on no better man. Any denunciation of Lucie or her daughter or her father will certainly not take place until after the execution tomorrow—probably not until two or three days afterwards—more probably a week afterwardss. You know it is a capital offense, to mourn for—or sympathize with—a victim of the Guillotine. She and her father would undoubtedly be guilty of this crime, and Madame Defarge would wait to add that charge to her case, to make it even stronger. You follow me?"

"I do."

"You have money and can buy the necessary tickets to travel to the seacoast as quickly as possible. You've already made your arrangements—several days ago—to return to England. Early tomorrow have your

horses ready, so that they may be ready to go at two
o'clock in the afternoon."

"It shall be done!"

Carton's manner was so passionate and inspiring,
that Mr. Lorry caught the flame, and was as quick
as youth.

"You are a noble heart. Did I say we could depend
on no better man? Tell her tonight what you know
of the danger involving her child and her father.
Emphasize that, for she will do anything to keep her
father safe." He faltered for an instant, then continued.
"For the sake of her child and her father, press upon
her the necessity of leaving Paris, with them and
you, at two o'clock tomorrow. Tell her that it was her
husband's last wish. Tell her that more depends upon
it than she would dare to believe or hope. You think
that her father—even in this sad state—will obey her,
don't you?"

"I am sure of it."

"I thought so. Without drawing unnecessary
attention to yourself, have everything ready out in the
courtyard here—right to the point of having everyone
in their seats. The moment I arrive, take me in, and
drive away."

"So I should wait for you no matter what?"

"You have my travel documents. Reserve my seat.
Wait for nothing but to have someone sitting in my
seat, and then for England!"

❷ Notice how carefully Carton words this instruction.

"Why, then," said Mr. Lorry, grasping his eager but
so firm and steady hand, "it does not all depend on
one old man, but I shall have a young and passionate
man at my side."

"By the help of Heaven you shall! But swear to
me that *nothing* will make you change these plans that
we've established here tonight."

"Nothing, Carton."

"Remember that promise tomorrow. If you change
the course—or delay—for *any* reason, no one's life can
possibly be saved, and many lives will be sacrificed."

"I will remember. I hope to do my part faithfully."

"And I hope to do mine. Now, good bye!"

Although he'd said it with a serious smile, and although he even put the old man's hand to his lips, he did not leave then. He helped Mr. Lorry put a cloak and hat on the dozing form of the Doctor, and to tempt him to try and find where the bench and work were hidden that he still muttered for in his half-asleep-half-awake condition. Carton and Lorry led the Doctor to his own home, and Mr. Lorry bid Carton a good night as he took the doctor up to his rooms.

Carton followed them into the courtyard and remained there for a few moments alone, looking up at the light in the window of her room. Before he went away, he breathed a blessing toward it, and a Farewell.

THIS IS THE END OF THE TWENTY-EIGHTH WEEKLY INSTALLMENT.

A Tale of Two Cities

CHARLES DICKENS

CHAPTER XIII
Fifty-Two

IN THE BLACK prison of the Conciergerie, the doomed of the day awaited their fate. There were the same number of condemned for the day as there were weeks in the year. Fifty-two heads were to roll that afternoon. Before they left their cells, new occupants joined them. Before their blood ran into the blood spilled yesterday, the blood that was to mingle with theirs tomorrow was already set apart.

Two score and twelve were counted off. From the seventy-year-old tax collector, whose riches could not buy his life, to the seamstress of twenty, whose poverty could not save her. The anger and thirst for revenge, bred by years of oppression and torture, make no distinction between people when choosing its own victims.

A score is twenty. Two score and twelve equals fifty-two.

Explain the double irony in this sentence.

Since his final imprisonment the day before, Charles Darnay sat alone in a cell and harbored no false hopes. In every line of the Doctor's document that he'd heard read aloud, he had heard his condemnation. He fully understood that no personal influence could save him, that Millions had condemned him, and that Individuals would not be able to help him.

Nevertheless, it was not easy to patiently accept his fate, especially with the face of his beloved wife always before him. His hold on life was strong, and it was very, very hard, to loosen. All of his thoughts felt hurried; his heart beat fast and furious, to avoid accepting his fate. If, for a moment, he did feel resigned to it, then the wife and child who would survive him seemed to protest and to make him feel selfish for having surrendered.

Eventually, however, he began to be encouraged by the realization that there was no disgrace in the way he was to die, that dozens—possibly even hundreds—died unjustly every day. Next followed the thought that his courage might bring his dear ones peace of mind. So, he gradually calmed himself into a better state, when he could raise his thoughts toward Heaven, and be comforted.

On the night of the day he'd been condemned, he thus began to prepare for his death. He was allowed have a pen, some ink, paper, and a candle. He sat down to write until he was ordered to extinguish his light.

He wrote a long letter to Lucie, telling her that he had known nothing of her father's imprisonment until she told him, and that he had had absolutely no idea of his father's and uncle's responsibility for that misery, until that morning in court. He had already explained to her that he had promised her father not to tell her his true name. He begged her—for her father's sake—never to ask whether her father had forgotten the existence of the paper, or had he been reminded of it by the story he'd told that Sunday evening under the old plane tree in their garden.

If he had remembered it at all, he certainly must have thought that it had been destroyed with the Bastille, especially when it was not listed among the relics of prisoners that had been discovered there, and published to the world. He begged her— though he added that he knew he didn't need to—to console her father, by telling him that he had done everything he could to rescue Charles from the Guillotine. He closed by commanding her to devote herself to their dear child and to comfort her father.

Remember in Book II, Chapter VI (page 113), the story that Darnay told about the ashes of a prisoner's letter found in a dungeon in the Tower of London, and Dr. Manette's strange reaction to the story.

Next he wrote to her father along the same lines, except that he told her father to comfort and care for Lucie and little Lucie. He hoped, by his letter, to ease any sorrow or guilt the Doctor might feel.

In a letter to Mr. Lorry, he wrote his last will and testament. When he finished that, he added many sentences thanking him for his friendship and his closeness to the family. And he was done. He never thought of Carton. His mind was so full of the others, that he never once thought of him.

He had time to finish these letters before the lights were put out. When he lay down on his straw bed, he thought he was finished with this world.

❷ *Why do you suppose Dickens makes it a point to establish that Darnay does not once think of Sydney Carton?*

But, the world called him back in his sleep, and showed itself in shining forms. Free and happy, back in the old house in Soho, unaccountably happy. He was with Lucie again, and she told him it had all been a dream, and he had never gone away. There was a pause of dreamlessness, and then he dreamed that he had in fact suffered. When he came back to Lucie, he was dead and at peace, but he walked and talked as if he had never died. Then there was another period of dreamless sleep, and he awoke in the somber morning, unaware of where he was or what was happening, until it flashed upon his mind, *This is the day of my death!*

Thus, had he come through the hours, to the day when the fifty-two heads were to fall. And now, while he was calm, and hoped that he could meet the end with quiet heroism, a new thought came into his mind.

He had never seen the instrument that was to end his life. How high was it from the ground? How many steps did it have? Where would he be stood? How would he be held? Would the hands that touched him be stained with blood? Which way would his face be turned? Would he be the first, or maybe the last? These and many similar questions forced themselves into his mind. These questions were not connected with fear. Instead, they originated in a strange desire to know what to do when the time came.

The hours went on as he paced back and forth, and the clocks struck the numbers he would never hear again. Nine gone forever, ten gone forever, eleven gone forever, twelve coming on to pass away. After a hard contest with his mind, he had gotten the better of it. He walked up and down, softly repeating their names to himself. The worst of his struggle was over. He could walk up and down, free from distracting fancies, praying for himself and for them.

Twelve gone forever.

He had been told that the final hour was Three, and he knew he would be summoned some time earlier, because the tumbrels jolted heavily and slowly through the streets. Therefore, he kept Two in his mind as the hour he would be called, and strengthened himself so that he might be able—when the time came—to strengthen others.

Walking normally back and forth with his arms folded across his chest, he was a very different man from the prisoner who had paced the floor at La Force. He heard One struck away from him, without surprise. The hour had passed like most other hours. Enormously thankful to Heaven for his self-confidence, he thought, "There is just one more hour," and turned to walk again.

Then he heard unexpected footsteps in the stone passage outside the door. He stopped.

The key was put in the lock, and turned. Before the door was opened, or as it opened, a man said in a low voice, in English: "He has never seen me here; I have kept out of his way. Go in alone. I will wait here. Don't waste any time!"

The door was quickly opened and closed, and there stood before him face to face—quietly studying him—with the hint of a smile on his face, and a silencing finger to his lip, Sydney Carton.

There was something so bright and remarkable in his appearance, that—for the first moment—the prisoner thought Carton was merely a figment of his imagination. But when he spoke, it was his voice. He took the prisoner's hand, and it was his real grasp.

"Of all the people on earth, I was the *last* person you expected to see." he said.

"I could not believe it to be you. I can scarcely believe it now." Suddenly a look of fear crossed his face. "You're not a prisoner?"

"No. I have some influence here, and it has brought me to you. I come from her—your wife."

The prisoner wrung his hands.

"I bring you a request from her."

"What is it?"

"There is no time for you to ask me *why* I bring it, or what it means. You must simply do as I say. Take off your boots and put mine on."

There was a chair against the wall of the cell, behind the prisoner. Carton, pushed Darnay down into it and stood over him, barefooted.

"Put on my boots. Quick!"

"Carton, there is no escape from this place. It can't be done. You will only die with me. It is madness."

"It would be madness if I asked you to escape. But have I asked you to try to escape? When I ask you to walk out that door, tell me it is madness and stay here. Here, take off your tie and put on mine. Change coats with me too. Here, while you're doing that, let me take this ribbon from your hair, and shake out your hair like mine!"

With wonderful quickness, and with a strength both of will and action, that appeared almost supernatural, Carton forced all these changes on Darnay. The prisoner was like a young child in his hands.

"Carton! This is madness. It cannot be done! It can never can be done! Others have tried, and have always failed. I beg you not to add your death to the bitterness of mine."

"My dear Darnay, have I asked you to go through the door? When I ask that, then you may refuse. There are pen and ink and paper on this table. Is your hand steady enough to write?"

❷ *So, what is Carton Doing?*

✔ *Dickens needs us to suspend our disbelief here and believe that Darnay does not realize what Carton is planning to do.*

"It was before you came in."

"Calm down, and write what I say. Quickly!"

Pressing his hand to his confused head, Darnay sat down at the table. Carton, with his right hand in his breast, stood close beside him.

"Write exactly as I speak."

"To whom do I address it?"

"To no one." Carton still had his hand in his breast.

"Do I date it?"

"No."

The prisoner looked up, at each question. Carton, standing over him with his hand in his breast, looked down.

"'If you remember,'" said Carton, dictating, "'the words that passed between us, long ago, you will easily understand this when you see it. You do remember them, I know. It is not in your nature to forget them.'"

He was drawing his hand from his breast. The prisoner happened to look up as he wrote, and the hand stopped, closing on something.

"Have you written 'forget them'?" Carton asked.

"I have. Is that a weapon in your hand?"

"No. I am not armed."

"What is it in your hand?"

"You'll know soon enough. Please continue. Only a few more words." He dictated again. "'I am thankful that the time has come, when I can prove them. That I do so is no cause for regret or grief.'" As he said these words with his eyes fixed on the writer, his hand slowly and softly moved down close to the writer's face.

The pen dropped from Darnay's fingers on the table, and he looked about him vacantly.

"What do I smell?" he asked.

"Smell?"

"Something that blew across me?"

"I don't smell anything. There's nothing here. Pick up the pen and finish. Hurry, hurry!"

As if his memory were impaired, or his mind

❷ *To whom is this letter going? What words is Carton referring to?*

clouded, the prisoner seemed to try to rally his attention. He looked at Carton with clouded eyes and his breathing was slow and labored. Carton—his hand again in his breast—looked steadily at him.

"Hurry, hurry!"

The prisoner once again bent over the paper.

"'If things had worked out differently,'" Carton's hand was again watchfully and softly stealing down, "'I would never have had the opportunity for redemption that you wanted for me so much back then. If things had worked out differently,'" the hand was at the prisoner's face; "'I would only have more sins to answer for at the end. If things had worked out differently ...'" Carton looked at the pen and saw it was trailing off into unintelligible signs.

Carton's hand moved back to his breast no more. The prisoner sprang up with an angry look, but Carton's hand stayed at his nostrils, and Carton's left arm caught him around the waist. For a few seconds Darnay feebly struggled with the man who had come to lay down his life for him, but, within a minute or so, he was stretched unconscious on the ground.

Quickly, but with hands as true to the purpose as his heart was, Carton dressed himself in the clothes the prisoner had taken off, combed back his hair, and tied it with the ribbon the prisoner had worn. Then, he softly called, "Enter there! Come in!" and the Spy presented himself.

"You see?" said Carton, looking up, as he kneeled on one knee beside the unconscious figure, putting the paper in the breast. "is your risk very great?"

"Mr. Carton," the Spy answered, with a timid snap of his fingers, "there is no risk to me at all if you are true to the whole of your bargain."

"Don't fear me. I will be true to death."

"You must be, Mr. Carton, if the tale of fifty-two is to be right. Seeing you in that outfit, I shall have no fear."

"Have no fear! I shall soon be out of the way of harming you, and the rest—God willing–will soon be far from here! Now, get help and take me to the coach."

"You?" asked the Spy nervously.

"Him, man, with whom I have changed places. You leave by the gate by which you brought me in?"

"Of course."

"I was weak and faint when you brought me in, and I am fainter now when you take me out. Saying farewell to my friend has overpowered me. Such a thing has happened here—too, too often. Your life is in your own hands. Quick! Call for help!"

"You swear not to betray me?" said the trembling Spy, as he paused for a last moment.

"Man, man!" returned Carton, stamping his foot, "have I sworn by no solemn vow already, to go through with this, that you waste the precious moments now? Take him yourself to the courtyard you know of, place him yourself in the carriage, show him yourself to Mr. Lorry, tell him yourself to give him no medicine but air, and to remember what I said last night, and what he promised last night, and drive away!"

The Spy left, and Carton seated himself at the table, resting his forehead on his hands. The Spy returned immediately, with two men.

"How, then?" said one of them, contemplating the fallen figure. "So afflicted to find that his friend has drawn a prize in the lottery of Sainte Guillotine?"

"A good patriot," said the other, "could hardly have been more afflicted if the aristocrat had drawn a blank."

They raised the unconscious figure, placed it on a litter they had brought to the door, and bent to carry it away.

"The time is short, Evrémonde," said the Spy, in a warning voice.

"I know it well," answered Carton. "Be careful of my friend, I beg you, and leave me."

"Come, then, my children," said Barsad. "Lift him, and come away!"

The door closed, and Carton was left alone.

Straining his powers of listening to the utmost, he listened for any sound that might denote suspicion or alarm. There was none. Keys turned, doors clashed, footsteps passed along distant passages. No cry was raised, or hurry made. Breathing more freely in a little while, he sat down at the table, and listened again until the clock struck Two.

Sounds that he was not afraid of, for he guessed their meaning, then began to be audible. Several doors were opened in succession, and finally his own. A jailer, with a list in his hand, looked in, merely saying, "Follow me, Evremonde!" and he followed into a large, dark room. It was a dark winter day, and he could but dimly make out the others who were brought there to have their arms bound. Some were standing, some seated. Only a few paced nervously and whimpered or moaned about their fate. The great majority were silent and still, staring at the ground.

As he stood by the wall in a dim corner, while some of the fifty-two were brought in after him, one man stopped and embraced him as though they knew one another. His heart pounded with the fear of being discovered, but the man went on. A few moments later, a young woman, with a slight girlish form, a sweet spare face which was pale as death, and large widely opened patient eyes, rose from the seat where he had seen her sitting, and came to speak to him.

"Citizen Evremonde," she said, touching him with her cold hand. "I am a poor little seamstress, who was with you in La Force."

❷ *Why would Dickens introduce this new character so late in the story?*

He murmured for answer: "True. I forget what you were accused of?"

"Plots. Though Heaven knows that I am innocent of any. Is it likely? Who would think of plotting with a poor little weak creature like me?"

The forlorn smile with which she said it, so touched him, that tears started from his eyes.

"I am not afraid to die, Citizen Evremonde, but I have done nothing. I am not unwilling to die, if the Republic—which is to do so much good to us poor—

will profit by my death. But I do not know how that can be, Citizen Evremonde. Such a poor weak little creature!"

As the last thing on earth that his heart was to warm and soften to, it warmed and softened to this pitiable girl.

"I heard you were released, Citizen Evremonde. I hoped it was true."

"It was. But, I was arrested, tried, and condemned."

"If I may ride with you, Citizen Evremonde, will you let me hold your hand? I am not afraid, but I am little and weak, and it will give me more courage."

As the patient eyes were lifted to his face, he saw a sudden doubt in them, and then astonishment. He pressed the work-worn, hunger-worn young fingers, and kissed them.

"Are you dying for him?" she whispered.

"And his wife and child. Hush! Yes."

"Oh you will let me hold your brave hand, stranger?"

"Hush! Yes, my poor sister; to the very end."

The same shadows that are falling on the prison, are also falling—at that same hour of the afternoon—on the crowded Barrier when a coach going out of Paris drives up to be examined.

"Who goes here? Who is in the carriage? Papers!"

The papers are handed out, and read.

"Alexandre Manette. Physician. French. Which is he?"

This is he, this helpless, murmuring, wandering old man pointed out.

"Apparently the Citizen-Doctor is not in his right mind? The Revolution fever has been too much for him?"

"Greatly too much for him."

"Hah! Many suffer with it. Lucie. His daughter. French. Which is she?"

"This is she."

"Apparently it must be. Lucie, the wife of Evremonde—is it not?"

"It is."

"Hah! Evremonde has an appointment elsewhere. Lucie, her child. English. This is she?"

"She and no other."

"Kiss me, child of Evremonde. Now, thou hast kissed a good Republican, something new in your family; remember it! Sydney Carton. Attorney. English. Which is he?"

"He lies here, in this corner of the carriage. He, too, is pointed out."

"Apparently the English attorney is in a faint?"

"It is hoped he will recover in the fresher air. It is said that he is not in strong health, and has separated sadly from a friend who is out of favor with the Republic."

"Is that all? That is not a big deal! Many are out of favor with the Republic, and must face La Guillotine. Mr. Jarvis Lorry. Banker. English. Which is he?"

"I am he. I must be, since I'm the only person you haven't spoken to yet."

It is Jarvis Lorry who has replied to all the previous questions. It is Jarvis Lorry who has climbed down and stands with his hand on the coach door, answering a group of officials. They slowly walk round the carriage and slowly mount the box, to look at what little luggage is on the roof. The country people hanging about, press nearer to the coach doors and curiously stare in. A little child, carried by its mother, has its short arm held out for it, so that it may touch the wife of an aristocrat who has gone to the Guillotine.

"Here are your papers, Jarvis Lorry. Approved."

"We may depart, Citizen?"

"You can depart. A good journey!"

"I salute you, Citizens. And the first danger is passed!"

These are also the words of Jarvis Lorry, as he claps his hands, and looks Heavenward. There is terror in the carriage. There is weeping. There is the heavy

Notice how the narrative style of this examination resembles Darnay's various trials.

breathing of the unconscious traveler.

"Aren't we going too slowly? Can you not force the horses to go faster?" asks Lucie, clinging to the old man.

"Then it might look as if we were trying to escape, my darling. I must not urge them too much. It would rouse suspicion."

"Look back, look back, and see if we are pursued!"

"The road is clear, my dear. So far, we are not followed."

They pass houses in groups of two and three, lonely farms, dilapidated buildings, dye-works, tanneries, and the like, open country, avenues of leafless trees. The hard uneven pavement rumbles under the wheels, the soft deep mud is on either side. Sometimes, the drivers turn into the mud, to avoid the stones that clatter and shake the coach. Sometimes the coach gets stuck in ruts and sloughs there. Then their impatience is so great, that they consider getting out and running—hiding—doing anything but stopping.

Out of the open country, back again among ruins of buildings, lonely farms, dye-works, tanneries, and the like, cottages in groups of two and three, avenues of leafless trees. Have the drivers deceived them, and taken them back to Paris by another road? Are they going in circles? Thank Heaven, no. They arrive at a village. Looking back, looking back, to see if they are followed! They arrive at the inn where their horses and drivers will be changed and fight to appear calm.

Leisurely, the four horses are unhitched and led to their stalls. Leisurely, the coach stands in the little street. Without its horses, it doesn't look as if it will ever move again. Leisurely, the new horses appear, one by one. Leisurely, the new drivers follow, sucking, and braiding the lashes of their whips. Leisurely, the old drivers count their money, make wrong additions, and grumble about being cheated. All the time, the overworked hearts of the terrified travelers are beating

❷ *Why does Dickens begin every sentence with the word "leisurely"?*

at a rate that would far outrace the fastest gallop of the fastest horses ever born.

Finally the new drivers are in their saddles, and the old are left behind. They drive through the village, up the hill, and down the hill, and on the low, watery grounds. Suddenly, the drivers exchange some words with much animated gesturing, and the horses are pulled up, almost on their haunches. They are being followed!

"You! Inside the carriage there. Speak up!"

"What is it?" asks Mr. Lorry, looking out at window.

"How many did they say?"

"I do not understand you."

"At the last post. How many to the Guillotine today?"

"Fifty-two."

"I said so! A brave number! My fellow-citizen here would have it forty-two. Ten more heads are worth having. The Guillotine goes handsomely. I love it. All right then, continue!"

The night comes on dark. The figure identified as Sydney Cartoon moves more. He is beginning to revive, and to speak. He thinks he is still in his prison cell. He asks another man—also named Carton—what he's planning. What if *this* Sydney Carton's ramblings are overheard and they are discovered?

The wind rushes after them, and the clouds fly after them. The moon follows them, and the whole wild night seems to chase them, but—so far—they are pursued by nothing else.

❷ *What key plot element has occurred in this chapter?*

THIS IS THE END OF THE
TWENTY-NINTH WEEKLY INSTALLMENT.

Research and Writing Opportunity:

Look up the story of Damon and Pythias. Write an essay in which you compare and contrast this story with how Sydney Carton saves Charles Darnay.

A Tale of Two Cities

CHARLES DICKENS

CHAPTER XIV

The Knitting Done

❷ *Who has most been associated with knitting in this book? What do you suppose will happen in this chapter?*

A T THE SAME TIME when the Fifty-two awaited their fate, Madame Defarge held a sinister conversation with The Vengeance and Jacques Three of the Revolutionary Jury, not in the wine shop, but in the shed of the woodcutter, who used to be a mender of roads. The cutter himself did not participate in the conference, but sat at a little distance, like a satellite who was not to speak until spoken to, or to offer an opinion until invited.

"But your husband," said Jacques Three, "is undoubtedly a good Republican? No?"

"There is no better," the talkative Vengeance protested in her shrill notes, "in France."

"Quiet, little Vengeance," said Madame Defarge. Frowning slightly, she lay her hand on the assistant's lips, "Hear me speak. My husband, Jacques, is a good Republican and a bold man. He deserves much from the Republic, and is a trusted friend. But my husband has his weaknesses. And he is very weak in his dealing with this Doctor."

"That is a great pity," croaked Jacques Three, doubtfully shaking his head, "he doesn't sound like a good citizen."

"Understand," said Madame, "I care nothing for

❷ *What is the horror in this conversation?*

✔ *Although much has happened in the last several chapters, this chapter began with the narrator's telling us that the Fifty-two condemned were still awaiting their fates. Thus this conversation is the day after Charles's second trial, the morning after Carton and Lorry planned the hurried escape.*

❷ *What literary convention is Dickens using here?*

this Doctor. He may keep his head or lose it for all I care. But, the Evremondes are to be *exterminated*, and the wife and child must die."

"She has a pretty head for the guillotine," croaked Jacques Three. "I have seen her blue eyes and golden hair, and they will look *charming* when Samson holds them up."

Madame Defarge cast down her eyes, and reflected a little.

"The child too," observed Jacques Three, enjoying the sounds of his words, "has golden hair and blue eyes. And we so seldom have a child there. It is a pretty sight!"

"In short," said Madame Defarge, "I cannot trust my husband in this matter. Not only do I feel—since last night—that I don't dare to include him in my plans, but I also feel that if I wait too long, he might warn them, and then they might escape."

"That must never be," croaked Jacques Three. "No one must escape. We don't have half the condemned as we need. We ought to have at least one hundred and twenty a day."

"Certainly," Madame Defarge went on, "my husband does not have the strong motive that I have for pursuing this family to annihilation, and I do not have his reasons for feeling any love or loyalty to this Doctor. Therefore, I must act for myself. Come here, little citizen."

The woodcutter, who was mortally afraid of this Madame Defarge, stepped forward.

"About those signals, little citizen," said Madame Defarge, sternly, "that she made to the prisoners...you are prepared to testify about them this very day?"

"I am!" cried the woodcutter. "Every day, in every kind of weather, from two to four in the afternoon. Always signaling, sometimes with the little one, sometimes without. I know what I know. I have seen her with my own eyes."

He gestured madly with his hands while he spoke,

as imitating some of the many signals that he had never seen.

"Clearly plots," said Jacques Three. "Clearly!"

"There is no doubt about the Jury?" asked Madame Defarge, letting her eyes turn to Jacques Three with a gloomy smile.

"You can count on the patriotic Jury, dear citizeness."

"Now, let me see," said Madame Defarge, pondering again. "Yet once more! Can I indulge my husband's affection for this Doctor? I have no feeling either way. Can I spare him?"

"He would count as one head," observed Jacques Three, in a low voice. "We really do not have enough heads. I think it would be a pity for him to go free."

"He was signaling with her when I saw her," argued Madame Defarge. "I cannot speak of one without the other, and I must not be silent, and trust the case wholly to this little citizen here. I am not a bad witness."

The Vengeance and Jacques Three protested that she was the most admirable and marvelous of witnesses. The little citizen, not to be outdone, declared her to be a stellar witness.

"He must take his chances," said Madame Defarge. "No, I cannot spare him! You are busy at three o'clock? You are going to see today's batch executed?"

The question was addressed to the woodcutter, who hurriedly said yes, and also that he was the most passionate of Republicans, and that he would be the saddest of Republicans if anything prevented him from enjoying his afternoon pipe while watching La Guillotine. He was so very excited, that it might have seemed that he feared for his own life.

❷ What is being implied here?

"I will also be there," said Madame. "After it is over—say at eight to-night—come to me in Saint Antoine. And we will give information against these people at my Section."

The woodcutter said he would be proud and

flattered to go with the citizeness. When the citizeness looked at him, he became embarrassed, evaded her glance as a small dog would have done, and retreated among his wood.

Madame Defarge beckoned the Juryman and The Vengeance a little nearer to the door. "She is most likely at home now, awaiting the moment of his death. She will be mourning and grieving. She will be in a state of mind to criticize the perfect justice of the Republic. She will be full of sympathy with its enemies. I will go to her."

"What a remarkable woman! What an adorable woman!" exclaimed Jacques Three, rapturously.

"Ah, my cherished!" cried The Vengeance, embracing her.

"Take my knitting," said Madame Defarge, placing it in her lieutenant's hands, "and have it ready for me in my usual seat. Save my usual chair. Go straight there, for there will probably be a bigger crowd than usual, today."

"I willingly obey the orders of my Chief," said The Vengeance, kissing her cheek. "Don't be late."

"I shall be there before it starts."

"And before the tumbrils arrive. Be sure you are there, my soul," said The Vengeance, calling after her, for she had already turned into the street, "before the tumbrils arrive!"

Madame Defarge waved her hand to show that she heard and went through the mud around the corner of the prison wall.

There were many women at that time, who were disfigured by their years of hard labor and starvation, but there was not one among them more to be dreaded than this ruthless woman. Truly she was a strong woman—fearless, shrewd, always ready, fiercely determined, with a kind of beauty forged by firmness and anger. Brought up as she was to dwell on wrongs and to hate the upper classes, this opportunity had developed her into a tigress. She was absolutely without pity. If she had ever had a drop of compassion

❷ What is Madame Defarge planning to do?

❷ Consider Madame Defarge and her actions from a psychoanalytic standpoint. Do her motivations redeem her as a sympathetic character in the readers' eyes?

in her, she had completely lost it long ago.

It was nothing to her, that an innocent man was to die for the sins of his forefathers. She saw—not him—but them. It was nothing to her, that his wife was to be made a widow and his daughter an orphan. To her, this was insufficient punishment because they were her natural enemies and her prey, and had no right to live. To appeal to her for any consideration or mercy, was pointless since she had no sense of pity, even for herself. If she had been slaughtered in the street, in any of the many battles she had fought, she would not have pitied herself. If she had been ordered to the Guillotine tomorrow, she would experience no emotion other than the desire to change places with the man who had condemned her.

This was the heart Madame Defarge carried under her rough robe. And, in a certain weird way, her hardness suited her as a garment. Her dark hair looked rich under her coarse, red cap. Lying hidden in her bosom, was a loaded pistol. Lying hidden at her waist was a sharpened dagger. Thus dressed, and walking with the confident step of a tigress, Madame Defarge made her way along the streets.

When Mr. Lorry was planning the escape from Paris, he was worried about what to do with Miss Pross. The carriage could only carry so many people, and the more people who were in the carriage, the more papers would have to be examined at each stop. Finally, he suggested—after anxious consideration—that Miss Pross and Jerry, who also had permission to leave the city, should leave it at three o'clock in a small, light vehicle that could travel quickly. With no luggage to weigh them down, they would soon catch up to the coach, and even pass it. Then they could arrive at the inn before the coach and order its horses in advance. This would greatly speed up the coach's progress during the precious hours of the night, when delay was the most to be dreaded.

Miss Pross was excited to be so helpful to the escape. She and Jerry had watched the coach leave.

This scene between Miss Pross and Jerry is another example of comic relief between the tension of the substitution in the prison, the escape, and Madame Defarge's coming, armed, to the apartment.

They knew who it was that Solomon had brought from the prison, had waited some ten minutes in suspense, and were just finishing their arrangements to follow the coach as Madame Defarge was making her way through the streets, drawing nearer and nearer to their apartment.

"Now what do you think, Mr. Cruncher," said Miss Pross, who was so nervous and excited that she could hardly speak, "should we start from somewhere else than this courtyard? Since another carriage has already left from here today, it might awaken suspicion."

"My opinion, Miss," returned Mr. Cruncher, "is as you're right. Likewise I'll stand by you, right or wrong."

"I am so worried about them all," said Miss Pross, wildly crying, "that I can't even think. Can you think straight, my Mr. Cruncher?"

"Respectin' a future spear o' life, Miss," returned Mr. Cruncher, "I hope so. Respectin' any present use o' this here blessed old head o' mine, I think not. Would you do me the favor, Miss, to take notice o' two promises and vows wot it is my wishes to record in this here crisis?"

"Oh, for gracious sake!" cried Miss Pross, still crying, "State them at once, and get them out of the way, like an excellent man."

"First," said Mr. Cruncher, trembling, with an ashen and solemn face, "if them poor things come out o' this all right, I never no more will do it, never no more!"

"I am quite sure, Mr. Cruncher," replied Miss Pross, "that you never will do it again, whatever it is."

Jerry continued. "Second, if them poor things come well out o' this, and I never no more will interfere with Mrs. Cruncher's flopping. Never no more!"

"Whatever housekeeping arrangement that may be," said Miss Pross, trying to dry her eyes and compose herself, "I have no doubt it is best that Mrs. Cruncher should be entirely in charge."

"I go so far as to say, Miss, moreover," continued Mr. Cruncher, with a tendency to preach like an energetic minister, "and let my words be took down and took to Mrs. Cruncher through yourself—that wot my opinions respectin' flopping has undergone a change, and that wot I only hope with all my heart as Mrs. Cruncher may be a flopping right now."

"There, there, there! I hope she is, my dear man," cried the distracted Miss Pross, "and I hope she finds that it meets her expectations."

"Forbid it," proceeded Mr. Cruncher, even more solemnly, more slowly, with more a tendency to preach, "that anything I ever said or done should undo on my sincere wishes for them poor creeturs now! Now's the time we should all flop (if it was at all convenient) to get 'em out o' this here dismal risk! Forbid it, miss! Wot I say, for-BID it!"

And still Madame Defarge, marching through the streets, came nearer and nearer.

"If we ever get back to England," said Miss Pross, "I will certainly tell Mrs. Cruncher as much as I can remember and understand of what you have just said. In any event, you may be sure that I will certify that you were completely earnest at this dreadful time. Now, pray let us think! My esteemed Mr. Cruncher, let us think!"

Still, Madame Defarge came nearer and nearer.

"Don't you think it would be best if you were to go now," said Miss Pross, "and stop the vehicle and horses from coming here, and were to wait somewhere for me? Wouldn't that be best?"

Mr. Cruncher thought it might be best.

"Where could you wait for me?" asked Miss Pross.

Mr. Cruncher was so bewildered that he could think of no locality but Temple Bar. Alas! Temple Bar was hundreds of miles away, and Madame Defarge was drawing very near indeed.

"By the cathedral door," said Miss Pross. "Would it be much out of the way, to take me in, near the great cathedral door between the two towers?"

"No, Miss," answered Mr. Cruncher.

"Then, like the best of men," said Miss Pross, "go right away, and make that change."

"I'm not sure about leaving you here," said Mr. Cruncher, hesitating and shaking his head, "We don't know what may happen."

"Heaven knows we don't," returned Miss Pross, "but have no fear for me. Take me in at the cathedral, at three o'clock, or as close to three as you can, and I am sure it will be better than our leaving from here. I just feel it."

This encouragement, and Miss Pross's two hands clasping his, energized Mr. Cruncher. With an encouraging nod or two, he immediately went out to alter the arrangements, and left her alone to follow as she had suggested.

It was a source of great relief to Miss Pross, that they had solved that problem. It was also relieving, that she had the task of getting herself ready for the streets to occupy her mind. She looked at her watch, and it was twenty minutes past two. She had no time to lose, but must get ready at once.

Afraid, in her extreme excitement, of the loneliness of the deserted rooms, and of half-imagined faces peeping from behind every open door in them, Miss Pross got a basin of cold water and began washing her eyes, which were swollen and red. Haunted by her feverish imagination, she could not bear to have her sight obscured for a minute at a time by the dripping water, but constantly paused and looked round to see that there was no one watching her. In one of those pauses she recoiled and cried out, for she saw a figure standing in the room.

The basin fell to the ground and broke. The water flowed to the feet of Madame Defarge.

Madame Defarge looked coldly at her, and said, "The wife of Evremonde—where is she?"

It suddenly occurred to Miss Pross that the doors were all open, and that that would suggest flight. Her first act was to shut them. There were four in the room, and she shut them all. She then placed herself before the door of the room that had been Lucie's.

Madame Defarge's dark eyes followed every one of Miss Pross's movements and rested on her as she blocked the way to Lucie's door. Miss Pross was not beautiful. Age had not tamed the wildness—or softened the grimness—of her appearance. But, she too was a determined woman—in her own way— and she measured Madame Defarge with her eyes, every inch.

"You look like the wife of Lucifer," said Miss Pross, in her breathing. "Nevertheless, you shall not get the better of me. I am an Englishwoman."

Madame Defarge looked at her scornfully, but still with something of Miss Pross's own perception that they two were at bay. She saw a tight, hard, wiry woman before her, just as years before Mr. Lorry found her to be a woman with a strong hand. She knew full well that Miss Pross was the family's devoted friend. Miss Pross knew full well that Madame Defarge was the family's dread enemy.

"On my way over there," said Madame Defarge, with a slight movement of her hand toward the fatal spot where the executions would soon take place, "where they reserve my chair and my knitting for me, I have come to pay my respects to *her* in passing. I wish to see her."

"I know that your intentions are evil," said Miss Pross, "and you may depend upon it, I'll hold my own against them."

Each spoke in her own language. Neither understood the other's words. Both were very watchful, and intent to figure out from look and manner, what the foreign words meant.

"It will do her no good to keep her hidden from me at this moment," said Madame Defarge. "Good patriots will know what that means. Let me see her. Go tell her that I wish to see her. Do you hear?"

"If those eyes of yours were bed-winches,"

> ✔ *This pairing of opposites— strong friend versus strong foe; English versus French; loving and devoted versus hating and vengeful—is called "antithesis." Dickens used the same technique at the very beginning of the novel when he compared England and France: "It was the best of times, it was the worst of times."*

> ✔ *A bed-winch was a tool used to tighten or loosen the tension of the ropes supporting the mattress on a bed.*

returned Miss Pross, "and I was an English four-poster, they shouldn't loose a splinter of me. No, you wicked foreign woman. I am your match."

Madame Defarge certainly could not follow Miss Pross's use of idioms, but, she could understand enough to guess that she was not going to get what she wanted.

"Woman! You imbecile and pig!" said Madame Defarge, frowning. "I take no answer from you. I demand to see *her*. Either tell her that I demand to see her, or stand out of the way of the door and let me go to her!" This she said with an angry wave of her right arm.

"I little thought," said Miss Pross, "that I would ever want to understand your nonsensical language. But I would give everything I have—except the clothes I wear—to know whether you suspect the truth, or any part of it."

Neither of them for a single moment released the other's eyes. Madame Defarge had not moved from the spot where she stood when Miss Pross first became aware of her. But, she now advanced one step.

"I am a Briton," said Miss Pross, "I am desperate. I don't care an English twopence for myself. I know that the longer I keep you here, the greater hope there is for my Ladybird. I'll not leave a handful of that dark hair upon your head, if you lay a finger on me!"

Thus Miss Pross answered her foe, with a shake of her head and a flash of her eyes. But, her courage was of that emotional kind, and it brought tears into her eyes. This was a courage that Madame Defarge mistook for weakness. "Ha, ha!" she laughed, "you poor wretch! You are worthless! I address myself to that Doctor." Then she raised her voice and called out, "Citizen Doctor! Wife of Evremonde! Child of Evremonde! Any person but this miserable fool, answer the Citizeness Defarge!"

Perhaps it was the echoing silence that followed. Perhaps something in Miss Pross's expression gave it away. Perhaps it was just a hunch unrelated to the

Throughout the book, Dickens has hinted at national pride, but here he makes it explicit.

silence or Miss Pross that told Madame Defarge that they were gone. She quickly opened three of the four doors and looked in.

"Those rooms are a mess. There has been hurried packing. There are odds and ends on the floor. There is no one in that room behind you! Let me look."

"Never!" said Miss Pross, who understood the request as perfectly as Madame Defarge understood the answer.

"If they are not in that room, they are gone, and can be pursued and brought back," said Madame Defarge to herself.

"As long as you don't know whether they are in that room or not, you are uncertain what to do," said Miss Pross to herself; "and you shall *never* know whether they're here or not, if I have any say in it. And you shall not leave here while I can hold you."

"I have been in the streets since the beginning of our Revolution. Nothing has harmed me. I will tear you to pieces if I have to, but I *will* have you from that door," said Madame Defarge.

"We are alone at the top of a high house in an empty courtyard. We are not likely to be heard, and I pray for the bodily strength to keep you here. Every minute you are here is worth a hundred thousand guineas to my darling," said Miss Pross.

Madame Defarge rushed for the door. Miss Pross, on the instinct of the moment, grabbed her around the waist with both of her arms, and held her tight. It was useless for Madame Defarge to struggle and to strike. Miss Pross, with strength of love—always so much stronger than hate—held her tight, and even lifted her from the floor in the struggle that they had. Madame Defarge's two hands punched and tore at her face, but Miss Pross, with her head down, held her round the waist, and clung to her with more than the grip of a drowning woman.

Soon, Madame Defarge's hands stopped punching, and felt at her encircled waist. "It is under my arm," hissed Miss Pross between her teeth. "You shall not

It was believed that drowning victims gained incredible strength and would drag potential rescuers to the grave with them.

draw it. I am stronger than you, I bless Heaven for it. And I'll hold you until one or other of us faints or dies!"

Madame Defarge's hands were at her bosom. Miss Pross looked up, saw the pistol and grabbed for it. There was a flash and a crash, and Miss Pross stood alone—blinded with smoke.

All this was in a second. As the smoke cleared—leaving an awful stillness—it dissipated in the air, like the soul of the furious woman whose body lay lifeless on the ground.

❷ *How has Dickens prepared the reader to accept Madame Defarge's death as just? What is the literary term for when a character receives the reward or punishment he or she truly deserves?*

In the first fright and horror of her situation, Miss Pross pushed the body as far away as she could, and ran down the stairs to call for help. Luckily, she realized what the consequences would be if help did come and Madame Defarge's body were discovered in the Manettes' deserted rooms, and she stopped calling and returned. It was dreadful to go in again. But, she did go in, and even went near the body, to get the bonnet and other things that she must wear to keep her appointment with Mr. Cruncher. She put these on out on the staircase first shutting and locking the door and removing the key. She then sat down on the stairs a few moments to breathe and to cry. Then got up and hurried away.

Fortunately she had a veil on her bonnet, so no one stopped her to ask what was the matter, why was she crying. By good fortune, too, she was normally so odd-looking that it was hard to say what was normal for her. She needed both advantages, for Madame Defarge's scratch marks were deep in her face. Her hair was torn, and her dress was torn, soiled, and disheveled.

While crossing the bridge, she dropped the door key in the river. Arriving at the cathedral a few minutes before her escort, and waiting there, she worried what would happen if the key were already caught in a net and identified. What if the door were opened and the body discovered? What if she were stopped at the gate, sent to prison, and charged with murder! In the midst of these fluttering thoughts, Jerry Cruncher appeared, took her in, and took her away.

"Isn't there any noise in the streets?" she asked him.

"The usual noises," Mr. Cruncher replied. He looked surprised by the question and by her expression.

"I can't hear you," said Miss Pross. "What did you say?"

It was useless for Mr. Cruncher to repeat what he said. Miss Pross could not hear him. "So I'll nod my head," thought Mr. Cruncher, amazed, "at all events she'll see that." And she did.

"Is there any noise in the streets now?" asked Miss Pross again, presently.

Again Mr. Cruncher nodded his head.

"I don't hear it."

"Gone deaf in an hour?" said Mr. Cruncher, thinking, his mind much disturbed; "What's come to her?"

"I feel," said Miss Pross, "as if there had been a flash and a crash, and that crash was the last thing I will ever hear in this life."

"Blest if she ain't in a queer condition!" said Mr. Cruncher, more and more disturbed. "What's she been drinking—to keep her courage up? Listen! There's the roll of them dreadful carts! You can hear that, Miss?"

"I can hear nothing," said Miss Pross, seeing that he spoke to her. "Nothing. O, my good man, there was first a great crash, and then a great Silence. And that Stillness seems to be fixed and unchangeable, never to be broken for the rest of my life."

"If she don't hear the roll of those dreadful carts, now very close to the place of the executions," said Mr. Cruncher, glancing over his shoulder, "it's my opinion that she never will hear anything else in this world."

And indeed she never did.

❶ *Notice how Dickens has waited until this moment to show the reader the rolling tumbrils. There is no suspense in the passing of the carts as the reader knows that Carton's plot has been successful and those he wanted to save are safe.*

❷ *What has been the purpose of this chapter? Where are we in the structure of the plot?*

A Tale of Two Cities

CHARLES DICKENS

CHAPTER XV
The Footsteps Die Out Forever

THE DEATH CARTS rumble through the Paris streets, hollow and harsh. Six tumbrils carry the day's victims to La Guillotine. The Guillotine is the gruesome combination of every flesh-eating monster ever dreamed of. And yet the conditions that made its invention inevitable had for generations been the "natural" order of things. The Guillotine was the fruit of repression, of torture, of cruel inequality. Whenever the Few reap the pleasures of life from the hardship of the Many, the Many will eventually rise up and make similar inventions.

Six tumbrils roll along the streets. Look around! You will see what used to be the carriages of absolute monarchs, the equipment of feudal nobles, the toilettes of blatant Jezebels, the churches that are not my father's house but dens of thieves, the huts of millions of starving peasants! The great magician who fulfills the will of the Creator, never reverses his transformations. The seers in the stories of the Arabian Nights are wise to tell the bewitched, "If you have been changed into this shape by the will of God, you must remain like this! But, if mere magic has made you like this, then return to what you were originally!" Changeless and hopeless, the tumbrils roll along.

✅ *Notice how the tone of this chapter changes. It is in the present tense, and the narrator addresses the reader directly.*

✅ *Jezebel was the Old Testament wife of Ahab, king of Israel. After marrying her, Ahab abandoned the God of Israel and worshiped the pagan god Baal. Jezebel is remembered infamously as a seductress, prostitute, murderer, and thief. The second allusion refers to the episode in the New Testament when Jesus drives out the moneychangers and merchants from the Temple and proclaims that the Temple was supposed to be a house of prayer and not a den of thieves. In these allusions, Dickens is clearly implying that the relics of the fallen monarchy and feudal system represent the evils of false ideals and misplaced values.*

As the six somber carts roll, the masses gathered in the streets part to allow them to pass. The effect looks like a great human furrow being plowed in the street by the wheels of the cart. The people who live in the houses on these streets are so used to the spectacle that there are no people in many windows. In others, the people do not bother to stop their work. In a few of the rooms, the resident has visitors who have come to see the sight. The host points his finger—to this cart and then to that one—and he seems to tell who sat here yesterday, and who there the day before.

The riders in the tumbrils study these things. They study *everything* on this, their last journey. Some merely stare impassively. Others look eagerly with a lingering interest in the life they will soon leave. Some are seated with drooping heads, sunk in silent despair. And there are some so focused on their appearance that they can't help but offer the crowd of spectators dramatic looks of bravery. Several close their eyes, and think, or try to collect their thoughts. Only one—a miserable, crazy-looking creature—is so terrified that he sings and tries to dance. But the hardened crowd has no bit of pity for a single One of the Fifty-two.

There is a guard of various horsemen riding beside the tumbrils, and the spectators often approach some of them in order to ask a question. It seems to be always the same question, for, it is always followed by a press of people toward the third cart. The horsemen beside that cart frequently point out one man. He stands at the back of the tumbril with his head bent down, speaking with a mere girl who sits on the side of the cart. She holds his hand. He has no curiosity about the scene around him, and always speaks to the girl. Here and there in the long street of St. Honore, people shout curses at him. If he notices them at all, it is only with a quiet smile, as he shakes his hair a little more loosely about his face. He cannot easily touch his face because his arms are bound.

On the steps of a church, awaiting the arrival of the tumbrils, stands Barsad (the Spy and prison-sheep). He looks into the first cart. Carton/Darnay is not there. He looks into the second. He is not there. He already asks himself, "Has he betrayed me?" His face relaxes when he looks into the third cart.

"Which is Evremonde?" asks a man behind him.

"There. At the back."

"With his hand in the girl's?"

"Yes."

The man cries, "Die, Evremonde! To the Guillotine all aristocrats! Die, Evremonde!"

"Hush, hush!" the Spy asks him, timidly.

"And why, Citizen?"

"He is going to pay the debt. It will be paid in five more minutes. Let him be at peace."

But the man continues to exclaim, "Die, Evremonde!" the face of Evremonde is for a moment turned toward him. Evremonde sees the Spy, looks attentively at him, and then turns away.

It is almost three o'clock, and the "furrow" plowed in the people is turning round, to walk to the place of execution. The gap of people closes in behind the last cart as it passes. Everyone is following it to the Guillotine. In the front row, seated in chairs, as if they were at a play, are a number of women, busily knitting. On one of these chairs stands The Vengeance, looking about for her friend.

"Therese!" she cries, in her shrill tone. "Who has seen her? Therese Defarge!"

"She's never missed before," says a knitting woman of the sisterhood.

"No. And she won't miss today," cries The Vengeance, crossly.

"Therese."

"Louder," the woman recommends.

Ay! Yell louder, Vengeance, much louder, and still she will not hear you. Louder yet, Vengeance, with a little curse, and yet it will never bring her. Send other women out to look for her. They'd have to go to the very depths of Hell to find her!

"What bad luck!" cries The Vengeance, stamping

❷ *What is the source of the Spy's compassion?*

The citoyennes tricoteuses, citizeness knitters, are famous in French Revolution lore. There are dozens of historical and psychological interpretations of their acts of unemotional knitting at the foot of the guillotine. Dickens clearly wants to portray them as heartless, like their leader, Madame Defarge.

her foot on the chair. "Here come the tumbrils! Evremonde will be executed, and she'll miss it!"

As The Vengeance steps down from her perch, the tumbrils begin to discharge their loads. The ministers of Sainte Guillotine are robed and ready.

Crash! A head is held up, and the knitting women, who barely lift their eyes to look at it, shout, "One!"

The second tumbril empties and moves on. The third comes up.

Crash! And the knitting women—never pausing in their work—shout, "Two!"

The one everyone thinks is Evremonde climbs from the cart, and the seamstress is lifted out after him. He has not let go of her hand in getting out, but still holds it as he promised he would. He gently places her with her back to the crashing blade that constantly whirrs up and falls, and she looks into his face and thanks him.

"If it weren't for you, dear stranger, I would not be so calm, for I am naturally a poor little thing, faint of heart. Nor would I have been able to think of Him who was put to death, so that we might have hope and comfort here today. I think you were sent to me by Heaven."

"Or you to me," says Sydney Carton. "Keep your eyes on me, dear child, and don't think about anything else."

"I'm not afraid of anything while I hold your hand. I will not be afraid when I let it go, if they are quick."

"They will be quick. Fear not!"

The two stand in the shrinking crowd of victims, but they speak as if they were alone. Eye to eye, voice to voice, hand to hand, heart to heart, these two children of the Universal Mother—so very different in every aspect but this one—have come together on the dark highway, to return home together, and to rest in her bosom.

"Brave and generous friend, will you let me ask you one last question? I am very ignorant, and it troubles me a little."

Note the metaphor of life as a journey. Carton and the Seamstress have met on the "highway."

"Tell me what it is."

"I have a cousin. She is my only relative and an orphan, like myself, whom I love very dearly. She is five years younger than I, and she lives in a farmer's house in the South. We were separated because of our poverty, and she knows nothing of my fate—for I cannot write—and—even if I could, how would I tell her this? It is better as it is."

"Yes, yes. Better as it is."

"What I have been thinking, is this: If the Republic really does good to the poor, and they come to be less hungry, and in all ways to suffer less, she may live a long time. She may even live to be old."

"What then, my gentle sister?"

"Do you think," her eyes filled with tears, and her lips parted a little more and trembled. "Do you think that it will seem like a long time to me, while I wait for her in Heaven?"

"It cannot be, my child. There is no Time there, and no trouble there."

"You comfort me so much! I am so ignorant. Am I to kiss you now? Is the moment come?"

"Yes."

She kisses his lips. He kisses hers. They solemnly bless each other. Her tiny hand does not tremble as he releases it. There is no expression on her face other than a naïve loyalty to the Republic that is about to take her life. She goes next before him. She is gone. The knitting women shout, "Twenty-two!"

"I am the resurrection and the life," said the Lord. "Anyone who believes in me will live even if he dies, and everyone who lives and believes in me will never die."

It is his turn. Many voices in the crowd murmur as his number is called. Even the knitting women pause in their work to watch. The front rows of the crows inch forward as everyone wants a better look. But the one they all think is Evremonde sees nothing of the crowd and the city when he hears the call, "Twenty-three!"

Throughout the City that night, they said that his was the most peaceful man's face ever seen there. Many added that he looked virtuous and prophetic.

Not long before, a Madame Roland, who was unlucky enough to be an influential member of the wrong Party, asked for pen and paper so that she could record the strange thoughts inspired by her imminent death. If Sydney Carton had had any Final Thoughts—if he had been granted the gift of prophecy as several of that days' witnesses claimed—he might have written these words:

Don't be confused. All of these final paragraphs are what Carton might have thought in the seconds immediately before his death.

"I see Barsad, and Cly, Defarge, the Vengeance, the Juryman, the Judge...long lines of these new oppressors—who have risen to power after the destruction of the old—destroying themselves by their own instrument of "justice." I see a beautiful city and a brilliant people rising from this pit. In their struggles to be truly free—in their victories and defeats—though still far in the future—I see the present evil and past evils, gradually repenting for themselves and wearing out.

"I see the lives for which I lay down my life, peaceful, useful, prosperous and happy, in England which I shall see no more. I see Lucie with a son on her lap, who bears my name—Sydney Carton Darnay. I see her father—aged and bent, but otherwise healthy. I see Jarvis Lorry—so long their friend. In ten years, he will pass to his own Ultimate Reward and leave to them all of the wealth he has accumulated on earth.

"I see that I occupy a Holy Place in all their hearts—and in the hearts of their descendants for generations to come. I see *her*—an old woman—weeping for me on the anniversary of this day. I see her and her husband—at the ends of their lives—lying side by side in their grave, and I know that neither loved the other more than they both loved and honored my memory.

"I see young Sydney, grown up to be an attorney, full of potential for a brilliant career. I see him winning

it so well, that my name is honored because of his. I
see the blots I threw upon my name, faded away. I see
him—a famous judge and honored man—bringing his
own son—Sydney Carton Darnay, Jr.—here, to this
place. By then it will be a beautiful spot, with no trace
of today's ugliness. I hear him tell the child my story,
with a tender and a faltering voice.

"I see that the Future I am creating today is far
better than my Present or Past, and …

"…It is a far, far better thing that I do, than I have
ever done; it is a far, far better rest that I go to than I
have ever known."

THIS IS THE END OF THE
THIRTIETH WEEKLY INSTALLMENT.

The opening lines of this story—It was the best of times, it was the worst of times…and these closing lines are among the most famous in all of English literature.

Research Opportunity:

The French Revolution set into motion a lengthy period of chaos that was not stilled until the rise of Napoleon Bonaparte. Research the historical and political causes of the French Revolution, and report on the figures that held power during the Reign of Terror. How was Napoleon instrumental in bringing it to a close?

Many historians consider this French Revolution to be a "failed" revolution because it resulted in the restoration to the throne of the same royal family that had been in power before the formation of the First Republic. Others see the French Revolution as the prototype of all later revolutions, especially the Russian Revolution in the early twentieth century. Research both views and report on the one you feel is most accurate.

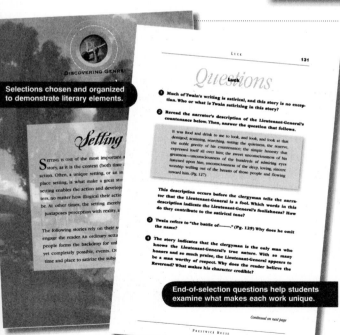

Insightful and Reader-Friendly, Yet Affordable

Prestwick House Literary Touchstone Classic Editions–
The Editions By Which All Others May Be Judged

Every *Prestwick House Literary Touchstone Classic* is enhanced with Reading Pointers for Sharper Insight to improve comprehension and provide insights that will help students recognize key themes, symbols, and plot complexities. In addition, each title includes a Glossary of the more difficult words and concepts.

For the Shakespeare titles, along with the Reading Pointers and Glossary, we include margin notes and various strategies to understanding the language of Shakespeare.

Special Introductory Educator's Discount – At Least 50% Off

New titles are constantly being added; call or visit our website for current listing.

		Retail Price	Intro. Discount
X200102	**Red Badge of Courage, The**	~~$3.99~~	$1.99
X200163	**Romeo and Juliet**	~~$3.99~~	$1.99
X200074	**Heart of Darkness**	~~$3.99~~	$1.99
X200079	**Narrative of the Life of Frederick Douglass**	~~$3.99~~	$1.99
X200125	**Macbeth**	~~$3.99~~	$1.99
X200053	**Adventures of Huckleberry Finn, The**	~~$4.99~~	$2.49
X200081	**Midsummer Night's Dream, A**	~~$3.99~~	$1.99
X200179	**Christmas Carol, A**	~~$3.99~~	$1.99
X200150	**Call of the Wild, The**	~~$3.99~~	$1.99
X200190	**Dr. Jekyll and Mr. Hyde**	~~$3.99~~	$1.99
X200141	**Awakening, The**	~~$3.99~~	$1.99
X200147	**Importance of Being Earnest, The**	~~$3.99~~	$1.99
X200166	**Ethan Frome**	~~$3.99~~	$1.99
X200146	**Julius Caesar**	~~$3.99~~	$1.99
X200095	**Othello**	~~$3.99~~	$1.99
X200091	**Hamlet**	~~$3.99~~	$1.99
X200231	**Taming of the Shrew, The**	~~$3.99~~	$1.99
X200133	**Metamorphosis, The**	~~$3.99~~	$1.99

PRESTWICK HOUSE, INC.
"Everything for the English Classroom!"

Prestwick House, Inc. • P.O. Box 658, Clayton, DE 19938
Phone (800) 932-4593 • Fax (888) 718-9333 • www.prestwickhouse.com